MY BROTHER'S KEEPER

By Thomas Cross

Introduction

The adventures of John Thorn, younger brother of Frank. In the year 2581, John leaves his home planet, Marmaris, near the centre of the Milky Way. Following his boyhood dream of joining the military, things do not turn out quite as anticipated. Then this is merely the start of a lifelong quest across the galaxy to find a role in life and, ultimately, a place he is happy to call home.

My Keeper's Brother - Chapter 1

Midday approached on the planet Marmaris. A hundred other points of light in its pale, blue sky joined the brightness of its sun. Night-time, there would be millions more stars of varying intensity visible. It never got dark.

For Marmaris was a world near the hub of the Milky Way galaxy. As near as could be considered safe, that is. It stood a respectful distance away from the centre, where an enormous black hole lived, eating up planets and stars.

The year was 2581 and 16 year-old John Thorn sat alone in the waiting room of the spaceport. This was only his second visit there. The previous year, he and his parents saw his brother off. Frank, three years John's senior, suddenly "got religious" and departed their home world to move to the theocratic planet Eden. They received word of Frank's enrolment at the university there and his steady progress. His brother resented it. For he had talked about leaving Marmaris for years; it was anything but a whim. John held onto his own quite different dream, and bugged his parents until they gave in.

Theirs was a poor world. The low fertility of the soil matched that of the population. Rarely did couples have more than a single chid. Folk said that the Thorns were fortunate to produce two healthy offspring. They also marvelled that such weak-willed people could beget such headstrong boys. A lifetime of struggle to keep their farm going had worn them down. Dipping into the last of their savings, they were financing John's journey.

Ever since his older brother's departure, he had pestered his parents. His lifelong fascination with militaria fed his ambitions to join the army. Whose army, he was not too concerned about, because Marmaris did not possess one. The impoverished planet belonged to part of a larger group, in this crowded part of the galaxy, and protected by them.

When John got to hear of the planet Andracon's recruiting drive for its space marine division, he, with his parents' help, sent a message applying for a post. He received a brief response instructing him to attend the barracks there. A selection process was not mentioned.

Were they so desperate for new recruits that they would accept anyone? Either way, after that, he would not rest until his parents agreed to let him leave and finance a one way, third-class passage.

More people entered the waiting room. A middle-aged couple sat down near him while their friends gathered round them and chatted. John felt more alone than ever, sad his parents were not there. They came to see Frank off, but their mother had gone downhill since then; old before her time. Father elected to stay with her.

Rucksack beside him, they already checked his case in. The handler being surprised at the old-fashioned "dumb" case, without an anti-grav unit. Then few folk from outlying farmsteads used this tiny, rundown spaceport, which would be regarded a joke on most worlds.

It would be a long time before he received a call for his ship. He looked through a book, *Spacecruisers of the First Intergalactic War - Part 1,* a much-thumbed volume. One of his favourites, he was well versed in its contents, his passion being the weapons and equipment of the first major conflict fought in space almost 400 years earlier. The history of that era was mostly lost. Yet he loved to look at the pictures of these mighty machines and read their specifications. The book's contents were speculative. Very few specimens survived, none in working order. They lost much of the technology in the cataclysm known as the Second Intergalactic War of the late twenty-third century. None of that put John off. Tales of ancient spaceships, wars of independence from old Earth, a planet long lost to his current civilisation, fascinated him.

The drone of a modern ship's engine outside penetrated the thin walls and possessed an hypnotic effect. Book on his lap, he nodded off to sleep.

"For the flight to Andracon, Xin Zhong and Fartac Three, please proceed to the boarding gate," came the crisp announcement over the loud speakers.

John woke with a start and looked about him. More people filled the waiting area now and they all rose from their seats as one. The middle-aged couple he saw before were on their own now, their friends having gone home. They were amongst the others, standing and getting their things together. John fumbled to put his book away in his rucksack and soon joined the line. His heart beat fast in anticipation. This would be his first ever flight. None of the other travellers looked as concerned as him.

Third-class passengers were the last to board and the seats in that compartment packed together. On this occasion, though, half of them were empty. He placed his rucksack on the empty seat next to him until a stewardess instructed him to store it in the locker provided.

The screen in front of him malfunctioned. He could not get it to work. It was only when the pilot addressed the passengers that he realised they had taken off. Inertia negators meant there being no sensation of movement. With no porthole or screen, he missed the moment they left the planet he had spent his entire life on. 'I never said "Goodbye Marmaris",' he mused.

John's understanding of modern space travel was rudimentary. He knew ships generated their own force field and that this invention, along with the UDS Drive, facilitated interstellar travel. The former protected travellers from cosmic radiation and the latter negated the time effects predicted by Einstein's theories.

Early ventures between the stars were risky and they lost many ships. Yet those stars provided a reason for man to strive and they kept coming. Safety standards had improved immeasurably by the late twenty-sixth century and while accidents still happened in the cold confines of space, they were a good deal rarer. The journey from Marmaris to Andracon, amidst an area crowded with celestial spheres, was a short, routine hop.

He knew little about his destination other than, unlike his native planet, it was not open. On the large majority of inhabited worlds, people lived under domes. Few were as fortunate as the folk back home, able to enjoy wide open vistas and a breathable atmosphere. Most were inhabiting self-contained living cells, "domes," outside of which lay an inhospitable environment.

"We will land on Andracon in five minutes," came the terse announcement, which prompted a buzz of activity amongst the stewards.

The small spaceship, a "planet hopper," operated between the tightly-knit worlds of this area. It descended without sound into a docking bay. Once landed, the sides of the dome rose to envelop the scene. The technicians established a seal and re-pressurised the area inside with that precious commodity - air.

Third-class passengers were the last to leave and John found the palms of his hands sweating and his breathing laboured. The reality of his decision to leave finally hit home.

Few people disembarked at this port. John found himself at the end of the short queue outside the ship. They soon reunited him with his luggage. As he shuffled forward, John saw they were moving towards a couple of kiosks above which a lit sign read, "Initial Processing." Before he got to a kiosk, he underwent a face scan. A green light meant he stepped forward to speak to an official in the kiosk.

John had been warned by a more experienced friend back home never to joke with an immigration official, because the authorities surgically removed their sense of humour when they began employment. The man looked none too happy, so the new arrival answered his questions in a serious, straightforward manner and soon found himself through to the waiting anti-grav sleds.

Luggage stowed, he sat down next to a young couple who said nothing. The vehicle took them silently along a lengthy corridor to the central dome. He alighted and stepped to one side, away from the busy people walking hurriedly in every direction.

The dome complex held to a standard design found on many worlds. Corridors of varying size led off from this central reception area in every direction. Above, stood a large window high on the ceiling. It struck John a waste of time, though, because, with the artificial lighting, it was a patch of black on an otherwise light-grey wall.

People of all ages and sizes were hurrying past, each filled with purpose. John, meanwhile, had two immediate aims: to send a message home and report to the barracks.

"Information Desk," proclaimed a sign and, mercifully, a human being manned it. He sighed with relief, picked up his case and made for it. A neatly-dressed woman, twice his age, was on duty. After having endured a dull morning, she perked up at the sight of a customer and smiled as he approached.

"How can I help you, sir?"

"Um, I'm wanting to get a message home."

"To Marmaris."

John paused, then realised that she must have known where he hailed from because of the ship freshly docked. In truth, one look at his distinctive yokel costume gave him away.

"Er, yes."

7

With a further smile, she helped him get a message back to his home planet. It was short and to the point, but his parents would welcome the fact that he had arrived. The price of this service took half his money, because it needed to cover the cost of the courier at the other end.

Some people ensured they surgically embedded their details into their bodies, often the backs of a hand. However, this was taboo in religious circles, because they declared it to be "the Mark of the Beast." John's parents were not religious, but still used an old-fashioned data card. Most people on their planet did that rather than have the operation. Medical facilities on Marmaris were both primitive and expensive, anyway.

The message sent, he asked about a rendezvous point for new recruits.

"Marines? Here," she said, pointing to a nearby terminal, "this'll give you all you all the information you need."

They provided a planet-wide, free intranet service and he soon discovered where and when he must go for the barracks. They would come for him, an hour hence, at a designated place in the reception dome fifty metres from where he currently stood. He therefore possessed the opportunity to learn more about his new world. He sat on the stool provided and immersed himself in the online encyclopaedia.

Andracon orbited at a mean orbit of 225 million kilometres from its sun. Surface temperature varied between 160 and 275 degrees Kelvin. So, at its very hottest, water briefly existed in liquid form before freezing again. Gravity was 0.95 ES (Earth Standard) and carbon dioxide composed the major component of its thin atmosphere.

. The single inhabited world in the solar system, Andracon belonged to the Xanthic Association of planets. Its population of a quarter-of-a-million was an eighth that of Marmaris, the usual difference between closed and open planets. John knew claims that, in the twenty-first century, some worlds' populations measured in billions, but he could not believe such nonsense.

His time expired. Rising from the stool, he heard the receptionist's voice, close to, ask, "You got one of these?"

Her hand held a TRAC, or personal computer. He knew what it was and noticed that everyone here owned one, strapped to their wrist. It was not an accessory owned by a poor farmer's son from Marmaris.

"Um, no," he admitted.

"Here, take it," she said, holding it out to him. When he hesitated, she explained, "They'll make fun of you if you don't wear one here."

"Are you sure?"

"I am. I've bought a new one, but this will serve you a turn. It's a reliable model, even if it's not the latest upgrade. Besides, you'll need to transfer any cash you have onto there. I can help you do that now."

She owned at least half a dozen old ones back home. Not that she normally gave them away, but she felt sorry for this young innocent from the sticks. There and then, she changed his physical money to credits on the computer. The process did not take long.

The woman said, "And if you'll take my advice, you'll lose the jacket. It doesn't do to look different."

She intended it as friendly advice and he saw wisdom in heeding it. As he removed the garment, it impressed her to see the young man's bulging muscles. He had been building up his strength over the past year to prepare for following his dream. John empted the single pocket and passed the jacket over the counter to the kind woman who hid it behind, assigned for disposal later.

He stood there, mesmerised for a while. A short period of silence followed his mumbling thanks.

"Over there," she reminded him, pointing to the rendezvous point. "Don't be late."

Fumbling to put some things into his trousers pocket, he picked up his case and slung his rucksack over his shoulder. As he left, he said, "Goodbye... and thanks again."

He waked across the floor of the dome, stopping half way to put the second-hand TRAC on his wrist and admire it before carrying on. Upon looking at its many functions, it surprised him to note it even possessed a self-destruct facility. The instructions told the wearer to keep a safe distance if they activated this in case it caused injury. It was one feature he had no intention of ever using.

The woman, enjoying a quiet day, watched him the whole time. She could afford the time and enjoyed a warm glow for having helped one of her few customers so much. Her actions were well beyond the call of duty, but she hoped they would not pick on the strapping young lad for being a country bumpkin. She said a silent prayer of protection for him.

Unaware of this, John moved to the rendezvous point, marked by a sign on the floor. He found one other young man there already.

"Peter Baum," he introduced himself and then confirmed that he was also there to join the marines. Tall, he towered over John and, with his tender features, he barely looked sixteen, the minimum age.

"I'm from Marmaris; where have you travelled from?"

"Galileo Three. I... I... come from Galileo Three."

Enthusiasm and nerves rising in equal measure, John volunteered, "This is something I've always wanted to do; join the army."

The reply, when it came, was half-hearted.

"Oh... I... I thought I'd do it 'cos I'd nothing else to do."

'I hope you stand the course then!' thought John, but the arrival of the transport curtailed further discussion.

The open anti-grav sled looked much like others that passed by, keeping within the designated lines on the floor. The driver, in neatly pressed military uniform, gave away its purpose.

"Hop on," he said cheerfully, "stow your things on the back."

No one else joined the duo, so it was Peter and John who heaved their cases onto the sled and climbed aboard behind the driver.

"Off we go," the driver announced, taking the vehicle off down a tunnel.

The vehicle overtook a gaggle of people walking beside the "roadway."

They emerged from the shaft into another, smaller dome, the driver barely slowed down as they crossed this area before diving into another tunnel. John's head was down, fiddling with the controls of his newly-acquired TRAC. His fellow recruit watched him for a short time. The sled's engine gave off a low hum and Peter spoke above the sound.

"A new toy?"

"Yes, I'm seeing how it works."

"Hmm."

"I won't have to use their intranet system."

"But you won't be able to contact your home world with that," the lanky youth said, nodding at the device.

"No?"

"Nah! Like the intranet, it's only planet-wide. Nations don't trust each other with access to their online systems. Galileo Three is in the Xanthic Association too, but they..."

He stopped talking because the sled had halted at the barracks entrance, terminus of yet another shaft. What a warren of tunnels! The 1st Andraconian Space Marines enjoyed exclusive use of the dome beyond.

An attendant ushered them to a building where a recruiting sergeant sat waiting for them. He was stationed behind an enormous table with a couple of other men in attendance.

"Ah, the stragglers," he boomed as they went towards him. John walked ahead, so they processed him first. The sergeant asked several questions, the most pointed of which concerned the volunteer's dealings with the planet Kupulla. John assured the man he had none.

Next, a medical officer inspected him, John stripped down to his underwear for the examination, which included a further host of questions. Pronounced fit, they accepted him for training. It appeared a somewhat perfunctory selection process, as if this nation currently took on any reasonably fit volunteer. The training would probably remove some people, but that was not his concern.

He stood outside, but did not have to wait long before Peter, having also been accepted, joined him.

"The MO said I needed to put on weight."

John did not comment. A marine then took them to their destination. Soon the newcomers were entering the barrack room, their base for the foreseeable future. In the small, oblong area, there was space for a mere half dozen recruits. The beds faced out from the walls, each with a compact locker and chair beside it. Others already occupied four of the areas, so Peter and John completed the complement as they took their baggage to the final two places. Brief introductions followed. Nicknames were the order of the day.

Rootsy caught one's attention. Lounging on his bed, he stared at them, sizing up the new arrivals.

"Hey, country boy!" he called out to John, deducing his origins from his attire, even without the jacket.

"The name's John Thorn," came the strong, defiant response.

"Okay, Thorn... Thorny it is!"

Next to him sat Billy. Fresh-faced with a fair complexion, he was perching on his chair the wrong way. When he saw Peter's height, he ironically christened him, "Midget" and called out across the floor, "Hey, Peanut, Midget here is almost the same height as you!"

The joke's target, a short, stocky individual, turned away, carrying on what he was doing.

All six occupants were of a similar age; none as old as twenty earth years. The final occupant to introduce himself had a swarthy complexion, thick, black hair with eyebrows to match. He walked up to John, shook his hand and declared, I'm Krisnan - Kris."

"Hi, Kris. When did you get here?"

"We four arrived this morning."

He welcomed this news. Arriving last was unfortunate, but at least they were close behind the others. Then Kris spoiled it by adding, "We've been waiting for you."

"Oh, I'm sorry."

"Not a problem. You can store your case behind that door."

"Thanks."

"The lockers don't have much space."

"I see."

"Welcome."

That last word meant a lot. John found tears welling up and had to turn his head away. Fortunately, with his bed being at the end, he could keep his face from the others as he unpacked.

Meanwhile, in between several rich swear words, Rootsy called out in a loud voice, "I hate them Kupullans!"

John had seen Kupulla mentioned on the intranet as another inhabited planet in this sector of the galaxy. Therefore, he knew what the young man was referring to. Before anyone could respond, the door shot open and a tall soldier marched in purposefully before coming to a sudden halt.

Taken by surprise, the new recruits were all arms and legs as they fumbled to obey the order to stand to attention at the foot of their beds.

"My name is Corporal First Class Roberts. You will address me as Corp."

The six new arrivals did their best to stand ramrod straight and look straight ahead. He then gave them a lecture. If the recruits gave their best, he would be more devoted to them than were their own mothers. But, if he found any of them slacking, he would be their worst nightmare. When he told them he would eat them for breakfast and still feel hungry, they believed him!

He led the group out to have their hair cut. How different each one looked with the shortest of crew cuts. John was glad he had seen them beforehand. Then they had showers and uniforms were issued. John noticed Rootsy checking out his muscles as he put his shirt on. Rootsy, quite muscular himself, apparently, needed to size up the opposition.

Training would begin the following day. After supper, they were back in their barracks with spare time before lights out. Some wanted to know their new companions.

Billy posed a question to John, "Do you hate the Kupullans, like Rootsy here?"

Straightforward questions deserved straightforward answers.

"The Kupullans? I know nothing about them."

From the corner of the room came Rootsy's stentorious declaration, "I (swear word) hate them Kupullans!"

Ignoring this, Billy asked a further question, "Did you come seeking fame and fortune, then?"

"Yes," John said automatically. He was then annoyed with himself for pandering to someone else's expectations and not being his own man. He was not thinking about fame and fortune. Yet, he did not want to stand out from the crowd. Better to be part of this group.

Then Rootsy began tirading about the bad Kupullans and how marvellous the Andracons were. He was a native of the latter. John noticed the others also getting annoyed by this speech. It concluded with, "No one should mess with us. Andracon is a great nation."

John asked sarcastically, "Did you make Andracon great, then?"

Rootsy looked puzzled, but did not answer. Billy smirked and the others enjoyed a few moments of peace.

Midget sat on his bed staring at the far wall, lost in thought. His mouth was wide open the whole time, which did not give him a flattering look. Eventually, he returned to the present and asked, "What are your interests then, Thorny?"

"The First Intergalactic War," he said without hesitation. "I like the ships they used and the ancient technology."

"Yeah!" the other enthused, "it's amazing what they could do in those days. I heard that, in the twenty-second century, they did head transplants! Can you imagine that? Your body's getting worn out and an' you just swap it for a new one. You keep your brain and all your memories, but you have a brand-new body. I guess the donor would have to be someone who'd died suddenly, someone who'd had their head crushed or something. Then they could donate their body to a rich guy who could afford the operation. They'd have their head transplanted onto the fresh, young body. Young heart, young limbs, they'd be able to live for another hundred years."

Billy laughed at this. He said, "Yeah, so you've got some old guy with a wizen old head, all wrinkly, deaf and his eyesight failing, on Peter Brabent's body!"

(Note: Peter Brabent was a famous twenty-sixth century athlete).

"Maybe it was just the brain."

"They suffered from dementia?"

Midget realised he would not win this discussion and fell silent while John carried on playing with his new acquisition. He noticed that everyone else in the room sported a TRAC on their wrist. Indeed, Peanut and Kris were both engaged in theirs. The latter then looked up, arose and walked across to John's bed. Once close, he asked gently, "Is this your first time on a domed planet?"

"Yes. I come from Marmaris."

"I know," Kris replied with a kind smile, "Your clothes gave you away."

"Oh. Where are you from?"

"Regnal Three."

"That's another domed planet?"

"It is."

"Naturally, I'd always heard of domed planets, and I knew this was one. But I figured there were lots of open planets, like where I come from."

Then, following a brief frown, Kris responded quietly, "Aren't you aware how infinitely small the chances are of a planet being able to sustain life and where humans can inhabit?"

"I know it needs water in a liquid state."

"That's a start."

"Plus you have to have to have a reasonable gravity. You couldn't live somewhere where you'd weigh half a ton."

"True, but there are plenty other factors you must take into consideration. You need a planet's core with enough volatility to produce radiation belts to keep out harmful radiation from the star. The atmosphere must be exactly right, both the mixture of gases and air pressure; that's a one in a million chance. The temperature has to be within acceptable limits; for the human body, that's a tiny range. Above 310K and you're feeling uncomfortable; below 275 and you need to wrap up! That's a tiny margin. Many worlds are hovering a fraction above absolute zero, others 700 degrees plus. We'd not be able to survive for ninety-five per cent of that temperature scale. You also need rotational stability, not too much seismic activity nor a prevalence of meteorites in the solar system."

"Oh."

"To name but a few factors," Kris added with a wink.

"I see."

John recognised the astronomy lesson for what it was, a kindness. A space marine ignorant of such basics could appear foolish. He therefore did not mind the lecture. It was well intended and he realised he needed to know more.

Meanwhile, there was nothing wrong with Rootsy's hearing. From across the room, he added his words of wisdom.

"I've visited Marmaris, a shit-hole of a planet. They have the luxury of an inhabitable, open planet and it's a complete pit. They don't realise how lucky they are!"

"What do you mean?" asked John defensively.

"Don't you realise how few inhabitable planets there are in the universe?"

"I'm beginning to."

"The vast majority of planets are uninhabitable except under artificial domes like this one. You'd get crushed like an eggshell by the pressure, fried or frozen. You..."

"Okay, okay, I get the message! We were very lucky on Marmaris."

"The chances of a planet being inhabited are trillions and trillions to one. That's why there are so few."

John, if he possessed a better knowledge of astronomy, could have pointed out that the Milky Way possessed trillions of planets. As it was, he made no reply and the conversation died a death. They had exposed his ignorance of this subject, but he was quite grown-up about it. He must possess more knowledge than them about other topics. Not afraid to learn fresh things, all this talk increased his interest in astronomy. He recognised that, as a space marine, he needed to learn more about the universe he would travel through.

No more talking took place that evening. Then came the five-minute warning buzzer followed by, bang on time, lights out.

John lay still in his bed. The mattress was thin and uncomfortable, plus he did not have enough pillows. Everything was different and, the exciting day having passed, he found time to introspect. His room contained a varied bunch. Peter, "Midget," appeared too immature for him and Peanut said little. Billy was flippant and Rootsy a boor. Could Kris be friend material? Time would tell.

Suddenly, he felt a sharp pang of homesickness. Swept away were his home comforts, both physical and mental. He had landed on an alien planet amongst folk so different from those in his experience. The image of his parents came into his mind, thin and worried.

John turned over, buried his head into his pillow and cried pitifully.

~ End of Chapter 1 ~

My Keeper's Brother - Chapter 2

They had no time to reflect once training began. In the early days, it was physical training to get the raw recruits fit. It pleased John that he had been on his own rigorous exercise regime before departing his homeland, because he needed every bit of strength and stamina now.

Others joined them, but, John and the men in his dormitory, B Squad, spent more time together. Corporal Roberts worked them hard, but that was to be expected. The young man from Marmaris simply wanted to perform well. He was always in the top half in any task. On some individual tasks, he came first.

Almost immediately, rivalry developed between himself and Rootsy, but he would not describe it as a friendly one. He could not take to the man. John felt most pleased at the rope challenge when he beat him climbing to the top, despite Rootsy's best efforts. That Peanut beat them both was irrelevant.

Marching and drill played a part in moulding this disparate group into a coordinated unit. B Squad fared pretty well, unless Midget, whose lanky arms and legs seem to fly in all directions, forgot his right from his left. "Right, right, right; left, left, left," he would say to his respective limbs of an evening until he mastered it.

Drill was no one's favourite pastime, but necessary. This phase seemed long, but once mastered, it ended.

Then the lectures began. A political officer gave the first one, talking about the tensions between Andracon and Kupulla. They held a long-running dispute regarding which of them controlled an uninhabited solar system equidistant from the protagonists. Dubbed Solar System 117114, it contained a couple of rocky planets close to the star. Further out orbited another unnamed, uninhabited planet thought to contain precious metals. Currently it was not being exploited.

Tensions were building, all because of Kupulla's actions, they were told. In order to reduce these, the Xanthic Association, which the two planets were members of, recently had declared a temporary exclusion zone around 117114. Both sides accused the other of violating it.

Complicating matters further, they had not banned neutral ships from the area, which stood on a direct flight path. Andracon accused Kupulla of sending their survey ships into the disputed zone disguised as merchantmen, an allegation strenuously denied.

"We do not want a war," the lecturer concluded, "but we must be prepared in case the Kupullans start one."

In other lectures, the new recruits learned the primary tasks of the marines included boarding and searching neutral ships, boarding enemy ships and missions on planets and planetoids. They would learn a great deal more in the coming days and weeks.

Following a long route march round the inside circumference of a dome, an officer gave them a stirring talk about the history of the regiment.

He informed them, "The Andracon Marine Division has a long and proud history." In particular, he regaled them with a tale of how one of their units held out to the last man on Ponoba Four, against overwhelming odds, during the Second Intergalactic War. It seemed inspiring stuff, until Billy burst the bubble somewhat by whispering, "That was a long time ago!"

"I found it interesting," Midget announced over their meal in the canteen a short while later.

The clatter of plates and buzz of conversation filled the large room. B Squad were all together except for a space on John's left for Billy. Midget asked about his whereabouts.

"He's in the bog," Rootsy said.

Not accustomed to such coarse language, Midget enquired what they meant. Rootsy then made fun of the less worldly-wise youth. John let it go at first, but, when he persisted, said, "Leave him alone!"

The bully swore at the intervention. Just then, Billy joined then which allowed the tension to disperse as he began regaling them with details of his constipation, now conquered. It amused the others, but it made John wonder if this was the sort of company he wanted to keep.

'What did you expect?' he asked himself, 'hoity-toity conversation and buttered scones for Tiffin? I'm not sure they are my kind of people.'

He found himself able to join in the merriment a short time later, though. Billy had stuffed his mouth so full that he could not answer a question straightaway without bits of food flying out of his mouth. Many exclaimed, "Urgh!" at the sight, but they still laughed. John sighed. He knew he must fit in if they would not pick on him.

Too late. That evening, he returned to the dormitory after the others. A strange atmosphere pervaded as he entered. On the surface, the others appeared engrossed in their own affairs. He saw Kris reading a book, while Rootsy and Billy were on their TRACs. Peanut was lying on his bed, playing with a fearsome-looking knife.

As he walked to his far end bed, something seemed amiss. Someone had folded down the sheets further than he left them. He turned the bedclothes back and found someone had made an apple-pie bed. Further, they had spread toothpaste all over the inside of the sheets.

John looked around, everyone was making sure their heads were down. He thought he heard a slight snigger coming from Rootsy's direction, but he could not be certain. Quietly, he stripped the bed and put the soiled sheets in a heap on the floor. That night, he slept between the blankets. He hoped that by not rising to the bait, he could diffuse the situation.

Next day all appeared forgotten, except for Midget, who, on the quiet, confirmed John's suspicions that Rootsy was the culprit for the bed prank. It was best to know, but he left it there.

The squad was in good spirits at the rifle range. They had been there before and John, like the others, improved his score. Whilst a lot of it entailed firing modern energy weapons, they also tried their hand at old-fashioned guns firing bullets.

It pleased John, who possessed a keen eye, to increase his rating from second class to first class. Only "marksman" lay ahead of that and, apart from Peanut, no one else achieved that accolade.

It proved difficult to get close to Peanut. He kept himself to himself and let his actions do the talking. Billy complemented him with the epithet, "a pint-sized marvel."

Around this time, they received a brief lecture from the chaplain. Bald on top, apart from some close-cut patches on either side of his head, he sported a short, neatly-trimmed brown beard and moustache. John guessed his age at around forty, but he was not at all sure. The man appeared most keen to emphasize his approachability.

"You can talk with me in absolute confidence any time of day. Whether you want to discuss your mortality, or why we do what we do, please feel you can come and see me. Problems at home, financial problems, I have a sympathetic ear, though I might not have all the solutions."

John thought this sounded fair, but he had no intention of confiding in him. Billy, as ever, held his own take on it. "Yeah, like I'm going to sneak out at midnight and speak to that sky pilot!"

The training had been hard, but bearable. More would follow, but the authorities granted them a forty-eight hour rest and recuperation break at this stage. With Corp's warnings regarding their behaviour still ringing in their ears, B Squad went as one to suss out the night life of Andracon.

There was a mini-casino attached to a bar and they headed for that. Spirits were high and forgotten was the antagonism between John and Rootsy, at least for now. Laughter and back-slapping accompanied the group as they entered the establishment.

A large, dimly-lit room appeared bustling, with customers drinking and gambling the evening away. To one side of the bar stood stools, mostly occupied. To the other, a traditional casino laid out in classical style: roulette, blackjack, nines and a host of other games available to the punters. Music played and whoops of delight came from the men and women indulging. Billy, Rootsy and the others were keen to get stuck in.

Under peer pressure, John changed over half his wages to chips and had a go on the roulette wheel. It amazed him at how quickly they disappeared. With the others carrying on, he retreated to the confines of the bar. He hoped the rest of his money would take longer to evaporate there.

"Hey, Thorny! Lend us some money, will ya?"

It was Billy, already a little the worse for wear after several drinks. Still trying to court popularity, John decided not to let him down. He asked how much.

"Seven hundred and fifty 'll do it."

John took his TRAC code and transferred the money over. It was half his remaining money. The other watched it go into his account with a grin, gave John a friendly punch on the chest and said, "You're a mate," then disappeared into the crowd.

'No chance of seeing that money again,' John mused.

Standing alone in the crowd, he resumed his move to the bar. All other members of B Squad stayed at the tables. As he ordered a drink and mounted a bar stool, the man on his right presented his back to him. As the figure turned round, he saw to his embarrassment that it was Corporal Roberts.

"Corp."

"Thorn."

Cursory exchanges over, John buried his face in his drink until the NCO addressed him again.

"Had enough, Thorn?"

"Um... I've learned that gambling is not conducive to a good bank balance."

Looking pleased, the other man replied, "A lesson well learned early on. What were you playing, roulette?"

"How did you know?"

"An educated guess. It draws most rookies in."

"Oh."

"It's a mug's game, nothing glamorous about it. They stack the odds against you. On average, you will lose."

"Unless you're lucky."

"Don't tell me you believe in luck!"

When John did not reply, he continued, "For every one winner, there are ten losers. The losers keep quiet, but the winners love to brag about their good fortune. It gives a false picture."

John nodded. These words made sense and he would take them to heart. However, the fact his superior was bothering to give him the time of day in a social context and the benefit of his wisdom amazed him... and he was not finished.

"You're an intelligent lad. My advice is to keep applying yourself, as you have been, and keep your nose clean. There may be some promotions coming up soon. We will be looking for outstanding candidates."

At that point, a fellow NCO appeared and Roberts turned his attention away from the trainee. Yet he had given John much to consider and the encounter boosted his morale no end.

The second evening of their leave, the others wanted to return to the casino. Not wanting to be the odd man out, John joined them, although he had no intention of gambling away what remained of his money.

"Give me a loan, Thorny! Lend me fifteen hundred for tonight."

"Okay, Billy. You give me back the seven hundred and fifty you already owe me and I'll be happy to lend you the fifteen hundred."

John knew that the man was broke, but his retort sounded cleverer than a flat, "No." Billy frowned, turned away and began hassling Kris instead.

Peanut and Midget were already exiting, the former's head not reaching the height of the younger man's shoulder. They looked a funny sight. Rootsy held back to speak to John.

"You think you're a smart arse, don't you! I saw you sucking up to Corp last night."

By explanation, John replied, "Sod off!" and hurried to catch the others.

It was not the most enjoyable evening. Instead of the bar, he found a vacant table in a corner. Sitting there, he imbibed an alcoholic drink in silence, oblivious to the surrounding sounds. Memories of Marmaris came back to him. He recalled Frank leaving the planet the year before. John had behaved badly, teasing his brother until told not to by his parents. He remembered an incident a few years before when a tornado devastated the crops. His father's face as he came in to relate the damage to his mother. Both parents were sick with worry. The farm would have gone under had not a government compensation scheme supported them. The stress and worry did them no favours. It could be why he and his brother hurried to leave that poor and backward planet.

A loud cheer from the blackjack table brought him back to the present. It looked like Billy was having a better evening. Maybe the fellow would pay him back after all, but he doubted it. He had written the money off. If it stopped him from being pestered for another loan, it was almost worth it.

Sipping his drink, he found the chaplain, of all people, settling down on a vacant seat at his small table.

'Oh shit!' thought John. 'That's all I need. Being seen talking with Corp was bad enough, but the chaplain...'

"Good evening," came the newcomer's opening gambit. John gave a less than enthusiastic response.

"Looking forward to your first tour of duty on board the ship?"

"Um, I think that's some time off, sir "

"No need to call me sir."

"Oh."

"Archie will do, that's what everybody else calls me."

John thought it strange that this gentleman would wish him to address him by his Christian name. Later would he learn it was, in fact, a nickname. Archie was short for Archbishop, an 'honorary,' ironic title.

"What are you drinking? Can I get you another one?"

"Oh, it's some kind of alcoholic gnat's piss, tastes horrible. No thanks."

The chaplain ordered himself a soft drink from a passing waitress and this instigated a conversation about John's background. He seemed interested, but John said as little as he could do without appearing impolite. Eventually, the subject returned to his drink.

"Why do you drink that stuff if you dislike it so much?"

"'Cos everybody else does. I don't want to stick out."

"Yet here you are, away from your pals by yourself."

"They're gambling and I've got little money left."

"But you drink that alcoholic concoction so as not to be different."

"It tastes horrible!"

"Why drink it then? Be your own man."

It sounded good advice, but, thought John, the chaplain should be wiser than that. He should realise that a young man wants to be seen blending in. Finally, with the dregs of his drink in his hand, he excused himself and went over to the rest of the gang at the gambling tables. Billy, it seemed, was on a winning streak; having a most successful evening. No others had any chips left and they hung on to their friend's every move. Cheers erupted from the group as their champion made another killing.

"My lucky night," Billy said. "I'm enjoying this!"

John joined them as the centre of attention vacated vingt et un and move to the roulette table. 'Oh dear,' he thought, 'this will end badly.' He knew the winner was too intoxicated, with alcohol and gambling success, to listen to any word of warning he might issue.

Rootsy shoved past him to get a prime position as B Squad descended on the roulette table. The girl on the wheel initially looked startled, then settled down when she correctly assessed the situation.

"Place your bets, please."

It took a bit of shuffling around before John achieved a good vantage point. During this time, Billy placed his first bet, with a sizeable tower of counters, on a single number.

"Straight up!" shouted one excited voice.

"Unlucky for some," called out someone else. This led John to think that he had placed the bet on number thirteen. This was wrong, they placed it on...

"Thirty three black!" the croupier called out to a loud cheer. To many observers' amazement, he had beaten the odds and scooped a huge reward.

'I should have got him to return my money in chips at that stage,' John thought to himself afterwards.

For it was downhill after that. Twelve red, eight black, eleven black... the "wrong" numbers kept coming up. Billy, in his last action, put the whole of his depleted pot on red... and up came black. Game over for Billy. Not that he minded at all. He was drunk and enjoying the moment. As soon as the last of his would-be fortune disappeared, the observers deserted him in search of fresh thrills.. The game continued without him. In fact, it went on with no members of B Squad, them having lost all their money. None seemed to care. They had experienced a good night out, they concluded, as they staggered back, laughing.

John, who at least had a few credits left, helped carry Billy, as the latter, much the worse for wear, had difficulty walking in a straight line. The others seemed inebriated, too. Peanut said little, as was his wont, but held an inane grin. Kris tried to focus his eyes and John got a scowl from Rootsy. They returned to their dormitory safely and without being told off. A restless night followed, with both Rootsy and Midget being sick, but they all reported for duty the following morning as training recommenced.

Several busy days passed with nothing of note happening. Midget was getting better at the physical exercises. Peanut beat John to the rope top again, but it was close on this occasion. They donned space suits for the first time for a jog outside the dome, an exhausting experience. More fun was a simulated hostile ship boarding exercise done inside. The training, whilst gruelling, continued to be varied and challenging. The lectures varied in quality, but they all appreciated a break from the physical activity.

One evening, before lights out, John was called out to collect some electronic notepads to be distributed to the squad members the next day. He returned to the dormitory with the box tucked under his arm. All was quiet when he re-entered the room, each person busy keeping to themselves. This struck him as odd, because they were quite boisterous when he left.

As he neared his bed, his worse suspicions seemed to be confirmed as he saw the disturbed sheet. Still holding the box, he said to Billy, "He hasn't done it again, has he?"

The reply was a facial expression which told him all he needed to know. Right! He spun on his heels and marched towards Rootsy's bed. The others all jumped up at this; a fight seemed inevitable.

"You bastard, Rootsy!" he shouted. No one had seen him half this cross before.

The accused, thinking attack the best form of defence, sprung from his bed and took a step forward, screaming back, "So what if I did?"

In a slow, deliberate movement, John handed the box to Billy, saying, "Hold this, will you?" before launching a ferocious right-hand punch at his tormentor. The box transfer distracted Rootsy and he was caught off guard. The punch landed in the middle of his face and he staggered back, towards the wall, dazed and unsteady.

A moment later, the door shot open and in marched Corporal Roberts. The squad members sprang to attention where they were.

Corp Roberts, being no fool, gauged that something was afoot. He scanned the silent statues before him and soon noticed Rootsy's red face, with even redder blood trickling from his nose onto the floor. Following a pause, he addressed him.

"I hope you're going to clear up that mess you're making when I've gone."

"Yes, Corp!"

"I should think so. Now listen you lot: there'll be no more tankering," (he meant messing about) "this evening. You've got a busy day tomorrow. In the morning, you'll have a lecture on tactics from retired Captain Kim Sun. I expect you all to be on your best behaviour. Is that understood?"

"Yes, Corp!" they shouted as one, just as the five-minute buzzer sounded.

"You heard that. Get into bed and stop tankering. Right?"

"Yes, Corp."

Then, a few decibels lower, he said to Rootsy, "You clear up that mess now."

"Yes, Corp."

Corporal Roberts disappeared as quickly as he arrived. Kris expelled air from pursed lips and, with the tension gone, John took back the box and went to strip his bed. Rootsy possessed no appetite for further confrontation and cleared up the small pool of blood at his feet.

Midget re-enacted the earlier confrontation, "Here, take this," he imitated John handing over the box, "Pow!" as he copied the punch. Kris smiled; he appeared impressed as well. Nevertheless, John endured a second night without sheets.

Some say that violence begets violence and it is never the answer. Maybe every rule has its exceptions, for, following that evening's episode, Rootsy never again tried the bed trick again. He did not seek any retaliation against John, in fact. The pair would never be bosom pals, but at least the persistent hostility finally ended. This strengthened the squad.

Next morning was a lecture on battle tactics. Retired Captain Kim Sun seemed ancient to the young recruits, although he was in his mid-60s. Short, with jet-black hair and classic oriental looks, he liked to keep his hand in by giving occasional talks to trainees. Their counterparts in A and C squads joined B Squad for the talk. They received warnings from their respective NCOs to be on best behaviour and respectful towards their lecturer. Besides, he came across as somewhat intimidating and with Corporal Roberts standing to one side, they would not mess about.

The man's first words were a bit mumbled and difficult to catch. He said something about "before" and "reminding ourselves." Then, he cleared his throat and was a good deal clearer as the talk proper began.

"The weapons of the ancient world differed completely from those employed today. Nevertheless, we can still learn from the successful generals of the past. Certain tactical methods are universal and can apply to any age.

"Can any of you name any famous generals of the Ancient world?"

John put his hand up straightaway. After all, passionate about military history, he knew a fair deal on the subject.

"Yes?"

"Hannibal, Julius Caesar, Alexander the Great."

"Admirable. What can we can learn from these figures?"

Putting his hand up again, John noticed that no one else had. Kim waited a moment before picking him again.

"Hannibal can teach us about keeping the enemy off guard. The Romans didn't expect him to cross the Alps and attack them in their own back yard."

" Admirable again. Buck up, the rest of you, you should know this. We've talked about it before."

As the lesson progressed, the same pattern continued, with John alone answering questions and none of the others knowing the answers. The lecturer was becoming frustrated at this. John enjoyed being praised for his correct answers, but it became more and more awkward for him. Captain Kim began slipping in comments such as, "You should remember," or even, "We've been through this." It belatedly dawned on the recruit from Marmaris that the lecturer was under the misapprehension that he had previously taught the class. However, he felt extremely awkward about being the one to point this out.

Following yet another insightful answer from John, the Captain enthused, "Well remembered. What's your name, marine?"

"Thorne, sir."

"Admirable, Thorn, but buck up the rest of you!"

This was getting embarrassing now. The topic turned to Alexander the Great. Kim spoke at length about the Battle of Issus, the critical importance of well-trained troops and good leadership. When he asked a further question to his audience, there was still only one person answering.

"He moved down into Egypt, sir."

"Again, admirable, Thorn. Why can't the rest of you remember?" Then, with a direct question aimed at John, he asked him if he knew the date Alexander the Great arrived in Egypt.

"Um, I'm not sure."

"Give me your best guess."

"333 BC, sir."

" Admirable. I wish the rest of you had been paying attention."

"Um, sir?" the same recruit, turning bright red as he caught the lecturer's attention.

"Yes?"

"I... I don't think you've taught us before. My private study taught me these things."

"Oh!" Captain Kim said. The revelation took the wind out of his sails, but at least he accepted the truth of it. The rest of the session ran without further controversy, much to everyone's relief, not least John's. In fact, there were no further questions.

Afterwards, his immediate colleagues gathered round him. He expected a roasting, but it was not like that.

"Hey, thanks for putting him right," said Kris.

"How come you know all this stuff?" Billy asked.

He did not answer, for Corporal Roberts was bearing down on the group. He was making a bee line for John and the others were parting before him.

"Well done, Thorn," he said, but the praise only added to his embarrassment. The NCO then commanded, "Now come with me."

The room emptying now, the trainees stepped aside for the tall, imposing figure of Corporal Roberts and his sidekick. They passed retired Captain Kim, speaking with another NCO. John glanced at him, but did not achieve eye contact. Where was he being taken?

John began wracking his brains to work out what he had done wrong. Was he about to be disciplined? His worst fears seemed to be confirmed when he arrived at the door marked "Captain Farnham." Corp gave him his instructions.

"You will march three steps in, halt, salute, and stand to attention while the captain addresses you. You are not to speak except in reply to a direct question. Once the captain has finished with you, you will salute, about turn and march straight out. Do you understand?"

"Yes, Corp!"

"Very well." Roberts pressed the door intercom.

"Come!" came a command from within. The electronic door slid open and John entered.

John marched in and gave his best salute, standing to attention, straight as a ramrod.

He had only ever seen Captain Farnham from a distance. He was captain of the space destroyer *ASS Excellent*, the ship that John would serve on if he passed his training. A handsome 48 year-old, he had been a top athlete in his youth. A wrinkled brow and chiselled features, this was a no nonsense commander. Yet he possessed an air of natural authority about him, which meant he never needed to shout. When he spoke, it was with the peculiar accent reserved for the Andraconian aristocracy.

"Trainee Thorn," he began, his tone measured but not unpleasant, "I have been receiving excellent reports about you. In three weeks, after completing your training, your squad will march out. On that day, you are promoted to the rank of corporal, second class. Make sure you live up to the faith being shown in you. That is all. Dismissed."

John gave another salute, turned to his left and quick-marched out. He only allowed himself a smile when he was back in the corridor with Corporal First Class Roberts.

"Well done, Thorn."

"Thank you, Corp!"

"You deserve it. Make sure you live up to the high standards you have been setting of late... and you handled Captain Kim well today, too."

This was rare praise from the NCO. He must ensure it did not go to his head. They marched together to the drill hall, where Corp made a quick announcement about John's promotion. It pleased the latter to witness the squad's reaction. Even Rootsy gave him a "Well done."

The next few weeks were a blur as they completed their training. The big day came when they marched past Captain Farnham and other dignitaries inside the largest dome allocated to Andracon's armed forces. They awarded John the white lanyard as the best trainee of the cohort, but then so was Peanut. Joint best then. John beamed with pride, as did the other recruits, some of whose family members attended the ceremony. Everything ran as planned. It pleased B Squad to be operational.

End of the year 2581 and they enjoyed a generous period of leave before their first deployment. Many visited their families off-world. Rootsy, a native Andraconian, was on poor terms with his parents and stayed in the barracks. A place was not immediately available in the NCO barracks for John. He had to stay put for now, but saw little of Rootsy. When he did, their exchanges were civil enough.

"I've got a baby sister!" Midget announced when he came back off leave.

"Congratulations," John offered.

"It's disgusting; my parents are *far* too old to be having sex!"

The others laughed. The man from Marmaris wondered why he had not gone back to his home planet during leave. He did not know why, he hung around doing nothing in particular. With the barracks deserted, he got a lot of reading done. He ventured to the casino/bar on one occasion and suffered a further conversation with the chaplain. It made him feel awkward, because after discussing mundane things, the man switched the subject to God and the meaning of life. He had neither the time nor inclination to talk about that sort of thing. He did not go back there. On his final full day, he got a message off to his parents telling them of the successful completion of his training and promotion to corporal, second class. Receiving no reply, he did not know if his communication got through.

The following week, they moved John to the NCO barracks. It felt funny dorming with Roberts; at least they were at opposite ends of the room. He no longer ate in the same canteen as the men he trained with. He still saw plenty of them. Corp ensured he kept the squad in tip-top condition with regular exercises.

Meanwhile, the international news was disconcerting. The Andracon government announced its intention to withdraw from the Xanthic Association. This, they believed, would give them more freedom of movement. Tensions between their planet and Kupulla were ratcheting up. It remained a war of words and wise heads did not want it escalating into something else. Rootsy, not qualifying as wise, continued to vocalise his wish for a shooting match with the bloody Kupullans.

Finally, they received orders that they were going on board the *ASS Excellent* for a routine patrol. Everyone knew, though, that with the current political situation, it would not be routine.

The *Excellent*, the newest ship in the Andraconian fleet, was a Prince Class destroyer and a state-of-the-art war vessel. When built, they expected her usual duty would be as an escort to one of the nation's three juggernaut battleships. Those behemoths were the nation's pride. They must protect them at all costs. On this occasion, *Excellent* would fly solo. Its mission was to show the Andraconian flag in an area of international space, some distance away from the disputed solar system 117114.

"Hurry, lads, get your kit stowed over there. We'll be in level 4B. Move along there!"

John stood impassively beside Corp as the latter issued orders. Their excited mood of the first day soon passed and they confined the marines to their quarters for the entire voyage. It seemed an anti-climax.

"Bloody hell, this is boring!" Rootsy declared on day three. "I want to see some action. We didn't do all that training just to sit on our arses."

For once, there was widespread agreement with his words. Meanwhile, as an NCO, John possessed a lot more freedom to wander the ship, although there were sizeable areas that he must stay away from. Although highly automated and with a crew small for the vessel's size, it still had plenty of men on board keeping systems running. From the galley staff to the laundry operatives, from the munitions officer to the fire suppression team, there were still many roles for human beings on a late twenty-sixth century ship.

John liked peering out of the observation port on level 2. Situated in a quiet section of the ship, there was no harm in it while nothing was happening. He had no immediate duty and he was not in anyone's way.

What a busy section of the galaxy they lived in. A myriad of stars and surrounding solar systems existed within a short distance of each other in astronomical terms. He had heard of solar systems colliding and planets, or even stars, being thrown off course and heading off on a dangerous vector.

None of that happening on one particular afternoon when John was peering out of the observation port. Not that the terms "morning," or "afternoon" held any meaning in space, but the destroyer, as with all ships, worked on a day/night cycle divided into 24 hours that had served mankind for millennia.

They parked *Excellent* in orbit around a huge, gaseous planet. By the light of a nearby star, he could see its blue clouds swirling round. One of its small moons passed between the planet's surface and the ship.

Engrossed at the sight, he did not notice someone approach until he was almost upon him. Looking up, he recognised Executive Officer Kovatz, second in command of the ship. They had not spoken before.

John felt guilty being there. He would have made a quick escape if possible. Yet XO (as everyone called him) bid him stay.

"All's quiet in the Ops Room and I'm taking a breather. Stay, let's chat."

"Yes, sir!"

"Corporal Thorn, am I correct?"

It astonished John that the second-in-command of the ship should know his name. Then he held a calm, friendly air about him, which soon put the younger man at his ease. Introductions were soon over and John studied the officer at close quarters.

Mid-forties by the look of him, his complexion did not appear too healthy. Was that the effect of the low, artificial lighting in this section?

A high hairline, what hair he possessed, he combed into a ridge at the top of his head. Studious-looking, he made it clear that he did not hesitate to engage the young marine in conversation.

"You've been studying Poseidon, then?"

"The planet we're orbiting?"

"The same."

"Yes, I was watching the blue clouds swirling round. It gets quite hypnotic after a while."

"Do you know what composes the clouds?"

"The clouds?"

"Yes."

"Um, no."

XO was in his element now. Having got his degree in astronomy, it was a subject that never ceased to grip him. He was happy to have a rookie to teach.

"Care to take a guess?" he began.

"I understand that hydrogen is the most common element in space, therefore my guess is hydrogen. It's a gaseous giant planet, right?

"Good guess. There's lots of hydrogen in its atmosphere, but large quantities of helium and methane as well. We class Poseidon as a super giant planet; you could fit Andracon into it many times over."

"If it comprises gas, could the *Excellent* fly straight through it?"

A genuine question, albeit a naive one. It was hard for XO not to chuckle. As he collated his reply in his mind, John added, "After all, we do have a force field."

"We do indeed, but the forces involved are unimaginable. Even a short distance into the atmosphere the pressure would crush us like an egg shell. Deeper down, comes an icy mantle and, in the centre, a small iron core. I say small, but I mean in proportion to the whole; it's still bigger than the whole of our planet."

"Phew, it makes us seem so small."

"Indeed it does."

No one else passed their way and it contented both men to keep the conversation alive. XO moved the topic onto a particular aspect which was a favourite of his.

"The early days of colonisation are a fascination to me," he confided to the younger man who was finding this enthusiasm infectious. "There's much that we don't know, because they lost the records... if they ever existed. We're told that many species of animal were extinct pre First I. W. But the colonists brought lots of different species of flora and fauna with them."

"Before they introduced the bio protocols?"

"That's right, they could transport animals in cellular form. It must have been amazing coming across virgin planets and deciding to colonise them. They visited planets never previously set foot on and went through decontamination until sure there were no alien viruses."

"What about terra-forming? Didn't they build great plants to enrich the oxygen on certain open planets?"

"They built such plants on several worlds, you're right, but with very limited success. It proved better to sow seeds from old earth and let nature do its bit. Not that it was always successful. Like an effective general, the early colonists had to pick battlegrounds where

33

they stood a good chance of success. There were lots of places to choose from, especially in this region."

"But I thought open planets are rare."

"It's true they represent a tiny proportion of the total, yes, but there are millions of planets within a couple of parsecs of here. Later colonists had to settle on a domed existence, after others snapped up all the best open planets."

"You mentioned old earth; do you think it's true that all life originated there?"

"In the known universe, it would seem to be the case, yes."

"But we've lost earth's whereabouts now, that's right, isn't it?"

"It is, thanks to the nihilists of the Second War."

"And there are other parts of the inhabited, colonised galaxy lost to us."

"That's true. I wish we weren't so introspective nowadays. I'd love to lead an expedition to rediscover the lost parts."

"Do you think you ever will?" John asked.

"Not me. There's no sign of it happening at all. There's no political will, nor anyone rich enough to finance such an expedition. I don't think I'm going to see it in my lifetime... maybe in yours."

A tantalising thought, but it was time to move on and they returned to their respective stations, not meeting again on that voyage.

Back in their ship's quarters, B Squad had been playing cards, but now sat back in the galley waiting for dinner. As John joined them, Midget was asking Kris whether he knew if this operation would be over soon.

"No idea," came the reply with a shrug, "but I hope so. All this inactivity is frustrating."

Rootsy, not wishing to be left out, said, "Yeah! You're telling me. It's doin' my 'ead in. I want to board another ship, kick some Kupullan flesh!"

It was Peanut who reminded him they were not at war yet.

"Yeah, too bad. Hey, Thorny, any news from above deck?"

"I'm afraid not, all quiet on the Western Front. It can't be too tense if XO has time on his hands. We're in orbit round a super giant planet named Poseidon right now."

He chuckled to himself at displaying the knowledge that he himself had only just learned himself. Still, image is everything and he enjoyed being able to show off the information that the unfortunates stuck below deck were not privy to.

The rest of the operation passed without incident for the marines. The whole thing had been a big non-event and an anti-climax. John considered the matter, deciding that an anti-climax was a great deal better than war. On the international front, peace talks were beginning with Kupalla on a neutral planet hoping they could avert conflict.

John never found out if they offered him a new post because of his conversation with XO, but it came following an extended period of inactivity base,. It was not an order, they gave him the choice whether or not to accept it. He was, therefore, keen to find out all that it entailed. The Captain's Assistant role promised a major departure from the marines, one offering variety and a far more interesting vantage point while out on operations.

Captain Farnham already employed a valet to look after his personal needs such as making sure the right uniform was ready and his room kept tidy. On operations, the Captain's Assistant's role came into its own. He would be stationed either on the bridge or Operations Room, responding swiftly to the captain's commands.

A major bonus was a room to himself whilst in the dome and on board ship. Most excitedly of all, he would have to fly a space launch. That clinched it; to learn to fly a space craft, even a modest one, would be an adventure and a useful string to his bow. He accepted.

Whilst B Squad sweated blood, training in space suits out on the surface outside the dome, he was learning to fly!

Computers controlled many of the space launch's functions. There was still plenty to learn, especially what to do if certain systems failed. Large enough to carry six passengers and a pilot, it would be his job to ferry the captain and any chosen dignitaries as ordered.

"Pity it has no guns," he said to the instructor. The latter ignored the comment, but his pupil's progress over several weeks pleased him. Indeed, he took to it like a duck to water. Coming in to land seemed daunting at first, he worried he might hit a dome wall. Yet he gained confidence and before long was docking like a professional ferry pilot.

His training complete, he enjoyed a mere two days break before *ASS Excellent* set sail again. Rumours said the mission was escorting one of Andracon's three giant juggernaut spaceships. He had never seen one, but, of course, knew of their existence. The prestige which came with these mighty warships, was hard to exaggerate. A colossal expense, they displayed a nation's power. Hence it was big news in the quadrant the previous day, when they were about to set sail, word came through of the loss of another nation's juggernaut in a nearby star system. It belonged to the House of Drakas in the Armana System. Mere names to John, but all emphasised the gravity of the loss. The reports stated it sailed straight into a star. Speculation why this happened, was rampant, but no one knew.

No time to dwell on the matter. For at 0530 hours the alarm would wake him to start an important day. It would be his first time on operational service in his new role as Captain's Assistant. He eagerly anticipated it.

~ End of Chapter 2 ~

My Keeper's Brother - Chapter 3

The *ASS Excellent* was a hive of activity the following morning.

"Careful! Excuse me. Can I squeeze through?" were some things John said as he made his way towards his cabin, two along from Captain Farnham's for operational reasons. Carrying a mini-computer with his right hand and a poly-canvas duffle bag slung over his left shoulder, he entered a part of the ship he had not visited before. He kept one eye on his TRAC with the ship's internal schematics displayed. Three more corridors and a final level change to his destination.

The automated supply-loader was malfunctioning. Neither a good omen, nor very impressive for a new spaceship. It meant a lot of essentials brought aboard the old-fashioned way: a chain of men passing them up the line into the hold. Earlier, as he hurried past, he noticed the familiar faces of B Squad on this duty. They did not spot him.

"Ah, Thorn! There you are."

It was the captain. John fumbled, trying to put his things down and salute. The other man waved it away, a gesture saying it was unnecessary, adding, "Briefing room in twenty."

With that, he left. John stood near his cabin, so he stepped straight in and breathed a sigh of relief. He would have liked to have pointed out to the captain that he was not late, but, afterwards, he felt glad he kept quiet. The captain possessed an air of urgency about him; there was no implied criticism of his new assistant.

Brushing the concern aside, he smiled as he considered he now had a cabin to himself. Okay, it may be tiny, not room to swing a cat, but it represented his own little domain. Space was precious onboard ship. It would be his bolthole if he had spare time.

He never expected to be included in the meeting held in the Briefing Room. Captain Farnham felt it best, though, that they included John in the operational picture. A stream of senior staff, most of whom he did not recognise, filed in. As John entered, he noticed Executive Officer Kovatz, who gave him a look of recognition. That cheered him up. The venue was not cavernous.

With large numbers present, no spare room could be found. John wormed his way to the back and the most inconspicuous station.

Captain Farnham introduced a couple of new officers to the rest and they all enjoyed a brief laugh at the expense of the logistics officer whose supply-loader had broken down. Then he announced, "And Thorn, over in the corner, is my new assistant." Heads turned towards him and there were smiles as he went bright red. The moment passed and it pleased him when the briefing began.

"Along with the *Revenge* and the *Glorious*, we shall screen the *Max* on a mission to Hydron in the Ravanis System. As you are aware, this is near 117114, so it's a sensitive area of space and we must be extra careful not to provoke anyone.

"There is a civil war being fought on Hydron, a messy business. *Max* will send a delegation down to meet with representatives of the friendly, southern force and gauge whether our operative on the ground will need to be extracted. We are not to get involved in the fighting. We are maintaining our official policy of neutrality in this conflict.

"Our job will be, with *Revenge* and *Glorious*, to enforce a 500,000 kilometre exclusion zone around the juggernaut. *Max* will send out vims to patrol round the planet as part of the operation."

As the captain, followed by the Executive Officer, went into fine detail, John tried to assimilate what he had already heard. He knew that *ASS Maximillian*, "Max," was one of Andracon's three giant spaceships of the Juggernaut Class. They named the ship after a twenty-fifth century national hero. Vims were vimanas, the pilotless, main fighting craft sent out from her hangars. Fast and manoeuvrable, these provided the ship's main "punch." *Revenge* and *Glorious*, like *Excellent*, were space destroyers. He did not understand the politics involved, but he expected that their potential enemy, Kupulla, would take a keen interest in what they would be doing.

Questions and answers followed, but soon the meeting ended and out they all trudged. John held back, because the captain still stood there, chatting to the XO. When Farnham finished, he looked up and said, "On me," and John left with his superior.

As they walked along the corridor on the way to the bridge, the captain quizzed him about his background.

"You're from Marmaris, that's right, isn't it?"

"Yes, sir."

"Family?"

"My parents are still there. I have an older brother. He's on the planet Eden "

"Ah, the religious planet."

"Yes,"

"Now!" the captain declared in a loud voice, showing the serious stuff was coming.

"You're a trained pilot, right?"

"Yes, sir, I've flown the launch."

They were nearing the bridge now.

"Good. When we rendezvous with the *Maximillian*, you will fly the liaison officer and myself over there. Once my meeting with Captain West is through, I shall be your sole passenger on the return journey."

"Yes, sir."

They entered the ship's bridge. Seated at their stations, the crew present were told "at ease" before they could stand. The captain's chair was central and dominated the room. John had never been on the bridge. They showed him his perch to the right, and behind, the captain. He sat there as they made orders, read out data and other announcements made. The automatic loader began functioning again as soon as they finished manually stowing the last of the goods.

To the front was a massive, oblong screen. They currently split it between an outside view of the docking dome and XO in the Ops Room. The latter looked up to respond to Farnham's enquiry.

"Everything set here; all systems green."

"Very well," the captain said as he pressed a button on his seat and a hot beverage rose from the arm. "Launch procedure, Mr Lee."

"Yes, sir."

Speaking to John much quieter, he ordered, "Go to the galley and get my scone."

Springing from his stool, he cried, "Yes, sir!" louder than he should have, and marched out at double speed.

He had spoken with Galley Master Bunsen on several previous occasions. The man's curious nickname came early in his career when he burnt the food. Ebony skinned and with a huge grin, he enjoyed his job. He gave the new captain's assistant a warm greeting when he entered his domain.

The place was empty apart from one other man contemplating his coffee. He did not have a duty. Bunsen's face looked stubbly that morning, a moustache topped his ample lips.

"Here you are," he said as he passed over a toasted cheese scone with butter, "just as Captain Farnham likes 'em."

"I take it this is a regular order."

"Daily! Yes it is."

"You enjoy your job, don't you, Bunsen?"

"I've been on service here eight years now. I'm pretty used to it now, but find I'm always tired..."

The other man, looking up from his drink, interrupted their conversation with, "I joined up to escape from a boring job. Life's never dull here; you don't know what your next operational task will be."

Before John could respond, the Galley Master cut in, "You'd better get that off to the good captain, Thorny, before it gets cold."

"Oh yes! Of course... thank you," he replied and hurried out.

If the scone had cooled down too much, Farnham never mentioned it. He ate it between issuing orders. The domed hangar was open and depressurised by now and the space destroyer lifted clear and hovered. Then UDS engines engaged and the craft shot up into space. They could feel no sensation of flying thanks to the inertia negators. The acceleration forces were so massive that, without this wonderful invention, it would have crushed those inside the craft instantly. One moment John was looking at the bleak planetary vista of a rock-strewn plain, the next a juggernaut spaceship filled the screen. John viewed it with awe, what a mighty vessel. Over 750 metres from bow to stern, with multiple decks and hangars for smaller craft at regular intervals along her sides, a magnificent sight. A few "vims" - pilotless fighting craft designed only for space use - circled her on patrol. They spied the other two destroyers in the distance.

Captain West of the *ASS Maximillian* came on the screen and welcomed his opposite number. Soon John sat at the launch's controls, about to take off with his cargo of two VIPs. He was nervous and only slowed his breathing down by maximum effort. He forced himself to relax and concentrate, reminding himself that his trainers well versed him in flying this craft.

Cleared to leave, he eased the controls and made the perfect departure, steering it towards the designated hangar on the juggernaut. There was plenty of space on board the massive ship and John set the launch down centrally. Perhaps his passengers had a little further to walk than necessary, but they did not comment.

The pilot stayed in the cabin during the meeting. *Excellent's* liaison officer would stay on board *Max*, but Captain Farnham came back for the return journey. He smiled as he embarked.

"Video links are fine, but you can't beat human contact," was his verdict.

After returning to the bridge, the operation began. The task force set off for the Ravanis System, a half hour's journey. Hydron was an open planet, renowned for its beautiful scenery and crystal clear lakes, the sole inhabited one in that solar system. So what did the inhabitants do? Start a civil war and fight amongst each other. John did not know half the politics involved, but gleaned that Andracon's declared neutrality was a deception. Their agent was working with the southern power.

The operation began with the *Maximillian* in synchronous orbit round the planet and the three destroyers keeping guard to enforce the exclusion zone round the master ship.

With a thick outer atmosphere holding perpetual storms, it forced them to send ships down to see the situation. These were the manned "interceptors," able to travel within and without the atmosphere.

The *Excellent's* crew concentrated on enforcing the exclusion zone round the juggernaut, not what was happening on the planet. They split the screen on the bridge between the *Maximillian* and XO in the Operations Room.

In the Ops Room, the nerve centre of the ship, they busily tracked ships throughout the quadrant. They knew the Kupullans may take an interest and send ships to observe. So when a pair of Kupullan spy ships arrived on the scene, no one panicked. They were keeping a safe distance.

"All part of the game," Captain Farnham said to no one in particular. Operations continued, then one operator noticed something suspicious on the edge of the exclusion zone. The sensors detected it for a split second, it was a shadow which disappeared. All the same, they took it seriously.

Various ways existed of cloaking a landed ship on a celestial body, but even they were easy to negate if you possessed the proper equipment. Such cloaking devises did not operate in space, because a ship's force field would not allow a cloak to form. Rumours abounded of undetectable stealth ships in space, but most people did not believe the technology existed.

They could not take any chances. They sent unmanned probes see if they could detect anything. "Could just be a space phenomenon," XO speculated. There was lots of activity in the Ops Room and they kept the captain informed regularly.

XO, coordinating the hunt, said, "It's been two hours and still nothing. I think we'll put it down as a false alarm and call the probes off."

"Agreed," said the captain.

"We're still keeping one eye on the ships going down to the surface," XO said.

"Mmm."

The XO replied, "You possess all the hi-tech equipment in the universe, but you still need someone to understand the data and decide. Having to monitor what the spy ships are up to adds complications."

Nevertheless, with no further scares, the interceptors came back to base for the night.

John breathed a premature sigh of relief, for one of the ship's main sensors began playing up. It was imperative to get it working. For that to happen, they must replace a key component. That meant a space walk out onto the hull of the ship. Technician Ajmal was a congenial-looking fellow with dark skin and a pleasant mien. He would replace the part, but needed someone to assist him. Out of the kindness of his heart, Farnham chose John.

"You've worn a space suit before?" the captain sought confrontation.

"Er... yes," his assistant replied, still in shock.

He had indeed done exercises in a suit on Andracon's surface, but this was far more scary. Plus, Ajmal was notorious or using technical language and having to be reminded to come down to the level of normal mortals in order to communicate.

Therefore he felt some trepidation as he donned his suit. As he did so, Ajmal, already suited up, explained John's role in the operation.

Seeing a look bordering on terror in the other man's eyes, he sought to reassure him.

"It will be a straightforward operation. Once the airlock has depressurised, it will remain open for the duration. We will anchor our harnesses in there, which means you cannot fly away. I will step out first; you follow me. The artificial gravity will not operate outside, but there are grab handles all the way to S.I.T.T. You will carry the T.S.H. and..."

"Sorry?"

"The device with the tools I'll need."

"Oh."

"And the sensor component. You will attach them to your suit so that you cannot launch them into space."

"That's good," said John with a smile.

"It is, because if they deducted its cost from your wages, you'll be paying them back for the next two hundred years."

He got the message; an expensive piece of kit. After a few further instructions, the pair completed their preparations, donned helmets and entered the air lock. Strapped to John was the heavy, box-like component, a cuboid thirty centimetres long, plus a board which held the tools.

'So, I'm the spanner holder!' he considered. 'Well, someone's got to do it.'

They checked intercoms before depressurisation. Then the outer door slid open and, one by one, they stepped out onto the hull of the ship. It looked massive from this perspective; whatever must the *Maximillian* seem like, John considered.

There were compensations with weightlessness. The component box no longer felt heavy. Following the example of the figure ahead of him, he took the grab handles one at a time as he progressed to the sensor. The technician stayed in constant contact with Ops, this being a vital operation for the ship to continue to operate effectively.

Once they made it to the array, it was John's job to open the tool holder and position it so that Ajmal could use them. With great precision, he took each one he needed for the moment and replaced it in its bay after use. Soon, he had the old component out and swapped it for the fresh one. As this operation proceeded, John looked up. He knew that the ship's force field was still operating a metre above his head, but decided against jumping up to test it. It

43

brought him back to the operation when Ajmal swore when his foot slipped. John shot out his arm and with his other hand on a handrail steadied the technician. No harm done and soon they completed the task. They made their way back, John holding the defunct component.

Back inside, he gave an enormous sigh of relief now it was all over. Ajmal thanked him, pleased it had gone smoothly. John did not wait for the result, but, next morning, he heard that the sensor was working perfectly.

"One hot, buttered scone."

"Thank you, Bunsen; I'll take it to him straightaway."

The second day began in similar vein. The interceptors kept leaving their mother ship and heading down to the planet. It was not John's place to ask what was happening. The Kupullans' spy ships continued to probe a short distance beyond the exclusion zone, but showed no outright hostile intentions. "We'd act similarly if the boot was on the other foot," the captain said.

Matters were taking on a routine feeling when, mid-morning, all hell broke loose.

"Unidentified ship," announced the operator sitting next to XO, "2828 by 253, vector 1.0"

While still some distance out from the exclusion zone, it was travelling steadily towards the juggernaut. *Excellent* sent out warning messages, but they ignored these. A large vessel, the sensors could not establish its identity at this stage. The destroyer needed to know what it was as early as possible. XO recommended action stations to be called and the captain agreed. A flurry of activity ensued as their training came to the fore.

"We need to identify before the threat increases," Farnham said.

The alert ended as quickly as it began. A merchant ship, unaware of what it was blundering into, changed course as directed.

"Confirmed neutral, stand down!" came the order and everyone relaxed again.

Turning to his assistant, Farnham rolled his eyes and said, "Just blundered into a war zone without checking their charts; pretty reckless behaviour. It could have interrupted operations. The idiot probably doesn't even realise what they've done."

Shortly afterwards, the screen was showing the *Maximillian* when a returning interceptor pilot misjudged his landing and crashed into the hangar. A huge fire erupted, but they extinguished it without too much effort. Casualties were low, but it destroyed two of the juggernaut's shuttles. With the third one out of service for essential maintenance, Captain West sent a request to his opposite number on the *Excellent*.

"We need a shuttle down on the surface, stat. Can you help?"

Worded as a question, only one answer could to be given. In next to no time, John was taking controls of the launch. Behind him sat an intelligence officer, the seat next to him remained empty. Further behind were some familiar faces: Corporal Roberts and marines Rootsy, Billy and Peanut. He exchanged a brief greeting with his former colleagues before taking off for the planet. With time of the essence, the intelligence officer briefed them en route.

"They have remotely programmed the coordinates for the rendezvous point into your flight computer from onboard the *Max*." he told John. "You will fly there and land on the lawn in front of the building." Then, turning to Corporal Roberts, but speaking for the benefit of all the marines present, he continued, "You are to form a defensive perimeter around the shuttle while I contact Agent X. As soon as he is on board, you are to re-embark. Then, pilot, we fly straight to *Max* hangar B."

"Hangar B, sir?"

"The one in the middle, starboard side."

"Right."

They made the rest of the journey in silence until they came to enter the planet's atmosphere. The dials went crazy when it battered the craft from both sides. The shuttle received multiple lightning strikes. It seemed surreal, because while the front screen showed a grey haze and read-outs going haywire, the inertia negators working overtime, meant no sensation of movement. John swore and Billy looked away from the screen as it made him feel sick.

Then they were through into clear air. The dials returned to normal and showed they were eighty kilometres above the surface of Hydron. No other aircraft of any description showed on the sensors.

With the launch flying on automatic, John had little to do as they descended. It would land itself on the designated patch of grass as programmed.

As they got nearer the surface, a scene laid out before them. A mixture of modern energy and old fashioned weapons were in use. They were flying straight into the middle of a raging battle and, with the limited shield capacity of the launch, its pilot was concerned.

The ship vectored towards a large building, a huge, white mansion on a hill with terraced lawns. An architectural monstrosity, the building sported a couple of round turrets of different heights and a flat roof.

As they got closer, they saw soldiers covering the lawn, trying to hold off a tidal wave of attackers.

John took manual control and said, "I can't land down there, the..."

"Over there, land on the roof," ordered the intelligence officer, pointing. He had spotted their man, waving like crazy, a couple of people beside him. Bullets and energy pulses filled the air as John laid the launch down on the top of the building. A low wall curved round the roof hid the craft from the attackers whilst there.

The intelligence officer headed for the door even before they touched the ground. The portal flew open and out he jumped, followed by the marines. Some sort of heated, but brief, argument followed before they all piled back in again, including Agent X, plus a woman and young child.

"Go, go, go!" Corporal Roberts shouted and as the second the door closed, the launch lifted off.

It hovered a moment before UDS engaged and it shot up into the sky. It was long enough for one blast from an energy weapon to hit it. The inertia negators gave in and it rocked them from side to side. The shield's integrity held and, with the inertia negators coming back online, they made their escape.

Tensions were high on board. Rootsy boasted that he had picked off some attackers during the few seconds on the roof. Meanwhile, the intelligence officer and Agent X engaged in a heated argument. John gathered that the man insisted on bringing along with his mistress and child, much to the other's annoyance.

John never found out the identity of Agent X. Both he and the intelligence officer, along with the unscheduled passengers, disembarked in hangar B, *ASS Maximillian*. He then flew the marines back, speculating in his mind regarding the whole incident.

Far from being mere observers, Andracon was providing support to one side in the civil war. He concluded they had aided the losing southern side and that air strikes from *Max's* interceptors proved unable to stem the tide of the advancing northern armies. Maybe the one that crashed into the hangar had sustained battle damage.

"Wait 'till we tell the others!" Rootsy exclaimed

Billy said, "You'll have killed half the enemy army by the time we get back to Mitch and Kris."

"How are they?" enquired the former marine, but they lost his words in the general hubbub. They all piled out except John, who needed to perform post flight checks. All appeared in order, despite the hit they received. They had been lucky. "I must tell the maintenance crew," he said to himself.

After backing the wrong side in a foreign war, the Andraconian task force set sail for home. The return journey was without incident. Back home, the crew cold enjoy some rest and recuperation before the next mission.

In the casino one evening, John sat away from the gambling area at a table by himself. He sipped a soft drink and watched the world go by. He felt in a philosophical mood, musing over an encounter he experienced a little earlier. A woman had engaged him in conversation. She mentioned her "boyfriend" a couple of times, but they could still discuss things in a civilized manner. It did not last long and she soon moved on.

He realised that this was his first meaningful encounter with a member of the opposite sex since he arrived on Andracon. Without a doubt, women were a foreign, exotic species in his eyes. It was a male-dominated world he lived in, there being no women on board ship. He knew other societies mixed the sexes in their fleets, but not the Andraconians.

'I won't be here for ever,' he considered. 'I've lived on this planet for two years but can't imagine I'll be here forever. Still, I'm not getting itchy feet yet. I want to see what happens here and keep involved. This captain's assistant's job is more varied than I'd expected. Never a dull moment, in fact.'

The place was not as full as normal and he noticed XO making a beeline for his table. He did not mind, because he quite liked the older man.

"Do you mind if I join you, John?"

"Not at all," came the reply. No need for formal titles here.

"By yourself this evening?"

"Yeah, I don't mind. I was thinking about things."

Feeling that the Executive Officer was someone he could confide in. He voiced some of his musings. In this current role, he found it difficult to have a sense of belonging. He was no longer in the marines, but did not feel part of the regular ship's crew either.

"Why not?" asked the other, surprised. "Captain's Assistant may be a varied role, but it's a necessary component in the machine that is the ship's company."

"So that the captain gets his morning scone?" came the cynical question, but XO was having none of it.

"I know what you did on our last mission. The space walk was no routine job and vital for the entire ship to continue. Then your heroics on Hydron with the successful extraction of our agent down there. I'll tell you for nothing that they considered you for a medal for that operation."

"Was I?" asked John, surprised at how eager his own voice sounded.

"Indeed. If it wasn't for the sensitive nature of the operation, you'd have got it. The intelligence department blocked it."

"Oh."

"It never happened."

John raised a chuckle before taking a sip from his drink. Their conversation flowed this way and that, but almost inevitably settled on the early planetary colonists. XO found a pupil eager to learn more.

"Early on, the colonists sent probes down to the surface of a likely open planet to search for pathogens and deadly bacteria before trying to inhabit it. They also passed through decontamination after visiting a new planet's surface, in case they picked something up."

"Would communications satellites orbiting a fresh planet be a priority?"

"Indeed it would, but they'd each have to generate their own force field."

"Why's that?"

"Many stars have volatile periods when they give of tremendous bursts of electromagnetic particles. Satellites, as much as the colonies on the ground, needed shielding from these. That's still the case today. A stable star is also needed for life to be viable."

"I see."

"For instance, there's an inviting world in the Akrana System with ideal gravity and water in its liquid state. Unless folk want to bury themselves deep underground, it's uninhabitable because of solar activity. It's cheaper to build a dome on another planet."

"Wouldn't a dome protect life on such a planet?"

"Often, but in that case, the discharges from the star are extreme and even domes with a sizeable force field would be vulnerable. We are talking about unimaginable forces here. The colonists soon learned quite how precious life is. All early predictions about the universe's abundant life turned out to be optimistic."

"So, life has to be nurtured, protected."

"Indeed it does. There is a vital need for a holistic approach, getting the fauna and flora in balance. It's no mean achievement to get it right."

"Must've been a huge enterprise, if the planet didn't possess any indigenous plants and animals."

"It was."

"Too much for private individuals?"

"Unless they were incredibly rich, yes. It's thought that the more likely route was that large companies started out trying to exploit natural resources."

"Such as mining companies digging for metals in high demand?"

"That's the idea. They started it off sometimes."

"How can we be sure?"

"Ah," said XO, "a good question. We cannot support this theory, because records for a long period of history after the twentieth century are so patchy."

"Can you tell me why many planets have the number three in their names? Most odd."

The other man said with a smile, "It seems that way because it's often the third planet from a star that's the optimum distance away to inhabit. Not that it's always the case. An inhabited number three means the existence of planets one and two, but you don't hear about them much. Most solar systems follow a similar pattern with the smaller, rocky planets close to and the gaseous giants further out."

"Why is that?"

"The energy from a star reduces as it gets further out, according to the inverse-square law. As electromagnetic radiation goes out, it travels in straight lines, as if it were covering the surface of an ever-expanding sphere."

"It's all in three dimensions."

"Exactly. This area increases in proportion to the square of the distance the radiation travels. The defining point comes at the frost line. That's the distance from a star where it is cold enough for volatile compounds such as water, carbon monoxide, methane, carbon dioxide and ammonia to condense into ice. You often get an asteroid belt just within this line, consisting of rocky material that never came together. Whilst beyond the line, further out, the gaseous giants are composed of volatiles driven further out."

"I see. Am I correct that the closer a planet is to a star, the quicker the orbit?"

"You are. Some planets, or planetoids, are incredibly close and orbit in a week, or less. Far too hot for habitation, of course. The star will swallow them up first."

"And there are precious few open inhabitable planets like Marmaris or Hydron, right?"

"There are, I'm afraid."

"That explains the fighting down there."

"Hydron?"

"Yes, fighting over limited resources."

"That may well be one reason, but I understand that there are multiple factors involved."

Then, changing the subject, John asked, "Do you mind if I ask you why you joined up?"

"Not at all. My father was in the force and he inspired me to join up and follow in his footsteps."

"Ah."

"And you?"

"It's something I've always wanted to do. Do you know when what our next mission will be?"

XO was not at liberty to divulge this information. He chuckled, then disclosed there would be a full briefing the day after tomorrow. "You'll get to hear about it then."

The faces at the briefing looked serious. That Admiral Jo-song himself gave it emphasised how important the occasion. They were about to learn the delicate nature of the operation ahead of them.

"In your mission, *Excellent* is to escort the merchant ship *Glad Tidings* through the disputed solar system 117114. They are carrying essential supplies to the planet Jacana Three, where a plague has broken out..."

The reference to that planet caught John's attention. He knew it was quite close, in astronomical terms, to Marmaris.

"... and is spreading like wildfire. Speed is of the essence and the most direct route is straight through 117114. Whilst that is unfortunate, our government has pledged to help them, so that is the task before us. Our duty is to escort the ship through the disputed area of space and make sure no one delays it. We have known the Kupullans to stop and search neutral merchantmen and even seize their cargoes. We have sent a message to Kupalla telling them what is happening. No reply has been received, we know they can be unpredictable. They have been heightening tensions and causing problems in the area."

Admiral Jo-song said that, while the Andraconians wanted peace, they must stand up to bullies. To send a juggernaut would have sent the wrong signals. He felt that a destroyer was a proportionate action.

That afternoon, *ASS Excellent's* crew boarded her for this sensitive mission. Proceeding to his cabin, John smiled at how quickly the route through the ship's corridors had become familiar to him. 'Not like the first time when I kept looking at my TRAC.'

Launch proceedings went through as usual and soon the warship was proceeding to its rendezvous point on the far side of the disputed solar system. There were no complications on the first part of the operation and, once in position, the ship sat stationary in otherwise empty space.

All was calm as the Ops Room plotted traffic over an immense distance.

"They're late," XO said across the link to Captain Farnham. No sooner were the words out of his mouth than they detected the *Glad Tidings* in the distance. She was travelling fast for a merchant ship.

When it got closer, they made contact, although after formal greetings, the merchantman's captain sounded dismissive.

"We're on a humanitarian mission. This can't be necessary."

"Our orders are to escort you through this sector," was all Farnham's response.

The two vessels proceeded beside each other and entered the disputed zone. Soon after this, they relayed a predictable message from the Ops Room.

"Kupullan vessel sighted. Coordinates 2937 by 411, vector 2.9."

"Red alert! Send out a probe," the captain ordered.

A small, unmanned vehicle shot into the void. The information it gleaned could give them the edge.

They identified the Kupullan ship as an F class attack boat. Tiny by the destroyer's standards, but still able to carry mines which packed a punch. They would be wary of it even as it stayed a safe distance away at a million kilometres.

"Communication from Kupullan ship being received, captain," XO announced.

"Put it through."

"Audio only."

All ears listened to what their potential enemy had to say. It started with an announcement.

"This is the Imperial Kupullan warship *Caracus*. We are approaching to get information."

In reply, Farnham said, "This is the Andraconian space destroyer *ASS Excellent*. We are on a humanitarian mission escorting an unarmed merchant vessel with emergency supplies. You must, under the Zynan Treaty, allow us safe passage."

They received no further communication and the Ops Room read out more coordinates. The tension on board the bridge was palpable.

"They're making their presence known," XO offered. "No weapons locked on."

"I'm concerned about them coming within effective weapons range," the captain replied. "You never know what they have under their sleeve. Five hundred thousand kilometres is my trip wire."

With the Kupullan warship starboard of the Glad Tidings, Farnham drew the *Excellent* between the two vessels. The merchantman was now half way through the solar system and not reducing speed.

A second Kupullan vessel appeared up ahead. The destroyer sent a message announcing themselves and demanding it move out of the way. The ship did not budge at first and they were bearing down on it fast. John found the tension unbearable.

The captain ordered a probe be sent on ahead with "code purple" instructions. The meaning was lost on his assistant, but the foreign ship then moved to one side and the merchant ship and her escort passed by without incident.

There were sighs of relief and they scaled down the alert level. It was only later that John learned that "code purple" was to do with disrupting enemy communications. Whatever it was, it did the trick.

Excellent continued to shadow the *Glad Tidings* until the merchantman passed by Andracon on way to Jacana Three. Farnham wished them "bon voyage" before issuing the order to return to base. "A successful mission well executed," was his verdict. "Well done, crew!"

On the return journey, XO came through to the bridge and passed words with Captain Farnham. Then he took the unusual step of pointing out an astronomical phenomenon to the captain's assistant.

"John, what are you seeing on the screen?"

"A star."

"Yes," came the patient reply, "and above the star?"

"Oh, it's a comet!"

"That's right. It's quite close to the star at present, so at its brightest. Can you see it has two tails?"

John confirmed he could indeed see two streams of white coming from it, one brighter than the other. XO advised further.

"The straight one which always points towards the centre of the star; that's the gas tail. The curved one is the dust trail."

He had the whole bridge studying the phenomenon now. However, the impromptu astronomy lesson was soon over and they were back to business.

Ground Control announced, "Cleared for docking," and the ship settled within its landing point. The dome sides rose even as the engines shut off. Operation over, unlike the previous one, this had been an unmitigated success.

The next several weeks, John spent between missions on Andracon. He was involved in a few military exercises during this time. Only on a couple of occasions did he leave the surface of the planet and they were solo shuttle flights for refresher training. A reorganisation of the force meant that he, and *ASS Excellent*, were now designated part of a newly-formed group named Attack Brigade A. In practice it seemed to make no actual difference. A reorganisation of the ranking system meant that they designated him as "Leading Rating." He preferred Captain's Assistant and everyone still referred to him that way.

The officers regularly left for intelligence briefings. For the international situation, reading between the lines, was grim. John overheard rumours that fresh, interplanetary talks were going nowhere, or even breaking down. Andracon was recruiting new soldiers like there was no tomorrow. The authorities had introduced a truncated training schedule to save time and money. When he joined, the *ASS Excellent* was the newest ship in the fleet. They had commissioned several more destroyers since then. More gossip said that a further fleet juggernaut lay under construction on another planet. One man said they had signed the contract to build it on the worst possible financial terms, because Andracon was desperate for it and the builders knew it.

'Why,' he asked himself, 'was Andracon so desperate?' They had always told him that this planet's forces were far superior to Kupullan's and would easily beat them in a fight.

A bout of "dome sickness" compounded these uncertainties. An unofficial malady, but one suffered by many who, raised on open planets, then spend too long under domes. He did not become so much homesick as have a general longing for wide, open spaces that domes could not offer.

He had heard precious little of his home world since he arrived; life was too busy for that, anyway. Towards the end of the year, when news of Marmaris came through, through, it was of the worst imaginable kind. A virulent plague was ravishing the land, killing people in swathes. Nothing could stop it. Maybe his parents would be okay, settled as they were on a remote farm. They quarantined the planet off from the rest of the quadrant. He made urgent enquiries, but had to navigate every bit of red tape imaginable to find out. When the news came, it stunned him. His parents were dead from the plague; their bodies, possessions and homestead all burned as per local government policy.

He hid himself in his room the next couple of days while the news sank in. He would never see his parents, or childhood home, again. On a short period of leave over Christmas, he considered going back to Marmaris. Yet even had they lifted the quarantine restrictions, there was no point. He had nothing to return to.

One evening, sitting in the corner of the refractory by himself, the emotional floodgates opened and he wept buckets. Hurrying to his room, he sat alone and cried some more.

The authorities on his home planet promised compensation, but he knew the government there possessed limited resources and, besides, how do you make monetary compensation for losing your parents? An obscene idea.

One thing he had to do, however, was inform his brother. As far as he knew, Frank was unaware of events on Marmaris. He made enquiries and learned that his brother still lived on Eden. He therefore sent him a video message telling him the sad news and adding more about his own current situation. A week later, John received a reply. It was brief. Frank still in shock, told his brother he could keep any compensation, He did not want it.

Meanwhile, they heralded in a new year, 2584. Indeed, there was a celestial herald that shot through Andracon's solar system at 300,000 kilometres an hour. One downside of living near the hub of the Milky Way, with stars close together, was that there were more rogue planets and stars. It could throw these bodies off their usual course if the gravitational pull of a nearby star, or black hole affected them. One such body came hurtling close to Andracon.

The strange, cigar-shaped object measured two kilometres wide and twenty long. It was, in fact, a conglomeration of rocks that adopted different shapes on its travels, depending upon the gravitational forces involved. The observers speculated it had broken off from a larger body when it got too close to its host star. The force of gravity sent the fragments flying off into space. If it hit Andracon's dome, it would have ended their civilization there and then. As it was, it passed by, but too close for comfort.

The large refractory screen was showing simulations of the object when John entered for a late supper one evening. Few people were there, but XO, sitting with an engineering officer, beckoned him. Feeling more sociable than of late, he walked over there with his tray of food.

"Some are saying it's a bad omen," XO remarked, tongue in cheek, at the object on the screen.

"I know you don't believe that," John said with a smile.

The engineering officer made his excuses, got up and left the table.

XO said, "Maybe not, but it's not the best start to 2584. Anyway, I haven't seen you of late."

"I've been having my meals brought my room. It's good that they do that."

Then John explained all about his parents and he got a most sympathetic response, which helped. However, XO then said, "I didn't see you at the mission briefing this afternoon either."

"Oh dear, was that today?"

"It was."

XO looked compassionate, he would not inform on him. "We need to report to our stations by 0600 hours tomorrow morning."

When John asked him, the Executive Officer explained their latest operation. The Kupullans had set up a station in international space between Andracon and solar system 117114. The *Excellent* was being sent to gather intelligence.

"Can't we just send a probe?"

"That would be a treaty violation."

"Would it?"

"Yes. We've got to suss out what they're up to. With international relations on the brink, this is a super-sensitive mission."

John knew the delicate situation. "The powers-that-be must think it's worth the risk."

"They do. Admiral Jo-song spoke to us again. 'A vital fact-finding assignment' he called it."

"What does Captain Farnham think?"

"I'm not sure I should betray that confidence. He is as concerned about the tightrope we are being asked to walk."

That evening, as John set the alarm on his TRAC, he wondered what the next day would bring. It sounded the craziest thing to do, provoke one's potential enemy when war might break out any moment. 'I could be there at the outbreak of war!' he thought. 'My ship might cause a conflict which is starting to seem inevitable.'

As he lay in bed, he forced his mind not to think of such things. Important to get a restful night's sleep if he was going to have his wits about him tomorrow.

~ End of Chapter 3 ~

My Keeper's Brother - Chapter 4

"Depressurisation complete, captain."

"Okay, take her out."

The *ASS Excellent* lifted off from its docking bay and passed the top of the dome. Then the UDS engines were engaged and she shot away from the planet on her lone mission to investigate the potential enemy's space station in an international zone.

In law, the Kupullans possessed every right to build a station there. While still some distance away from Andracon and in international space, it did seem a provocative act at a time of heightened tension. They tasked *Excellent* with discovering the station's purpose. No one believed the "scientific research" excuse touted by the Kupullan news channels. Yet was it an intelligence gathering post, a docking facility for warships, or a platform for invasion?

No unnecessary chat took place on the bridge that morning; everything was business-like. Captain Farnham even waved away the scone when offered it. His assistant ate it himself, hoping his commander would not look round and ask him a question when his mouth was full.

Once the space station came within range, the destroyer took on a holding position. Almost immediately, a Kupullan destroyer appeared on their port side, but it kept a safe distance away.

Excellent's sensors began scanning the space station, but no sooner had this operation begun when they detected a second Kupullan destroyer on the starboard side.

"They've locked their weapons," XO said. "They're sending a message, audio only." However, *Excellent* received no verbal message. The two potential enemy ships then both started coming closer, but at a slow speed. The message was obvious enough.

Captain Farnham's orders were not to back off. It crossed his mind to try the same probe trick that worked on the previous mission. That had not been against two destroyers, though, both *Excellent's* equal. Deciding that discretion was the better part of valour, he ordered, "Reverse speed, one quarter."

As the vessel eased away, they received a successful audio message. It said, "Thank you for complying with my previous instructions. The Council charges us with maintaining peace and security in the region."

They had avoided confrontation. It might have meant a loss of face for Andracon, and Captain Farnham may have to answer some tough questions when they returned, but they averted conflict for now.

Back home, they enjoyed the evening off and John headed to the bar with some other crew members. Most hailed from his ship, but a couple from a deep space patrol vessel tagged along. Captain Farnham's problems not being their own, they concentrated on the room's video feed. It was reporting worrying developments.

"Kupullan pirates have seized the Andracon merchant ship *Ocean Bay*, kidnapping the crew and holding them to ransom..."

Plainly, something important was brewing, but they had little truck with the biased reporting. The group moved to a vacant table.

"The ship strayed into their space, the idiots!" said one.

"Yeah, that 'holding them to ransom' part sounds over the top," said another.

John put in, "It's like they're ratcheting up the rhetoric to prepare us for war."

"Doesn't surprise me," the first speaker said, "I don't expect to take leave any time soon."

Later on, the topic changed despite of the continued broadcasts. One crew member said, "This is something I've always wanted to do. I never thought about anything else. Always busy, I'm told what to do, I don't have to think for myself."

"Like you, Thorny," said another.

"How do you mean?"

"You're the captain's lap dog. 'Fetch me my scone, fetch me my slippers.'"

This attempt at humour was poorly received by all present. They told the speaker to get lost. Nonetheless, the comment stung.

"Don't listen to him, Thorny," another said. "He always talks nonsense."

One man shared his musings. "I hate being parted from family for long periods, but I force myself not to think about it."

"You're on long range patrol aren't you?"

"Yeah, it can be bad, but my comrades get me through; make the time go quicker."

Someone shouted, "Look at the screen! look at the screen!" They did and saw the Andraconian President giving a rare address to the nation. The background music stopped as the room stilled. Then they could focus on the President's message.

"... And the intolerable provocations. Citizens of Andracon, these upstarts will no longer boss us about. It is high time we made the Kupullans pay for their violations of international law. It's my solemn duty to stand up for all that is right in our great nation. Therefore, I must announce that, as of 2300 hours this evening, a state of war exists between Andracon and Kupulla."

They fixed all eyes on the screen. No one spoke. The brief address played again from the beginning. John and his colleagues stared at each other. There was no Rootsy there to cheer; John did not currently know the whereabouts of B Squad. Everyone looked shocked. It was one thing to be heading towards an interplanetary war, quite another to find war declared.

Before anyone had time to explore that question, military police poured in and ordered everyone back to their barracks. As he hurried along a corridor connecting two domes, John got a message on his TRAC. An order to report to his ship at 0600 hours the following morning. There would be no delay in beginning operations, it seemed.

John woke before his alarm and jumped out of bed. He got changed, then double-checked he had everything before making his way to the ship. The entire planet seemed abuzz with people on the move. Other folk did not register with him, though. Here he was, marching off to war as countless generations of soldiers, sailors, airmen and spacemen had done before. He would most surely be involved in a battle.

Fear did not register. He knew Andracon possessed a large, up-to-date fleet of warships. On board one of the newer destroyers, well-equipped and with a fully-trained, highly-motivated crew, there was every reason to be optimistic.

The usual launch routine seemed no different on the surface, except that there was an extra spring in everyone's step. The *ASS Excellent* took off on schedule. Once in orbit, Captain Farnham announced to the crew.

"We are to rendezvous in Sector Blue with the main fleet..."

John was not the only one to raise his eyebrows. Well beyond Quadrant Echon and away from solar system 117114... not what the crew expected.

"... from there we will proceed to the Kupullan home world. We are going to hit them with everything we've got. *Excellent's* mission will be to provide cover for *ASS Maximilian.*"

He gave further details as the destroyer, flanked by two similar vessels, made its way to the rendezvous point. When they arrived, they displayed the scene on the bridge's big screen. What an amazing vision met their eyes. All three Andraconian juggernauts lined up in battle array, with a vast host of support warships around them. It was hard not to be moved by the sight. John swelled with pride for a nation's cause he had adopted. What a huge, powerful fleet! How wonderful to be a part of this mighty force. He almost felt sorry for the enemy, having this massive firepower coming down on them.

They were a long distance out from their target and would attack planet Kupalla from an unexpected angle. John detected little sense of urgency, he would have preferred them to get on with it. Instead, he flew Captain Farnham over to *Max* for a pow-wow with Admiral Jo-song. It could be done remotely, but, in that culture, they valued personal, face-to-face contact.

The captain was in good spirits as they boarded the shuttle. Ships' hangars did not have doors. They kept the air from escaping by invisible, discriminating force fields. They allowed craft with the correct access codes to pass through them, but nothing else. As they left *Excellent*, John found the *Maximillian* took up his entire screen, so large was the vessel.

Max soon nestled them in one of her vast hangars, following a smooth hop over to the juggernaut. It may have been large, but currently offered precious little room for him to land, being crammed full of attack vimanas ready for the fight.

John sat in the cabin, set for a lengthy wait. In the event, it was not, Before he knew it, he was flying the small craft back. An quick, uneventful return journey followed. Soon they were once more on the bridge and getting ready to move out.

"My tablet!" Farnham cried, fumbling round his seat. "Dammit, I put it down in the shuttle."

Dispatched to collect the device, it frustrated John at missing seeing the fleet move out. He hurried down the corridors to the destroyer's hangar, now familiar to him. Climbing inside, he began looking round for the captain's tablet. He closed the door as he searched. As he reached between the seats, he caught the sleeve of his uniform and tore it. How annoying!

'Why can't he use a TRAC like everyone else?' he thought. 'Ah, here, down the side of...'

Without warning, the entire vehicle gave a tremendous jolt and it threw him about inside. He collected himself and sat up in the shuttle. Its nose faced outwards, only the force field between it and the cold void of space. The sight which met his eyes shook him to the core.

The *ASS Maximillian* was on fire from stem to stern. Small craft darted all around it and projectiles hit it from every angle. Even as he looked on, an Andraconian destroyer slid past his field of vision, equidistant between the burning leviathan and where he sat. In a vertical position from his vantage point, it split in two as he struggled to comprehend the scene. It was made surreal by the absence of sound.

Then the force field at the hangar opening failed and several objects shot out of the spaceship. Clamped to the deck, the shuttle went into another upheaval, caught in the *Excellent's* convulsions. Twisted metal beams began giving way.

With no air in the hangar he could not step outside. The ship was in severe trouble. He did the one thing he could do. Preparing the engines and releasing the clamps, he steered the shuttle out of its bay. Out of its bay... into utter pandemonium.

The entire sector seemed to be a mass of spaceships in their death throes. Parts were breaking away, others with streams of fire venting into space. Debris flew this way and that. Some rained against the shuttle, its force field keeping it from damaging the hull.

Everything happened in a flash. A glance at the rear view monitor told him that *Excellent* was in severe trouble with huge chunks breaking off. A small warship of an unfamiliar design shot past in front of him. Were those bodies thrown out of a destroyer with its hull broken in three?

Making his mind up, he put the shuttle to maximum forward thrust and shot away from his mother ship, fleeing from the cataclysm engulfing the fleet. His hanging around would help no one. He thought he was getting clear when a loud bang occurred and the craft, still speeding forth, began spiralling. Nothing he did with the controls made any difference. The thrusters were not working. Alert messages rang in his ears, along with an alarm sounding and warning lights flashing. Not wanting these distractions, he turned them off.

The inertia negators, the most protected system on board, were uncompromised. Otherwise, the force would pin him to the side wall of the craft. He strapped himself into the chair for comfort; it had little practical use. The screen showed stars and vessels whizzing round and round and he switched that off also, before he was sick.

Then the sensors packed up, so he was flying blind while being projected like a spinning top into deep space. He tried getting the on-board computer to work again and ended up re-booting it. It took time, all the while the shuttle moved further and further away.

The computer came back online. "At last!" he said, relieved, but the readings were haywire. He tried the manoeuvring thrusters again and this time they worked. The spinning slowed by degrees until it stopped. The speeding shuttle, a way from the battle, had no other ships were anywhere near. He slowed the velocity and turned the screen back on.

Sensors came back online, but parts of the ship's computers still malfunctioned. For instance, the star charts could not show his position.

All of a sudden, a planet appeared right in front of him. Staring at the screen, reading the data, he learned it was an open planet with all the conditions to sustain life. What luck! The stars in the area beyond were far fewer than anywhere he travelled whilst on the *Excellent*. None of this made any sense.

Not wanting to look a gift horse in the mouth, he began descending into the atmosphere. With everything on his mind, he overlooked calling ground control. The automatic pilot was still offline and he had to steer the craft down himself. As he did this, he noticed the atmosphere increasing.

As re-entry progressed, the inertia negators finally gave way and external forces buffeted the little ship. He wrestled with the controls. The force field kept the re-entry heat from burning up the hull, but he was having a struggle to keep the shuttle stable. Thick clouds obscured the screen. Alarms within the cabin came back on and filled his ears. 'I thought I'd turned them off!'

In a flash, he was through cloud and into clear air... and hurtling towards the ground! By firing retro-thrusters and pulling hard on the controls, he avoided a dive straight into the planet. Instead, he came in to land at a shallow angle over trees and other vegetation. He crashed onto the earth with a terrible thump and the shuttle rocked this way and that while it dug a furrow in the soil as it decelerated. John was glad to be harnessed in. Shaken up, he was losing consciousness. Then the craft came to a safe halt... and he passed out.

He was aware time had passed when he regained consciousness. He lay in a wide, comfortable bed, surrounded by bright fabric walls. All was white and quiet.

Disorientated, he struggled to raise himself up. Images flooded through his mind of the juggernaut on fire and the crash landing ploughing up the ground. A tent flap parted and a young woman entered. Piercing blue eyes, thin eyebrows, she possessed a wan complexion. Her mid-length blond hair was over her right ear, but tucked behind her left. She would have been attractive if she smiled, but she looked distressed at the sight of him. Before he could say a word, she sicked on the floor, then fled.

'That's a strange greeting!' John said to himself. He wondered, 'has a crash injury disfigured my face?' Not that he felt any discomfort there, but he touched his features. Everything seemed in place.

His thoughts settled. He realised he had survived the crash with no discernable injuries. The kind folk here had put him in bed and he felt, to his immense surprise... great!

Now to get up and explore. He stopped when the flap parted again and two people entered. One was a tall, neatly-groomed gentleman with curly grey hair and close set features. The other, a short, dark woman, immediately busied herself clearing up the sick.

"I'm sorry about that," were the man's opening words, "but she's a sensitive soul." He ended the sentence with a compassionate smile. "How are you feeling?"

John tried a reply, but got tongue-tied and it came out all wrong. He gave up and let the man continue.

"Don't worry, you've been through a trauma. It's quite understandable. But you're safe now; let nothing concern you. My name is Bastrem, by the way."

"John Thorn," came the response. Then he tried to answer the question again, with more success.

"I'm feeling okay, thanks. I think I can get up."

When the man offered no objection, he eased himself out and, somewhat to his surprise, found he had no pain. He stood there for a moment, grinning at the rather snazzy pink pyjamas they dressed him in. Bastrem shared in his mirth and pointed to the neat pile of clothes on a nearby chair.

"Where am I? Why am I here? Did you extract me from the shuttle?"

The other man said, "Why don't you get dressed, come outside and then we'll talk? I'll answer questions."

It sounded a reasonable proposal. As soon as he was alone again, he got dressed. They were the same clothes he arrived in, but cleaned, pressed and mended. He could not even detect the tear on the sleeve. Before he exited, he glanced at his TRAC, but, it was not working. He pressed it and even tried a voice command, but to no avail. He would have to leave it.

Stepping outside into the sun, the temperature was not too hot. Just perfect, in fact. Looking back, he saw he had emerged from a large, white, round tent. About half a dozen identical structures stood on a grassy plateau.

The vista to the front was breathtaking. He stood a hundred metres from a large lake. On the far side were vertical white chalk cliffs, mostly covered by greenery. To the right, conifers of regular height covered a gentle slope leading down to the water. In the foreground, the grass gave way to large, smooth stones down to the edge of the crystal clear water. The backdrop to the entire scene were majestic, snow-capped mountains. Small, fluffy, white clouds dotted a blue sky. All was still. The fresh air held a faint scent from some nearby flowers.

"Admiring the view?" Bastrem's voice came from behind. It was soft for a man's.

John said, "I've seen nothing quite like it, not in real life. Yes, there are pictures and holograms, but thy don't match the real thing. Nothing even comes close."

"You have some questions?"

With a chuckle, the pilot thought, 'Where do I begin? I must have a million questions!'

As if reading his mind, Bastrem suggested they walk to a nearby log to sit down.

"... And I'll see if we can answer them to the best of our ability."

He led the way, walking slowly with an upright gate. Once seated, he allowed the new arrival to begin.

"Did you extract me from the shuttle?"

"We did."

"I expect it looked a right state after ploughing through the ground as it landed."

"Battered, yes."

"Did you see me come down?"

"We saw your craft approaching."

"Incredibly lucky for me to discover this place. A beautiful open planet and it appeared right in front of my ship."

Bastrem's sole response was a compassionate look, but then John had formed the words as a statement, rather than a question. He therefore asked another.

"How long did I lay unconscious?"

"Only a day. There were no serious injuries."

It was then that John realised how hungry he felt. Possibly a coincidence, but at that point, Bastrem asked if he wanted to eat.

"Oh, yes... please. That would be great."

As he got up, Bastrem responded, "Come, I'll introduce you to some more people."

He led them back towards the tents. John enquired, "How is that young woman who first called in on me? I felt sorry for her when she was sick."

The listener found these words amusing. He replied, "Ursula is fine, but thank you for asking. She isn't used to meeting people from other worlds."

"Oh."

"Here we are."

They arrived at the tent without seeing another soul. Inside, however, were three people reclining round a low table upon which there lay a large array of food. Two women and an elderly gentleman, they appeared to be waiting for them to arrive. As they took their places on the cushions provided, Bastrem made introductions.

"John Thorn here is staying with us for a while. John, this is Diana, this is Arinal ... and Ursula, you've already met. Diana was another blond, but she looked a lot less serious. Her dark brown eyes and bright red lips set off a cheeky look. She seemed amused by his presence. Arinal was a dignified, elderly man. From his greyed-over eyes, he was blind. He propped himself up on one elbow and paid close attention to the proceedings.

"Hi!" John said in a general greeting. Then, thinking this inadequate, he said to Ursula, "I'm glad you're feeling better." She gave a brief acknowledgement, but kept her serious face.

"Do eat up!" Bastrem declared and everyone, including John, tucked in. The meal contained a vast selection of delicacies, all of them vegetables, some he did not recognise. Brought up a strict vegetarian, this was no problem for the visitor. It fascinated him to experience tastes and textures he had never come across before. One looked like fibre optics, which amused him, but tasted like spaghetti. He commented favourably on the fare and they met his words with smiles.

The locals ate in silence until Arinal commented, "A military uniform."

"Um, yes," John responded. Someone must have told him. Seeking to justify himself, he added, "I'm a captain's assistant. I was piloting his shuttle craft."

Diana, sitting opposite, then enquired, "What were you doing out here by yourself? It looks like a short range vessel and you had no supplies on board."

"I was escaping from a battle. Um, it's a bit of a long story, but I was sitting in the shuttle when they hit its mother ship and she began breaking up. I had little choice. I'd have died if I'd stayed."

The young woman studied him as he spoke, keeping an amused expression. She responded, "Fascinating. Would you mind if I asked you some more questions?"

"Diana, please!" Bastrem interjected, "let the young man eat. I know he has questions of his own."

John came to her defence. "It's okay, I don't mind at all." To Diana, he asked "How can I help you?"

"How long have you been a soldier?"

"In Andracon's defence force? Two-and-a-half, three years."

"And were you press-ganged into it?"

"Not at all. It's something I'd always wanted to do."

"You were born and raised on Andracon?"

"Not at all. I was born on Marmaris. I moved to Andracon to join the marines when I turned sixteen."

"And have you fought many battles?"

"Oh no, this was my first. But I've been on several operations."

"How do you feel about killing other human beings?"

That blunt question took the wind out of his sails. Yet she asked in a spirit of enquiry; her tone did not sound judgemental. He groped around for an answer.

"Um, er.. I, I don't see my job in those terms. Maybe that's dishonest of me, for I was a marine to begin with and they taught me to kill. It's all very impersonal on board a spaceship. You don't think about who your enemy is." He paused before adding, "I mean, I don't know my enemy at all. I've never been there, or met any of them. I guess they're the same as me."

He had run out of steam and Bastrem gave the inquisitor a look and she desisted. Then he turned to John to apologise.

"Please forgive Diana's curiosity. She got carried away, we don't have many visitors."

"No need to apologise," John leapt to Diana's defence. "I have nothing to hide. I'm curious about you, too. Don't you travel to other planets the way we do?"

Bastrem replied, "The way you do, no."

"And are you from a town nearabouts?"

"There are few of us here. There are no urban areas on Sitnalta."

"Sitnalta? I can't say I've heard of your planet before."

This statement elicited no response and the group fell quiet for a while as they concentrated on their food.

Then, out of the blue, Ursula asked him, "Have your parents passed recently?"

"Yes, they have."

'How in heaven's name does she know that?' John thought.

She said earnestly, "They want you to know that they are well and no longer suffering."

His mind was abuzz. So, "sensitive" meant she was a medium. Not having met one before, this was a fresh experience for him. He would have called himself a sceptic before this encounter. How could she have made this up? It could not be a coincidence and he had said nothing about his parents since he arrived. Being fully occupied of late, they had not been on his mind. She must be genuine.

"... And they don't want you to feel any guilt about not returning home."

John felt tears welling up and he put his head down. He had told no one, absolutely no one, about feeling bad about not returning to Marmaris. He barely registered it to himself.

As he began to weep, Bastrem whispered admonishment to Ursula for saying too much, but John interjected. "No, it's okay. In fact, it's a tremendous release. Thank you, Ursula."

The rest of the meal passed without incident. Afterwards, Bastrem asked their guest whether he would like to accompany him for a walk.

"I'd like that very much."

Leaving the others, they withdrew from the small group of tents and climbed the gentle slope away from the lake. Before crossing a ridge, he glanced back at the scene. The still water reflected the bright white clouds and a couple of birds flew over the encampment. Everything was peaceful.

Bastrem waited for him. The visitor tore himself away from the enchanting sight and allowed himself to be led over the ridge to face another breathtaking panorama spread out below them. Beautiful countryside right to the horizon. It dotted small turquoise lakes between majestic mountains, with no sign of human habitation at all. They walked on, staying on the vantage point of the plateau. John seized the opportunity to take it all in.

It was time to find out more.

"Where are the rest of your people? Presumably, the tents are a temporary thing."

"A temporary abode, yes. We move about the countryside as it pleases us."

"But there are other, larger settlements?"

"Mmm," the man considered, "some are larger."

"You told me you have no towns or cities."

"That is correct."

"Or spaceships, like mine."

"That is also the case."

Thinking it through, John realised he would have to stay on this planet until another ship came by, one that did not crash-land. How long would that be? These gentle folk said they experienced few visitors, but that made no sense. A beautiful, open planet like this would be a magnet for colonists. Maybe these people fattened up any travellers on delicious food, such as he had enjoyed, then ate them following a human sacrifice.

"No need to worry," Bastrem said. The comment was out of the blue.

"Did I look worried?"

"We will impose no restrictions on you. You have perfect freedom... and you can stay here or go whenever you please."

How in heaven's name he could leave without a working spaceship? Bastrem clearly did not have a clue. John did not wish to state the obvious. Besides, why not stay here a while? It was all so lovely. The man spoke further.

"Although I should say that Ursula and Diana seem quite taken with you and would like to learn more about your worlds."

"They're both beautiful women."

With a chuckle, Bastrem said, "A little old for you, I fear."

This baffled the visitor, who came back, "I'm nineteen; they must be in their twenties."

"Ursula is two hundred-and-forty-three years old."

John opened his mouth to say something, then shut it again. Years here must be a lot shorter than Earth Standard. It was not worth pursuing the matter.

"Ah, here we are. Watch your step on the large stones."

The path dropped away and they descended from one large boulder to the next. Looking across, he could see that they were entering a narrow canyon. On the opposite side, strata of white rock interspersed with horizontal lines of vegetation. They worked their way down. It was easy work for anyone with reasonable fitness. At the bottom lay a flat, pebbled surface, leading to a pond fed by waterfalls on the opposite side. Weeping willows overhung the water. The whole spectacle was beautiful beyond belief.

"It's paradise," John said. He had never seen such a place.

"Come, sit," said the other, taking advantage of a convenient wooden seat at the water's edge. From there, they could see tiny fish swimming close to the shore.

It was time for further questions.

"The elderly gentleman at the end of the table, the blind man. Is he your leader?"

Again, one of his questions evoked a chuckle from the host, who replied, "Arinal is a lot less blind than most people with the use of their sense of vision. But he is not our leader. We do not order our society that way."

"You have no leader?"

"We do not."

"But that'll lead to anarchy!"

"You are quite right, we have an anarchic society," he said softly.

"No, I mean chaos."

"Anarchy and chaos are different things."

"Aren't they?"

"Do we seem chaotic to you?"

John conceded they did not. Yet he still sought to justify his comments. "But what if someone doesn't want to contribute to your society? Who will make him work?"

"No one."

"Would you still let him eat the food you've prepared?"

"Of course."

"But it wouldn't be fair. He'd be sponging off you."

"That individual needs to work it out for himself. Is being lazy the best manifestation they can make of their life? If not, they will want to contribute. If they cannot yet see any clearer, we will not compel them to contribute."

"Do you have any people like that?"

"We do not."

Then, making it personal, John said, "I'd like to do my bit while I'm here!"

"Good," the man said. "Perhaps you would like to go fruit picking with some of the group tomorrow."

"Yes," came the firm reply.

He continued to probe and ask questions and Bastrem never held back with his answers. Yet the heart of the matter remained elusive. How could this completely unknown paradise planet, spring up out of nowhere before him? It is one thing to land on your feet, but this was ridiculous. Then why worry about it? He could enjoy a rest and recuperation here on Sitnalta and concern himself with getting back later. The battle must be long over. He could not return and help them even if he had a ship to fly.

That night, alone in his tent, he soon fell asleep. He then woke around midnight. He stepped outside to consider the cloudless night sky. No artificial lights disturbed the view and everything was quiet.

The vision before him made his jaw drop. There were no constellations he recognised, and, indeed, few stars visible. He had never experienced a night sky like it. It belonged to outer space, not from within the Milky Way.

Tiredness returned and he went back to bed and slept before waking refreshed in the morning. Rootsy and Billy occupied his last dream. He wondered if they still lived, but knew they did not. The idea flashed through his mind to ask Diana to contact their spirits, then he thought better of it.

Before he got up, they brought him a bowl of warm water to wash in, plus a towel. The carrier was a gentleman named Zabadiq. Younger than the other menfolk encountered on the planet, his skin was dark brown skin and his black beard full, but closely-cropped. Appearing wary, he neither said a word, nor looked at John. Nevertheless, he provided the means of ablution and that was an act of kindness.

Later that morning, John got his opportunity to contribute to the community and went fruit picking with Ursula and Diana. On the way, they approached a tall, broad copper beech tree. With the sun's rays coming through it from behind, it almost appeared golden.

Beyond that, an orchard of fruit trees stood and the trio set about gathering some of the crop. The visitor did not recognise the oval, green fruit he was picking, but it did not seem to matter.

Diana, in a flippant mood, played with the fruit, imagining them as earrings. Yet it was the quieter, more controlling Ursula whom John found alluring. She may be two-hundred-and-forty-three years old, but he was attracted to her. He told himself not to allow his emotions get the better of him. It would be foolish to allow himself to fall for her.

He knew this idyll could not be a permanent state for him.

71

That evening, they were back in the tent where the community ate their meals. John was enjoying relaxing with pleasant company, having run out of questions for now. Instead, he found himself on the receiving end of enquiries from the blind Arinal.

"Pray, tell me about your home world."

"Marmaris? It's near the centre of the galaxy, in the Kronos Sector. It's orbiting a star with only five-hundred-thousand years of it life left. We're only a hundred and fifty light years away from a large black hole too. It's not as beautiful as your world, although it is open. It's predominantly small agricultural communities and... I guess it's a pretty fractured society. They recently suffered a plague there and I don't know what current conditions are like."

"And how long have they colonised it?"

"Since before the First Intergalactic War. After the Second War it remained with what we call the civilised universe. Because it cut off lots of planets, then... you probably know."

"Is that how you measure time?"

"Sorry?"

"In wars?"

John pulled a face. It said little for his "civilisation," that their history did indeed measure time in terms of their wars.

The elderly man broke the embarrassing silence by apologising. "I meant no judgement of your society. You have been very open with your answers, refreshingly so for an off-worlder. I was curious, that's all."

Considering he had nothing to hide, John decided not to sweeten the pill. Glancing round, he saw all eyes fixed on him.

"Our society is warlike, I can't deny it. We can't seem to resolve international disputes half the time without recourse to arms. We seem incapable of learning from our mistakes of the past."

"You will," Arinal said, "you will in time."

"If I can offer you a word of helpful advice, be wary of other planets. I'd hate you to be conquered by one of our warlike peoples."

His attentive audience did not appear at all alarmed. He concluded with a solemn promise. Looking them in the eyes, he declared, "I want you to know that, when I return, I won't tell a soul about Sitnalta. I don't want unscrupulous men coming here and taking advantage of you."

Warm smiles met this announcement. They left it to Arinal reply on all their behalf. He said tenderly, "We believe you, John Thorn."

The days and weeks sailed by and the stranger from a different universe got used to life on this beautiful world with his peaceful, angelic hosts. It could not have been easier to get along with such kind, unselfish folk. 'Why can't all humans be like this?' he mused.

The sole additional inhabitant he encountered during this period was Sita, an elegant lady with long, black hair and dark eyes. She looked about thirty-five, therefore she must be about five hundred, John joked to himself.

One curious thing about Arinal was that, although his eyes did not function, he operated as if he possessed sight. He never walked into an obstacle and, if someone passed him an object, he always stuck his hand in the right place to receive it. John felt too awkward to ask.

As time passed, he fell into their way of living. Everything here was so perfect and he accepted things as they were. Questions remained, but he suppressed these as he enjoyed the simple life. His old life faded away as he got used to their unsophisticated ways. He laughed, though, because his brother had gone to a planet named Eden. Here *he* was in an absolute Garden of Eden. An innocent land where war and conflict were unknown. He wondered if it was all too good to be true. For instance, how did they escape detection from belligerent powers who would give their eye teeth to get their hands on a such planet? These were fundamental questions, but, lulled by the beauty of it all, his curiosity evaporated.

They still lived in the same place. John learned that they moved the tents occasionally to different locations, but there was no sign of that happening. The tents appeared to be in pristine condition, as if brand new. Did nothing wear out in this paradise?

One day, he was alone in a tent with Ursula. He enjoyed her company the most, but uncertain whether it was because of her sweet nature, or that he fancied her like crazy. Either way, she provided pleasant company and he did not want to ruin it by making a move on her.

She was at a spinning wheel and he was sitting nearby on an upright chair watching her as they talked. A few weeks before, he had helped Diana and Zabadiq harvest some balbar plants.

"The balbar fibres must be separated from the rest of the stalk before I can spin it," she explained. "I pull the fibres through combs to remove the last bits of straw."

"And you call the resulting cloth...?"

"Sinet."

"Sinet," he repeated.

"It needs to be spun into a smooth yarn."

"That's the material you use to make the bedclothes?"

"It is."

Silence reigned before John plucked up courage to ask something on his mind. First, he thought he should ask her if it was alright to ask her something personal.

Looking up from her work, she stopped to give him her full attention. "Of course it is; ask me."

"That first time you walked into my tent and was sick... Forgive me, but I got the impression that you were okay until you saw me. Did I have that effect on you?"

"It was your thoughts," she confessed, "they were so confused and they did not attune me at that stage..."

"My *thoughts* made you sick?" he asked, amazed.

"I am sensitive to thoughts," she said, sounding a little defensive.

Seeking to reassure her, he hastened to tell her she had not insulted him, but this was beyond his experience. Then he enquired, "Can you tell me what I am thinking now?"

Amused by the question, she gave a rare giggle before answering, "It's not like that. One's thoughts give off astral matter from the region around your head. I can see them as different colours; for example, brown is depression. I see red with anger, green for selfishness... but not everyone sees the same colours. Arinal taught me for many years."

"Oh, but I guess he can't see them any more."

"Why ever not?" she asked, not understanding.

"Um, he's blind."

"Ah," she responded, figuring out the question now. "He sees through his third eye. I would trust his sight ahead of yours or mine."

John frowned. His confusion could be seen without clairvoyance. She went back her previous topic.

"The astral colours you give off, called thought forms, build up during childhood. By early adolescence, the individual has a flow of habitual thought colours around them. That is called an aura. I can see what someone is like by studying their aura."

"And I was so horrible that I made you sick!"

"You were confused and your thoughts all over the place. No one prepared me. It was not your own fault."

"Okay. Dare I ask what my aura says about me now?"

He sat motionless, as if this should help. Ursula adjusted her posture and concentrated on him. When she spoke, it was with a tenderness that put him at ease.

"You are still very young and have veins of selfishness, as expected. John, you go with the flow, not wishing to stand out from the crowd. You are capable of loyalty and are trustworthy to a good degree. My advice to you would be to give yourself freedom to think for yourself. People influence you too readily."

"It's difficult to think for yourself when you're in the army under orders."

"And you could not leave the army?"

He did not answer; he was too busy taking it all in. She told him things about himself which rang true, but which he had not realised himself.

Then she added, "You are not bad for a person from a primitive society, John Thorn, but there'll be some major forks in your road the next few years. You must make the right decisions. You still have most of your life ahead of you."

'Now she's sounding like a cheap fortune teller,' he considered, then was concerned that she would read his thoughts. He picked up on something she said.

"How can you call where I come from a primitive society? We build colonies on uninhabitable planets, have modes of transport to go between the stars. We communicate across vast distances and... and invent amazing things."

Unflustered, she replied, "And what do you do with all these wonders? Fight, be selfish, commit murder, have so many wars that you have to number them. The destruction, the violence, each individual in it for themselves. Your worlds are in chaos, not working together for the common good. From what you have told me, you went to war, helping to kill other sentient beings whom you've never met and knew nothing about. Are those signs of an advanced civilisation?"

Her tone was more one of sadness than judgement. She had given the game away, though. These people were no simple fools; but fully aware of events around them. It was time to ask a fundamental question.

"Your planet, Sitnalta, how come I could find it... I wasn't even looking for you. But thousands of ships flying through the galaxy don't know you're here?"

"Because we manifested ourselves to you."

"What? Do you have a kind of cloaking device for the entire plant? A force field?"

"No," she smiled at the thought. "It is Sitnalta's collective consciousness which chooses to keep us hidden from primitive peoples. It is within our choice."

"Gosh!" he exclaimed. "I believe you. With everything I've seen and heard, I believe you. It's so lovely here, but I will move on in time. I won't tell anyone about Sitnalta, not a soul. I'll never betray your presence."

"I know you won't," she said with a knowing look.

~ End of Chapter 4 ~

My Keeper's Brother - Chapter 5

That day spent with Ursula meant the end for John's stay on Sitnalta. He knew now that, far from being the simple, peasant society that he imagined, they were, in fact, an advanced race, having evolved far higher than his own civilisation.

The universe, he learned, is teeming with life, much of it at the etheric, or super-etheric levels, meaning a vibrationary rate too high for human detection. They have to lower their rate of vibration to manifest in the material world. These beings normally keep themselves apart from mankind, because of the latter's propensity to violence. It was difficult to argue against that.

John lived amongst a race more advanced than humanity by a billion years. Ursula really was two-hundred-and-forty-three years old and some others a good deal older. He realised he did not belong. No matter how much he enjoyed living there, no matter how welcome they made him feel, he would have to move on.

As he faced this reality, his mind turned to his previous life. XO, Captain Farnham, Rootsy, Peanut and the rest, where were they now? Were any of them still alive? The Andracon fleet was having a terrible time of it when he left. Would they treat him like a deserter if he went back? Would their Kupullans enemies have destroyed their homeland? What sort of situation would he be returning to? After all, he possessed little idea of how long he had spent on Sitnalta. Time could function differently here for all he knew.

One morning, he sought Bastrem after breakfast and declared his desire to leave. "You've been wonderful hosts and I've learned a tremendous amount. I'll never be able to repay you."

"It's been to our mutual benefit. We've enjoyed hearing what you have to say."

John's resolution caused no surprise, almost as if it had been expected.

He asked, "How are you going to do it? Flag down a passing ship, or teleport me onto another planet?"

With a chuckle, Bastrem replied, "Let's leave teleportation to science fiction, shall we? Heisenberg's Uncertainty Principle means it can never happen in the real world. No, we've prepped your craft, it is ready to go. You may leave at any time. We have always said that."

John, incredulous, wondered how in heaven's name they could repair the shuttle? It was in a terrible state after his crash-landing. Yet, when they took him round to see it, there the vehicle stood. Not only repaired, it appeared spotless as if fresh off the production line. His host smiled at his look of astonishment.

"No!" cried John, "I'm not even going to ask how you did it. I'm amazed."

"You're all ready to go now."

This struck John as being too sudden. "I must say goodbye to everyone. May I stay for lunch?"

Unusually, his guide sought to tease him, replying, "Oh dear, I'm not sure... well, alright then."

The pair laughed as they made their way back. Everybody from the small settlement appeared for the farewell meal. John was full of thanks for all the help and goodness shown to him during his stay.

"I've experienced the most wonderful time," he declared. "Never will I forget the kindness and I'll try to make wise decisions, like you said. I'll try to be good and be thoughtful of others. I will always remember you."

As he spoke these last words, his eyes alighted on Diana. She winked at him. Her expression, usually amused, now appeared touched by... sadness? Pity maybe? He was not sure.

She came with him after the meal, along with Bastrem and Ursula. The three of them stood lined up, a short, but safe distance from the space craft. These people, being minimalist, owned few possessions. He realised, as he climbed on board, that he was not taking a souvenir with him. However, as he got into the pilot's seat, with the door still wide open, the most beautiful glass paperweight sat in the receptacle between the seats. It contained a scene of the lake, with the mountains in the background. Turning it round in his hands, he found they etched his name on the bottom. He felt it inappropriate to dwell too long on it now, for he was keeping them waiting.

"A present from us," called out Bastrem.

"Thank you. Thank you so much! I shall treasure it," he shouted back, fighting the lump in his throat.

They all waved and called out goodbye. Then he closed the door. 'What if the engines are dead?' he considered.

He need not have worried. Perfunctory pre-flight checks completed, he set the craft on its way. After hovering momentarily, it shot upward with speed. As he flew away from the planet Sitnalta, he watched it on his rear-view monitor. John glanced away and when he looked back, it was gone. Nothing but open space and a few distant stars.

Back on the ground, Diana turned to Bastrem and gave her verdict.
"A nice young man. I hope he can stay true to his resolutions and make something good with his life."
He said, "Yes, we have embedded these things deep within his subconscious to influence his decisions in the future."
"Indeed. Maybe there's hope for his species if they can learn not to be influenced by others of their kind."
"Evolution must run its course, Diana, but they will make it. We all know that."

John Thorn was flying the shuttle alone. Everything happened in a flash. A glance at the rear-view monitor told him that *Excellent* was in severe trouble, with huge chunks breaking off and escape pods being launched. A small warship of a design he was unfamiliar with shot past in front of him.
The entire sector seemed to be a mass of spaceships in their death throes. Parts were breaking away, others had streams of fire venting into space. Debris flew this way and that. Some rained against the shuttle, its force field keeping it from damaging the hull.
Engaging maximum forward speed, he shot away from his mother ship, trying to escape the cataclysm engulfing the Andraconian fleet. He thought he was getting clear when a loud bang occurred and the craft, still speeding forth, began spiralling. Stars and ships flashed round before him. It made him nauseous, so he turned the screen off. Just as he did, the spinning stopped.
'That makes no sense,' he considered. 'I was whizzing round like a top; I did nothing to stop it.'
The monitor showed only stars, plenty of them, near and far. He recognised the scene from many training flights he had taken. What was going on? Switching from rear to forward monitor, there, in front of him, stood the planet Andracon.

"What in heaven's name is going on?" he cried, incredulous. A moment ago he was in Sector Blue, engaged in a tremendous battle. Now he was approaching his adopted home world. Sensors showed no other ships in the vicinity, which of itself was unusual.

"Unidentified ship, state your business; identify yourself."

"Um, this is the shuttle from *ASS Excellent*, pilot John Thorn. Requesting permission to land."

The controller hesitated before they asked him to repeat what he said. He did, word for word. A longer pause this time before a different man's voice said, "We clear you for landing, docking bay A."

'That's huge! It'll dwarf the shuttle in there,' thought John, but he said nothing.

He landed without incident and undertook the post flight checks. As he did this, he noticed the most beautiful paperweight next to the seat.

'Must be the captain's,' he considered as he picked it up for inspection. No, someone had inscribed his name upon it. Baffled, he stuffed the trinket into a pocket before alighting.

He set the ship down near the exit, so he had a short walk. A couple of handlers stood watching him with astonished expressions. Hardly surprising, but he tried to ignore them. Earlier that morning, the shuttle was on board the destroyer as they departed for battle. Now he had returned by himself, what were they supposed to think? This was all most confusing.

A squad of military police ran in. He recognised the squad leader who, in the most serious terms, addressed him.

"Are you John Thorn from the *ASS Excellent*?"

"Enlai, you know me well enough."

"You are under arrest for desertion of your post. You will come with us."

He followed, flanked by the security detail, but not restrained. He wanted to cry out, "I can explain everything!" but he could not. Marching down a corridor, a dishevelled man approached and begged for money. They brushed him aside. The fellow's associates rested on a pile of blankets at the side. John never saw the like on Andracon.

With his mind still working overtime, he found himself the lone occupant of a military police cell looking at four grey, metallic walls. He considered the facts.

'They were pretty quick off the mark, weren't they? How do they know Captain Farnham did not send me back from the battle? Have they received telemetry of the fight yet? Have I got to be the one to give them the bad news? I wish I understood quite what happened out there!'

His TRAC clicked back to life before they took it from him, along with all other personal possessions. There was no chance to check his wrist computer first.

'They *must* know what's happening. They'd have sent probes to record the battle for the folk back home. The authorities would want to show a glorious victory. Maybe they are trying to hush up the disastrous defeat. I'm sure about what I saw. They won't be able to keep the lid on it for long, but it'd explain why they want me in here.' He considered further, 'What am I to say, though? No one will believe I found myself half a light year away from my position in the blink of an eye. Had the enemy destroyed the fleet, knocking them out before the probes transmitted to Andracon? I'm not too keen on being the bearer of bad news. But none of this explains why they were so quick putting me in here...'

Round and round went his thoughts, but he got nowhere. For a whole day he did not see another soul, although they supplied food and drink by an automatic panel in the wall. He continued to wrack his brains to the point of exhaustion. How could he expect anyone to believe his story when it made no sense to him? Soon, he lost track of time.

The door slid open and they ushered him out to meet his defence attorney. John disliked the speed things were moving. Still, it relieved him to see another human being, even the emotionless guards. Then, directed into a room larger than his cell, a diminutive figure sat towards the end of a table. Old enough to be John's father, his close-set eyes and worried expression injected little confidence in the accused. His goatee beard was turning grey, so too the little hair that remained on his head.

"I am your representative, Marcus Ridge."

"John Thorn," the other said, sitting down. He let the other man speak first.

"These are grave charges, John, but I need to hear your testimony first. There may be mitigating circumstances."

"The charges being?"

"Desertion in the enemy's face is the most serious, but others, treason, for instance."

"Gosh, they don't hang about! It only happened this morning."

Undistracted, Ridge responded, "You account, please."

"Okay. We'd rendezv..."

"We?"

"The ship, the *ASS Excellent*. We rendezvoused with the rest of the fleet as planned, ready to launch an attack on Kupalla. I ferried Captain Farnham to the *Maximilian* to see the admiral, then back again."

"Mmm."

"Once we got back on *Excellent's* bridge, the captain sent me back to retrieve his note pad. Um, I expect it's still in there, in fact. Anyway, I was there in the shuttle, trying to find it, when all hell broke loose. Have you received any reports on the battle?"

"I'm afraid so. Continue."

"And the entire ship, the destroyer, seemed to break up. I couldn't step outside, because the force field had failed, therefore I made a run for it in the shuttle."

"I presume there are some space suits stored on board the shuttle?"

"Yes, but I hadn't time to don one; the whole hanger was cracking up!"

"Go on," the lawyer said without emotion.

"I shot out of there as quickly as possible and found complete mayhem. Pulse cannon and other weapons were firing in every direction. The *Maximilian* was belching fire and it looked terminal. I didn't have time to survey the scene. I just tried to get away."

"What happened then?"

Running out of fuel, John stopped. When urged to say more, he confessed, "I'm not sure."

"It was confusing?"

"Very."

"Tell me what you remember."

"Um, okay. I'll tell you, but nothing makes sense."

"Go on."

"I hadn't got far when they hit the shuttle. It spun round and round and I don't know, maybe I lost consciousness. Because the next thing I remember is the spinning stopped and I ..."

He trailed off. How could he say the rest? It sounded too absurd. When the lawyer insisted, he gave it a go.

"Next thing I knew, I was coming in to land here."

"Sorry?"

"It stopped spinning. At least I thought it went into a spin after they hit me. It stopped and I was no longer in Blue Sector with the rest of the fleet, I was coming in to land. I know it sounds crazy. It's the truth."

"You remember nothing in between?"

"Nothing at all."

"You have no memory of the previous half year?"

"What!?"

Not a great deal happened in the week that followed. In between rare exercise breaks, they gave John plenty of time to brood. Early on, his lawyer informed him he was considering an insanity plea. That compounded his confusion.

It seemed crazy, being told he had been missing for the six months since the battle. It was a period he possessed no recollection of. His lawyer gave the accused little confidence. John suggested they test the area for Chang Tides, that mysterious phenomenon in interstellar areas said to distort time and space. His representative refused, saying that they remained a mere theory and not a proven fact. Besides, even their advocates theorised they move about. It would be pointless after this long.

Ridge needed an explanation why the shuttle was in such a pristine condition. If, as his client contended, the enemy hit it so hard during the battle, even with a force field in operation, the electronic flight log would have a record. Yet it wiped the log for the last half year. Above all, John could not account for the missing time.

As for the battle's outcome, he received no further information at this stage. Forbidden to speak with anyone else, his lawyer evaded the issue when quizzed. It frustrated him. This state of affairs was unchanged for the ten days after he first met his attorney. Morning of the eleventh day, the guards led him out once again to the interview room. Only on this occasion, he received a most unexpected visitor.

"Midget! Are you a sight for sore eyes? How are you still here?"

The other man held up his hand to stop further questions. "Hold on, hold on; I'll tell you what I know."

Midget seemed much matured since John last saw him. It was not the couple of weeks that his brain told him. He had beefed out and no longer wore a marine's uniform. Dressed as a smart intelligence officer, he looked the part. From the conversation that ensued, it was apparent that he had built up a network of useful contacts. First, however, John wanted to learn the outcome of the battle and how his former colleague survived it.

"I wasn't aboard the *Excellent* that day. Medics rushed me to the infirmary after I got acute appendicitis. Never known such pain, but as the medics saw to me, the fleet sailed."

"And the battle?"

"An ambush. So confident of victory, they streamed a video of the fleet in real time from probes sent especially. We enjoyed a ringside seat all right... of a catastrophic defeat! Somehow the enemy found out about our rendezvous point in Blue Sector and, appearing from nowhere, pulled our fleet apart. The enemy destroyed all three juggernauts and most of the support ships.

"The *Excellent*?"

"Destroyed, but it appears some of the crew survived, although it's not known who. I saw some escape pods leaving. They built the bridges on the newer destroyers to be one big escape capsule. I've studied the footage and there wasn't a clear view of our old ship as she broke up."

"Tragic!"

"Yeah. If they escaped, then they're still being held as prisoners of war on Kupullan. Our government is trying to negotiate their release."

"But the battle ended in total defeat for us?"

"The whole thing was over in minutes. A massacre!"

"Did they come to attack Andracon?"

"They came, but the government here surrendered straightaway. Either that or have the domes destroyed. Since then we've experienced two changes of government, a harsh peace treaty imposed by the Kupullans and a breakdown in society here. Many folk emigrated, those who could afford to. New Spain a favourite destination. There were riots, food prices rocketed, beggars now roam the streets, it's a complete mess."

"But Andracon kept her independence?"

"Sort of, but the Kupullans have emasculated us."

"Us?"

"Yeah, I guess I see Andracon as home now."

"If it's as bad as you say, I'm surprised you didn't go back to your home world."

"Gallilo Three has little going for it. Here, they offered me this job," he pointed to the badge on his sleeve, "at more than double the pay. I attend an exclusive restaurant out of bounds to most and I'm earning enough to send money back home to my parents. When reports come in, I see them. I've taken an interest in your case ever since I first heard you got back. I wanted to have solid information to tell you when I saw you."

"Yes please!"

"In the battle's footage, you can see your shuttle exiting the *Excellent* after she's in trouble. It vectors out, then gets hit. It whirls round like a top..."

"That's right! That's what I've told them," John shouted.

"The spinning slows down and the..." he hesitated before completing the sentence, "it disappears."

"Disappears?"

"Yeah. A well defined picture, it's baffled the experts. We got several angles of it from the hologram projectors on the probes sent there to record the event. They all showed the same thing. Of course, the authorities have suppressed all records of the battle and destroyed the data stones..."

John growled, "Oh, typical!"

"... but I know for a fact the Intelligence Corps has got copies of them all."

"Hmm."

"Plus, I copied a set myself, just to make sure. They're safe."

Midget's cheeky grin met the other man's look of relief. He did not understand it all, but the footage, such as it was, corroborated what he told his lawyer. The intelligence officer had more.

"Ridge..."

"My lawyer."

"... has been busy working your case. He's not as hopeless as he looks. He's made quite good progress with an insanity plea..."

"Oh, thanks!"

"Latest thinking is the Kupullans captured you and returned you as a spy, or an assassin."

"What? Subconscious conditioning, you mean?"

"Yeah."

John swore, then pointed out, "They could do a mind-probe; that would reveal the missing memories."

"They can't compel that under Andracon's constitution. Ridge has been arguing against it."

"But I think I'd rather know. I know nothing on a conscious level. If I volunteer for one when it's not compulsory, would that not be held in my favour?"

"Perhaps, but you're an embarrassment to the authorities right now. There's political pressure to let you go... away from here, I mean."

"Oh."

"Andracon's in a mess, anyway. Under the peace treaty, they have shrunk our armed forces to a fraction of their former size. It's not as if there's a job for you here. Unemployment is rife. The short to medium-term future for this place is pretty grim. I'm hanging on for now. There's no way I'd earn this salary anywhere else. I'm going to milk it for as long as I can."

"Don't blame you."

"I've spoken with Ridge often."

"Have you?" John, surprised.

"Yeah; I'm trying to point him in the right direction. It's going to be a political decision, not a military court. The military, what's left of it, has lost its power and influence. They promised a victory after mortgaging the nation to the hilt with an arms build-up, then suffered total defeat. A few weeks ago, Kupullan announced the annexation of 117114 and renamed it... er, something or other. Andracon has to pay them tribute every six weeks. It's a humiliating defeat."

"Don't you think they might treat me as a scapegoat? Execute the enemy spy?"

"There's no appetite for that. The latest bunch of politicians in power are busy feathering their nest and your case is an unwelcome problem. I've been whispering in the right ears, helping towards your release."

Now, that shocked the hearer. The marine recruit of three years ago now exercised influence amongst people in authority!

"Besides," he continued, "with your windfall, you'll be able to purchase a decent little ship outright and fly to the stars... or whatever."

"What? What are you talking about?"

"Oh, didn't I mention it? You've got twenty-thousand credits coming to you from the authorities that look after Marmaris; compensation for your loss."

"That much? Are you sure?"

"I am. Here, look," and he showed copies of the relevant documents on his TRAC.

"Wow, that's a lot more than I expected."

Any qualms John might have held about accepting compensation for losing his parents he now forgot.

"Not all your home world was affected. Besides, they're talking about re-colonising the ravaged areas. They're also considering a new political system."

"Yeah, we all need more politicians," John said before continuing. "Anything you don't know, Midget?"

"Sure, plenty. Like where you've been the last half year."

They laughed and chatted some more. His visitor had been working tirelessly behind the scenes on his behalf, ever since John's return. He only revealed himself when he had enough material to make it worthwhile. What a pal!

Within a week, he found himself freed on a neutral discharge. He was informed this was between an honourable and a dishonourable exit from the armed forces. He would take it rather than argue. The accused explored the mind-probe idea with his lawyer. Prepared to go along with it, John found himself released anyway, so they did not proceed with it. It being an expensive procedure with no funding available. Midget gave him advice, wise for his tender years, to grab the opportunity for freedom without a fuss. If he could have remembered the past six months, he would have fought to clear his name. As it was, it made sense to go before anyone in authority changed their minds.

The Andracon government even provided him free passage to the next star system. They returned his few belongings to him. These included the TRAC in perfect working order and showing the twenty-thousand credits, plus the curious paperweight. The beautiful scene drew one in. He stared at it on the flight after saying goodbye, and thank you to Midget. A beautiful scene, but too amazing to be real.

Almost a year later, John was a resident on Leisure Space Station Four, which orbited a moon named Invicta. The moon went round the gaseous giant plant Vestiga Supremo in the Wellinger Sector. Several solar systems away from Andracon, the station employed artificial gravity set at one-point-zero ES (Earth Standard) which was an advantage. With the rent reasonable and the space ship he bought docked, it pleased him to spend awhile there to rest and relax. He frequented the gym to keep trim and liked to look out of the observation deck's giant window and watch the scenery.

After leaving Andracon, he travelled to Van Der Plast, an open desert planet. Such an extensive selection of small, private space craft were for sale that they spoiled him for choice. For an important purchase, he needed to be careful to get it right. In the end, he picked a red second-hand runnabout. A two-seater, it also possessed a spacious bagged compartment. He currently owned little baggage, but it might come in handy. It displayed the name *Shooter* along the starboard side and he quite liked that. He employed an expert to check it over. They gave him the thumbs up and, with a price tag of ten-thousand credits, it took up half of his money.

"Got a type IX UDS drive, so she's quite nippy," the dealer told him. The technical details meant little to the buyer, but the craft handled well and the sale delighted him.

Now he sat in a corner by himself at one of the space station's several bars. It was a quieter one with subdued lighting, which he preferred. Quite happy with his own company, the realisation dawned on him he was becoming something of a loner. Not that he disliked company, but ever since the battle, he experienced strange dreams. He wondered about his sanity. Not that the dreams were disturbing, quite the opposite, in fact. Wonderful scenery, beautiful people, how could he not like it? Yet the recurring nature and intensity of them unsettled him.

He held no regrets for having joined Andracon's defence forces and none for leaving either. Now approaching twenty, he felt an urge to be more independent, not taking orders the whole time. Or should he dismiss such ideas as escapism? He would have to take obtain employment one day.

In the event, employment found him. Lost in his musings one evening, he did not notice a stranger approaching until he was upon him.

"Excuse me, are you John Thorn?"

John started a bit and looked up from his drink.

"I'm sorry, I did not mean to startle you."

The speaker was a man, well into his sixties, with long, fluffy white hair covering his ears. His neat beard and moustache were white too, but his eyebrows black. He wore a faun polo-neck jumper under an expensive mid-brown suit.

Collecting himself, John confirmed his identity and asked how he could assist this wealthy-looking gentleman.

"My name is Oleg Rosing. A mutual acquaintance put me on to you."

"Oh?"

"Martin Kovatz, he said you would be a good person to ask."

"Are you sure you have the right person?" asked John. The name of the contact meant nothing to him.

"You were on Andracon?"

"Yes."

"You come recommended. May I sit?"

Getting his brain more into gear, John ordered a drink for the new arrival as he realised this was *the* Oleg Rosing, head of the Rosing Corporation. They owned vast amounts of real estate in the quadrant. What would he want with him? Not something underhand, he hoped.

"Mr Thorn, I understand you are unemployed and I would like to offer you a one-off job. It's not something I can ask of my regular employees, but it isn't illegal."

"I'm glad to hear that."

"But it is dangerous." When the younger man did not respond to this statement, he continued. "Have you heard of the planet Diyu?"

John frowned before saying the name was not familiar with him.

"I can send you the specs to your TRAC, for I don't want you to go into this blind. In short, Diyu, in the Canas System, is a small rocky planet with a toxic atmosphere. It has a weather cycle whereby rain falls every few days and that rain is not water, it is acid, concentrated. My son, Advar, went there on a fool's mission a month ago. They heard it held large deposits of gold. A rock fall in a cave killed my son. The other members of the party abandoned the body there. I want him brought back home for a proper burial. If you are successful, I would reward you."

"Why not use machines?"

"The terrain is too rocky for wheeled vehicles. Tracks would slip on the shale and the resonance signal in that area rules out anti-grav machines. Besides, nothing has the dexterity and general versatility of a human being. I need second volunteer. You operated as a pilot, I understand."

"Yes."

"Will you consider the job?"

With a shrug, John said that he would consider it. He then asked the reward on offer for a successful mission. When informed, he tried to keep his composure and not fall off his chair. It was a lot of money, which rang alarm bells as to the dangerous nature of the task. He said that he would consider it. Why not? He could consider every angle before committing himself.

"I must rely on your discretion. News of this operation mustn't get out before it happens. Do you understand?"

"You can rely on me."

"We meet again here, same time tomorrow," Mr Rosing said.

"Okay. I'll have your answer then."

Rosing pointed out that John was using his right hand while taking a sip of his drink.

"Yeah, what of it? I'm right-handed."

"Good! That is what I was told."

"Why?"

"Oh, I find it hard to trust left-handed people."

With that, Oleg Rosing departed.

John himself left the bar soon afterwards. He returned to his cabin to study the files already downloaded onto his TRAC. From looking at the hologramic images projected from the device, he learned a lot more.

Mean daytime temperature around four-hundred Kelvin and with an atmosphere comprising of CO_2 and H_2S, this was not the galaxy's nicest world. The planet contained many active volcanoes too.

Gravity registered half Earth Standard. The name, Diyu, meant "hell"; not at all inappropriate.

It did indeed rain acid, but according to the best information available, this was on a predictable cycle. They would time any mission to coincide with a dry spell.

Schematics showed the proposed landing site and where the cave was in which lay the body. Mr Rosing had done his homework, but then he struck one as the type not to leave anything to chance.

A basic payment was on offer if they did not find his son's body. The reward for a successful mission, though, was generous. Then the retrieval of the body of his only son meant a lot to Mr Rosing. It meant more than wealth.

Studying the files took half the night. He could have a lie-in the next morning. The documents included a report on the gold prospecting expedition which ended in tragedy. Advar Rosing died after being hit by a rock fall inside this cave system and his five confederates abandoned his body. John doubted if their actions pleased the father, but that was none of his business.

He looked further. Rosing's company would provide a ship, the suits and everything else required. The importance of secrecy was unclear, but that did not concern him. Whom would he tell?

Deciding to sleep on it, he retired for the night. In reality, he had already made his mind up. The money was a real incentive. However, not having been able to bury his own parents, he empathised with Mr Rosing and thought he understood why he so wanted his dead son's body back.

A lazy day followed. He got up late and ordered them to send a meal to his room. He glanced at the download, but John had given them such a thorough inspection the night before that he felt confident he could remember the pertinent details. A shower, a walk round the observation deck and discussing star patterns with a visitor passing through. Before he knew, it was his usual time for heading to the bar. Mr Rosing was already there, this time with someone else beside him. They sat in a dark corner. As he got closer, he inspected this fresh character. His fellow adventurer was wide-bodied and muscle-bound. Two slits punctuated his fat face for eyes. He appeared a most unsavoury fellow, but then John reminded himself that he was there to consider a job, not to make lifelong buddies.

Rising from his seat, Mr Rosing made the introductions. "John Thorn, this is Nestor Gurevich; Nestor, this is John."

"Hi," said John, while the other grunted.

"Before we start," Mr Rosing said, "I want you to know this YJL will thwart any attempts to eavesdrop on this meeting." He tapped a small device sitting in the middle of the table. "So," he continued, eagerness in his tone, " are you prepared to help me?"

"In principle, yes, but I need to discuss details before committing myself."

They spent the rest of the evening going through the operation in depth. Gurevich, whilst paying attention, let the other two do the talking. It slipped out in conversation that he was an ex-mercenary, still offering himself for hire. John felt he could not criticise, because he was also open for this unorthodox job.

A well considered enterprise, it was hard for John to pick holes in the plan. One of Mr Rosing's large spaceships, with a shuttle craft on board, would transport them to the planet. John would pilot the shuttle down to the surface, taking Gurevich with him. The timing between acid rain storms being vital.
Landing near the cave, it should be a short walk.

An unmanned probe, sent to the planet earlier, revealed a wide opening to the cave. It got stuck when the machine flew into a narrow tunnel off the main cavern and ceased broadcasting after a while.

Rosing criticised the other men on the original prospecting expedition in which his son lost his life. While they declared Adva had died by an internal rock fall, the details were sketchy. The father could not forgive them for leaving the body there. John and Gurevich would take a stretcher, climbing gear and plenty of other equipment they might need. With the gravity so light, they should be able to carry a good load.

Things could go wrong on the hostile surface of Diyu; they must satisfy John that there were contingency plans for all eventualities. By the end of the evening, it convinced him they had tried to ensure the operation was as safe as possible.

Seeking confirmation, John said, "And the astro-meteorologist on board will not sanction our leaving the mother ship until it satisfies him there is a dry spell."

"Yes!" Rosing confirmed. "That's vital. They've been studying the weather patterns for a long time and are confident they'll get you the window of opportunity you need."

"Okay, I'm satisfied, I'll do it."

It delighted the bereaved father that his evening had not been in vain. Pieces were falling into place, but further preparation needed doing before they could leave.

A week later, the freighter *Maverick* made its way silently through outer space on its way to Diyu. An automated craft, the crew was small and, apart from the astro-meteorologist, regular Rosing employees. John had spent much of the previous few days training alongside Gurevich. The ex-mercenary's taciturnity was getting on his nerves. He kept telling himself that the operation would not take long. It would soon all be over and he was not there to make friends. So he gritted his teeth and bore it.

The freighter possessed an observation deck and the captain halted the ship near one particular star to have a look out. He explained to John, "We're early and it won't matter of we stay here a while. I wanted to look at that."

What fascinated him was a giant planet orbiting too close to its star.

"It's famous," the captain said, "but I wanted to see it with my own eyes."

"Why, is it unique?"

"Unusual. It's a gaseous giant orbiting every eighteen hours and has a surface temperature of one-thousand-two-hundred-and-fifty degrees. Soon, tidal forces will rip the planet apart. The star'll then consume it."

They stood for a while watching the celestial bodies in motion. It held less interest for him than for the captain. Besides, another matter concerned him.

"It surprised me Mr Rosing didn't come along with us."

"He's a busy man."

"Yes, but he's taking a keen interest in our mission."

"I think he felt it might tempt him to interfere if he was here. As it is, we've organised a live video feed from the shuttle, so that he'll be able to watch you on the surface."

"I see. Anyway, I think I'll go along and check it once more before we get into orbit around Diyu."

"You're right," responded the captain, dragging himself away from the observation window. "Back to work."

John visited the shuttle in its housing on board the freighter. Although called by the same designation as the *Excellent's* craft, this was different. He would have to land vertically on the planet's surface, not horizontally. The pair would have to descend a ladder from the craft's underside. John had flown one of these in simulations, but not real life. He held a slight concern about this, but remained confident he would manage.

Soon they reached Diyu and established the freighter in synchronous orbit over the landing zone. Attention now fell on the astro-meteorologist, because it was he who would declare when it was safe for the mission proper to proceed. He bent over his instruments and screens for some time before he delivered his verdict.

"We're in luck! We have a twelve hour window right now. The next one won't appear for a week."

The decision to proceed was unanimous, although John considered to himself, 'We should be okay, but we'd better get going straightaway, 'cos there isn't a huge margin for error.'

He and Gurevich suited up before entering the capsule. This task took some time, but once completed, they sat inside, ready to leave. The many pre-flight checks were gone through, then they were okay to go.

"Release clamps, launch shuttle, engage engines," the commands came and the craft moved out of its depressurised bay into the void. A few minor manoeuvres proved necessary. Then, once free of the freighter, he made for the uninviting orange sphere below.

The two-man crew did not feel the atmosphere's buffeting. Meanwhile, the ship's force field ensured that the acid clouds did not have a detrimental effect on the hull. Passing into clear air, a red-brown surface came into view.

"Vector 9.2, reading 204," John read out.

"Roger, shuttle," the controller on board the freighter said. "Maintain course."

The landing area soon appeared. The pilot had familiarised himself with the terrain during simulation. All was going according to plan. A nice, even, boulder-free area presented itself seven-hundred-and-fifty metres from the cave entrance and, manoeuvring the craft, John began a controlled final decent.

"No, land closer!" cried Gurevich, the first time he spoke since leaving the freighter.

An unwelcome distraction, the pilot ignored him. Making landfall, he turned the engines off and breathed a sigh of relief before reporting in to the controller.

"Safe landing achieved, all instruments green; settlement three-point-five degrees from level."

It was close to a perfect landing, but his passenger was unhappy.

"Should have landed closer to the cave. We'll have to walk much further there... then back again carrying the bloody body!"

John could not ignore him this time. Leaving the screen on, he pointed at the scene and said firmly, "Look! It's far rockier there, if one foot had hit a boulder we might have crashed. We're almost perfectly flat here. Nearer the cave and we'd almost certainly have ended up at an angle. In this ship it'd spell trouble when we come to take off again."

The other man brooded, but said nothing. So John added, "Come on, we mustn't waste time, let's get prepped."

They spoke no further word as they donned helmets, re-checked that their suits and oxygen supply were good. Then the pair shuffled to the cramped airlock in the shuttle's bottom. The folded stretcher being stored there, Gurevich picked it up as decompression took place. Then they boarded the ladder. The floor compartment slid open and they descended to the surface.

They knew that gravity on Diyu was a mere fifty percent Earth Standard, but their heavy, industrial spacesuits and equipment carried compensated for this. Once down, John released the force field just long enough for them to step out beyond. Once re-applied, they began the trek to the cave.

Walking in this gravity and over the rocky terrain took some getting used to. It proved quite tiring, even for fit individuals. The thought occurred to John that his companion was right regarding landing closer to their destination. Nevertheless, he knew he had made the most sensible decision.

Nearer the cave stood an enormous bank of smooth pebbles which they must climb. For every two steps up, they slid one back.

Progress was slow and frustrating, but it pleased John that the other man said nothing further.

Reaching the top with their hearts beating wildly, they stood for a while to catch their breath. John glanced at the bright orange sky, a strange sight. Looking back at the ship, he remembered that Mr Rosing would watch their every move. He tried checking in with the controller on the freighter, but his suit's transmitter was too weak to connect.

"Forget them, let's go," snapped Gurevich.

John glanced at his oxygen dial, he had used thirty percent already. That alarmed him. At least they were at the cave. They lit the lights on their helmets and entered.

The floor of the cave was smooth except for the stalagmites dotted around. The ceiling stood so high that their lights only showed it up if they tilted their heads. A few stalactites hung down, but the lowest was well above their heads. John issued a warning.

"Don't walk under one of those if you can help it, they might drip liquid with a high acid content."

Gurevich grunted a response.

John turned on the sensor instrument he carried, designed to detect organic matter. He walked round for a while. None registered and they seemed to go circles. Carrying on round the cavernous area, John felt helpless. Would they find the body? A faint register on the instrument stopped him in his tracks.

"Something?" the other man asked.

"Um, not sure. Wait a second... yes! There it is again. It's very faint. Over here."

It led them to a pile of small rocks. Peeling these away, it revealed what they came for, the body of Advar Rosing, in its spacesuit. The scene was not a rock fall, it was a distance from the side. It looked more like a makeshift grave made of stones. The previous expedition came looking for gold, the current one only for a body.

They said few words. Gurevich removed the last of the rocks and opened the stretcher. They loaded the corpse onto it. John was at the front as he led them back to the opening.

Emerging from the cave, he checked his oxygen level again. Forty percent left. He reminded himself that he also possessed a small emergency tank, so he would not panic yet. Descending the pebble bank should be faster than going up.

The light seemed changed; less bright. Peering up, it was noticeable how much darker the clouds appeared. Had he been on Marmaris, even accounting for the different coloured sky, he would have forecast rain.

With a cascade of stones, they surfed down the pebble bank. All the while they held onto the stretcher. It was a good start. John struck out for home, but he heard Gurevich on his radio, "Slow down, damn you! It's a lot harder being at the back."

Half way across, the man complained again and John suggested they swap places. With the clouds looking ever more menacing, it meant precious time wasted. They got going again, getting closer to the shuttle with every step. Then it rained.

The first drop landed on the stretcher. John watched in horror as, in a matter of seconds, it burned its way through. Gurevich had seen the first few drops too and began running with the stretcher. As further drops fell, and they were a hundred metres from their destination, the ex-mercenary dropped his end of the stretcher and made a run for it.

John cursed. Self-preservation was a real motivator, it would only take a few drops to burn their way through his suit and expose him to the toxic atmosphere. Yet he could not look Mr Rosing in the eye if he dumped Advar's remains, not now they were so close. With a monumental effort, he picked up the body and put it over his shoulder in a fireman's lift. Thus encumbered, he ran the last stretch. Gurevich ahead of him, tripped over a rock and fell down head first.

Arriving at the shuttle, John de-activated the force field briefly to pass through it. He put his load under the craft and spun round. He re-activating the force field and was ready to reduce it when the other man arrived. Gurevich, forty metres out, got up onto his knees when the heavens opened.

Before John's eyes, he witnessed the man die an agonising death. Screams filled John's radio as Gurevich perished in a shower of acid. It burned through his spacesuit in next to no time.

John was powerless to help. Concerned that his own suit may be compromised, he wasted no further time. Mounting the ladder with the body, he hauled them up into the air lock. Pressurisation took longer than usual, but then he hurried into the capsule itself. As quickly as possible he took the spacesuit of. An acidic smell filled his nostrils, but he was unhurt. A quick look at Advar's suit showed tiny marks, like bullet holes, caused by raindrops. John was still in shock and found his hand shaking as he sought to re-establish contact with the freighter.

"John Thorn to controller, I'm back on board, but..."

"We saw what happened," came the reply. Nothing you could have done. Prepare to return to orbit."

"Commencing lunch sequence... and tell that meteorologist fellow that I'll be giving him a piece of my mind once I'm back on board!"

~ End of Chapter 5 ~

My Keeper's Brother - Chapter 6

A week later, John sat at his favourite bar on Station Number 4 waiting or Mr Rosing to arrive. He had come extra early, realising how fortunate he was to be there. What if he had tripped instead of Gurevich? What if the shuttle, its hull integrity compromised by acid, had broken up before making it back to the freighter? No use dwelling on it.

"Ah, my boy!" Rosing greeted him like a long-lost son and, as John stood up out of respect, the older man gave him an enormous hug.

The industrialist's lawyer came in tow. A tiny, mousy figure, he ended up speaking not a word. His boss, on this first encounter since John got back, was full of praise.

"You are my hero! I watched it live, biting my fingernails to the quick. When that rat, Gurevich, ran for it, I was certain you'd do the same. I underestimated you. Martin recommended you, I'm glad I listened to him."

A puzzled John replied, "Yes, this Martin..."

"Martin Kovatz."

"I don't re..."

"The former executive officer on the *Excellent*."

"Ah, XO as we always knew him. He survived!" The young man sounded astonished, but Rosing had other things to discuss.

"Thanks to you, I have Advar's precious body back. In time, I will give him a proper burial back in our home world, next to his mother."

After carrying on in similar vein for a while, he revealed something truly shocking.

"They examined my son's body and it revealed a bullet wound."

"What!?"

"It took a while for them to find it amid the acid burns. The murderer used an old-fashioned gun. The authorities have issued an international warrant for the immediate arrest of the other expedition members. I will make sure they bring them to justice."

"Oh, Mr Rosing, I'm so sorry."

"Do not concern yourself, John, it is my problem. But there's one thing I need to tell you."

"Yes?"

"Have you checked your TRAC?"

"Er..."

"Your remuneration went in an hour ago. I'm sorry it's late."

"Oh, that's okay, Mr Ros..."

"And I've given you Gurevich's amount, too. He didn't earn it, but you walked the extra mile and I shall always be grateful for that."

John considered protesting that this was not fair, that the other man's relatives might be glad of the money. Then he decided against it. After all, the ex-mercenary almost certainly did not have a family, he considered somewhat illogically. Definitely not the family man, while such a double payment would be a tremendous boost to John's diminishing coffers. He checked his wrist computer there and then. It was true, he was wealthier than he had ever been.

Mr Rosing left soon after that, leaving a young man sitting pretty, delighted at how the situation had concluded.

After receiving his windfall, John decided it was time to leave. He did not want to spend the rest of his life on Space Station Number 4. Where to go, though? That was not at all certain. He was unsure where to move even after a fortnight's contemplation.

Open planets held appeal, of course, but they were few. He enjoyed studying details of these different worlds, but it was a tough decision to make. Still undecided, he perched on his favourite pew at the bar. The place had yet to fill up.

John sat in a brown study, his mind elsewhere when someone walked across the room, straight towards him.

"John?"

"Um, yes?"

"Martin, Martin Kovatz," the man introduced himself.

John hesitated before the penny dropped. When it did, John stood up and grasped the man's hands, crying, "XO, wonderful to see you!"

"May I sit down?"

"Of course."

"I'm afraid I'm no longer XO. That life is in the past."

"Let me get you a drink."

They paused while a waiter did this. As the other man took his first sip, John studied him. A year and a half had passed since they last met, but Kovatz looked ten years older. With his head shaved, he looked quite different. No wonder he was not recognisable at first. Time had etched deeper the lines on his face, but, as he set his drink down, he appeared cheerful.

"Good to see another survivor!" Kovatz said.

"Yes indeed, it delighted me when I heard you were okay," John said.

"I thought you'd been killed."

"Did you?"

"Sure; we saw the shuttle launch on the monitor. You were still in sight when hit you. We thought you'd had it. We couldn't dwell, the ship was breaking up at that point."

"How did you get away?"

"The *Excellent* was the first of the fleet's ships fitted with a bridge escape pod. In effect, the entire area became one big life raft. Put to the test, it worked well."

"Captain Farnham?"

"I'm afraid not. He insisted on leaving the bridge and seeing to... I don't know. The captain insisted on going down with his ship in the ancient tradition."

"Oh, a pity, I liked him. I don't suppose you know if any of the marines survived."

"No idea, I'm afraid. I encountered none on Kupullan. They might not've make it; there wasn't time... although they launched one or two life pods."

"And they took you prisoner?"

"Yes. Spent a year in prisoner of war at their facilities. Some on their home world, one on a moon orbiting the planet. Most of these were quite small. The Kupullans separated me from my fellow *Excellent* survivors; they held them elsewhere. There were a substantial number of survivors from other ships, although we lost thousands."

"How were you treated?"

"I can't complain. They interrogated me. I..."

"No thumb screws, I hope," interrupted John, who was then annoyed with himself for making such a crass joke. He need not have worried, for the Kovatz laughed.

"Nothing like that, I can assure you. During the interrogation, I told them everything they wanted to know. It seemed silly not to. They annihilated our fleet, our nation utterly defeated... nothing to be gained in resisting."

"How long did they hold you?"

"About a year. Back on Andracon, the conditions had deteriorated. There was no prospect of finding employment. I heard about your survival, though, which amazed me. The stories I heard about it sounded too fantastic to believe."

"What were you told?"

"I'd rather hear it from you."

John then described everything he could remember, which, of course, was very little. He was at pains to stress the veracity of his account. "I swear on my mother's grave that what I've told you is the truth, XO."

"I believe you," said the other man. What else could he say? "But it's Martin, please. My XO days are long past."

"Martin, okay; I'll try to remember. Please be patient with me if I slip up again. Oh, and thank you for putting that job my way!"

"Mr Rosing?"

"Yes, it proved lucrative."

"Good."

"So, what are you doing now?"

"I'm an officer on one of Rosing Corporation's freighters."

"A comedown from a destroyer."

"You could say that."

"Sorry!" John apologised. Why could he not control his tongue?

"It's okay," Kovatz assured him. "It's a temporary post. They have offered me a place on a deep exploration ship."

"An exploration ship?" the younger man echoed.

"That's right. It won't set sail for another three months and I'm filling in time."

"Where will you go?"

"Classified, I'm afraid, but I expect the voyage to take several years."

"How exciting!"

"I think so. You and I used to talk about the early colonists and I feel like I'm following in their footsteps."

"I enjoyed our discussions."

"As did I."

"How big is the ship? How many people are on board?"

"Again, I'm sorry."

"Classified!"

"It is."

"But I bet you're excited about following the old traditions of deep space exploration."

"Too true. It's the first such expedition we've attempted in years. So frustrating, these days, the lack of motivation. I want to visit fresh worlds and explore astronomical phenomena like the explorers of old. It's rare for people to have that sense of adventure nowadays. I'm thrilled to be on this."

They spent the rest of the evening talking. The room got busier, but the two men stayed oblivious to anyone else. Kovatz could give few details away, but John gleaned that an enthusiastic businessman funded the expedition. John wondered if they could consider him for a spot on the adventure. After all, his piloting skills might come in handy. Yet he pulled back from asking and Kovatz never suggested it. It was late when they retired.

"I hope you're not leaving here soon, Martin. I'd love another chat tomorrow."

"Sorry, but my job calls. I've got to be back on board at 0600 tomorrow. No peace for the wicked."

"I am so glad you came to see me. It's been great seeing you again, find out what happened and learn your plans. Plus, I got the opportunity to thank you for your word in Mr Rosing's ear."

"You're welcome."

"Good luck for the future, XO."

Kovatz smiled before turning away.

"Hope we'll meet up again one day," were John's last words, but the crowds swallowed the other man up. He never saw him again.

The following two years were poor ones for John. He stayed on Space Station 4, money not being a problem. Making friends was. He was one of the few long-term residents there. If he began forming a bond with someone, they soon moved on. After a while, he stopped making the effort.

Few unattached females frequented the station and women were an alien species to him. He had no father figure to give him helpful advice.

One evening, a heavily made-up woman approached him while he drank alone at the bar. Brought up to avoid such people, he surprised himself when he agreed to go back to her cabin. Half way there, walking behind her along a narrow corridor, he had second thoughts. Embarrassed, he apologised as he turned and hurried away. She called back, her unkind comments stinging him.

After this, he fell into a deep depression. He did not feel like doing anything. His gym visits stopped and he did not frequent the bar so much. One morning, after a day and a half spent in bed, it shocked him to see the gaunt figure staring back at him in the mirror. Finally, he got the impetus to do something about it.

John, sick of being confined, decided it was time to leave. He needed to find an open world to live on.

Realising how foolish it would be not to do some research first, he spent hours on his TRAC doing precisely that. Nothing seemed ideal. Either the mean temperature was uninviting, the society sounded off-putting or the gravity wrong. Eden was one planet he perused and it amused him, because, as far as he knew, Frank still lived there. He did not want to cramp his brother's style, though. Besides, a society run by priests was not his thing at all.

Then he discovered a planet which appeared perfect. Belovo enjoyed the right gravity, atmosphere, temperature range, in fact, everything. The aviation museum most attracted his attention. The write-up said that they held the remains of a 1st I.W. warship there. That captivated him and provided all the impetus he needed. The following day, his long stay at the station ended and he prepared *Shooter* to leave.

The one thing against Belovo was its location. It sat a long way away, towards the edge of the area of the current inhabited universe. He considered this on the journey.

Whole chunks of the populated galaxy became detached following the 2nd I. W. generations before. The war, the greatest calamity ever to befall mankind, still shaped the society of John's day. Robophobia and the all-powerful Dycon Inspectorate were two products of that conflict. Another was "losing" earth, the mother planet and vast areas of colonised space, now unknown to the civilization John lived in.

Spread across countless worlds, populations were small. Most planets, being domed, could only accommodate limited numbers. Belovo might be open with ideal living conditions, but it was stuck away and no one would visit it on their way to anywhere else. Wide open spaces were the result, while the populated areas held a "frontier town" feel about them.

When he arrived, John laughed at the space port, so small and amateurish it seemed. Still, with pleasant staff on duty, they made him feel welcome. 'A lot less officious than on some planets. They could teach the others how to treat visitors.'

His ship parked, they directed him to a hotel a kilometre and a half away and he elected to walk. The exercise would do him good and his one medium-sized case employed an anti-grav unit. 'My whole life contained within one case!' he considered. 'Not a lot to show for twenty-two years' existence.'

The building material here was wood, timber being in plentiful supply from the extensive forests. One or two cars drove along the town's high street as the sun set. A larger proportion of people walked, but a tranquil mood purveyed.

Finding the hotel, he enquired about a room and it pleased him when told there were several available. He chose a single room at the quieter rear of the building.

"Have you travelled far, sir?" the desk clerk enquired.

"I have, the Wellinger Sector."

Raising his eyebrows at this, the employee mentioned that, while the hotel took payment from his TRAC, many places would insist on physical money. "You will need to change credits into coins and notes."

It was John's turn to show surprise. He had not been on a planet with physical currency since he left Marmaris. He enquired where he could get physical money.

"We can do it here, sir. Maybe after we settle you in your room."

"Of course, thank you."

The room offered basic amenities, but that did not concern John. A comfortable bed was of primary importance. Enjoy a good night's sleep and explore in the morning. That was the plan. He wanted to find the museum.

Yet, that night, sleep evaded him. Midnight, he sat up in bed and read more data about this planet on his TRAC. Third planet from an aging main sequence star, the temperature here at the equator held constant. It stayed between two-hundred-and-seventy-five to three-hundred Kelvin; most pleasant. The more he learned about this place, the better he liked it.

It was involved in the 1st I.W. with fighting taking place both on the planet's surface and in the space surrounding it. They were lucky during the 2nd I.W. for the conflict left the planet alone. The information did not state the population size, but when he descended in his ship, the town appeared small and isolated.

Turning off the device, he looked out of his window at the night sky. Light pollution being low for a town centre, on this cloudless night the widely-spaced stars stood clearly visible. 'Where are they all?' he considered, for the view here, pointing away from the centre of the Milky Way, contained fewer stars than he could ever remember. It proved an extraordinary sight to eyes accustomed to seeing entire skies filled with lights great and small. Yet, was this not like those strange, recurring dreams he still experienced?

As he pulled away from the window, he dismissed this, drew the curtains together and climbed back into bed.

Following a lie-in, he got up, showered and dressed. John was ready to meet the day. It proved easy to exchange online credits for physical cash as the counter clerk had said. Not having a proper container for it, he stuffed the money into his pockets.

With the hotel's bar and restaurant closed for refurbishment, he ate breakfast at a cafe the other side of the road. Muffins and fruit, it was quite tasty and inexpensive. Everything on this planet seemed enchantedly old-fashioned to him. He double-checked the whereabouts of the museum with the waitress. It was a straight walk across town. Again, he welcomed the open air exercise and it did not tempt him to take one of the taxis on offer.

Getting to the quarter where the aviation museum stood, John walked past it at first, not recognising the shack for what it was. Locating it, he paid the minimal entrance fee and stepped inside for a look round. A family-run enterprise, it appeared amateurish and the exhibits, such as they were, poorly displayed. With plenty of time to study them, though, he did not hurry. No other visitors were there. The items were at least labelled. A compressor from a Type III

106

freighter; the landing gear, the caption said, belonging to an original colonists' ship...

'A pile of junk!' was the visitor's verdict, 'they could have salvaged that from any scrap heap and we'd be none the wiser '

The piece de resistance, and the exhibit he had come from afar to see, was the 1st I.W. fighter Already an aficionado, if not an actual expert on the subject. It proved an enormous disappointment. The pile of burnt, mangled wreckage was unidentifiable! He spent some time walking round, inspecting it, but was far from impressed.

The museum displayed a mock-up hologram of the ship in its prime. The visitor shook his head. The cabin was positioned incorrectly and the colour scheme wrong. He found no curator nearby to tell and gave up. Why bother?

'Oh well,' he mused upon coming out into the fresh air, 'there's more to this planet than its crummy museum. I'd like to go hiking in those mountains.'

A few kilometres south of the town, the tree-covered slopes looked inviting. A surge of delight ran through his body at the prospect. Having used up half the day already, he decided it would be his project for the following morning. That afternoon, he bought some firm walking boots. From the moment he tried them on, he knew they were right. A drinks flask and lunch box with a strap to put round his neck were useful purchases too. The quality of these items seemed fine. Produced on the planet, they were cheap to buy. Still possessing the bulk of the money he received for the Diyu operation, he could stay on Belovo a considerable time without needing work.

'I wish I'd come here sooner,' he considered, but his spirits were lifted as he walked back to his hotel.

Now a creature of habit, he sought a bar to prop up that evening. With the hotel's own facilities closed, he stepped once more onto the high street. He would find somewhere else.

The town took on a different aspect after sunset. There were more people outside. In no rush, he wandered along the road looking in bars. No shortage of such establishments on this planet, he checked several out before choosing. As he progressed, it became apparent that he was entering the more seedy part of town. Paint peeled off the walls, the road had pot holes and a shutter hung loose, swinging in the breeze.

With the buildings up ahead thinning out, he tried one final establishment. Written on a large, but somewhat shabby sign above the door was the word "Majestic." It amused him, for it certainly did not look majestic. Having come this far, he might as well try it.

"Can you spare a credit for the poor, brother?" a man wearing a grey costume asked him.

"No, thank you," John said as he pushed past.

Inside, it was rather dingy, but not too dark. The odour of beer met his nostrils, but then what did he expect? The conventional establishment sported a long bar with stools lined up by it, then an area with tables and chairs. It was a scene repeated on a thousand and one planets.

A gaggle of customers propped up the bar and occupied almost half the seats. He had seen busier places. A short flight of steps led from the road to the bar area. Hesitating inside the door while he considered whether to stay or go back to one of their rivals, he noticed the person behind the bar. A woman, just a few years his senior, she was pretty with dyed blond hair cut with a fringe "Cleopatra" style. With no one to serve, she was doing some tidying up behind the bar. Drawn to his stare, she glanced up at the figure inside the door. When their eyes met, she gave him a sweet smile. It made his mind up.

His foot slipped on the last step. Only by grasping the banister did he avoid a fall. A few people glanced round and he flushed bright red.

"Are you sure you haven't drunk enough already?" the barmaid quipped once he arrived at the bar.

Not expecting a tease, this opening remark took him aback. He did not appear drunk as he walked across the room.

"I'm sorry, I shouldn't have said that," she added. It's my silly sense of humour; please don't take offence."

She was apologising too much and he was at pains to set her mind at rest by telling her he had *not* taken offence. Satisfied that he would not complain, the woman took his order and, upon receiving his drink, he established himself at the far end of the bar, which was free. He would have spoken further, but another customer came up and she was busy.

Quite happy sitting on the stool, back propped up against the wall observing the scene, he let his drink last as he took his time taking it all in. From the clientele, he could guess this was the less salubrious quarter, even if he had not seen the outside. Some customers looked rough around the edges. A contretemps broke out between two men at a nearby table. Wiser heads intervened and calmed the situation in a few moments.

On several occasions, he thought the barmaid was coming over to speak to him, but each time a fresh customer waylaid her. John told himself not to be so silly, it was his imagination.

"Whisky, large one, no ice, no water!" an obese, middle aged man demanded of the barmaid after waddling up to John's end of the bar from his table. The latter was thinking him rude when the man asked what he was drinking.

John did not consider the man too rude to accept a drink from him, so he said, "An Orange juice, thank you."

"Orange juice," repeated the man with disdain, "is that all?"

"Yes."

"If you'll have a proper drink, the next one'll be on me."

"How is an orange juice not a proper drink?" enquired John.

The other grunted, turned his back on him and finished his transaction with the barmaid before returning to his table.

As he took another sip, John found the barmaid apologising to him again.

"I'm sorry about that."

"It wasn't your fault. You're saying sorry a lot tonight."

"I'm sorry," she said, then they both laughed.

"I'll forgive you. It's busier than when I first arrived."

She glanced round at this, but there was no one to serve. "You've recently arrived on Belovo?"

"Um, yes. I wanted to see the aviation museum."

"That old thing!" she exclaimed, rolling her eyes. "I hope you haven't come light years for that; it'll disappoint you."

"I already have been disappointed, I visited this afternoon. Not the most impressive place."

"Oh dear."

"But it's not the sole thing I came for. I wanted to spend some time on an open planet."

"Your first?"

"Oh no, I was born and raised on Marmaris."

"Hmm," she considered, "I can't say I've heard of it."

"No reason you should. It's a long way from here."

"Most places are."

"It's open like here, but not as beautiful as your planet."

She gave a slight laugh, but John wanted to keep the conversation going, so he said, "A beggar accosted me as I came in here, called me 'brother'!"

His superior tone did not impress her and she said, "That wasn't a beggar. He'll be a member of the Brothers of Compassion; they help the poor around here. They're a religious order with a vow of poverty."

It was his turn to apologise. He did not want to offend this attractive lady. "I'll make sure I give him something on the way out."

"You do that. Excuse me."

Another customer came up and she served them. In fact, they kept her busy after that and John sat there and brooded.

'Damn!' he thought, 'stupid of me to say that? Am I trying to impress her with my arrogance? How idiotic!'

Time passed and it was getting late. He had no further chance to speak with her that night. Downing the last of his drink, he slipped out and headed for the door. There was no sign of the charity worker outside, so he made his way straight to his hotel.

On the way, he asked himself why he felt so cross about his comment. It kept playing again in his head. He must find a Brother of Compassion tomorrow and give them something. Why? He wanted to please that attractive barmaid, that was why.

Next day, he got up in good time ready for his trek. He ate breakfast in the cafe across the way again, then bought food supplies from them before departing. The air felt cooler this morning, he noted as he made his way along the high street. Before long, the buildings lay behind him and he entered a pine forest, the ground soft and springy beneath his feet.

No one else was in sight as he went deeper into the woods. A gentle incline became steeper as he ascended. The pine trees stood tall and erect. Many had shed their branches in their lower parts.

There were no extensive forests back on Marmaris and it thrilled him at the forest's huge expanse. He anticipated a good view from the top above the tree line.

110

Nearing the summit, he came across a bare outcrop of rock. It was an ideal vantage point, with an unobstructed view of the countryside. Here he sat on a patch of grass and got his packed lunch out. All that climbing gave him an appetite.

A beautiful landscape spread out before him. The woodland was indeed extensive and filled his view from left to right and ahead where, beyond, the town lay. There was little variety of tree and, away from the immediate area, a uniform dark green blanket covered the countryside. In the far distance stood a much higher range of snow-capped mountains. The atmosphere was clear and fresh. Little industry was in evidence on this remote planet from what he could tell. He filled his lungs with clean air and it felt good.

Finishing his food, he sat for a while, enjoying the moment. He was unsure how long he would spend on Belovo. Apart from wide-open spaces, it did not appear to have a great deal to offer. No need to decide quickly. One certain thing was where he intended going that evening.

Back in his room after supper, he took a quick shower and put on a clean shirt, his best, before setting forth.

'What if she doesn't work this evening?' he asked himself. 'What if the bar is extra busy and she hasn't time to talk?'

Only one way to answer these questions; he picked up his pace the nearer he got. Arriving earlier than the previous evening, it was not dark yet. He rounded the corner and his eyes lit up when he spotted the Brother of Compassion at the Majestic Bar's door. Fingering the coins in his pocket, he took them out and pressed them into his hand before the friar opened his mouth.

"There you are."

"Thank you, sir!"

"My pleasure," he said, beaming. Then, with a deep inhale, he stepped inside.

A barman was on duty, serving customers. John's heart sank as he came down the steps, carefully this time. Taking a few paces over to the counter, she appeared from behind it. She had been hunting for something.

Her face looked concerned. Was she worried about something? Either way, it lit up when she spotted him and greeted, "Hello, soldier, would you like the usual?"

This being his second visit, the reference to "the usual" amused him. With a smile, he answered, "Orange juice, please... but how did you know I used to be in the army?"

"I didn't," she replied as she prepared his drink, "it's just a greeting."

"Oh."

"There you are, one orange juice, a real drink," she said with a cheeky wink.

He paused before telling her, "I gave some money to that Brother of Compassion outside a moment ago."

"Good for you!" she said sweetly, but then another customer needed serving and he retreated to his favourite spot at the end of the bar. It stood free despite the place being busier that evening. There he sat, sipping his drink and watching the barmaid's every move.

The evening wore on and she was busy. Her worried look had returned and she seemed unhappy. When she found an opportunity, she seized the initiative and approached him.

"Like another one?"

"Um, yes please," he said, downing the last drop before handing the glass over.

"You're not the last of the big spenders, are you?" she said with a glint in her eye as she got his fresh drink. The cloud over her most of the evening lifted momentarily.

He laughed, not minding being teased by her. Then, plucking up courage, he commented, "You looked worried."

"Hmm," was all she responded as he handed over the money for the drink.

"Anything I can help with?"

"Not unless you've got two thousand credits to spare," she said, more to herself.

"Yes, I have!" John came back.

She hesitated. A colleague was serving another customer at the bar. Sounding suspicious, she enquired, "And what would you want in return?"

"Nothing! Um, maybe the chance to take you for dinner on your evening off." When she smiled, but hesitated, he introduced himself.

"I'm Stella," the barmaid replied. "If you're paying for the food, then tomorrow evening's my night off."

"Great! Shall I come and pick you up?"

"I'll find you; where are you staying?"

They arranged details before she hurried back to deal with a fresh order. He tried not to grin too much as he sat there, his heart pounding. Tomorrow evening could not come too soon for him.

Stella's story was a complex one. A rollercoaster life saw her wanting a lasting relationship, only to find them turning sour.

She was born on the thirty-fifth of July 2563 on the open, but remote planet Belovo. This world's single companion was a large, uninhabited moon. With a stable, temperate climate, breathable atmosphere and gravity 1.02 Earth Standard, it had a lot going for it. With poverty rife, and its low birth-rate and distance from most of the rest of civilization, it meant the population remained low.

The days there were approximately twenty-five hours Earth Standard, but the planet took four-hundred-and-four days to circle its sun. Long before Stella was born, they decided to split their year into eleven, thirty-five day months, plus a twenty-nine day February. The arrangement worked well, but it caused confusion with their nearest neighbour, Varnis, some light years away, because it could be April on one planet and October on the other. The authorities on Belovo disdained falling into line with General Standard Time. No one on their world minded.

Growing up, Stella did not realise quite how poor her family was. An only child, she saw little of her father, a big man and heavy manual worker. Her disabled mother was also feeble at decision making. Stella herself was small for her age.

Her mother did, however, take her daughter to church each Sunday. Stella enjoyed hearing the tales of Jesus' exploits and rather fell in love with this ideal man, kind both to children and women.

A major change to her insular life came when Stella started at the local primary school. There she got in with a couple of girls who led her astray. They were into "pranks," starting off with simple capers such as knocking on peoples' doors and running away. Soon they progressed to "dares" which amounted to little more than acts of vandalism.

Matters culminated one day when they were in a public building with a flower display on a plinth in the corridor near the entrance. An easy target, the three girls together trashed the display, leaving a rude sticker on the wall in its place. They ran away laughing, but even as they did so, it pricked Stella's conscience. She remembered Jesus' words about treating others as you would like them to treat you. 'I would not like it if someone smashed up a flower display I had taken care to put up,' she told herself. Ashamed, she resolved to confess to the crime. Very well, but she was commanded to inform the adults her accomplices' identities. She did.

They set the trio to work in the centre's garden as a punishment, with Stella given the job of weeding a flower bed while the other pair whitewashed a concrete shed. When she spoke to them, they told her they would "get her" for the betrayal.

Frightened by the threat, Stella hurried home once she completed her duty. Her mother stood in the walled annex outside the back door on that clement day, ironing some clothes. The little girl started building a barricade out of boxes to shield her from her former friends. Their threats came to nothing and the whole thing blew over. Nevertheless, these events convinced her parents to moved her to a different school.

Stella never forgot her first lunchtime break there, standing alone in the playground full of children she did not know. She had grown quite a lot in the preceding year, but still cut a forlorn figure. Then a girl she had noticed in her new class come over to her.

"Hello, I'm Bianca," she said in a low-pitched voice for a girl so young, "do you want to be my friend?" The speaker was tiny, but moved, spoke and acted with an inner confidence. Jet black hair and large, bushy eyebrows the same colour, she stood out from the crowd.

Turning down the offer was not an option and a beautiful friendship began. The girls were soon inseparable, playing hopscotch in the playground, or spending their spare time going for long walks in the woods. Why a confident, popular individual would want to pick a poor, insecure girl as a friend, Stella did not know, but it pleased her she had.

One day, early in their association, Stella stood outside the school gates waiting for Bianca. She was playing with a ball, bouncing it off a wall. Some older boys came up and "asked" to borrow it. Intimidated, she was about to hand it over when her friend arrived. Dwarfed by the boys, Bianca told them to go away. Faced with such determination, they complied. The boys departed and Stella kept her ball.

The years passed and they progressed to secondary school. Biology and language were Stella's favourite subjects, while Bianca excelled in drawing and mathematics.

One summer's afternoon, they sat alone, under a plum tree. They had eaten their full of the ripe fruit. Stella read a poem out loud, one by her favourite poet, Yamashita.

"Pale moon rising into the sky
Liquid orb surveying its subjects
Round and grey,
Glaucous sphere
Why do you torment me so?"

Bianca laughed, saying, "I don't see it, sorry. The moon is just a great big rock circling our planet. Why try to make it something it isn't?"

"I like the words," Stella replied, disarmingly. She would not defend a poet dead two-hundred-and-fifty years. Her friend listened; that was enough for her.

"You like the words? Oh well, each to their own. But, shouldn't I bow to she who came top of the class in biology and who won the Moreland Prize for the best essay?"

Stella did not mind her friend's teasing, for she knew she did not mean it maliciously. Their time at school would end soon. Bianca was getting serious with her boyfriend, Fabian, while Stella eyed further education.

"I've put my nursing collage application in," she said.

"You'll get in, no trouble."

"I'll need the scholarship, though, it'll be impossible to survive without that support."

"Hey!" Bianca cried, "if you're not awarded it, then it'll be a travesty of justice."

Fortunately, everyone saw justice done as they awarded a generous scholarship to Stella. She plunged herself into her studies, having set her heart on nursing. There was much to learn. As well as the theory, she undertook protracted training at the local hospital. This institution was well equipped for a poor planet. Stella found the days long and tiring, but most rewarding.

Years passed and Stella's hard work paid off. Now a qualified nurse, she worked in the general ward at the hospital. Connecting well with staff and patients alike, she got great job satisfaction from her role.

Being busy, her church attendance suffered, but she made sure she kept in touch with Bianca as much as possible. The latter then announced her engagement to Fabian. Tall, thin and prematurely bald, he was as quiet as a mouse. "Then," Stella reasoned, "they say that opposites attract."

Meanwhile, she learned the strict hierarchy at the hospital, each job having its own coloured uniform. Cleaners, porters, nursing assistants, nurses, junior doctors, registrars, consultants and, at the very top of the pile, surgeons. Therefore, it flattered Stella when she found one consultant taking a keen interest in her. Dawud was a fair bit older than her, but quite dashing and confident in his manner. He owned a big house in the wealthiest district of town, a modern construction with a minimalist interior.

A whirlwind romance ensued, and before long, she moved in with Dawud. Their relationship was a physical one right from the start. She wanted to seal it with marriage, but the strong-willed man dismissed the idea. Best not to pursue it and rock the boat, she concluded. A baby soon arrived, and calling him Benjamin, she insisted on having him christened. Dawud did not attend the ceremony. Giving up work to spend time with the baby, it contented her at first. Living within a palatial home, with no physical needs and her offspring to care for, life should have been wonderful. It was not. With each week, Dawud became more and more controlling.

~ End of Chapter 6 ~

My Keeper's Brother - Chapter 7

Another year passed for Stella and Bianca sat over the breakfast table with her husband. Her mind appeared elsewhere and Fabian guessed the reason.

"Thinking about Stella?"

"I feel pushed out by her; I don't understand it. Did our friendship mean nothing to her?"

Pointing to his TRAC, he suggested sending her a message, but she said, "I've called, I've sent messages until I'm blue in the face. There's never any answer."

"Go along there to see her. Go today."

"You think I should?"

"Why not? You've got nothing to lose."

"Except my pride," she responded dryly.

"Salvaging a friendship is worth any amount of pride, I'd say."

The frown left Bianca's face as she said, "You're right, thank you. I'll go this morning like you said. After all, I have the day off."

Her resolve firm, she did indeed go. She approached the front door when she knew Dawud had departed for work. No answer, but then, out of the corner of her eye, she spotted a figure at a ground floor window. Working her way round to it, Bianca got the shock of her life.

It was Stella alright, but in a terrible state. Haunting eyes stared from a thin bruised face. Bianca immediately made her mind up.

"Let me in!" she demanded. "You're coming home with me."

"I can't," Stella responded pathetically, "the door's locked." It was and the toughened windows were unbreakable.

"I'll come tomorrow with help."

Back home, Bianca reported the situation to her husband. "He locks her in whenever he goes out, so that she can't escape. Not that she seemed to show much sign of wanting to escape. Her spirit seemed broken from the short conversation I had through the closed window."

"What are you going to do?" Fabian asked.

117

"You're coming back with me tomorrow. We'll gain entry, even if we have to smash a window, and remove her."

"It'll be a type three composite; you'll need a battering ram to break that."

"What about the door, then? You're the electronics expert."

"Did you take a picture?"

"No!" she snapped, "I can't say I did."

"Did you check it out?"

"It looked similar to ours."

"Hmm, if it's in the Monarchy range, I should be able to decode it."

"You'll come with me then?"

Fabian was used to obeying his wife's instructions. That she phrased it as a question surprised him.

"Of course I'll come with you, dear."

The following morning, the couple set off at the same hour. On this occasion, Bianca went straight to the window while her husband, armed with a little bag of tricks, set about breaking the electronic combination lock on the front door. A mere one-hundred-and-ninety-four-million combinations to consider.

"Stella, it's me," her long-term friend told her through the same window, "we're going to take you home."

"Are you sure?" the feeble response came from bruised lips.

Bianca felt like screaming, "No, I've come for the hell of it!" but she restrained herself. Instead, she turned to her husband, a metre and a half away, "Will you be able to do it?"

He stood upright and, with a grin, answered, "I will."

"How long's it going to take?"

"I've already done it."

He had indeed.

"Oh, you marvel!" Bianca said and planted a big kiss on his lips. He responded by telling her he had also disabled the alarm. She shook her head in amazement, then stepped into the house.

"My God!" she exclaimed upon seeing Stella close up without the filter of the window. "What has he done to you?"

The life had been sucked out of the gaunt figure standing before her. Her bare arms were thin and her face displayed multiple bruising.

"It's not his fault," she said.

118

After a tirade of swearing that would make a trooper blush, Bianca told her, "And don't you dare tell me you walked into a door! You're coming with us."

"But I love him."

Bianca counted to five in order not to say anything she might regret, then ordered in her loud voice, "Show me your room!"

Such a command must be obeyed. A quick escalator took them up to her bedroom on the first floor. Then Ben, who had been asleep, started crying. While his mother saw to the baby, the couple gathered Stella's clothes and shoes.

"Bring his things. You two are coming with us."

They had to go back into the house several times to collect everything. They piled their car high with her possessions.

"Right, let's go," came the command and Fabian pressed "home" and the vehicle returned them.

The operation to retrieve her turned out to be the easy part. Over the following weeks, Stella needed to be de-programmed. Dawud had abused her physically, sexually, financially and psychologically. She seemed like an automaton and several times Bianca stood in the doorway to stop her friend from going back to him.

"How can she even *consider* it?" she exclaimed to her husband in her frustration.

Quietly, he said, "I can't imagine how anybody would want to treat another human being like that."

Things got easier as the weeks passed. They managed to convince Stella that she no longer loved Dawud and that he had mistreated her shamefully. There was no point in reporting it to the authorities. The hospital consultant possessed key friends in high places and would never be called to account for his behaviour - in this life.

Slowly, the old Stella emerged from her cocoon. Ben had also been traumatised by the ordeal. Now released into a loving environment, he caught up on his development. Bianca beamed when she saw mother and son playing together. Having recently learned herself that she was expecting a baby, it overjoyed her at the thought of becoming a mother.

Only once did Dawud call at their home. With Stella out, he faced the formidable figure of one-and-a-half metre tall Bianca. She did

119

not know how he tracked them down, but she sent him off with such a flea in his ear that he never bothered them again.

"I can't go back to the hospital," Stella informed them one day. "I'd rather die than set foot in there again."

As she improved, she considered returning to work. With Bianca's baby expected soon, all agreed it best if she could try to stand on her own two feet again.

Bianca and Fabian owned a track of woodland. They had bought it on spec when prices were low, but the promised property boom showed no signs of materialising. It remained a piece of undeveloped land, a hectare in size, on the edge of town where no one went. After a family conference, they decided that Fabian, along with some of his friends, would build a cabin there for Stella and Ben to live in. The town was close enough, but it gave her the privacy she wanted.

The cabin, or a rather crude shack, was sufficient for her purposes and they settled into their new home. Around the same time, Stella secured a job at the Majestic Bar in town. It was low-paid employment, but with no rent to pay, she could make ends meet. A couple of aunts helped with childcare while she worked.

On her evening shifts, she encountered the Brothers of Compassion, a religious order dedicated to a simple lifestyle and giving relief for the poor. When she could, she attended services at their church. It felt good to reconnect with God. Things were looking up.

The attractive barmaid often had men trying to chat her up. She was in no mood to enter another relationship, but one fellow was persistent and used to getting his own way. Haroon, a component salesman had the gift of the gab. She abandoned the shack and moved in with him, before even she knew what had happened.

The man was compulsive gambler, she belatedly discovered. Stella even lent him an amount of money from her meagre resources. It was a bad move, because, under Belovo law, it made her liable for his debts. So, when he abandoned them and fled the planet, Stella discovered her appalling financial situation, owing an amount of money from which she could not pay the interest off, let alone the capital sum.

Back to the shack, now with a heavy debt to pay, she continued with the bar job, but with a huge worry hanging over her.

During that time, tragedy struck. Bianca contracted a serious illness and died soon afterwards. Stella attended the funeral in a daze. A devastated Fabian left Belovo for good. As a parting gesture, he signed over the land containing the shack to Stella. She did not care that it was a worthless plot of land.

Stella took solace in her faith. Resolving not to have anything to do with men again, she concentrated all her energies on her little boy, Ben, but also in keeping her bar job. If she had not owed a large sum of money, life might not have seemed so bad. Not feeling owned by anyone anymore, she enjoyed the simplicity of being unattached. Sometimes, she forgot her worries and could laugh and joke, joining in with the banter at work with regulars at the bar.

Then, one evening, a dark-haired, strongly-built stranger came into the bar. She found herself drawn to him. He showed none of the sophisticated flare of Dawud, nor the easy tongue of Haroon. Junior to her, John was pleasant, without being pushy. Easy to chat, Stella surprised herself by finding herself teasing him and enjoying it. John seemed young in his manner and, unless she was mistaken, he was a man without deceit. It was an instant attraction for her, so when he asked her out, she happily agreed.

John thought the evening would never come. Now he stood waiting outside his hotel extra early. Marking time there, it did not matter... as long as she showed. As the hour approached, John found his heart racing again and doubts flooded his head.

'She agreed only to get rid of me. She's older than me, I bet she doesn't show...'

Yet now she appeared, coming towards him, only fifty metres away. In a smart dress, she looked lovelier than ever. His heart missed a beat and he took in a big gulp of air before greeting her.

"You look nice," he added.

"Thank you."

"Um, I wasn't sure which place to take you. What's your favourite restaurant?"

"Let me see... there's Claudio's. They do a mean pizza."

"Okay, let's go there."

It was a short walk and a waiter ushered them to a spare table in the corner, which John felt ideal. He wanted to start a conversation after ordering, but his mind was blank. Stella guessed correctly that this

121

young man was inexperienced in the ways of dating and helped him out.

"You served in the army, then?"

"That's right," he replied, pleased that she picked a topic he could respond to. "I got involved in a big space battle, but I retired after that."

She found this amusing, for he was a little young to retire. Wanting to keep the conversation going, though, she asked, "And whose army was that?"

"Andraconian. We went to war with the Kupullans."

"I can't say I've heard of either of them. And did you win?" she enquired, her tone amused.

"Er, no, we came second. Bet you haven't heard of those places, or Marmaris, where I was born?"

"I'm afraid not; far too insular, I confess. I've been born and brought up here on Belovo and I know nothing else."

They kept the conversation light until the waiter served the food and they paused. Studying her face, he noticed that her right eye was a fraction less open than her left. For some unfathomable reason, this minor imperfection increased her beauty in his eyes. Meanwhile, she found herself attracted to her date. He exuded an air of inexperience, which brought out, if not a mothering instinct, a desire to encourage and buoy him up.

In between bites, they continued talking and he seemed to relax a bit. John spoke about his background on Marmaris and one or two of his experiences. She learned this young man, who had so rashly offered to pay her debt, was not born to wealth.

Stella then got something off her chest, declaring, "I have a son." It sounded more dramatic than she intended, but he was eager to let her know it did not put him off.

"Yes? What's his name?"

"Ben, he's my life."

"I'm sure."

Then it all came out as she relayed more details. "I lived with a man until recently. A dreadful gambling habit gripped him. It got worse and he became uncontrollable. He'd use any money he could discover in the house. I had to find fresh places to hide it from him! I kept my job at the Majestic, which helped me put food on the table. Matters got out of hand..."

"I see."

She paused from her tale of woe to quip, "Perhaps I wouldn't have minded him gambling so much if he was any good at it! He wasn't; he kept on losing."

"And you got into debt?"

"He began borrowing money. 'I'll pay it all back when my lucky streak returns,' he said. It never did. When he scarpered for it, they forced me to take on his debt under the local law. He left me high and dry."

"Oh, I'm sorry, that's terrible!"

"Hmm, I shouldn't say this, but it felt a godsend when he left. I'd fallen out of love with him and my life had become a living nightmare. It's not wonderful now, but at least I know where I am."

"The debt?"

"Yes, like I said, they passed it on to me. I appealed against it, but it seems I'm not appealing enough, for they wouldn't budge. So, I'm working all hours now, but I'm not even paying of the interest. I don't know what the future holds."

"I see."

"Sorry!" she said. Instead of enjoying a rare night off, but found herself cataloguing her problems to this young man kind enough to treat her to a meal.

Not that John minded, he was enjoying the company of attractive woman. The scenario she described sounded familiar to him. He knew of families on Marmaris held in virtual slavery by debts to unscrupulous people. While Stella's situation was not the same, there were definite similarities.

"Two thousand credits, is that right?"

"Give or take."

"I've got that money spare. Let me give it to you," he said earnestly.

With a look of tired scepticism, she retorted, "And why would you give two thousand credits to a complete stranger?"

"'Cos I like you!"

"How can you like me? You don't even know me."

"But I'll like you when I get to know you."

He was incorrigible. She knew from what he told her he had not been born into wealth. This was no rich boy playing Lord Bountiful. She badly wanted the worry and burden of debt lifted from her shoulders. Yet it would be unfair, taking advantage of this sweet, unsophisticated man, junior to her years and lacking most of her acquaintances' cynicism. Torn between accepting and rejecting this life-changing offer, she found her head spinning with these thoughts.

"I'm tired!" she declared with a sigh.

"Oh, I didn't think it was that late."

His face was a picture of disappointment, so she sought to reassure him.

"Not of being here. I'm tired of the situation I'm in; all the worry."

"Let me help you, then."

"And what would you want in return?"

The implications of this enquiry did not deter John. Without hesitation, he said, "Nothing. It would be a gift. If you turn round afterwards and say you don't want a relationship, I would respect that. I wouldn't regret it; it would please me knowing that I could help another human being."

He was incorrigible! Faced with this pressure, she agreed and gave him her TRAC code and he transferred the money. She asked him to bear with her while she there and then forwarded the money to her debtor. There was no time like the present.

John said he did not mind and sat watching while she made the transaction. After hesitating for a minute as she studied her wrist computer, she announced, "There, paid off!" With her face showing great relief, she said, "Thank you so much, John. I'm more grateful than I can out into words."

Delighted that he had pleased her, he noticed how even more beautiful she looked with a tearful smile on her face. With his words, he played his actions down, although they both knew that this was no mean favour.

"I made a payment earlier this week," she said, looking back at her TRAC. "They've confirmed the debt's settled, but there's a little left over. I'll send it back to you."

"No! Keep it, please. It would make me happy."

The meal finished, they ordered extra drinks and sat chatting into the night. Stella was a woman transformed, thanks to a tremendous burden being lifted from her shoulders. This young, handsome man, eager to please, had solved the major problem in her life at a stroke. How could she not be grateful? Even apart from the tremendous help, he was pleasant enough. Why not accept his offer of a second date?

"Good," he said, matching her smile for smile. "Where do you live? Can I walk you home?"

"I live in a cabin in the woods, beyond the far side of town. But I'm staying with a friend close by; she's got Ben for a couple of days. I don't mind if you escort me there."

Escort her he did. It was not a long way. Before they parted, he plucked up the courage to ask her for a kiss. She proffered her cheek and he gave it a kiss, followed by a last goodbye. He floated on air back to his hotel. He considered it a perfect end to a perfect evening.

Meanwhile, Stella walked into her friend's home to be told that her son was asleep before being quizzed about her date.

"I enjoyed it. I wasn't sure what to expect. He seemed so enthusiastic, so... young." She did not want to tell her friend about her financial assistance from John, because she felt guilty, if relieved. Instead, she said, "I'm going to see him again. He's different from what I'm used to."

"Ha!" the friend exclaimed, "you haven't been the best of pickin' 'em, have you? Maybe different is good."

"Maybe you're right," Stella replied, her face aglow.

The next few weeks saw a whirlwind romance. A second date, watching a local show, was fun. From then on, there was no stopping them; they enjoyed each other's company every day. Stella took him to her place in the woods. It struck John as crudely built, but at least it looked homely inside.

In this region, mature trees stood, spread out ten metres apart. So uniform was this distancing that John wondered if they planted them that way.

"Friends bequeathed me this land," Stella answered one of his questions. "Few folk come this way."

Her home was by itself, being several hundred metres from the edge of town. He worried for her safety and insisted on escorting her every evening. His concern amused Stella, who thought it unwarranted. The crime rate in this small, closely-knit community was low and she had never experienced problems before. She enjoyed his company, though, and did not mind indulging him.

Stella had lived in the town all her life and possessed many friends to meet. It meant a lot of names for him to learn. The most important person she introduced him to was three-year old Ben, her son. John played with the boy which his mother appreciated.

One day, he took her deep into the woods and showed her the outcrop of rock he discovered with its panoramic view. She enthused about it, not telling him she had been there a hundred times before.

The biggest change came when she asked him to move in with her. Earlier, John, still living at the hotel, considered suggesting they get a place together in town. However, he realised that his new love liked her "cabin" in the woods and did not want to move from there.

Meanwhile, Stella brought up the "M" word (marriage) but got a poor response. Perhaps it would come later. She hoped so.

She kept her evening bar shift, but reduced the number of hours she worked. After her previous experiences, she did not want to become dependent on a man. Besides, it gave her a sense of purpose. Prior to John's arrival, her aunts looked after Ben in the evenings, but now that was unnecessary. Her new man struck her as reliable and trustworthy, which was a relief. In particular, he never thought to control her and she was able to relax. She experienced a proper loving relationship for the first time in her life.

John found Stella spoke little about her wider family, but he gleaned she had several aunts in town. He also learned that both her parents were deceased. That was something they held in common. Some of her friends showed concern at how quickly she threw herself into the new relationship. He soon won them over with his openness and relaxed manner.

"He's not your usual type," an aunt commented.

"How do you mean?"

"All worldly wise. This one seems naive."

"John's straightforward; what you see is what you get."

One morning, Stella and John lay in bed together, having not long woken up. Neither of them had yet spoken. Outside was hushed, other than the birds singing. Ben was not making a sound.

"Good morning," he said suddenly.

"Good morning," she echoed in a whisper.

Just then, her tummy made a long rumble and she giggled at the sound.

"Good morning, tummy!" he said and they both laughed.

Later, over breakfast, Stella announced, "I want to do some washing today. The weather should be good for drying. You got any plans?"

"I'm considering going into town a bit later and buy myself a fresh shirt. Did you say Ben could do with some fresh clothes?"

"I'm not sure now. I found some stuffed in a drawer. He's growing so fast that he'll need some bigger ones soon. Both my aunts are busy knitting, but I think they'll have to increase the size a bit. That last cardigan could hardly fit him when they gave him it. It's awkward... John, are you okay?"

He was frowning at his TRAC, but dragged his eyes away in order to reply to her.

"Um, checking my balance. A little lower than I was expecting."

"Dammit!" Stella exclaimed, for the bag of potatoes she picked up burst open and the contents poured out across the floor. John hurried over to help her pick them up. They forgot financial concerns for now.

One mid-morning, John was by himself in the middle of town, wandering up to the green grocers. In this backwards society, no one made home deliveries and the customers collected their wares themselves. Stella was doing an unusual daytime shift and Ben was spending the day with an aunt. The streets appeared busier than usual and when he stepped into the road to avoid a group of people walking the opposite direction, a passing car narrowly missed him. He skipped back onto the path and carried on. Up ahead, a spaceship, a freighter, shot up into orbit, a rare sight on Belovo.

His TRAC rang and he expected it to be Stella. He was about to greet her when a male voice enquired, "Is that Mr Thorn?"

"Yeah!" he said, surprised. With no hologram coming up from the device, he asked the caller's name.

"This is the space port. We have received a long-range transmission for you."

"Oh, I see. Do you want to put it through?"

"I'm sorry, sir, but we cannot do that. If you come to the port, you will retrieve the message here."

With spare time and fine weather, he did not mind. He therefore made his way there, choosing to do the modest distance on foot. Inevitably, he wondered as to whom the message was from.

'It could be my brother, Frank. I wonder what he wants. I can't imagine who else it would be.'

He got to the space port and explained his purpose. Ushered through to a private booth, he played the recorded message.

"Mr Thorn," began the face on the hologram, "my name is Porinev. I am a broker. My sponsors have charged me with finding someone for a delicate operation for the Flores family on Grande Verde. You come recommended. It is a two month contract and the pay is exceptional. Please call me back in order that we can discuss details and you can let me have your decision whether you accept the contract."

This was not what John expected. The names in the message meant nothing to him. There was a pre-paid reply, so he called straight back. It surprised him that, without hesitation, he got straight through to the gentleman who sent the message. The line was clear too.

"Thank you for getting back to me promptly," he said. "Allow me to flesh out some details for you."

"Please do."

"Have you heard of Grande Verde?"

"No."

"It's a few solar systems from your current location. A large population, it is the single open planet in their sector of the galaxy. Your employers will be the Royal Family itself: King Alberto and Queen Isabella Flores..."

"King and queen? How archaic!"

"Maybe, but they need a bodyguard, someone discrete. They have asked for someone off-world. I understand, between you and me, that there are trust issues there."

Further details followed. The two months was a trial period; with an extension optional. The pay would be generous. When John heard how much, it tempted him. It would be a major boost to their finances. Bodyguard to an ancient royal family? It sounded pretty straightforward.

"When do you need an answer by?"

"Yesterday!"

"How about tomorrow?"

"Without fail?"

"Without fail, I promise."

"Very well. I shall send a further credit. Call on this line in twenty-four Earth Standard hours. I shall expect your answer."

The excited young man took a taxi back into town. If he was about to get a substantial payment, he could afford it. He arrived at the Majestic soon after. Stella came out, having finished her extra shift. It surprised her to see him draw up in a taxi, but he was keen to tell her his news.

At her aunt's house, and with Ben playing on the floor in front of them, he told her the details.

"That's a lot of money for two months work!" she said.

"Yeah, it'll be a great help. I know I'll be away for that time, but I don't think I'll extend the contract, even if I'm offered it. I'll want to get back."

"I'm glad to hear it."

"I'll come back as soon as I can. As soon as I'm paid."

"What about your interplanetary travel?"

"Private shuttle, all paid for."

"They can't be short of a credit or two, can they?"

"I don't mind."

"But why you?"

"Um, I forgot to ask."

"Forgot?"

"The conversation moved on. I'm assuming it's because of that job I did on Diyu for that fellow. Gosh, I can't remember his name now."

"You think he put in a good word for you?"

"I can't think who else it would be. I didn't look for this job, it came looking for me. They say you don't look a gift horse in the mouth."

Stella said dryly, "Don't they also say you should look before you leap?"

"How do you mean?"

"My mother told me if it seems too good to be true, it most likely is."

"I'm not sure that's fair," John responded. "The broker explained they wanted someone who wasn't a native of their planet, because they can't trust them."

"That doesn't sound very good."

"Um, I think they want someone who isn't involved in their political systems and might want to harm them. I don't know."

Stella thought he was making it up as he went along, unsure he was thinking it through. She said, "I only want you to be safe."

"Okay. I mean, it's a bodyguard job, which must mean there's some element of risk. Otherwise, they would not bother to have me."

Stella thought of saying they needed an off-world sucker now their local bodyguards were killed, but decided to keep quiet. His eagerness did not convince her he had looked enough into this matter. His mind made up, he was doing it for her, or rather the three of them.

"Just don't be a hero, my darling. If twenty hired assassins come to murder the king, you slip out the back door... but make sure they transfer the money to your TRAC first!"

She was teasing now and he took it in good humour. He interpreted this as her blessing to go.

"Thank you. I'll go to the port again tomorrow and tell the broker I accept. I got the impression they don't want any delay."

"Mmm."

"I can see myself leaving before the end of the week."

That evening, John spent much of the time on his wrist computer, looking up details of the planet Grande Verde. He started with zero knowledge, so anything he learned might be useful.

It was, the data file informed him, the sole inhabited planet in the Baracon System and boasted a long and proud history. Then most planets seemed to. It was one of the first group of planets to declare independence from earth. This sparked the First Intergalactic War, or, as folk there called it, the Grande War of Independence.

The Royal Family traced their ancestry back to the Mother Planet and exercised more power than a constitutional monarchy. Much loved by the populous, they ruled Grande Verde with gentleness and wisdom, the report said.

"No doubt where the writer's sympathies lie," John said after reading that section to Stella.

"Anything else of interest?"

"There are disreputable republican factions who don't have popular support."

"Yet the fact that they see fit to mention them shows a society with factions and unrest. Please don't get too mixed up in other nations' squabbles."

Sage advice, but as a royal bodyguard, he was duty bound to be on one side. Best not to pre-judge the situation. He would find out soon enough.

"Okay," he concluded, "I'll contact the broker tomorrow as arranged and confirm that I'll take the job."

A small spaceship slipped silently through cold space, its lone passenger in an anticipatory mood.

'This is a different assignment,' John realised. 'A private shuttle to take me there! You'd have to be unbelievably rich to afford this.'

It was only right to take advantage of the fully stocked mini-bar. He sat there enjoying an exotic fruit drink and some cookies. Yet the novelty wore off and it pleased him when he came into land at a space port on Grande. For a heavily-populated planet, it seemed tiny, he considered, until told that it was a Royal Family facility.

"Look around you. As far as the eye can see it's one of the Royal estates."

"Ah, of course," he said. "I must get used to this."

An employee, dressed in the maroon Flores family livery, escorted him to the edge of the field and a mettled road. Here, he showed John his means of transport to take him to the Royal Chateau.

'A bullock cart!' he considered, astonished, but he was polite enough to say nothing.

It looked a poorly maintained vehicle. The painted lettering on the side, "Flores Royal Estate," being faded and chipped. The driver, an elderly, dour man, loaded the traveller's light case without comment. Up front there was no space for passengers; John travelled on a rear bench seat. Around him lay an assortment of tools, plus a contraption like a lobster pot. This was a strange introduction.

A sunken road took them straight to their destination. Most of the way high banks flanked it, topped with bushes. Up above, the sky was blue, except for the occasional stationary white cloud.

Thinking he might gain some insightful knowledge from this local, John asked him a few questions.

"Is the chateau part of a town complex?"

Following a period of consideration, the driver replied, "I'm not sure as y'can say that."

"Is there another spaceport nearby, or is it just the royal one?"

"Hmm, I don't rightly know that."

"Are you directly in the king's employ?"

"I'm not sure as y'can say that."

This was going nowhere; John gave up. In any case, soon, up ahead, a wall came into view at ninety degrees to the road. It encompassed the inner estate, containing both the chateau and royal gardens and stood as far as the eye could see both ways. They were headed for a modest gate in it, manned by a lone guard in the same maroon uniform as the employee wore at the spaceport. He let them through without a word and the bullock cart continued its leisurely pace up the long drive to the royal residence. No other soul was in sight.

The occasional tree punctuated the lawns on either side. The grass needed cutting, but the trees were well worth studying. Some were giant specimens of a type unknown to the new arrival. Up ahead stood the chateau. As they travelled at a slow walking pace, it gradually got bigger. He soon realised that this was a magnificent building.

Built of white marble, the central section was seven stories high, with identical, lower, wings to either side. Stone balustrades topped these wings. Rows of tall, oblong windows lined the structure. Above the lintels were triangular pediments and they had covered the roof in grey slate tiles. Tall, ornate chimneys stood out against the skyline, each with an ornamental topping. The visitor found the entire structure most impressive.

Before they reached the building, the drive opened up to a large, paved area. A few royal servants were standing together as his reception committee. They were conversing in low tones. Everyone wore the same uniform and John realised he would have to get used to the colour maroon. As the vehicle ground to a halt, John hopped off the cart in one bound. He was travelling light and carried one small case which a man took off him. Thanking the driver, he turned again to see the reception committee. One of them came forward to greet him while the others dispersed. It struck him odd, but John did not have time to dwell on it, for he was being addressed.

"You're Thorn?"

"I am."

"Good!" the other said, showing great relief, "you've arrived in time."

"For what?" the new employee enquired, but the servant ignored question and led John inside. Before they entered the building, he thought he heard faint crowd noise in the far distance. The sound disappeared as they stepped inside and he dismissed it. Of more concern to him was the lack of personnel. Still, in such a vast building you could lose an army.

Led to a room, they instructed him to change into a uniform. There were several sizes to choose from. Finding himself hurrying because of the man's demeanour, he soon looked the part in maroon Royal livery. He slipped the I.D. badge and pass onto his wrist.

"You can use one of these?" the man asked as he handed over holster containing a pulse pistol.

"Yes, I can," John assured him. He took it out of the holster to check. It was of a precise type he had used in training and was charged, so he spoke with confidence. Re-sheathing the weapon and donning the holster, he was all set to go.

First, standing his ground, he wanted a couple of questions answered before he took another step.

"I need to be told my duties. I've been told very little."

"Simple," came the reply without expression, "protect their majesties."

"From what? I need to..."

"Malcontents. Now we must get going."

Not wanting to antagonise him, John followed the servant out of the room. Upon arrival at the lift, they explained that the electricity was intermittent and the pair took the stairs.

As they ascended, John considered the strange mixture of old and the new here. Space shuttles, bullock carts and unreliable electricity. After a few flights, they entered an enormous, wooden-floored hall with paintings on the wall. A gaggle of concerned-looking people were milling about a short distance away.

Ordered, "Wait here," John did so while his guide had a brief, mini-conference. As he waited, the new bodyguard heard the crowd shouting in the distance again.

Back in the stairwell, the ascent continued. There was the most odd atmosphere here; he hoped someone would tell him what was going on.

Once at the correct floor and, two corridors on, they arrived at a pair of double doors by which were stationed some armed guards. After showing their passes, they went in.

Inside, huddled together, stood a group of our men plus one woman in the middle of a spacious living room. John's eyes flashed round to take in the chamber. There was a modicum of furniture, but it was of exquisite quality. He noticed a sideboard with intricate marquetry built into the design. On its surface, a golden figurine of a soldier on horseback slaying a dragon. Above it, a painting of a unicorn. They must be mythical beast lovers. Crystal chandeliers hung from the ceiling and the pile on the carpet was so deep that one's feet seemed to sink into it. Everything screamed opulence.

None of the group had sensed the fresh figures in the room. One agitated man was talking at length. He was dark, with a mop of black hair on top of his square-shaped head.

"The Varano District has succumbed; now reports of revolution in Stacancia are being received. We..."

"You are not to use that word!" snapped the only woman present.

"Revolution, Your Majesty? We have to face realty."

"Let him speak, dear," said an older man. His face was white, except for a patch of colour in his cheeks. Quite overweight, his neck was thick and flabby, with multiple fold of skin.

The excited man was about to resume when he spotted the interlopers. Not unhappy with the intrusion, he stepped forward to greet them while the others looked on.

"You must be John Thorn."

"Yes, sir."

"Thank you, Danilo," he dismissed John's escort, then addressed the new arrival. "My name is Fabio Locche, advisor to the king, this is my brother Claudio." The similarity was obvious, but the quieter character was younger and with less well kept hair. "And this is Henio." The latter gave a perfunctory nod, indicating he had more important things on his mind. "Come, let me announce you to the king and queen."

He introduced King Alberto, the overweight one, and Queen Isabella to John. He noticed the lacework on her dress. The low neckline stressed her own, long neck which was covered in a large necklace of precious stones. It was the first royal couple he had met and probably his last. He gave a slight bow and said, "Your majesties," following the form of address given earlier by Fabio.

The queen gave half a smile and the king nodded once, then rejoined the discussion.

"I'm glad you're here," Fabio said, then re-joined the others.

Outside, the chanting got louder. Claudio walked to the window and, upon his return, told them the crowd was getting both larger and more vociferous.

John was uncertain what to do. Being bodyguard against an assassin was one thing, but was he supposed to stop a revolution single-handedly? He stood, rooted to the spot, unsure whether to go back outside, or step away a few paces. Not being dismissed, remaining a safe distance seemed the best course of action. What followed, he found bizarre in the extreme.

The group of five's circle expanded to include him. All the time they were debating the current crisis in their land.

"Parliament is being no help," Fabio was saying, "they're afraid of the uprising and have refused to sit today."

"The situation gets worse by the hour," his brother chipped in.

"Elements of the First Regiment have joined the revolutionaries. I have seen soldiers in their uniform in the crowd."

The king bemoaned, "We don't know who to trust."

"If the crowd out there gets any bigger," Claudio recommenced, "I can't see the few guards outside holding them off."

"The shuttle's on its pad?" enquired the queen.

"Yes, but the pilot's absconded."

It tempted John to tell them he could fly a shuttle, but he thought better of it. While they had, most strangely, let him into the circle, no one asked his opinion. Quite the opposite, none of them so much as glanced at him. John was thinking this was a madhouse.

His mind wandered and he was imagining these five people in the back of a bullock cart, fleeing to their private spaceport. The intrepid bodyguard trying to hold off a baying mob from the rear of the cart with a single pulse pistol. What had he let himself in for? No wonder the pay was so generous.

"For the revolution!" shouted a voice in the room and, before anyone knew what was happening, royal advisor Henio produced a large, sharp knife and began slitting Claudio's throat from behind. Everything happened quickly. The king and queen stared in disbelief; Fabio screamed his brother's name and John pulled out his pulse pistol and shot the murderer straight between the eyes.

Even before Claudio's body hit the floor, Henio was following it, a black hole in his forehead.

The attack coincided with the crowd outside making a tremendous roar. John sprang to the window to see the mob surge forward, overpowering the few guards still on duty. There was no stopping them. Fabio knelt by Claudio's body, covered in his brother's blood, cradling his head in his lap. The man died within seconds, his blood had spurted everywhere. John knew he acted instinctively in killing the assassin. There had been no time to think. He put the weapon back in its holster, aware that the rabble was pouring into the building unchecked. Even a newcomer like him could assess what would happen next. Addressing the royal couple, he spoke to them hurriedly.

"You want to escape to your shuttle?"

"Yes," said the queen firmly.

"Which are the best stairs down?"

"Not down, up. It's on the roof."

"Oh."

"But we don't have a pilot."

"I can fly. I'll fly you."

Relief washed over the royal couple's faces, then the queen's hardened again as she cried, "We must hurry, the mob will be charging up the stairs by now and if they find us, they will tear us to pieces!"

~ End of Chapter 7 ~

My Keeper's Brother - Chapter 8

Spurred into action by the Queen, the remaining four people moved towards the door. This included Fabio, who dragged himself away from his brother's body. He realised he could gain nothing by staying there a moment longer.

John threw open the door to find that the guards had evaporated. Out in the corridor, they heard sounds of shouting coming from inside the building. They were getting closer. The mob homing in on its prize.

"Come!" commanded the Queen and she led the group along the passageway and up a single flight of stairs onto the roof. There sat a sight for sore eyes; a small space shuttle on its pad. Close by, stood a lectern-like flight console with display.

They were on top of one wing of the chateau. John glanced down from the stone balustrade to see outbuildings on fire. Further plumes of smoke rose in the distance. He knew nothing of Grande Verde's politics, but a change of regime was happening before his eyes.

"Get to the ship!" Fabio screamed at him. "If the revolutionaries get here, they'll kill us all."

John ran to comply and, as the Royal couple took their seats, he piled into the pilot's seat and surveyed the controls before him. It was a while since he last flew himself and some instruments looked quite different. The fundamentals seemed familiar enough and he quickly concluded that he could fly it.

Fabio fiddled at the console as John started the engines up.

"Hurry!" the Queen urged, worried that even then her enemies were storming the last stairs to the roof.

Increasing power, the pilot waited until Fabio jumped on board before taking off. At least they tried to, because the craft did not move.

Fabio swore, saying the clamps must still be on. He frantically opened the door again and jumped out. Running to the console, he released the clamps, just as the first revolutionaries burst onto the roof. Task accomplished, he turned towards the shuttle, but an agricultural implement speared him in the back and he fell to the floor.

The shuttle's occupants watched all this. As the revolutionaries slayed her trusty employee, the Queen shrieked. Her husband shouted to John, "Go, go, go!"

Even as the door closed, the spacecraft was lifting off its pad. Various missiles came its way, but fell short. One attacker fired an energy rifle, but John engaged the force field in time and its shots had no effect. Then the shuttle streaked skywards, to the intense relief of all on board.

As they achieved orbit, their heart rates settled and they could assess the situation. John realised his payday had gone by the way, but that was the least of his current concerns.

Queen Isabella shook uncontrollably and her husband, noticing, put his large hand over hers. In the space of a few minutes, they had witnessed their three chief advisors killed. One of them had proved a traitor, to their shock and horror. Then a thought occurred to them both. They now found themselves at the mercy of a complete stranger. Could he be trusted? It was the Queen who raised their concerns, asking, "Where are you taking us?"

The reply came, "I'm in your hands, Your Majesty. Where should I take you?"

Relaxing, the Queen said, "The next solar system is the Apollus System, a light year away. A pleasure station orbits a moon of the largest planet there. If you program destination 'Rati Kama,' then the shuttle will take you. The pilot did and the craft left Grande Verde's orbit and headed off.

'They hardly need me to fly it,' thought John, but he knew he had saved their bacon down on the planet. He contemplated how he was to get home after dropping the Royal couple off. Having already written off getting his fee, he wondered if getting home would also be a problem.

He enquired, "Will you still require my services after we get to the space station, Your Majesty?"

The Queen acted as spokesman for both of them. She said, "Once we are on board Rati Kama and reunited with our family, we will consider your further employment."

That would have to do. If their family stayed on board a pleasure station, presumably they kept their money after all. He must sit back and enjoy the ride, as there was little choice. They would soon navigate an asteroid belt before passing a couple of gaseous giant planets and heading out into deep space between solar systems.

As he began to settle, the dramatic events of the day caught up with him. He had killed a man at point-blank range. Either that, or the murderer would have attacked the others. Why did political fanatics act that way? Yes, he killed a man, but his action prevented something worse from happening.

He was still trying to justify his actions to himself when the control panel lit up red and a warning alarm sounded. It made a terrible din in the cabin. Throwing himself forward, John turned off the racket, but it frightened his passengers. Seeking the reason for the warning, the pilot soon found it. Unidentified ship up ahead, possibly a pirate ship. That was what the shuttle's computer told him.

"Do you have pirates in this region?" he enquired, without turning round.

"Not lately," replied the Queen, sounding concerned.

"Well, we might have one up ahead. It's passing that big planet over there, coming our way. I'm going to head straight for the asteroid belt; try to hide there."

"Good," came an automatic response from Queen Isabelle.

John glanced back, his passengers looked very worried. He said, "If we've detected them, then the chances are they've done the same about us. I'm going to hide behind one of the larger asteroids. We have enough oxygen on board for quite a while. It might be a bit cat-and-mouse, but their ship is a lot bigger and a lot faster. While that ship is in the vicinity, we cannot make a run for it."

The shuttle shot into the asteroid field and John needed to decelerate as soon as they got there. He looked for a suitable place to hide and his passengers remained silent and left him to it. Presently, he found a small asteroid which possessed a couple of distinct advantages. It showed a smooth surface to land on and, second, the rock was not spinning in relation to the belt's collective orbit around their star.

"I'm going to stop here for a while," John said. He glanced back and saw that, while the Queen was hanging on his every word, her husband slouched fast asleep!

The shuttle touched down on the surface. With such an infinitesimal gravity, any slight movement would knock them off. It was important to turn the engines off to make it difficult for another ship to detect them.

"I've turned the force field off," he explained to his one conscious passenger. "That will help conserve energy. It makes us a lot more difficult to be spotted by another ship's sensors. There's a useful setting whereby it engages again if a solid object is about to hit us."

"Meanwhile, we wait," Queen Isabella whispered.

He presumed the whispering was so as not to wake her husband. As the time passed, it surprised John to find this royal lady wishing to converse with him.

"I can't believe what happened today," she confessed. "Henio betraying us like that... he's been with us for years! Your quick thinking saved us all."

"I'm not sure that thinking came into it; I acted on instinct."

"Thank goodness you did. But tell me more about yourself."

So, he did. It passed the time and took their minds off the fact they were hiding from a potential enemy. She found his escapade on Diyu most interesting. He did not set out to blow his own trumpet, but it sounded good when he told her about his exploits.

"You are an honourable man," she said. It was nice to hear her verdict, but a bit of a conversation stopper. A long period of silence followed this.

There was no question of them breaking cover. They must be patient. After a while, John felt he had nothing to lose from trying to strike up a fresh conversation, learning more about his passengers.

"Your Majesty..."

The Queen jumped a bit at this sudden breaking of the quiet.

"...do you mind if I ask you something?"

Collecting herself, she said amiably, "No, I don't mind."

"Forgive me, but I was wondering, have you always lived on your planet?"

"Grande Verde? No, I was of the House of Praxoa in the Trastacon System. Three small inhabited worlds, all under domes, ruled by my father. I never left the palace an'..."

"Palace?" John blurted out.

"That's what they called it. It wasn't as imposing as our place... our former place on Grande Verde. They betrothed me to Prince Alberto here when I was thirteen, before we ever met. They took me to Grande Verde two years later, at fifteen, when we were married. I know it was a long ago now, but it seems more like someone else's life. So much has changed..."

Now she was talking more to herself than John. When she trailed off, he felt it wisest not to re-kindle that fire. As a result, the embers of conversation died.

An hour passed, then another half hour. No sign of the other ship. Was it a pirate ship? Could this all be a waste of time? The King then woke from his slumbers.

"Your Majesty, I suggest we leave it another half hour and if..."

He stopped in his tracks, for, right overhead, passed the other ship. His blood seemed to freeze in his veins as the hull moved slowly past, so close he felt he could reach up and touch it. It was easy to see the markings along its bottom, not that they meant anything to the observer. The three shuttle occupants watched it through the ceiling window. Frozen in their seats, they held their breath, as if the slightest movement would draw attention.

'How in heaven's name can they not see us?' thought John as, wide-eyed, he watched the ship slide past.

Once it was clear, they still dare not relax, because it might return. Instead, it moved on and, once a thousand kilometres free of the asteroids, it shot off toward Grande Verde.

John needed no prompting after this. Within seconds, he fired up the shuttle's engines and manoeuvred the craft out of the belt of rocks and planetoids. As with the bigger ship, once into empty space, they shot off at maximum speed, but in the opposite direction.

A fortnight later, John sat back in the cabin on Belovo with Stella. She was listening as he completed his tale.

"As we approached the space station, I was wondering if this royal couple had secured enough money off-world. After all, they left Grande Verde in a great hurry. I needn't have worried. They had a lot of their relations resident on the space station, or pleasure station, as they called it. They rented an entire wing. The Royal Family settled in for the long haul, despite the station being dedicated to leisure activities such as gambling."

"How the other half lives!" exclaimed Stella.

"They must have stashed away an enormous sum. I'm not too bothered; they were decent to me. They paid me my full fee and got me on a ship back here."

"But you haven't explained the reason for the revolution. Why did they overthrow this royal family?"

"Um, I never understood that. The revolutionaries were a pretty fanatical lot. They hacked that advisor to pieces up on the roof. It was horrific. I wasn't there to get involved in the politics. The Royal Family was good to me. We're wealthy now and won't need to worry about money for ages."

John spent the next few years on Belovo with Stella. It was a simple life and he began growing a lot of their vegetables. His upbringing on the farm on Marmaris came back to him. This enterprise proved so successful that they took to selling spare food on the town's market once a week. The growing Ben helped with this.

In time, though, John sensed strains in his relationship with Stella. She appeared dissatisfied and was always getting at him. "I can't seem to do anything right!" became his theme in life. It concerned him they were drifting apart.

She was not insensitive to these developments. While Stella would still have said she loved him, she became increasingly annoyed at some of his habits, wandered to town without telling her, being clumsy at home and, worst of all, never listened to her when she spoke to him. She got fed up with having to repeat herself.

Then, in 2592, an opportunity came up which, John hoped, might help. The space liner *Alphelion* was taking a cruise through the stars, stopping at several interesting-sounding places. A luxury trip, he had enough money to pay for them both. Ben would stay with an aunt.

Wanting it to be a surprise, he booked it without telling her. Over supper one evening, he gave her the good news.

"How much did it cost?" she demanded.

"We can afford it."

"How much?"

When he told her, she blew her top. It cut no ice that included in the price was the shuttle hop to the liner.

She calmed down by the following morning and he could give her some details.

"The ship will stop at several open planets and astronomical phenomenon; it'll be the trip of a lifetime!"

"It better be at that price!"

Her negativity frustrated him. Still, he did not rise to the bait and bit his tongue. Stella eventually came round and enjoyed packing her case on the eve of the trip. She thought it through.

It was irresponsible of him, when he did not have a proper job to support them. Still, there seemed no point in discussing a fait accompli. She should prepare for the flight of a lifetime.

On the day, they left early by taxi for the space port. Nothing but the best for their holiday. Ben had gone to a relative the previous day, so they took care of everything.

The high street was busy that morning. The couple entered the space port and walked straight to check-in. He pressed buttons on his TRAC, but the automated system would not take the code. He called an employee across to help. Then the horrible truth came out.

"The shuttle for the *Alphelion* left a week ago, sir."

"What?"

"Yes, see the details on your TRAC."

The man was right. John had got the date wrong; he had no one to blame except himself. Which meant no cruise and no rebate, meaning a large sum of money down the drain.

"Oh, that's bloody typical!" was Stella's assessment, but she saved her full salvo until they got home. She gave a long rant about how hopeless he was. There was little he could say.

All the rest of that day, he was walking on eggshells, afraid to speak lest she jump down his throat.

The following morning, he rose extra early and loaded down with vegetables, headed by himself to the market. Ben was still with the aunt and Stella at home. John had a lot of stock to sell and enjoyed a productive morning. With most of it sold by lunchtime, he packed up early. As he did, a regular customer approached him.

"Hey, John, waddya doin' here still?"

"Oh, they cancelled our cruise."

"How d'yer mean? I thought you were goin' t'be on that there cruise liner."

"I was, but something happened and we couldn't go."

He would rather not discuss that "something." The other man continued.

"It was the *Alphelion*, wasn't it?"

"Yes, it was," replied John, surprised that the fellow could remember that detail.

"You were due to sail on the current cruise, but never did. Is that right?"

What was he doing, rubbing it in? Trying to remain patient, John confirmed, "That's about the size of it, yes."

"You haven't heard today's news then?"

"No, what?"

"The *Alphelion* disaster. Everyone on board killed."

"Huh?" John went, then stood open-mouthed.

"Yup," the man confirmed. "They say its inertia negators failed and an asteroid hit it... or were it a comet? Either way, no survivors."

The news stunned John. He packed up his things in double-quick time and hurried home to tell Stella. It amazed her, their good fortune in cheating death. She thanked God for their lucky escape. She still could not get over what she considered a terrible waste of money.

One extraordinary fact John had no way of knowing was this: a passenger on the salvage ship that claimed the wrecked *Alphelion* was none other than his brother, Frank. Then life has a habit of serving up strange coincidences.

The relationship between the couple stuttered on another couple of years, but living together was no longer enjoyable for either of them. John made enquiries at the space port for off-world jobs. He heard nothing for a long time. Then, in 2595, after turning thirty years old, an opportunity arose. He fed the details through to his wrist computer and he studied them while by himself one evening in the cabin.

"Kratos in the Halma Sector is looking to expand its armed forces. Men with previous military experience are especially welcome to apply..."

'Halma Sector,' considered John. 'That's further from the hub. It might be what I need to get away and recommence my military career. I'm going to volunteer.'

For Stella, the news came as a relief. From her point-of-view the previous few years had been both the best and worst of times. She found much to love about John. He was kind, with a sense of fun. Ben and he enjoyed a great relationship and she enjoyed having John as a father figure for her son.

Yet there were frustrations. She wanted marriage, but yet again she found someone not interested in the institution. He would not even countenance it to please her. She learned not to raise the subject after a while.

Plus, there was his need for adventure in his life. She did not argue too much regarding his mission to Grande Verde. It was for a limited period, the money generous and it was clear he set his heart on it.

'I listened to every word upon his return,' she recalled, 'but he seemed to be like a big kid. That's his problem, he's taking a long time to grow up.'

Considering the matter, she realised she had not helped the relationship by becoming hyper critical. Her cross words became more frequent. She found herself getting increasingly annoyed by his ways even though, deep-down, she knew she was still in love with him. Maybe she wanted too much. There was an aching gap between her ideal of him and the real him. She told herself to be reasonable, nobody can live with an image of perfection.

For all her dwelling on it, she still did not understand this bad patch in their relationship but she was wise enough not to blame him completely. Maybe, she reasoned, a period apart might be enough to re-kindle the flame of love, currently burning low. She hoped so.

If a nation is rapidly expanding its armed forces, there is usually one reason: it is heading for war.

Whether it ended that way, time would tell. However, as the twenty-sixth century drew to a close, Kratos appeared to be headng in that direction. Its antagonism with the planet Typhon had been simmering for years. Now matters threatened to boil over. Spanning two solar systems, the Halma Sector contained five populated domed planets. The other three, Pricus, Erebus and Attis, were unwilling to take sides. Instead, they tried to broker a peace. "It's like having to bang two unruly children's heads together!" as one exasperated Attisan diplomat put it.

Tension increased over the last year because of the large asteroid 542/SN. It had been a known astronomical body for years, in a thick asteroid belt in Kratos's system. No one worried about it until a geological survey team from Typhon discovered huge deposits of precious metals on it. The body's composition was evenly spilt between metal and rock. Word leaked out and Kratos sent their own geologists. Before long, both nations employed mining operations on opposite sides of the planetoid, while claiming full rights to the entire deposit. Kratos could point to the fact it was in their back yard, while their rivals pointed out that the Karrins (natives of Kratos) showed no interest in it until Typhon made the discovery.

John Thorn thrust himself into the centre of this situation, hoping to find longer-term employment. Matters were not improving between him and Stella and he felt relief at getting away. Not having given up on their relationship, he wondered if a period of absence might make the heart grow fonder. Besides, it would be welcome to get a regular salary for a while. He gave most of his remaining money to Stella because her need would be greater than his if his application succeeded. It was a big incentive to make this venture work.

John's flight was the longest one he had been on. It also took him further from the hub than he could remember. The stars and worlds were spread thinly here.

As the space liner descended into a dome's docking area, John wondered what he was letting himself in for. There were several would-be recruits from different worlds heeding the call to arms. They all looked younger than him.

Shuffling out of the re-pressurised dome, he gave a wry smile to himself. Was it sensible to give up the forests and wide-open spaces for this claustrophobic existence?

The Karrins were ready for the fresh arrivals. Once the officials completed formal identity checks and passport control, they ushered them to another dome given over to their recruitment drive. Multiple interviews took place in temporary booths erected for the purpose. John found himself with an affable, elderly gentleman with long, unkempt hair whose own military career was well past. He had suspended his retirement to "do his bit" for the cause. The authorities here would reject few candidates, but it was important to put them into roles which suited their skills and expertise. The interviewer was most interested in learning about John's previous experience.

"That's right, I served as Captain's Assistant on board a space destroyer. I was involved in a major space battle involving fleets of juggernauts on both sides. I don't know if you've heard of the conflict between Andracon and Kupalla several years back."

"Er, yes, I think so," came the unconvincing response. "And you were involved in this battle?"

"In the thick of it," said the would-be recruit. He never mentioned his side lost, but then the man never asked.

"And you were Captain's Assistant, you say?"

"Yes, sir, on board the *ASS Excellent* under Captain Farnham."

The names meant nothing to the Karrin, but these confident answers impressed him. What struck him more was the fact that this recruit, more mature than most coming in, could not only point to space combat experience, but held the senior rank of Captain's Assistant, most impressive.

He punched something into his computer and studied the results. Then, with a cheerful look, he announced, "We will be delighted to have you join our ranks, Mr Thorn, and we have just the post for you. As military advisor, we will involve you with decisions here on Kratos at the very highest level. I will get the paperwork completed today and we will show you the ropes once this process has been done. Orderly!"

Reference to paperwork was, of course, figurative. As the orderly came round the corner, he received his instructions, "Direct Mr Thorn here to living quarters A, senior officer level. Usual stuff, canteen, emergency procedures, etc."

They escorted John to his quarters and he found he would enjoy a suite of rooms all to himself. He would not complain, but it was quite clear they had made a mistake. Still, he would tell no one. If they wished to make him a military advisor, then so be it. He did not mind advising people if they paid him handsomely and gave him a suite of rooms and a servant, which they did. Some time later he found out "Captain's Assistant" meant something different on Kratos. It being one of the most senior ranks in their forces.

One thing he considered peculiar was the fashion for men to have long hair. It was the universal style here. Often they held it off their faces with clips, some brightly coloured. It was a cultural thing unlike any he had met.

Yet his biggest cultural shock was this society's use of religious commissars at the highest level. Spanning both the civil government and military decision makers, these monks held a great deal of power. The Karrin constitution laid down that they give the religious branch influence in all decision-making. This extended to their fleet, with every warship having at least one commissary on board.

"They're not all bad," Erik, an ordinance officer, told him.

A man a few years his senior, Erik, befriended John early on. Possessing a ready smile, there were laughter lines on his face. A native of Kratos, he had served in the fleet since leaving education, so far without seeing action. Considering the current, steady build-up of their armed forces, he wondered how long that would be. "I think I still have something to offer," he said. With his fair hair, arranged in the local style, and piercing blue eyes, he looked a friendly fellow. He was a big help to John in those early days, explaining some subtleties of Karrin power politics.

"My advice is to stay in with the commissaries. It would be a mistake to underestimate their influence, if not darn right power, that they hold. Some military types find them more of a hindrance than a help. But I don't want to give you the impression that all commissaries are bad, obstructive, or unhelpful. That is not the case. On board ship, a huge amount depends on the chemistry between them and the captain. I've served on board ship where they get on well and effectively worked together."

"But it's best not to cross them?"

"I'm not saying be afraid to offer your own opinion if it differs from a monk's, but show due respect. More than a few military officers have shown their disdain and come unstuck."

"Thank you for the advice, Erik, I shall make sure that I take it to heart. But tell me more about your political system."

"Okay. The Durbar is, in theory, the body in charge here. Containing both secular and religious members, it is too slow and cumbersome to make effective decisions. In recent years, the Durbar Committee, usually known as 'The Committee', runs the show. Benefactor Amri presides over this, he..."

"Amri, you say?"

"Takoda Amri, yes. He's a bit of a wet one, to be blunt. He followed his father as Benefactor, but now he's becoming more of a figurehead than anything else. His deputy, Quintin Black, is a more able man."

"Oh, I think I saw him on the vid screen, the news bulletin."

"Most likely you did. You could do worse than follow the news. There's a lot of propaganda, of course, but you'll gauge the mood.

That always helps. Did you say your first committee meeting is next week?"

"That's right."

"I'm sure it'll go well for you."

"Any last advice?"

"Think before you speak."

It was sound advice to be sure and he would try his best to heed it.

"And be wary of the commissaries. They have cut many a military career short by underestimating the monks. They learn the hard way and end up in charge of a basement department overseeing socks and shoes' supplies for the military."

"I see."

Backtracking, Erik added, "Not that soldiers' footwear procurement should be despised, but it's not as glamorous as commanding a juggernaut of the line."

This was John's opportunity to show his historical knowledge and he would not miss it.

"You could say they lost the American Civil War on old Earth because of poor footwear."

"Really?"

"Yeah, the advancing Confederate army went to Gettysburg because their troop' shoes were wearing out and they heard of a factory there with a large supply. General Lee might not have made his disastrous frontal assault if faced with different terrain. His order was as out of character as it proved disastrous."

Erik beamed, for he loved military history too and, once the pair got onto the 1st I. W., they spent half the afternoon discussing it. Both enjoyed the chance to show off their knowledge, whilst learning from the other. It was an excellent introduction for John, finding a pleasant friend.

During this "honeymoon" period before commencing his new role, John made sure he learned something about the history of Kratos.

It was yet another planet boasting a long and proud past. It survived a blockade during the 2nd I.W. three-hundred years before. Each year, they held a glorious celebration on the anniversary of its lifting. John had missed that year's party. He was told the Karrins shared the universal disgust of the whole civilized universe regarding battle robots. The Dyclan Inspectorate was always welcome there.

Made up chiefly of carbon dioxide, the atmosphere beyond the domes was dense. The temperature never got as high as the freezing point of water. Most activity took place within the domes. With few mineral deposits discovered, there was little surface activity. One exception being the setting up of anti-ship batteries on the plateau a few kilometres from the main dome. If anyone needed a reminder of the ongoing tensions with Typhon, this was it.

John soon discovered that the extensive array of domes and connecting tubes was not the complete picture. There was a vast labyrinth of levels carved out of the hard rock beneath. Most people lived there. An elaborate system of self-sealing doors ensured a dome breach would not drain precious air from elsewhere.

Some of the tunnel-building had been haphazard, with central government not always involved in its planning. As a result, it was a maze. He downloaded an app for his TRAC, which told him his position and the quickest way to any destination.

John still enjoyed a few days' grace before he would begin his duties. They told him this was standard procedure and he should not draw any negative conclusions. Given full access to roam, he took advantage of this free time to become acquainted with the place.

He found much of it was like a thousand other domed worlds. They employed none of the quaint little, old-fashioned market stalls here. Citizens must order everything on the local intranet. The domes' walls stood bare with little imagination employed in the decor of the public spaces. It still pleased him to familiarise himself with the set-up here and did not take long to teach himself the settlement's layout.

There was another meeting with Erik during this initial period on the planet. Mid-afternoon one day, they met up together at a public observation window looking out on an all-too familiar rocky landscape. It sat within its own room with the lights dimmed. The ordinance officer said, "We should return here in the evening."

John asked why.

"The Atherids are passing."

"I'm sorry?"

"They're an annual phenomenon, shooting stars, well worth a look."

"Okay, I've got nothing else on. Earlier you spoke about a special restaurant we could go to this evening."

"Yes, it's quite an exclusive one here, but novel, too."

"Go on."

"You cook your own food."

"Oh," said John, less than impressed.

"Don't look like that, it's rather fun. They have every ingredient under the sun. You go along there beforehand to order your ingredients and they have them prepared when you return to cook."

"What if they haven't got hem?"

"That's rarely the case. They have a tremendous range and get in fresh every day. Like I said, it's rather fun."

John was catching the other's enthusiasm, it sounded something novel. It was not a concept he had met before. Erik explained some more.

"They've an army of chefs and helpers to assist, but the customer is in charge. The staff may offer advice and one would be wise to heed it. They will also answer questions you may have, but unless there's a good reason, they will not stop you. I come here with my friend, Julian, a great deal. He's an excellent cook. I'd introduce you, but he's away on business off-world, at present."

"Where's that?"

"Oh, I don't know. He's a high-flier, frequently called away on business, often for weeks at a time."

An attractive woman then walked past and Erik noticed John's eyes following her. He asked, "You like women?"

"Of course I do!" John replied, thinking it was a bit of a daft question. Erik returned to the subject of the restaurant.

"I wondered if you'd like to come for a meal tonight. I'll go along there and order the ingredients if you say yes."

"No!" John said firmly, but grinning.

"No?" the other man was taken aback.

"I'd like to cook *you* a meal!"

"Oh... are you sure?"

"Sure, I'd enjoy that. Am I allowed to have an assistant from outside, say yourself?"

"I believe so. They have strict hygiene rules and we have to follow their guidelines, but it should be okay. We can go along and find out. Shall we go?"

"Can you peel potatoes?"

A couple of hours later, John sat down at the dining room table with a sigh. It felt good finally to be off his feet.

151

"What do you think?" he enquired.

"Give me a minute!" Erik said, chewing. "I'm still on my first mouthful."

He ate in peace for a few moments before giving his verdict.

"Not bad, not bad at all. When you said you'd be dishing up a vegetarian meal, I had my doubts. I do like my meat. But I'm enjoying this, I must admit. Do you cook often?"

"I don't. Didn't you notice how many times I referred to the cooking instructions on my TRAC? Potato goulash was one of my mother's special dishes. It's a long time since I last ate one."

"I'm not sure you'll convert me to vegetarianism," Erik confessed, "but it's something different."

John took this as a compliment, whether or not intended. He did not want to press it.

"You mentioned meat, but it's not real meat though, is it?"

"From an actual animal? Of course not, although I'm rather enjoying the image of a dome being given over to farming!"

"It makes you think."

"What does?"

"All this artificial crap that's eaten on domed planets; it can't do us any good."

"You're right," the other man sighed, "but I don't see the alternative."

"I wonder; is it the reason behind the low birth-rate?"

"Who knows?"

"But I know I want to retire to an open planet."

"Young to be contemplating retirement, aren't we? You've only just got here."

John laughed, "Yes, sorry!"

"It's all right. I hope you enjoy your stay here on Kratos."

"I'm looking forward to getting started with my new role."

They completed their meal, chatting some more on a host of subjects. Erik finished the potato goulash. He had eaten worse in his time. The restaurant provided a second course sweet. When the bill arrived, the local man insisted on paying fifty-fifty.

Later on, they went once more to the observation window. They were not alone this time. For a large group of interested spectators had converged to watch that year's Atherid meteor shower. John and Erik found a good vantage point where their view was unobstructed.

The light show had already begun, with one shooting star every minute. As time passed, the frequency increased.

"This is an annual event, you say?" John sought confirmation.

"It is."

"And do you come every time?"

"Used to, as a kid, although I haven't been for several years now. I thought you'd be interested."

"I am!" John enthused.

They watched some more. The meteorites appeared individually and plotted a zigzag, rather than a straight course, something the first time observer found intriguing. He had a question for Erik.

"Would it be possible for one of them to hit the domes here?"

"No chance; they burn up in the atmosphere. Besides, they're on a different course."

"It's nice to know we're safe."

Erik turned and placed his hand on John's lower arm. He said, "You're quite safe."

Feeling awkward at this gesture, John raised his hand and scratched an imaginary itch on his face. The hand withdrew and nothing was said.

"Oh, look!" someone cried out as a couple of meteorites, followed by a third, shot across the sky. The observers were getting their money's worth now.

"I'm glad you told me about this," John said, "because I wouldn't have known anything about it otherwise."

"You're welcome."

The light show fizzled out; it had not lasted very long. People drifted away, John and Erik amongst them. The latter said, "I'm back on duty tomorrow, but I hope to see you around."

"Of course, that would be nice."

"Goodnight, John."

"Goodnight."

He made certain he watched that evening's news broadcast, because there was a development in the tensions with Typhon.

"For too long the Typhons have supported pirates operating in this sector," the biased newsreader announced. "But today we can report a breakthrough. Our glorious defence forces uncovered a pirate base on asteroid 699RP." The vid screen showed footage which John

153

found difficult to make out. The announcer continued, "The pirate base had been hollowed out of the rock. This was a large and sophisticated operation for which they required assistance."

The obvious implication, even if unstated, was that the Typhons were aiding the pirates. The entire mood here and the building up of armed forces held frightening parallels for John. It was too close to his experiences on Andracon for comfort. That did not end well. Perhaps, in his role as advisor, he could be an influence for peace.

The day arrived for John's first Durbar Committee meeting. He arrived early, only to be told the venue had changed. Instead they held it in the Benefactor's study. A large carpeted room, the members sat round a central oak table. All, that is, except for the Benefactor himself, who was otherwise engaged.

Deputy Benefactor Quintin Black therefore led the gathering. Oriental-looking, he tried to comb his thinning hair down at the front to hide his receding hairline. Tried and failed, was John's verdict. He gave their new advisor a warm welcome and introduced him to the three other members present.

Foreign Minister Balina Jemonova, with straw-coloured hair moulded round her face, gave off an air of someone who meant business.

Next, they introduced him to Dux Vincent. Only later did Erik inform him that Dux was a senior army rank and not a Christian name. The man, in his late forties, had a furrowed brow and a pronounced widow's peak.

The last figure was the religious representative, Brother Jon-Francis. John's informant may have prepared him to meet the monk in some respects, but not in appearance. Wearing a dark grey habit, he sported the most enormous hair growth of both head and beard. He looked fearsome, something like an old warlord of myth. The newcomer was quite take aback, but tried not to show it. For want of conversation, he commented that he and the monk shared the same Christian name.

"My name is Jon-Francis," came the terse response.

Vincent came to the rescue by enquiring, "Is it true you come with actual space combat experience?"

"I do."

"On board a juggernaut?"

"No, a space destroyer, although there were juggernauts involved."

That seemed to satisfy the military man. Introductions completed, the Deputy Benefactor lost no further time in getting down to business.

"The revelations coming from 699/RP are most concerning. They carved a huge base out for the pirates' operation."

He spoke further and John was glad that he had followed the news and was aware of what they were talking about.

Balina declared, "We should send a strongly-worded message to the Typhons telling them that this kind of interference has got to stop. It is intolerable that they should support piracy in this way."

Vincent pointed out that unequivocal proof of their involvement had not been obtained.

"Fiddle faddle! They're up to their necks in it and everyone knows it. It's foolish to pretend otherwise."

The voice of compromise came from Brother Jon-Francis. He commented, "Sending a message direct to Typhon would play into their hands. It would make it look as if we've been hasty in making up our minds. I suggest that we rather send a message to Halma High Command, I mean involve the three other nations in our sector. Then they'll see us to be reasonable and not jumping to conclusions. We mustn't be in a hurry, or we'll face the harsh judgement of history."

John nodded at these sage words designed to pour cold water on a situation otherwise in danger of boiling over. When the meeting concluded, he realised that his exaggerated nodding had been his sole contribution to the proceedings. He was unhappy with that, feeling a need to justify his position. Then wiser thoughts occurred to him. To speak too much at his inaugural meeting might not be the best play. It could make him look superficial and trying too hard to impress. Better to let himself in gently. That way, when he finally did open his mouth, they would be more inclined to listen to him.

In the event, they sent Kratos' complaint to the body overseeing all five planets in the region. A short while late, Typhon answered, saying that they did not believe the pirates existed. Rather, they were Kratos' own ships on a misinformation exercise. That infuriated the Durbar Committee. Yet, deprived of their base, the pirates quit the region and this particular ticking bomb was diffused.

A few weeks passed and John attended further meetings. These were more routine. The regulars became familiar to him and he could make calm and considered contributions.

Then an opportunity arose, one too good for him to turn down. The Kratos juggernaut *Astoria* was to make a routine patrol flight. Would he like to join them as an observer? Yes, he would!

~ End of Chapter 8 ~

My Keeper's Brother - Chapter 9

Astoria was the ship that Ordinance Officer Erik served on board. It was nice to have his Karrin friend there. John's official role on this flight was observer. He therefore relaxed to a degree and enjoyed the ride.

Two senior officers accompanied him on the shuttle up to the monster ship in orbit around the planet. Captain Xernon Wallace and Commissary Brother Keith. He therefore got an early introduction to the secular and religious commanders of the *Astoria.*

Captain Wallace, at thirty-nine the youngest ever juggernaut commander in the nation's history, hailed from one of the wealthiest families on the planet. That fact never hindered his meteoric rise. It had taken a while for John to appreciate the vast class divide on Kratos. The underclass harboured little hope of great advancement, while the local aristocracy looked after their own interests. He realised now quite how fortunate he was to be classed with the "haves." That initial misunderstanding at his interview played right into his hands. His categorisation as a member of the ruling elite being a tremendous stroke of luck. John was not a political animal, still less a social revolutionary. He would relish his good fortune and give the role of military advisor his best shot.

He saw some snobbish behaviour towards the lower ranks, but not all of them behaved so. Erik, for example, was polite to all and popular with the crew.

Back to the shuttle and John studied the captain, nine years his senior. He sported a fresh face with pale pink skin and small eyes. His fine head of hair ran halfway down his back. Speaking in a nasally voice, he welcomed the observer.

"A mere routine patrol. We'll be heading round three stars and taking in the planet Erebus as we pass. Not planning on stopping anywhere, it is all about showing our presence."

Meanwhile, Brother Keith contrasted with the only other commissary he had met to date. Also from a fabulously wealthy family, Brother Keith gave up all that opulence to lead a religious life. In this role, he might not cling to money, but he kept power and influence. Besides shorter hair than any other male Karrin encountered so far, he displayed a neatly clipped moustache, the end of which reached down either side of his mouth. Economic with his words, he gave off an air of someone born to privilege.

"Greetings," was the one word he offered to John after being introduced by the captain. Yet his expression appeared welcoming.

A short flight took them up to the orbiting spaceship. As they got closer, John studied it through an observation port. It looked a colossal beast, then so had the previous juggernaut he witnessed, crippled and ablaze from end to end. He hoped the Karrin fleet did not go the same way as Andraconia's.

Once on board, he found the scale of the ship breathtaking. Nine decks, this floating military city possessed every imaginary facility on board. A rating escorted him to his room. There, he dumped the few things he had brought along. It was a lot smaller than his facilities down on the planet, but adequate for a patrol designed to last a mere eight days.

Before long, he was working his way towards the bridge, again using his TRAC to direct him there along a multitude of corridors on several levels. A warm welcome greeted him from Erik when he arrived. They gave John a seat with a good vantage point, where he enjoyed an excellent view of the screen. This showed the forward view of star studded space. Routine pre-flight checks took place before the *Astoria* left orbit and headed out into the void.

The first day was uneventful and John slept well in his cabin. The food quality in the officer's canteen for breakfast was better than expected. Brother Keith struck up a conversation with him over a post-meal coffee.

"You've come from afar, John?"

"I've been living on Belovo. It's a fair way, you're right."

"Is that where you came from originally?"

"Oh, no. Marmaris, near the hub."

"I can't say I've ever heard of it..."

"Nobody seems to've."

"... but then I'm not as well travelled as you. I've been on the three planets."

"The three planets?"

"Pricus, Erebus and Attis, all here in the Halma Sector."

"Ah."

158

"But the world I'd most like to visit is called Eden. Have you heard of it?"

John, laughing, answered, "I have. My brother lives there."

"Does he?" the animated man asked.

"The last time I checked, he did. He's into that sort of thing."

"Have you visited Eden?"

"No."

"You're not close, you and your brother?"

After pondering the question for a while, John replied, "I don't suppose we are. He got this religious thing when we were teenagers and I couldn't see it myself."

The monk gave him a warm look, but said nothing. The ship's alarm sounded and both men sprang to their feet and bounded off to the bridge. The other man led, John being happy to follow.

When they arrived, the place was abuzz. "Man overboard!" came the cry and sensors had located the spacesuit.

"We've despatched a shuttle," Erik told the two men as they took up their stations.

The captain, meanwhile, appeared distracted. He was fiddling about with his seat controls, rather than paying attention to the drama. The crew called out sit reps, ignored by the man in charge.

Tensions amongst the rest of the crew were high as the small vehicle approached the object floating in space. It was a Karrin spacesuit sporting the *Astoria's* name... but it was empty.

An investigation revealed the whole thing was a prank started by a couple of bored ratings. They spent the rest of the voyage in the brig.

As promised, the ship navigated past the planet Erebus, one of the three planets in the Halma Sector, trying to calm tempers between Kratos and Typhon. John got sight of it on the screen as they passed close by. However, clouds enveloped the globe and there was nothing interesting to see.

After this, the most bizarre episode occurred. A decision needed to be made regarding the route home. There were two usual ways taken, either via an uninhabited planetoid, or direct. The captain was uncertain and did not ask anyone's opinion. John sensed Brother Keith's exasperation at the secular leader's indecision.

Positioned in the command chair, Captain Wallace sought counsel in... a fortune cookie!

'My goodness,' thought John in amazement, 'the man's being serious!'

He was indeed. All eyes trained on the captain as he opened the fortune cookie. After reading the message, he at least had the decency to read it out loud.

"Getting there is only half as far as getting there and back."

Brother Keith rolled his eyes, Erik stifled a guffaw and the rest of the crew present turned their heads away. Then, seizing the initiative, the military advisor sought to earn his keep by suggesting, "Shall we travel back the most direct route, then?"

"Good idea!" Captain Wallace responded and gave the order.

The ship sped home and no further incidents occurred on this patrol. John felt pleased with himself for having broken the impasse. The following evening, home and in the comfort of the officers' bar, Erik congratulated him.

"You saved the day," he said with a smirk, "well done."

He was joking, of course, but the situation had a serious side. John asked, "What'll happen to him now?"

"How do you mean?"

"He's experienced a mental breakdown and we can't allow him to carry on in the role."

Lowering his voice, the other said, "Mustn't get caught speaking like that. You know he's flying the void" (a local expression for insanity) "and so do the rest of us, but he's from a wealthy family. Even Brother Keith knows he has to live with it. It's the reality of life here on Kratos. The upper classes are interbred and produce more than their fair share of mad people."

"I thought you said the monks were powerful. Can't Brother Keith have him removed?"

"Wallace is still the blue-eyed boy of the fleet. Brother Keith knows how difficult it would be to have him removed. He won't want to pursue a cause he stands a good chance of losing."

"Forgive me," John persisted, "but you sound blasé about it all."

Not taking offence, the other man said, "It's the reality I've lived with all my life."

"But what if a split-second decision is needed in the heat of battle?"

"I'd like to think the commissary would bark some sane orders and the crew would follow him. Folk know the score and make allowances. Hell, I shouldn't be talking to you like this. My family is part of the upper crust here."

"But you come across as sane."

"Why, thank you, John, that's the nicest thing you've ever said to me!"

Matching his grin, the advisor said, "Are there enough upper crust officers to go round with the rapid expansion of Kratos' armed forces? I know that no less than three destroyers have entered service in the past fortnight alone. We purchased two from abroad."

"You're right. From what I hear, the recruitment campaign has been an enormous success, drawing in lots of talent. How long our economy can fund this expansion is another matter."

"They might have to tax your super rich class more."

"As they are running the show, I can't see it somehow. Besides, we're never short of fresh ways to indulge ourselves."

"It's all very civilized here on the surface."

"You hit the nail on the head!" said Erik. "On the surface, we are the model of respectability."

The following evening, the pair were back again discussing a different topic. Their friendship blossomed, because they shared the same sense of humour and could rely on each other's discretion. It was pleasant to be free to talk about anything.

Erik said, "An elderly friend of my father's said he was looking into getting a body transplant. I didn't think that possible."

"Hmm, I heard someone else talking about that once before; they said it was possible before the 2nd I.W."

"Do you buy that?"

"What?"

"They lost a lot of technology due to that war."

"It wouldn't be the first time in history that's happened. We know for sure they lost a lot of data. I don't think anyone would dispute that. They devised library planets designed to house all known knowledge. The nihilists targeted them and, the accepted wisdom goes, civilization lost a tremendous amount."

"Indeed."

John continued, "This must have included technological information, not just historical facts."

"I guess it's difficult to catalogue what they lost, because it's been... lost."

161

"It's funny that a conflict occurring such a long time ago still affects us today."

"The fall of Rome affected European history for centuries."

"The Dycon Inspectorate is as important today as it's ever been."

"Try telling that to the inhabitants of Tangeot!" Erik exclaimed.

"Sorry?"

"Haven't you seen the news?"

"No."

"Tangeot was due to be inspected and has refused to admit the deputation."

"The Inspectorate itself?"

"The same."

John looked shocked, saying, "I've never heard of that before."

"Neither has anyone else."

"They must have something to hide."

"That's what everyone's saying, of course. Still," the ordinance officer concluded, "it'll blow over. You watch; the Inspectorate will force them to comply."

They were right that the Second Intergalactic War cast a long shadow. An eight-year conflict, three centuries before, it was a war on a scale unprecedented either before or since. The combatants wiped out entire planets and the extensive use of humanoid battle robots and genetic weapons horrified the civilized universe. So much so that they drew up treaties forbidding their development and/or use. The body assigned with the authority to enforce these regulations was the Dycon Inspectorate. They possessed unprecedented powers to search for and destroy any facilities they deemed in contravention of international law.

While the Inspectorate's aims still held almost universal support, by the end of the twenty-sixth century, the body was a byword for corruption. Either way, the situation regarding Tangeot was unprecedented and needed to be resolved.

The Karrins, caught up in their own neighbourly dispute, pushed such considerations into the background. If not planning for it, they were doing nothing to halt the slide to war.

After further wrangling, they expelled the few remaining diplomats from Typhon. John was present when one of them was being escorted out. He overheard him say, "I've been here ten years. I'd

162

been hoping to settle down here after I retire." John found it all rather sad.

However, pathos was the order of the day when, several weeks later, the planet held a show trial. The charge was treason, spying for the enemy camp. Then the accused, a Karrin national, committed suicide in his cell. The case proceeded, but with a corpse on trial. John knew it best to hold his tongue, but to him, it provided the ultimate proof these people were completely mad.

This event sated the desire of those baying for blood, for a while at least. Matters calmed down in the half year following. It was during this period that John received news from Stella. She had a new man in her life. Having moved on himself, he felt pleased for her.

As the year 2595 drew to a close, he was finding himself busy. A fresh development had arisen and his opinion was being sought.

The Benefactor presided over the meeting with a full turn-out of committee members. With his long, floppy white hair, Benefactor Amri was a familiar sight to John these days. He was unconvinced the older man could run a planet, though. Other committee members got used to swaying the opinion of this weak ruler's judgement and he seemed to go along with the views of whoever could shout the loudest.

On this occasion, he presented some interesting news to them.

"A large Typhon cargo vessel recently got into difficulty and made an emergency landing on one of our asteroids. We've impounded ship and crew pending a decision on what to do about them. The cargo was mostly mechanical parts, especially for anti-grav motors, but it also held two tonnes of gold bullion bound for their home planet. The question is, what should our next step be?"

"Confiscate the lot!" declared Foreign Minister Jemonova, who wanted to get her answer in first. "Under international salvage law, it is our right."

Dux Vincent was thinking along similar lines. "Two tons of gold would be enough to build another juggernaut," he pointed out.

"Have we that right, simply to take it?" Brother Jon-Francis' distinctive voice sounded. He looked none too happy at the way this debate was going.

"Yes we have! Under international salvage laws, we have no duty to keep anything if it has landed on our soil."

"John?" the Benefactor asked.

The advisor, confident in giving his opinion these days, had not wanted to speak straightaway. By holding back first, his opinion seemed more considered when he voiced it. Fixing his stare on the Dux, he said, "Just because something is legal, doesn't mean it's the right thing to do. We have a golden opportunity before us to improve relations with Typhon at a stroke. By handing back the ship to them unplundered, it will send a conciliatory message. Especially if we treat the crew well and repair the ship."

"Do you think they'd do that for us?" asked the exasperated Dux.

"I don't care. It's more important that we take the moral high ground by making a magnanimous gesture."

This marked the high point in the debate from John's perspective. After that, the arguments swayed both ways. Brother Jon-Francis was subdued, while Deputy Benefactor Black seemed to be influenced by the hawks. In the end, Benefactor Amri dismissed the group and said he would take all opinions into consideration before making a final decision. John was uncertain which way the man would jump and hoped that his more moderate, conciliatory view would prevail. That hope died when he saw a government news bulletin the following day.

"The legitimate forces of Kratos have impounded a rogue cargo ship, bound for the Typhon regime. Under international law..."

He turned off the vid screen in his room, having heard enough.

Fortunately, this proved insufficient to provoke Typhon and, when the new year arrived, John still hoped for a peaceful solution. The other three planets in the Halma Sector had not given up hope, anyway, and their diplomats shuttled between the protagonists trying to keep the dialogue going and prevent a conflict.

By this time, John was becoming a permanent fixture on board the juggernaut *Astoria*. He fitted in patrols with the ship in-between committee meetings. Both the monk, Brother Keith and ordinance officer Erik, encouraged the connection for the same reason. They perceived that Captain Wallace was being weaned off the fortune cookies and starting to rely on John's advice. A most welcome development in their eyes.

On one such patrol. they spotted a small cargo vessel going through their solar system on an unusual course.

164

"Unidentified vessel, state your name and business," the message from *Astoria* demanded.

"This is Ethan Linberg of the freighter *Hope*. We are attending on a planet in the Xanthion Sector "

"Stop your vessel and prepare to be boarded under International Law."

Suspicious, Captain Wallace said, "I bet they're taking banned goods to the Typhons."

Brother Keith pointed out that they were not heading in that direction at all. The captain said, "It could be a ruse; they'd double-back once they were clear of the asteroid belt. We can't be too careful. I'll send a marine detachment to search the vessel."

"Would you mind if I went along with them?" John enquired.

"Huh? I don't see why not."

Shortly afterwards, John was donning a spacesuit with a marine squad and boarding a shuttle to take them across. There was banter amongst the men, all of whom struck John as very young. It took him back to his first days on Andracon, but he said nothing.

The flight and docking on the *Hope* proceeded smoothly. Their captain was at great pains to comply and only requested they exercise care in the search. The marine officer asked what their cargo and purpose were.

"We are carrying a large consignment of insects bound for a planet in the Xanthion Sector. It's a newly discovered world, yet unnamed, thought viable as an open planet."

The marine officer looked unimpressed and turned to give directions to his troops with the help of a couple of scientific crew members. That left John alone with the captain on this highly automated vessel. He introduced himself.

"Hi, I'm Ethan Linberg," came the reply. "I trust we will not be detained long."

"As long as they find nothing suspicious, no. We'll have you on your way in no time. Insects, you say?"

"That's right. Billions of them and plenty of species, bred for the purpose. Diversity is vital in a new world."

"I'm guessing such new worlds don't turn up every day."

"Quite right, it's off the beaten track, you might say."

"And yet to be given a name?"

"Mmm."

"You could call it 'Hope,' after your ship. That'd be quite apt for a new world, wouldn't it?"

"Indeed it would. I can put that to the committee."

"You're terra-forming; is that what you call it?"

"It could be called that, but we're not doing it with machines. Everything has to be coordinated - the plants, the insects, the animals. We're also carrying parts for a desalination unit and other equipment, but as an entomologist myself, it's the insects that interest me the most."

"I see. Will you be staying there on the planet to oversee the operation?"

"Oversee my part of it, yes, but..."

The return of the marine officer interrupted them. He wanted some equipment explained to him. John did not follow, because the compartments were cramped.

They soon completed the operation and John made a point of thanking Captain Linberg and wishing him well in his enterprise. The scientist looked relieved that the ordeal was concluded and he could get underway again.

On the way back, the marine officer gave John the benefit of his considered opinion. "It's a load of old bugs! Bloody silly if you ask me." John received this wisdom with a faint smile. No point talking to such a man. Anyway, they were soon back home with another successful operation completed.

Back on Kratos, further news was coming through regarding the Tangeot dispute. A Dycon Inspectorate delegation landed there, only to be told they could not disembark. Following a stand-off, they had to leave. Further planets were getting involved, most on the side of the Inspectorate. One or two supported Tangeot by saying the Inspectorate was being heavy handed. Nothing like this had ever happened before. It was a regular topic of conversation between John and Erik at their favourite bar.

The former said, "Tangeot cannot be building combat robots. The very thought chills the blood!"

"If not, why aren't they letting the Inspectorate in?"

"That's the obvious question, but I don't have the answer."

"No."

"But I have been considering something."

When he halted, Erik said, "Carry on, don't be mysterious."

"I was wondering if I should apply to join the Dycon Inspectorate."

"What!"

"Why not? It's a cause I believe in. No one wants to see battle robots careering up the streets again..."

"Of course not."

"... and the Inspectorate's a cause for good."

"Agreed, but it would be difficult for you to carve out a career there unless you enjoy connections." When the other man didn't respond, Erik continued, "It's all done on a buddy-buddy system, you must be aware. Unless you're in with the right people, you'd be stuck on the ladder's bottom rung."

"If you put it that way..."

"Besides, we need you here! It's good for Kratos to have a sane voice in committee."

It was nice to get such a vote of confidence. Yet even as the idea of volunteering for the Dycon Inspectorate turned sour, he wanted to justify their cause.

"You must agree that we should do everything to stop robots being made again."

"Of course," Erik said with a laugh. "No sensible person would think otherwise."

For racial memory of the 2nd I.W. stood as strong as ever in the collective consciousness of this civilization. Parents brought up children on tales of battle robots massacring civilians. It was the ultimate horror; machines designed to look somewhat like human beings, but containing nothing but cold, programmed logic. They had not challenged the accepted wisdom of a complete ban on them for generations... until the Tangeot Dispute.

The *Astoria* had another mission. The new year 2597 having turned, reports came in of a fresh pirate base in the asteroid field. The juggernaut was being sent to investigate. Another mission was welcome, but it seemed overkill. He would have sent a smaller, more manoeuvrable ship into the confined spaces of the asteroid belt. With the decision made, he felt it pointless to kick up a fuss. Besides, he wanted to share some personal news with Erik as he entered the bridge prior to the operation getting underway.

"I learned from a friend of a friend that my brother, Frank, was on the planet Kostroma Shuya. Not a million light years from here."

"No, it's not. A domed planet, I visited it once, many years ago."

"Have you?"

"Yeah, when I was a teenager. My father called there on business. It's quite beautiful to look at, because it has rings round it. Not much fun on the surface, though."

"Why's that?"

"The gravity is too heavy or my liking. It felt like I was walking round with a sack of potatoes round me the whole time. Most wearing, I..."

He stopped speaking, for Captain Wallace had entered the bridge. The commander appeared distracted and ignored his crew as he made for his chair. Sitting down with a thump, he got out a small mirror and began scrutinising his hairline. "I hope I'm not going bald," he mumbled loud enough to be heard.

He looked up, discarded the mirror and, returning to the matter in hand, began pre-flight checks. John caught Brother Keith's eyes and they exchanged glances. It boded ill for the mission.

They were soon on their way and the captain appeared well focussed as the giant spaceship cruised to its destination. Addressing both Commissary and advisor, he said, "This is a fact-finding operation. If we discover a base, then it's more important that we find evidence of Typhon involvement than anything else. I'm not going in all guns blazing."

'Thank goodness for that,' thought John.

They arrived at the asteroid belt without incident. A swirling multitude of objects, from tiny grains to planetoids, revolving round the star, a short distance within its frost line. There were minor breaks in the belt; some sections being more sparsely populated with rocks than others. The section they needed to scan was not one of these gaps. It was full of medium-sized rocks weighing between one and ten million tonnes each. These could take down even a juggernaut's force field if hit at speed. They therefore must treat them with respect. First, the *Astoria* moved into synchronous orbit with the belt at eighteen kilometres a second round the star.

"Send out the probes," ordered Captain Wallace and the unmanned craft shot silently from the ship.

A couple of hours passed, but they found no leads. The ship moved up the belt a short way to a natural break between rocks, about a kilometre and a half wide.

"Hmm," began the captain, "we could manoeuvre her into that gap to get a closer look. Were I a pirate, this would be the ideal entrance for my ships into the asteroid belt's centre. An excellent place to hide. Let's take her in."

"You're thinking of flying us in there?" asked John, disbelieving.

"It'll be tight," Brother Keith pointed out, supporting him.

"We can do it!"

John said, "Wait. Pirates would set up mines in an approach like this."

"Nonsense. Our probes have detected none."

"But we've moved up since they deployed them."

"Enough. Helmsman, steer a course into the asteroid field."

No point in arguing further, because Wallace had made his mind up. John hoped his fears were unfounded. He reconsidered. 'No mines so far. History tells us it doesn't pay to be over-cautious. There was General McClellan who...'

"Bang!" The entire ship jarred as the inertia negators failed momentarily. An alarm rang and the lights dimmed.

"Shields are down!" cried the helmsman.

Captain Wallace uttered a swear word, which barely cleared his lips when there was another explosion. "Are we under attack?" he queried, confused.

"I don't think so, sir," came a reply. "I think we've hit a couple of space mines."

John looked away from the captain. He tried catching Erik's eye, but the latter was making sure he did not look up.

The captain ordered the ship to a dead stop relative to the circulating asteroids. As it did, debris from the juggernaut surged forward away from the vessel. The *Astoria* had hit two space mines. The first disabled the force field; the second did considerable damage to three decks, causing some loss of life.

After having had his advice ignored, John was at full liberty to say, "I warned you!" but there seemed no point. Everyone on the bridge knew it. They waited while the technicians redeployed the force field, then the ship slunk back home in silence.

"There'll be a board of enquiry," Erik told his friend the following day. "You'll get called to be a witness. It could mean the end of Captain Wallace's career. If it all comes out, and it should, then I can't see even his family connections saving him."

169

"I'm not sure I want to end a man's career!"

"You'd be doing us all a favour; Kratos, as well as his immediate crew. The man's a liability and this is the golden opportunity to get him sidelined. Twenty-two crew killed and extensive damage that'll take time to repair. I can't help thinking it's a let off, 'cos if war with Typhon comes, we don't want a liability like Wallace in charge."

The following week, war came. Yet it was not a petty squabble between two planets, it was on an altogether bigger scale.

Tangeot had been plotting with sympathetic neighbours to breakaway from the rest of civilization. Together, they formed the Confederation of Independent Planets. Knowing that the rest of the human galaxy would not stand for this, they decided attack was the best form of defence. They launched pre-emptive strikes on a host of loyalist worlds with a good deal of initial success.

It took a while for the remaining worlds to get their act together. Forming The Alliance of Loyal Planets, those allies sought to impose the majority's will on the rebels. These nations sidelined the Dycon Inspectorate as they chose force of arms to bring Tangeot and her allies to heel. What was to become (erroneously) known as the Third Intergalactic War had begun.

John had no doubts as to his next course of action. A confirmed loyalist, he felt compelled to join in a crusade for restoration of the rule of law. With his military experience, he could make a difference. Many planets were rallying to the flag, but the Halma Sector's where he currently resided, were not amongst them. They were too busy with their own affairs.

"It's true then?" Erik asked, "you've resigned your commission?"

"Yes, it's true. I'm following my conscience."

"I'm sorry to see you go, both on a personal level and professionally."

"I don't leave without regrets. You've been a great friend and I'll miss our chats."

"What about your witness evidence at Captain Wallace's court martial?"

"I've left video evidence. The military police made special dispensation because of the international situation. I told them everything, I didn't hold back. Anyway, won't he get off with a slap on the wrist thanks to his family connections?"

"Maybe, but Brother Keith and I are going to corroborate your evidence, I'm sure. He may escape serious punishment thanks to his connections, but I can't see him ever commanding a ship of the line again, thank goodness."

"The punishment should fit the crime."

"How so?"

"Put him in charge of a mine sweeper!"

Both men laughed. Erik asked about his plans. John told him he was heading for a recruitment centre on a space station.

"There's a huge call to arms. The rebels have made sweeping gains and must be contained as swiftly as possible. I want to do my bit."

"Of course you do," his friend said. "I might even have joined you myself if I didn't have news of my own."

"Oh?"

"I've got an interviewed for a ship's captain's job."

"That's great!"

"I'm hopeful, but they won't be putting me in charge of a juggernaut any time soon. If I'm successful, it'll be a modest ship, but I can work my way up."

"Congratulations; well done"

"Hey, we mustn't get ahead of ourselves. I have to pass the interview first."

"But you're confident?"

"Yes."

"Good luck then."

"And you, John, you show those rebels a thing or two. They must be brought to heal, for our very civilisation is at stake."

As he sat in the departure lounge in civilian clothes, he saw another young man in similar attire, in the next seating bay.

"Are you joining up?" he asked him.

"I am," the other man replied, amused that John had guessed correctly. "My two brothers have both done it. I'm going to meet them."

The brief conversation ended there and both men buried their heads in their respective TRACs. Time dragged. He was alone in his seating bay until a boisterous group of people invaded the area. A glamorous woman, accompanied by a younger, plain one and a posse of men. He sized them up. The woman dripped wealth, a representative of the privileged class here on Kratos. Her entourage were her hangers-on and sycophants.

Ignoring them seemed the best strategy, but then a fierce-looking bodyguard stood right in front of him.

"This is the VIP section," he growled.

"I know," John said in measured tones, flashing his pass courtesy of having been a senior Kratos officer. He went back to studying the sunspot activity of the local star on his TRAC, a most riveting subject.

After a pause, the man demanded, "Move up, madam wishes to sit there."

"No," said John, matching the man's stare with his own.

"Leave him, it doesn't matter," the woman said, diffusing the situation. John sat with the bodyguard and woman servant on either side. He continued to sit there defiantly until his flight was called. With great deliberation, he gathered his few belongings together and made for the gate. As he passed the other recruit he had spoken with earlier, the seated man gave a hand signal which said, "Well done," or "Good for you!" He had appreciated John's small act of resistance against the ruling class of the planet Kratos.

Said planet was soon a diminishing orb as the space liner pulled away. In his seat in the first-class compartment, John was well catered for. He could relax and consider the previous five years of his life. In a hierarchical society, he had been fortunate they accepted him into the higher echelons. 'All because of an early misunderstanding!' he mused. 'Anyway, it should look good on my curriculum vitae in the future. I'm going to aim for an officer rank in the allies' army.'

Serving on board a mighty juggernaut had been a thrill. When he departed Marmaris, being an officer on one of these extraordinary ships was a complete dream. Yet it became a reality. Kratos had provided varied experiences, but he would take some fond memories with him. The Durbar Committee was exciting at first, but in the end the political manoeuvring frustrated him. Erik's friendship had been an unmitigated joy.

What of a war between Kratos and Typhon? That was receding into the background now. The Halma Sector moved on from that. They now all declared for the allies against Tangeot and their rebel confederates. The once potential enemies would fight as allies.

Ironically, had John stayed, he would have fought for the same cause he left to join. Anyway, he had made the decision and he would not turn back now.

Besides, he was not over-impressed by Kratos as a fighting force. There were many weaknesses. At the highest level, the Durbar members were trying to score points off each other rather than arrive at the best collective decision. Their ships' crews were often disunited by having command split between the secular and the religious. Erik warned him about the monks exercising great power, but having seen Brother Keith in action, he believed the man did not stand up to the captain enough. Some men in authority displayed insecurities. Take Captain Wallace, a man promoted because of the family he belonged to rather than any ability he possessed. John also disagreed with the way they sent juggernauts out on patrol without an escort. That was asking for trouble.

As he sat in the space liner, he pondered the idea of producing a full audit with all these points and sending it to the Durbar Committee. He never did. He wished to look forward, not backwards.

Space Station *Recruitment 47* was a former pleasure station requisitioned for the war effort and imaginatively re-named. It orbited an uninhabited rocky planet with an unstable rotation. Frequent minor adjustments needed to be made to the station's orbit to keep it on track.

Other would-be recruits disembarked from John's ship. Another docked soon afterwards, which meant large numbers of people milling about. The call to arms had caught the public's imagination and volunteers, men and women from a thousand different worlds, were coming forward. Many made it to this recruitment centre.

Standing in a disorderly queue, John spotted a couple of older men and considered them too long in the tooth to enlist. A further glance round made him realise that, at thirty-two, he himself was older than most.

First, he went through several identity checks and scans. Before one, the operator joked it was to check he was not a robot. At last, John *hoped* it was a joke.

Eventually, they diverted him into a cubicle where a woman sat behind a table. After going through some further formalities, she asked him some different questions.

"Why do you want to join?"

"What do you feel about battle robots?"

"Do you think it's right we ban genetic research?"

He realised it was a politico / psychiatric test. Afterwards, he hoped he had come across as a loyal citizen and sane, The lady gave nothing away whilst it was going on.

Being told he would received a message on his TRAC when the next part in the process was due, he settled down for a canteen meal. Macaroni cheese tasted good for mass produced food and he tucked in. People bustled past, but he was concentrating on the news bulletin being played on the vid screen nearby.

"The gallant forces of Acre Minor held out to the end. Their heroic defence has helped buy time for the Alliance to build up their forces for the counter offensive. We will reimpose law and order on..."

No matter how they might spin it, another planet had fallen to the rebels. Were they using battle robots? There were no confirmed reports of such. John was not alone in hoping that the Alliance would get their act together soon.

Three days on the station and, following numerous mini-interviews, both with machines and humans, the process seemed interminable. He endured boring waits in between and, after a while, John felt desperate. Did these people want him or not?

'What a shambles!' he considered. 'No wonder the rebels are running amok.'

Called to another interview, he hoped this one would produce something tangible. A ginger-haired man of indeterminate age sat waiting for him. When he opened his mouth and invited John to take a seat, it revealed a sizeable gap between his upper, front teeth.

"I see that you've served as an officer in the past."

"Yes, I have." Had it taken them this long to pick up on that?

"Good!" the recruiter said. "We've found a post near the front line that suits your command experience and qualifications."

'Finally we're getting somewhere,' thought John as he waited to hear details.

"There's an officer post on Space Station 236 that I think you would fit into. It's further from the hub, nearer to where the action is taking place. I've been there myself recently and I can tell you it's a pretty busy centre. Lots of comings and goings. I can see it becoming ever more important as this nasty business takes shape."

John waited for the big reveal. What exactly was the role?

"They have recently reorganised the department I'm thinking of and it needs someone with excellent leadership skills to hold things together."

"Yes?" the listener said, encouraging him to say it.

"It's an accounts department, sorting out the salaries of the brave warriors of the Alliance."

"Accounts!?" went John in a tone a cross between disdain and disbelief.

"Indeed," the man responded. "It's a vital cog in the great machine we are seeking to build up. An efficient payroll system will be an important factor in our victory. It is essential for the troops' morale that we pay them on time. Good morale leads to good fighting spirit and good fighting spirit leads to victory."

Thought John sarcastically, 'So winning the war is down to the payroll department!'

It was hardly the frontline role he had anticipated, but those were being allocated to volunteers ten or more years his junior. It was a job and it would aid the war effort, he agreed. Maybe he should grant it the respect it deserved. More to the point, nothing else was on offer at that juncture. Trying not to show too much disappointment, therefore, he accepted the post.

~ End of Chapter 9 ~

My Keeper's Brother - Chapter 10

John passed almost two years on Space Station 236. Orbiting uninhabited planet Vesta Primus, it was indeed an important hub for the Alliance cause. There were many comings and goings, including planetary dignitaries. The longer-term inhabitants liked to imagine themselves at the beating heart of the war effort.

Being at the beating heart of the payroll effort was not as glamorous, but he kept reminding himself that even the biggest machine contained vital little cogs. He tried to console himself with these thoughts.

Heavily automated, his accounts department was an extremely small one. Three people worked under him, two of them women. Talia Sanz, a young, emotional programmer, sported long dark-ginger hair and a wide mouth. India Garcia, darker skinned with big, frizzy hair, was her tormentor.

On one occasion, John called India into the interview room for a telling off. Across the table, he said. "Talia sat in here with me earlier. You made her cry with your unkind comments!"

"I never made her cry!"

"Yes, you did. Look," he said, pointing at the drops of water on the table as evidence, "those are her tears!"

Looking back, it seemed an absurd episode, adding to John's frustration.

Then there was Michael Long, young, handsome and shy. All the women in Space Station 236 liked him. He was not so keen on them. All John cared about was running an efficient department. In fact, it ran smoothly most days and there were few errors and complaints.

Life on board was tolerable. The food at the canteen being better than tolerable, in fact. The good quality of the fare was due to the important personnel passing through. John enjoyed attending the gym most days. It kept him fit and the room had a small, external, filtered window with a view of the planet's sun. Inside, it boasted a sophisticated artificial lighting system with a full spectrum range. This mitigated against vitamin D deficiency. Besides, prolonged life in domes, ships, or space stations could make one yearn to stand outside in the open and soak up a sun's rays.

Leave being rare in wartime, John appreciated an opportunity, before New Year 2599, to visit the planet Voniz for a fortnight. It was open, all right, but a salty sea covered most of the planet. A single island towered out of the Great Ocean. Life there was pleasant enough. He enjoyed his stay, relishing the open sky above him. John learned his brother had visited the same world a matter of weeks before. Frank, having given up on Eden, was making his own way outwards from the centre of the galaxy.

Meanwhile, the war raged on, a conflict on a scale unseen for generations, involving multiple solar systems and regions. The fighting was fierce, not to say fanatical, with entire worlds de-populated. While rumours persisted, no confirmed reports existed regarding the use of battle robots. Observers, though, could see the Alliance gaining the upper hand. They had wiped out most of the rebels' early successes once the allies got their act together. Now their forces, superior in every way, were making their way to the enemy's heartlands.

"It's taken long enough!" one local said to John.

"Yes, but the end's in sight. I wished to see action before it ends, but I don't think that's going to happen."

Back on the space station, his boss invited him to a special luncheon. He was told that a VIP, a General Lebouran, would be attending. It pleased John to say yes, because it would be the best cuisine.

The visiting dignitary stared at John as he entered the dining room with a gaggle of other officers.

"Hello!" the general cried, "how wonderful to see you."

"Erik? My goodness! So you're General Lebouran."

"The same. I didn't know you're stationed here."

The general insisted that his friend from a couple of years back sat next to him. There was an instant reshuffle of personnel. As the meal began, Erik was excited to hear the other's news.

John concluded, "Although I'm assured my role is most helpful to the war effort, I'd rather have seen some action."

Not trying the patronise him, Erik said that he understood. Then, when prompted, he told his own story.

"I got the captain's badge..."

"Oh, good."

"... a week before the Halma Sector joined the Alliance. We sent our new fleet, accompanied by the Typhons of all people, to stem the tide of the rebel advance. Our task force became involved in a major engagement soon afterwards. We had lots of good fortune. The gods smiled down on us and we found ourselves in the right place. Anyway, we scored a major victory and lost only one juggernaut."

"Not the *Astoria*, I hope."

"No, the *Montpelier*. They did not critically damage her in the battle. She struck a mine on the way home and that began a chain reaction. A skeleton crew had stayed on board. Anyway, we..."

"Did they give the engagement a name?"

"I believe so."

An aide jumped in, saying, "The general is being modest. It was the Battle of the Argon Nebula."

"I've heard of it," said John. Well, he might; it being the allies' first victory of the war and a major one. The rebels gained no more planets after that.

Erik continued, "I then moved on to captain a juggernaut for a short time. More recently, they invited me on to the Allies General Staff where I am now."

His friend gave him enthusiastic congratulations for what was a meteoric rise over the past few years. The general noticed most of the table waiting on him and John. Most sat with empty plates, but the pair were so busy catching up that they had barely begun! They corrected that by digging in and letting the others do the talking.

The visitor was not staying on the space station and, following the meal, John said goodbye. The last thing Erik said was, "And your minor problem, leave it with me."

Not feeling like returning to the office again that day, John excused himself. That was one perk of being in charge of his department. He went back to his cabin. It felt good to lie there and re-live in his mind the most enjoyable couple of hours he had experienced on Space Station 236.

A couple of routine days in the office followed. India was being nice to Talia for a change and they achieved all their targets.

"Sir," called Michael, "I've been investigating this woman's complaint."

"Yes?"

"It's for back pay."

"Go on."

"She said that she should have received an extra allowance whilst serving on a destroyer out of Columbus."

"And?"

"I've contacted the base, but the officer I need to speak to never seems to be available."

"Try them again; if they're still not responding, then go to their superior officer."

"Yes, sir."

John thought, 'It'll please me when that young man takes on a bit more initiative.'

Just then, a woman entered. He recognised her as one of Admiral Xian Wenjing's aides.

"Can I help you?"

"Lieutenant Thorn, the admiral would like to speak with you... now."

He left straightaway.

'I wonder what the problem is,' he immediately thought. 'That obnoxious captain complained the other day. I wonder if he's kicked up a fuss...'

He saluted as he entered the admiral's room.

"At ease, John. The war situation is improving, but that doesn't mean we should ease the pressure. In view of this, and your previous experience, you are being transferred to the 435th Fighter Wing based out of Dolos."

With a puzzled look, John asked, "To do their salaries, sir?"

"Goodness no! You have flying experience, don't you?"

"Yes, sir."

"Your file says you have. Following familiarisation training, you will pilot one of the new manned vimanas. I cannot give you precise details, but Dolos is a mere two systems up from Tangeot."

They spoke further. John would leave straightaway for his new role. The strike against the rebel home world was imminent and he needed briefing.

Within a week, he sat in a state-of-the-art manual vimana in a hangar-dome on Delos. John could not believe the speed at which his life had changed. From what he considered being a dead-end desk job to a frontline fighter pilot, it seemed too good to be true. Maybe he should have held a more balanced view. For every fighter pilot, there existed a hundred and fifty personnel doing a host of occupations such as cooks, engineers, manufacturers, accountants, technicians, strategists - oh, and payroll clerks - to ensure the pilots could function properly. Having no consideration of this truth, he was living the dream. For wartime meant extraordinary things happening, but he felt certain who was behind this dramatic change in fortunes.

"Thank you, Erik!" he said out loud in his room whilst sitting alone. With the move came a promotion to Senior Lieutenant in the Alliance force.

Most of the previous day, he undertook regular training with the new spacecraft. Automated fighting machines needed to be so, for no human could compute the data quickly enough for the incredible speeds involved in space. A few manned craft existed for command and control purposes.

Well motivated, John threw himself into the intense training. His teachers were most impressed at how quickly their latest pupil got the hang of it.

He needed to, because a mighty fleet was being assembled. Although not announced, the target was surely Tangeot. The same planet had been the cradle of the revolt and possessed huge symbolic significance. If Tangeot fell, it would be the beginning of the end for the Confederation.

John had little time to acquaint himself with the other members of the 435th Fighter Wing. He was relieved when cleared for operations by his tutors in time for the big show.

The First and Fourth Alliance Air Fleets combined to make a concentrated strike force the scale of which the galaxy had not seen for centuries. Destroyers, juggernauts and many support ships, it was a powerful armada. Being stationed close by, John's unit would not fly from a mother ship, but go directly from Delos.

They gave a detailed briefing the evening before. Command confirmed early on the open secret that Tangeot was the target. Their unit would not be involved in the first wave of attacks against enemy space mines, flight bases and command and control centres. Once these were neutralised, the Alliance would send a final ultimatum to the planet. If they did not meet the demand for unconditional surrender, a bombardment would begin. John's task was with those screening the attack monitors. They would have to eradicate threats coming from the surface and stop any rebels escaping.

The fleet was already heading to the target when the Delos fighter wing launched. In fact, the initial pin-point strikes had ceased by the time John's vimana, call sign 1147A, took up synchronised orbit over Tangeot. Looking around him, he saw an entire sky full of warships, big and small. Destroyers, electromagnetic jamming corvettes, the mighty juggernauts and, near John, a squadron of attack monitors. These last were platforms for launching nukes against planetoid targets. Prior to the current conflict, they had used none in a long time. In this third year of the war, however, the gloves were off. The rebels could expect no quarter if unconditional surrender was not forthcoming.

Around all the capital ships, waves of unmanned vimanas patrolled. They must protect the fleet. John controlled over a dozen of these. Although automated, he could override that and redirect them from his controls. He sat in his cockpit and awaited developments. It was not a long wait.

"Bombardment will now commence," came the terse announcement over his radio.

Almost immediately, a series of flashes came from the attack monitors on either side of him as they released nuclear warheads. These hurled down onto the sphere below like an ancient god releasing his thunderbolts. They designed some of these projectiles to burrow deep into the planet's core before detonating. The attackers knew Tangeot employed underground industrial plants.

With little cloud cover, the observers could see the massive explosions from orbit. John looked on, somewhat detached. After all, it did not seem real from this distance. It was best not to dwell on events on the surface. Besides, he had a job to do.

Talking of which, as the planet's surface became more and more obscured by nuclear mushroom clouds, a couple of missiles came up towards the firing platforms, but the vimanas soon dealt with those.

Then a unfamiliar object appeared from the same direction. His ship contained sophisticated scanning equipment. This marked the object out as an unarmed shuttle crammed with people, heading in his direction. John neutralised the vimanas under his command. He then sent a direction to the shuttle to come alongside his ship.

This operation was still progressing when he received a transmission from the nearest juggernaut. "This is Captain Zarif of the *Excalibur*, you are to destroy that enemy ship!"

John froze in his seat. 'Was he talking to me?'

He was.

"Vimana 1147A, I am ordering you to destroy that enemy ship immediately!"

A juggernaut captain well outranked a senior lieutenant, even if from a different command chain. To disobey a direct order was a serious offence. Yet to destroy an unarmed ship full of human beings was beyond all humanity. He sized up the situation.

The juggernaut in question could not destroy the Tangeot craft itself, because an attack monitor stood in the way and his vimanas controlled the relevant section of space. Within a few seconds, he decided.

Switching channels, he called his direct commanding officer and requested permission to escort the unarmed Tangeot shuttle back to base. The commander, unaware of the other captain's order, granted permission and dispatched a reserve, manned vimana, to take John's place in the line.

Not replying to Captain Zarif, he pulled away with the shuttle and, together, they made their way to the base on Delos. It all took place faster than the juggernaut captain could respond. Besides, his hands were soon full with other issues.

"When the history of this conflict comes to be written, they will refer to Tangeot's destruction as a key event. You can tell your children that you were there! We are sounding the death knell of the rebellion. It is a key victory and your contribution has been invaluable."

The speaker was John's commander a couple of days after the engagement. It delighted the leader that they had reduced an inhabited planet to a nuclear wasteland. Of more immediate concern to John was his superior's response to his actions during the battle. He learned that Captain Zarif put in an immediate complaint following the victory, but the man in charge of the fighter wing dismissed this.

"You did well not to follow such a barbaric, illegitimate order."

The shuttle turned out to contain top Confederation officials and their families. Whilst showing clemency to the latter, the former leaders of the rebellion would make excellent viewing for the show trials to come.

With the Tangeot action, and others elsewhere around the same time, large-scale resistance by the rebels ended. The year almost spent, the single question on people's lips was whether the war would be over before the twenty-seventh century began.

The last free rebel units now converged on the planet Rakass-Hist in the Sub-Sierra Region. An anomalous area of space subject to strange gravitational and other forces, it affected most modern equipment. There, on the planet's surface, pulse rifles and other energy weapons did not function. Neither did electronics, anti-grav units and a host of other types of equipment. The remaining fanatical rebels set up defensive positions on Rakass-Hist to make a last stand. Over a year had passed since fighting began on the planet. Now, however, the final remaining rebel forces fled there, strengthening their presence. The Alliance needed to respond. They could not leave this last enemy stronghold unbroken. Bombardment from space was not an option, because the desperate defenders had taken important hostages. It would have to be stormed using infantry with old-fashioned guns and bullets. A large invasion force was needed to reinforce the Alliance troops already present.

Some worlds were already winding down their forces and not contributing to this final effort. They acted as if the war had concluded, but fighting continued in this area. Alliance command were experiencing difficulty in assembling sufficient forces to see the conflict to its conclusion. The soldiers on the planet called themselves The Forgotten Army. Their commanders were grateful for the trickle of volunteers still coming forward for the cause, seeing it to the end.

John never held any doubts. He volunteered and, retaining his senior lieutenant's rank, they put him in charge of a platoon, the 968th Rifle Group. These soldiers had, in fact, been together several weeks already. He was taking over after they recalled the previous lieutenant home when her husband became ill. There, within one of the large domes, he met the soldiers under his command.

Prior to going into combat, the authorities stationed them on large asteroid 741998BQ. This planetoid was located on the edge of the

183

Sub-Sierra Region, or "Chaos Zone" as it was known. He took instantly to his number two, Sergeant Peter Ongogo. A tall man with dark chocolate skin, he possessed a ready smile which displayed a set of bright, white teeth. This NCO's apparent easy form of leadership could have fooled the casual observer. He was, in fact, a stickler for the rules, but displayed a non-confrontational style of command. John realised the platoon were devoted to their sergeant and would follow him to the ends of the galaxy.

Corporal Ian Bradman made a formidable sight with his bull neck, small mouth and cropped hair. He, too, could be relied upon to keep the troops in order.

The unit had its share of characters. Della-Mura must have possessed a Christian name, but he was only ever called by his surname. A handsome, cheeky young man, he wore a non-regulation black chequered scarf round his neck the entire time. No one minded this breaching regulations, so John decided that neither would he.

"No fear," was his declared personal motto. Events would judge the truth of this slogan. One thing certain was that Della-Mura loved telling stories about his experiences in twenty-four years of existence. The trouble being he had a limited repertoire and repeated the same stories several times. His colleagues joked about this, shouting out, "Heard it before!" when he began a tale, regardless of whether they had. This formed part of the general banter enjoyed by the platoon. John hoped they would all live to hear some fresh tales by the end of this operation.

Liu Lou was the sole female member of the platoon. A sniper by trade, she kept to herself and preferred reading gun manuals in her spare time to human intercourse.

In an early conversation, John mentioned he had taken leave on the planet Vonis. One of his troopers was a native of that world. Nicalino Robles was a tiny fellow, but robust. His dark bushy eyebrows contained almost as much hair as his close-shaven head. He was a popular member of the team. Relaxed in his lieutenant's presence, he talked about his childhood.

"My parents brought me up in a cult on Vonis. The People of the Silver Cord. I take it you visited the reservation during your stay?"

"Um, no, I can't say I did. Someone mentioned it to me, but my time there was limited and I never got round to it."

"A good thing. Our culture was supposed to be protected, but it came at the price of allowing visitors to come and gawp at us. They lacked respect; whole families came to point at us and giggle."

"That's not nice."

"Hmm. Anyway, as I became a teenager, I questioned the core beliefs of my parents and those in the group. You don't realise how daft they are when you're indoctrinated your entire childhood. But I held my doubts inside until I made the mistake of confiding in a friend. Before I knew it, I was sitting in the middle of the Council of Elders with a score of disapproving faces staring at me. You wouldn't believe the pressure you feel under, unless you'd been in my shoes. I almost broke... but they didn't know that I kept a flame of rebellion burning deep within me."

"What did you do?"

"I ran away. They'd have brought me back, kicking and screaming, if they'd caught me. An artist named Paddy took me in. Very kind to me, he taught me a lot about the outside world - de-programming me, if you like."

"That's kind."

"Yeah, but his paintings were shit!"

Both men laughed before Nicalino said, "But he was an effective con artist and sold his crappy wares for exorbitant amounts to unsuspecting tourists. You didn't buy one, I hope, sir."

"Ha ha, no, I didn't."

"But he was kind to me and paid for my flight off planet... and I travelled here."

Rocket-powered transport and "old-fashioned" guns with bullets were the order of the day on Rakass-Hist. Recently, they had built a small arms range on the asteroid for weapons familiarisation and training. A hastily-constructed concrete bunker, it contained several firing aisles. The platoon spent time trying out an assortment of weapons. The instructors gave them a mere week-and-a-half on firearms familiarisation. It was an intensive course, but they were a dedicated bunch and took it most seriously. They needed to, for their lives may have to depend on having to strip their weapons down, clear a blockage and reassemble it all in the pitch black.

In shooting practice, John quite fancied himself, having used firearms before. In the event, the platoon leader made a decent showing. He wondered quite how old some of the equipment they tried out were, some of them veritable antiques. Yet they were still effective fighting weapons and not to be despised. He got a tight cluster with a .22 hand gun and again with a 9mm revolver. When he shot a .5 hand gun, he tried rapid fire and found his accuracy drop considerably. Bringing the target up close, though, the large holes the weapon made looked much bigger than the previous ones he fired. 'I wouldn't want a hole that size in my body!' he thought.

Whilst shooting, he felt little pin pricks on his face. It took a while for him to find the cause. Tiny flakes of concrete were flying off from the neighbouring aisles and ricocheting back to him. He decided not to say anything.

Later, there was a session on a rifle range. They commandeered a tunnel between domes for this. That way, they could fire a greater distance. It pleased John that he achieved a score of 78%. Then he heard that Liu Lau had got 100%, the perfect score. Planet-side, she would have a rifle with a telescopic sight.

"I'm glad she's on our side!" Peter commented.

The evening before they were due to fly out, John seized an opportunity to have a pleasant chat with his sergeant. The platoon were enjoying a raucous, but good natured time at the bar whilst these two older men stood by an observation window. In the background, the vid screen played a news item, saying the last enemy remnants would have to surrender. No one was paying it any attention.

Artificial lights from the facility illuminated a foreground view of light grey rocks and craters. This made it difficult to see the sky, although one or two brighter stars still showed. They knew that Rakass-Hist was close, both in terms of distance and time.

"They're having a torrid time down there, I hear," said Peter.

"Is that so?"

"Yes. I have a cousin in the 222nd which needed to be withdrawn from the line following heavy casualties. That was in the northern front, where we're heading. He didn't paint a pretty picture: boggy terrain and permanent fog, damp and cold. Plus faced with a fanatical enemy with their backs against the wall. We're going to have our work cut out."

Exhaling some air at the sound of this, John said, "We're supposed to be getting a final briefing regarding conditions before we leave

186

tomorrow. I suspect their assessment might be more upbeat. They're the vibrations I've been getting from the senior officers. From the number of hospital ships passing through here, though, they're not having a picnic."

"You have a good team under you, sir, they won't let you down."

"I'm sure you're right, sergeant. Plus, this is a cause I believe in. If we'd allowed the rebels to get away with it, civilisation as we know it..."

He allowed his voice to trail off. It did not need saying. If the age-old protocols on robots and genetics broke down, then it would threaten society's core. Some lines should not be crossed.

The sergeant said, "I'm sure there's no lack of motivation amongst our crew, sir. The rebels have shown themselves an evil bunch. Those Charkons annihilated whole populations early on before we stopped them. I know it's not on the same scale as the Second War, for..."

"I know what you mean." The officer then mentioned conditions on the surface. "I understand it's a bit of a mixed bag on both sides down there, soldiers from many worlds. It can't make it easy for command and control."

"It would be wonderful if we could sit up here and watch them nuke the place, like they did Tangeot. Serve the bastards right!"

John kept quiet about the fact he was present at that engagement. Instead, he replied, "But you know why we can't?"

"The hostages."

"Yes, we don't know how many they have taken, but VIPs from a dozen worlds are being held according to our best intelligence. No way of telling where."

"Or whether they're still alive."

"We're working on the assumption they are."

"Of course," Ongogo concurred.

John said, "Not long to wait now. Tomorrow we go down to the surface. We're told that the gravity is Earth standard and there's a breathable atmosphere, but they're about the only normal things in the Chaos Zone."

"What about inertia negators, sir?"

"Nope. It'll be a bumpy ride!"

"I can't wait to get on with it. The platoon is ready; at the height of readiness, in fact."

"You're right. I want to get on with it."

Strapped in for the journey, clutching the sick bags provided, the warriors lined both sides of the fuselage of the rocket taking them to Rakass-Hist. The earlier banter had ceased. Trying not to show their nerves, they now sat, waiting for the engines to start up. The seats faced the direction they would be travelling. They etched a measured stoicism on their faces. Outside the artificial gravity platform, they were weightless and the technicians tied everything down.

Della-Mura's voice cut through the air with, "Did I ever tell you the story...?"

"Yes!" at least three of them chorused and he fell silent again.

John shifted his position. This was a fresh experience for them all. Command had issued each of them with an old analogue watch. John glanced at his. At their destination, other types were unserviceable. He began musing about how the rebels picked the ideal place for a last stand. Conditions in the Sub-Sierra Region negated much of the Alliance's superior firepower at a stroke. Unfortunately, this remnant needed weeding out, but they must do it to bring the war to a conclusion.

A brief announcement from the ship's captain cut his thoughts short to tell them they were about to take off. A small craft by the standards of the day, it held space to transport one platoon and their equipment. Amongst the latter was a heavy piece that Liu Lau was getting Della-Mura to carry for her. John did not understand what it was, but believed it to be an aid for her sniper's role.

A tremendous roar shook the entire structure. It was more than a little disconcerting. Corporal Bradman shouted, "I wonder where they dug this old rust-bucket out of!" but they lost his words in the general din.

The shaking increased before they felt the transport take off. The escape velocity from the asteroid was minimal, but it pressed them into their seats for what seemed an age as the rocket accelerated. Once they achieved the required speed, the engines turned off and the ship continued through the void.

A quick hop by conventional ship, this antique would take eighteen hours to arrive at the planet. John glanced across at Nicalino using his sick bag. He would have sworn the man's pale face had a green pallor.

At least the noise and the shaking stopped. John gritted his teeth and waited for it all to be over. Before he knew it, he had fallen asleep.

"This is your captain speaking. Brace yourself for deceleration."

Another ordeal of buffeting ensued before the rocket came in to land. An excellent landing by twenty-second century standards, for people used to twenty-sixth century technology, it was a horrible ordeal. The craft settled and the platoon took a collective sigh of relief.

Della-Mura let off a row of expletives. The rest of them felt the same. They sat in a dazed state when a loud "hiss" announced that the external door was opening. A head poked in and a crew member said, "Come on you lazy lot, we've got a tight schedule!"

Unharnessing themselves, the soldiers released their stiff bodies and stood up. They assembled outside. Those who had not used their bottles relieved themselves behind some nearby bushes. Others stretched their limbs.

"Shall I call them to order?" asked Sergeant Ongogo.

"Let's give them a few moments more," John said. It would make little difference and they were all shell-shocked after their journey.

It was impossible to see the landscape as they stood on the landing strip's damp, grassy verge, in a thick fog. In the immediate vicinity were gorse bushes, dark green with small, bright yellow flowers. It was a welcome splash of colour in an otherwise grey scene.

"Lieutenant Thorn?"

John spun round and, there before him, was the liaison officer, another senior lieutenant.

"My name's Cavendish, I'm to take you to the base."

They shook hands while the sergeant fell the platoon in. Off they marched the two kilometres to the local Alliance HQ. The route took them along a sunken lane and, with the swirling mist, they could not see beyond the verges.

When they arrived, the only buildings in sight were a few wooden huts. A city could have laid beyond for all they knew. They heard little. As well as debilitating their sight, the fog had a strange quality of dampening sound.

Morale surged when the platoon found a buffet meal awaiting them. John and the sergeant left them to it, going next door for a briefing. They ate sandwiches as they stood over a map of the area. Cavendish was apologetic.

"I'm sorry for the one-man reception party, but there's something afoot at present. All hands on deck, if you know what I mean. I can explain things to you."

That he did, with the aid of the large-scale map. The new arrivals were dismayed when they learned the current situation in this sector. Stalemate, with trench warfare, was the order of the day. The Alliance for weeks had made precious little progress. There was a manpower shortage because of some Alliance worlds withdrawing their forces. The commanders on the ground complained about shortages of both personnel and equipment. Far from the rebel forces being hopelessly outnumbered as expected, local intelligence estimated there was one for every two Alliance soldiers.

"That's not enough for effective offensive operations in such conditions. The frontline troops are getting used to stalemate, not wanting to take the initiative."

"I hardly think my platoon's going to shift the balance."

"Maybe not, but every contribution is welcome. Earlier this week, we received a sizeable force from New Galway, plus a contingent from Columbus. The former are well-stocked with artillery. So we're going ahead with the offensive tomorrow. It'll be a big push."

"We've arrived nicely in time," the sergeant said with a note of irony.

Staying serious, Cavendish responded, "You'll be heading up to the support trench in the morning, but you won't be in the first two waves. You're with the back-up troops exploiting the breakthrough."

'Always assuming there'll be a breakthrough,' thought John. With his knowledge of military history, it all sounded rather familiar and a little overconfident. He asked, "Do we know the state of the rebels on this front? Command had led us to believe they were on their last legs."

"Don't underestimate a cornered snake, isn't that what they say? From deserters, we've heard vague stories of rebel factories behind the lines producing wonder weapons. We don't know the truth of it, but the sooner the show is over, the sooner we go home."

"Wonder weapons? I thought no advanced weaponry was supposed to work."

190

"You're right, it doesn't. The reports are vague, like I said, but we mustn't take any chances."

"I see... and when do you expect the fog to lift?"

"Never."

"Really?"

"It hangs around during the day, some nights are clear. By day, it's unusual to see two-hundred-and-fifty metres. More often, it's a hundred metres, or even less. Mustn't keep sentries on duty for long periods or they begin seeing ghosts."

"Ghosts?"

"Concentrating for a long time produces imaginary shapes. We've suffered casualties from our own side in the confusion."

"And electronic communications don't work here, correct?"

"That's right. Those things are useless..." he pointed to their wrist computers. "... and we end up relying on runners to get messages through. Most unsatisfactory."

"You been long here on Rakass-Hist?"

"Um... must be eight weeks now. Seems more like eight years."

"And is it always this damp?"

"Yes. Socks need changing every day. Sometimes the trenches flood..." the liaison officer then corrected himself. "... the trenches flood and we have to watch out for trench foot."

If the man was trying to sell Rakass-Hist as a holiday destination, then he was failing. The newcomers pressed him for more details about the enemy.

"A mixed bag... a bit like our own forces in that respect. Some from Tangeot, others from other worlds. We're facing a fanatical enemy here who more often than not will die rather than surrender. They haven't got half the heavy weapons that we have, but are masters of infiltration and camouflage. You think you've overrun an area and then they pop up from holes in the ground behind you!"

"Thanks for the warning."

"I don't think there's any doubt that they're short of both heavy weapons and ammunition. But this place is an enormous leveller and, hunkered down in their trenches and dugouts, they'll still cause us headaches."

"But we'll win in the end!" John declared.

"Yes, of course," said Cavendish with his first smile since he greeted them on the airfield. "We have assigned support units and everything is in place for the push."

The briefing took time and they discussed the fine detail of the coming operation and the platoon's role. In a nutshell, they hoped this major effort would result in a breakthrough into open countryside and the taking out of whatever facilities the enemy possessed there. If they were going to taste victory before year's end, the Alliance would need to get going.

Once the session concluded, John noticed a print of a spaceship on the otherwise bare wooden wall. He said, "A 1st I.W. ship isn't it?"

"It is," said Cavendish, pleased at someone other than himself taking an interest in it.

Moving closer, John said, "Looks like a Napoleon class battle cruiser."

"Bravo! You know your stuff."

It was a welcome lighter moment and the pair discussed their mutual interest for a couple of minutes. Then the present reality beckoned and they dragged themselves back to it.

"Over the top at 2300 hours tonight; you'll be having to get a move-on soon. I shall provide you with a guide."

They would not spare the platoon any further familiarisation time. It was up the line straightaway.

Next morning, John woke up in a dugout in a trench, the third one back in an elaborate defence system. The commanders had postponed the previous night's offensive a day. The actual rotation time on this planet was twenty-four-and-a-quarter Earth Standard hours, akin to the mother planet's. They should spend a day in the line before seeing action.

The smell of cooking lured him up the wooden steps and out, into the trench. He found his unit lined up and getting their breakfast. Many of them were wearing the latest headgear issued the night before. The helmets gave a measure of protection against bullets and shell splinters. They were far lighter than the steel helmets of old.

"I was about to bring yours down to you, sir," said trooper Chin, assigned to look after the officer's needs.

"That's okay, I'll eat up here," he replied and sat down beside Sergeant Ongogo.

The sky looked a lot brighter than when they landed and the morning mist allowed visibility to two-hundred metres. The mood was relaxed. Two trenches ahead of them meant they did not have to worry about immediate contact with the enemy. John joined the sentry looking out at the landscape ahead. It was a muddy mess with little greenery. In front of the trench stood a long row of pointed wooden stakes angled towards the enemy. He doubted they would stop anything, but they looked good.

Climbing back down, Della-Mura asked him, "So, what's happening, sir?"

"No change in our orders. When we launch the attack, our platoon moves up to the first trench and hold it. That'll be this evening. It could be a long night. Try to get some rest and..."

He cut off because of some large detonations close by. Further explosions went off further away down the line.

"Nothing to worry about, a few stray shots."

The fresh voice belonged to an unfamiliar figure who joined them. An officer of the same rank as John, who stepped forward to greet him.

"You must be Lieutenant Thorn."

"That's right."

"I'm Lieutenant Thanapol Jaturanrasamee..." When he saw the other's face drop, he added with a smile, "But I'm known as Than."

"Than it is," a relieved John said and shook his hand.

"I'm your familiarisation officer. I'm sorry I couldn't be here when you arrived; a bit of a mix-up. There's a lot happening currently."

"That's okay. We're settling in, as you can see."

Than scanned the fresh platoon. Most had finished eating by now and some were drinking hot beverages.

"I'm sorry to break up the party, but I'm to take you up the line."

"So soon? I thought that was for later."

"It was; change of plan. Anyway, it's up to the second line, not the first trench. Before we set off, a few words of warning. There's a hundred metres between the first and second lines. The rebels' frontline trench is another hundred metres on."

"Got it."

"Which means on a fine day like today, you'll be able to see the enemy front line."

"Good."

"Only it's best that you don't."

"Oh?"

"They employ a lot of snipers and they can pin-point anyone foolish enough to stick their head above the parapet."

Addressing his unit, John called out, "I hope you're taking this all in!"

"Yes, sir!" they chorused.

Than said, "We've a damn shortage of periscopes at present; they keep getting knocked off. Best to keep your heads down. You won't be there long... unless things change of course."

With this wise advice ringing in their ears, the platoon packed up all their equipment and made their way along the zigzagging communication trench to their new temporary home: Trench B. With his troops settling in to their new surroundings, and to a background of occasional shell-bursts in the far distance, John asked Than, "Have you got to dash off now?"

"No, I'll be with you for a few hours."

"Good. I need to learn more. Learn fast."

"That's wise. Oh, I should have said: welcome to Hades!"

John took a while to survey their fresh surroundings. A wider, deeper and better constructed trench than the one they had vacated. The firing step stood unoccupied at present. He could just identify the tips of another row of pointed wooden stakes at the top of the trench. Duck-boards lined the bottom. Standing water lay under there, but overall conditions were not too bad. Against the wall away from the enemy sat a low shelf with... a couple of dead bodies lying on it.

"Oh, I'm sorry about those," Than began, "they should have disposed of them, or at the very least covered them up."

Even as he spoke, stretcher bearers came to remove the offending objects.

"Sorry about that," the familiarisation officer said, annoyed that this had happened. It was not the best introduction for the new platoon. As the bearers took the corpses away, John noticed the unnatural pallor of their faces. As if reading his mind, the other officer remarked, "They turn that colour soon after death. I..."

"How?"

"Sniper."

"I see. I guess that'll be a wake-up call to us all."

Later that morning, Than joined them for lunch. It pleased John to have him stay longer, because he wanted to pump him for more information. In answer to one of his questions, Than said, "Next in line is an irregular army unit They're a rag-tag group of volunteers who hate rebels and want to get at them."

"Really? Where are they from?"

"All over, I gather. They're a bit of a law unto themselves and my advice is keep well away. Their commander is a real psycho. The tale goes he found a sentry asleep on duty one night. He shot him dead where he lay."

"My goodness!"

"Still, on the plus side, they have no more sentries falling asleep."

"I guess not."

At that point, Liu Lou came up; John broke away to see to her.

"Permission to set up my cupola, sir."

"Go ahead."

Initially, he was unsure about this heavy piece of equipment Della-Mura carried for her. It turned out to be a protective hood for placing on the lip of the trench to provide protection while she operated her rifle. At sniper school, they taught her that a good proponent should move location after each shot. Nevertheless, she wanted to give this gadget a try. It offered a good protection. John hoped it worked. Either way it gave her something to do. Than was speaking again.

"If tomorrow you capture one or two prisoners, that would be helpful. Few are taken."

"I was told they are fanatics."

"Hmm, that, plus a lot of shooting prisoners under the excuse of them trying to escape. Not a lot of love lost, I'm afraid."

"I guess not; they're enemies after all."

"This war is different," the man said. "There's a lack of respect... I don't like it. I've witnessed a lot of horrors down here; friends I've known dropping dead beside you. You get de-sensitised after a while."

John noticed that Than's hands shook. Then, becoming up-beat, Than said, "Anyway, good luck. I must return. You know your orders. I hope to see you again once this little show is concluded."

As he spoke, a salvo of shells landed further up the line. The allied batteries replied with a few shots of their own. They were keeping most of their ammunition for that night's bombardment. Liu Lau sat back with them, busy cleaning her rifle for all it was worth. In the middle-distance to the side, they could hear further troops working their way past them, along the communications trench, to the frontline.

The familiarisation officer left and John considered his orders. The bombardment would begin 2130 hours and creep forward once 2300 hours came and the assault began. He would then move his platoon up to Trench A with orders to hold it against any enemy counterattack should the Allied assault fail. Strangely, there was nothing about following up the first wave. From the plan's wording, John got the impression that, having suffered so many failures in recent weeks, the High Command were not confident of a breakthrough. He hoped that tomorrow's events would be a rare success.

~ End of Chapter 10 ~

My Keeper's Brother - Chapter 11

The day dragged. Desultory artillery fire continued from both sides, with the allies trying to make it appear that everything was normal. No enemy shots landed near John's 968th Rifle Group and that was all he worried about. Most of his troopers heeded the advice to rest. Many opted to stay in the trench rather than huddle in a dugout. John insisted on them wearing their body armour and helmets at all times whilst outside. Liu Lau spent hours on the firing step under the cover of her camouflaged cupola. She hoped for her first kill, but no targets presented themselves that day. After a time, John ordered her down.

As days on Rakass-Hist go, this was a nice one. No sign of the sun, but the morning proved bright enough. The fog was less thick than the day before. As the sun set, Sergeant Ongogo came over to share a warm drink with his lieutenant. They sat on a couple of empty ammunition boxes in the bottom of a trench.

"Not long to go now, sir."

"I hope so, I could do without another postponement. The attack's bound to happen eventually, but if it's put off again, it'll play havoc on the nerves."

"This whole scenario reminds me of World War One in the history books."

"Except there are no aircraft, or tanks, or barbed wire. It's more like the siege of Vicksburg in the American Civil War. They dug trenches similar to these."

"You know your stuff!" said Ongogo and they both chuckled.

It concerned John that the sergeant could see him as showing off, so he apologised, "Just an interest of mine."

"I bow to your superior knowledge," said the sergeant, flashing his whiter than white teeth.

Reinforcements appeared and made their way past towards the front line. There was little intercourse between these units and John's. If there were manpower shortages, they must be pooling resources in this sector.

Darkness fell and time dragged even more. Eventually, the hour approached. The lieutenant told his troops to do their ablutions if they needed to. Then a junior staff officer turned up and his heart sank. Not another postponement?

"You all set, Thorn?"

"We are ready to go."

"That's the spirit! The moment the bombardment lifts, you go down this communication trench to the frontline. You are to hold it at all costs if there's an enemy counterattack."

Instructions given, he hurried off to the next group, no doubt to repeat the same set of words. Then, right on time, the bombardment began.

The platoon was unsure whether the scale and ferocity of the avalanche of projectiles surprised the enemy. It surprised them. Amidst the deafening roar, they made out some individual shells. Different classes of guns made unique sounds and the allies had assembled an awful lot of them. 'I wonder if they raided a few museums,' he thought to himself.

The enemy's batteries started up a counter barrage. They had pre-ranged the Alliance positions and the shells landed far too close for comfort. Ready to move forward any moment, diving into dugouts was not an option. They clung to the earth for all they were worth, wishing the ground would swallow them up. One or two men even adopting the foetal position. Clods of earth rained into the trench and pieces of jagged shrapnel whizzed overhead. John thought afterwards, 'How is it possible to describe how those few minutes felt under fire? The utter terror. Knowing that they could extinguish your life at any moment. An experience like no other. '

The Alliance bombardment continued, but, mercifully for their infantry, the enemy batteries faltered. The occasional "friendly" shot landed short, but none close to John's Rifle Group. After a while, they deduced from the altered tone that the barrage was creeping forward. That meant the assault would begin now. Popping his head above the parapet, he saw a clear nighttime scene. He beheld flashes in the distance, although these did not coordinate with the sound, as the latter took longer to reach them.

By now, little enemy artillery was firing. The allies had either knocked them out, or they were short of ammunition.

"Platoon, fall in!" Sergeant Ongogo bellowed and, even before the batteries had expended their last shells, John led them down the narrow, twisting communications trench. With the clouds parting, a host of stars came out. Some were close and gave enough light to illuminate their way. As a result, they made their destination without a problem and manned the line. In the middle-distance, they heard shouting accompanying gunfire, but it was impossible to tell what was happening. Those sounds ended abruptly.

The rest of the night proved an anti-climax for John's unit. Come dawn, nothing else had happened and all ahead of them was quiet. Sporadic firing recommenced, but it seemed a distance away and soon stopped. John stood half his troops down. He would have liked another visit from an intelligence officer. Meantime, with no fresh orders, they stayed put.

"Sir!"

"Yes, Della-Mura?"

"Permission to get breakfast under way."

"Of course."

John thought he meant to crack open the iron rations they all held, but no. The trooper said there were enough supplies and cooking facilities for a proper meal. He would not ask the whys and wherefores. As the morning sky brightened somewhat, his platoon tucked into a basic, but most welcome, hot meal.

They were still eating when a large infantry unit appeared from the rear. Wearing distinctive uniforms with a dark maroon top, the officer in charge halted briefly to explain to John. "We're the Second Cohort, Third Legion of the Columbus Expeditionary Force. Our orders are to advance to the enemy trench, reinforcing gains made last night."

"Very well, good luck."

The allied soldiers ascended the ladders and began plodding forward over the broken ground. John had a peek and, ascending the firing step next to Liu Lau, looked out. The swirling mist had descended once more and he estimated visibility at a hundred-and-twenty-five metres.

A minute or two passed after the Columbus contingent disappeared into the vapour. Suddenly, a cacophony announced a fresh bombardment from the allied guns. Then the explosions of bursting shells shook the ground.

"What the ****?" screamed Corporal Bradman and they nearly all jumped to their feet.

The shells were landing short, some so close to the old front line that earth and stones fell around them.

"Into the dugouts!" John screamed.

They dashed underground as more shells ripped into the earth.

Della-Mura said, "They *are* ours aren't they?"

"Yes, something's gone..."

He stopped speaking because, as quickly as it started, the shelling stopped. Maybe someone in the artillery realised they had made a terrible mistake. Whatever it was, it fell silent again and John and his sergeant scrambled back up first. With no further shells falling, they ventured a short way over the top.

Then they came. Soldiers of the Columbus contingent running back in dribs and drabs. The first ones they saw had no physical wounds. Having thrown down their weapons, they were fleeing the battlefield. As they got close, John saw the terror in their eyes.

The rest of his command emerged from the dugouts and stood in the trench's bottom as the first Columbus legionaries hurled themselves in amongst them. Without a word, they pushed past to get to the communications trench and disappear down it.

"Let them pass," cried the lieutenant.

"Poor bastards!" was Sergeant Ongogo's verdict.

A brief salvo of their own side's heavy artillery had cut this allied unit to pieces. Soon the injured survivors came staggering back and Corporal Bradman ordered a couple of troopers to get stretcher bearers. Some climbed out of the trench to help the retreating soldiers.

Fewer and fewer appeared out of the fog. Any walking wounded who survived the barrage were back. It was a small, pathetic remnant, John's unit cared for the wounded to the best of their ability.

"Okay," shouted John to his troops still in no-man's land, "come back, you lot. You never know when our idiot artillery will strike again."

As he spoke, some medics arrived. Some hurried into the fog to assist any injured lying out there.

"Heads should roll for this," Ongogo said.

"Hmm," was the only response his officer gave. He had lived long enough to suspect it would be hushed up. Someone in authority should learn about it, though. Still standing in no-man's land, he resolved to write a stiffly-worded account and send a runner to deliver it. Before he climbed back into the trench, he glanced into the mist. As he did so, the most pathetic sight merged from it. A single figure staggered towards them. He was naked.

Without hesitation, John ran across to assist him. As carefully as possible, he helped him back towards Trench A and the attending medics. Burns covered the man and he shook uncontrollably. His eyes stared forward and his teeth chattered. He spoke not a word. In a most strange event, the blast of a shell somehow ripped all his clothes off! John would not have believed it had he not seen it himself. As he got to the lip of the trench, waiting hands stretched up, receiving the casualty. Soon, the medical personnel took the wounded men out of sight.

"Do you think he'll survive, sir?" Della-Mura asked.

"Who knows?"

Soon afterwards, they received orders to advance through no-man's land to what had been the rebels' trench. John hoped they would not share the same fate as the Columbus contingent. He did not send his complaint about the allied artillery before having to move out.

They hurried across the shell-pocked ground in double-quick time. This was no easy feat, travelling through such churned up terrain. Muddy water filled some large shell holes and the advancing soldiers had to avoid them. Dead bodies, old and new, strewed the ground. John noticed one in particular. A Columbus legionary, he lay on his back, his face already turning the grey colour of the dead.

Having reached their immediate destination, they dropped into the former enemy positions, only to find them occupied.

"You can't stay here!" a colonel from another regiment informed him.

"My orders are to come and occupy this trench, sir."

"Hmph! I'm not having you stay here," the stuffy colonel said. "You'll have to move on."

"Move on, sir?"

"Keep going, advance," and he pointed in the direction beyond.

"And do what, sir?"

"I don't care! I want you out of my bloody trench. Go and kill some damn rebels."

Amidst sniggers from the colonel's hangers on, John considered. He could not turn a blind eye to this superior officer's command. He therefore ordered his troops to continue their thrust into... into what? Enemy territory. John presumed the existence of a second line of defence, just as the allies employed three lines.

The whole situation was most unsatisfactory. A lack of orders and coordination was poor. The confounded mist exacerbated things, because it made them feel cut off from events elsewhere.

After leading a short way, John called his unit together. He crouched down, speaking to them there and then. Pleased to be free of the obnoxious colonel, he spoke a little above a whisper.

"We're on a reconnaissance patrol. Keep your eyes peeled and your ears open; there may be an enemy position ahead of us."

They stood up and began moving forward. No sooner than they started when two rebels appeared out of the fog and fired on them. Armed with antique, single-shot rifles, one missed and the other hit the stock of Della-Mura's own gun. Its composite material shattered, but at least he was unhurt.

The platoon returned fire, it being John himself who pumped a group of bullets into the leading rebel. Both assailants fell dead. The engagement happened fast, but it was enough to shake them up. John felt a revulsion at having killed someone at such short range; somehow it differed from when he shot Henio on Grande Verde. It was never easy to predict how one would react in extreme circumstances. He forced himself to pull himself together, but, like the others, could not resist gawping at the bodies. In truth, it was from morbid curiosity, not pity. Pity being a luxury when it was kill, or be killed.

They crept forward, arms at the ready. John peeked at the compass setting of his TRAC, but the arrow had gone crazy, spinning round like a top. Further they went, the constant mist would have made their clothing damp were they not made of advanced material. At least that worked.

If an enemy support trench existed, they would have come across it by now. After a while, the landscape changed. Fewer shell holes here and less muddy. Gorse bushes started springing up, too.

Still, the fog milled around. They stopped and listened, but there was no sound. It was as quiet as the grave. John sent two men on ahead with orders to reconnoitre and then return. They did that while the others huddled together, far closer than they should have. Human nature meant no one wanted to get detached from the group.

Seemingly an age later, the scouts returned, reporting no sign of enemy activity. John had a powwow with the NCOs. He spoke in a whisper, hiding nothing from them.

"We're in shit street. Going back is not an option; we'd probably get shot at by our own side. We don't know what lies ahead. There have been no specific orders. In short, I'm open to suggestions."

"We could..." Corporal Bradman began, "travel at ninety degrees to our trench for a distance before working our way back to the frontline from there."

That suggestion was not taken up. Sergeant Ongogo said, "I'm for pushing further forward and finding a defensive position to hunker down for the night."

"Yes," John said, "but I'd like to put a positive spin on it. We can class it as long-range reconnaissance; see if there are any worthy targets for our army to attack in strength. After all, they must follow up soon. My original orders said we were amongst the force exploiting the breakthrough. But we don't know if we've broken through or not; the enemy has melted away. If only communications here were better; these TRACs are useless."

Ongogo asked, "May I speak plainly, sir?"

"Please do."

"I can't help feeling that this whole op is a complete cock up by our senior commanders."

John chose not to answer the NCO, but the communication and organisation displayed appalled him. The entire operation appeared a shambles and he witnessed fatal results of such incompetence that very day. From his knowledge of military history, he knew that, usually, the side who made the fewest blunders won a war. Brilliant generalship was rare. Not wishing to pass on the example of poor communication, he made sure his platoon knew his plan. They were a self-contained, deep reconnaissance unit spying out the land, preparing for the main force.

Off the group set again. This time, the lieutenant organised their formation. Two troopers out front, flankers either side, all of whom were under orders to stay within sight (about a hundred and fifty metres) of the main body who would advance in two parallel files.

After twenty minutes, those at the front returned, reporting they had sighted two small buildings. He gave orders to surround the structures while a group armed with sub-machine guns and grenades crept forward. A few quiet minutes later, they reported the buildings as empty. Empty of people, that is, the first one contained a stock of food jars. The containers were made of modern composite materials. Sergeant Ongogo insisted on inspecting them before declaring them safe. It was a most welcome find and he charged Corporal Bradman with distributing the cache amongst the troopers.

"A wonderful find, sir!" Ongogo declared.

"Yes indeed. We deserve a break after the sort of day we've experienced. Have they inspected the other building?"

"We've established it's safe, sir."

"Okay, I'll have a look myself."

"Watch out for tripwires, or other booby traps we might have missed, sir."

"Oh... yes. Thanks for the warning."

The second building, like the first, square in construction and single story, appeared derelict. John stepped through the open doorway. To keep his breathing quiet, he kept his mouth open... and got a mouthful of cobwebs. Trying to spit them out silently was not easy. He peered in and saw an inside covered in rubble and burnt timbers from long ago. He gave it up as a poor job and came out again.

"There's nothing in there," he said.

The troopers spent a long time completing their search of the first building. Once they finished foraging, the platoon gathered round their leader and waited for orders.

"I know there's time, but we don't want to stay here tonight. It's too obvious a place and we'd be sitting ducks if an enemy patrol came along. We'll find somewhere else."

No one questioned this order, because it made sense. So they set off once more, going deeper into enemy territory. With the restricted visibility, they needed to be careful not to fall into one of the large craters. Long since grassed over, it was not clear whether these were old shell holes or abandoned mine workings. The usual rubbish that littered the battlefield was absent. No sign of enemy activity.

John said, "Not sure there's any point in moving until it gets dark. Do you think we should stay here tonight?"

Framed as a question, the NCOs were free to give their opinions. Both thought it a good idea. They posted sentries and settled down in a series of hollows amidst more gorse bushes. The fog then got denser and it drizzled.

The troopers unpacked their waterproof groundsheets and ponchos before settling down for a meal. A certain amount of swapping food jars took place before they tucked in. Morale, their lieutenant considered, was holding up well in the circumstances.

Time passed and they finished eating. Some of them chatted, but they kept the noise level low. John, lost in his own thoughts, jumped at the loud clatter of sub-machinegun fire close by. The troopers jumped to their feet and grabbed their weapons in a moment. Their officer dashed to the sentry, who had ceased discharging his weapon.

"I thought I could see some enemy approaching, sir," he explained, breathlessly.

John peered into the swirling fog, but he could see nothing. Corporal Bradman jumped forward and found no one there. He twizzled back and began laying into the sentry for being a complete imbecile for putting their lives at risk for firing at visions formed by the fog. The lieutenant, remembering the advice not to keep the sentries on duty for long periods, cut the tirade short. There was no point being harsh on the poor soldier.

"We'll draw a line under this," he said and, after getting a fresh sentry posted, ordered them all to hold perfect silence for the following half an hour. This time passed without incident and they could breathe more easily again.

As the sun set, the mist drifted away and, with it, the drizzle. It was the most curious weather, with another clear, cool night.

Waking with a jolt, John looked round and saw it was daybreak. Della-Mura stood nearby on sentry duty and the rest of the platoon lay fast asleep. He decided not to lie any longer on that uncomfortable ground and got up. His limbs were stiff and his hands numb with cold. He took a few steps over to the sentry and engaged him in conversation.

"Have you been on duty long?"

"No, sir."

"All quiet, then?"

"Yes, sir. The mist is coming back."

Della-Mura was right. John recognised this moment as his best opportunity to see into the distance. With fog laying thin, the light dawned bright enough. He made note of the sun's position, barely visible though in an overcast sky, as he needed to keep track of it. Going round in circles was a genuine possibility in these conditions. Using his binoculars, he spotted a small river up ahead. Fresh water to fill up their canteens would be a good thing. They could then follow the stream's progress as it meandered further the way he wanted to go. Waking Corporal Bradman, he got him to rouse the others, saying, "Not too much noise, please."

"Right, sir."

The group consumed a light breakfast before John briefed them on his plans for the day ahead. They would march deeper into what he still believed to be enemy territory, doing general reconnaissance and looking for any targets of opportunity. When they picked up their kits, Della-Mura told Liu Lau in no uncertain terms that he would no longer carry her heavy cupola. No one volunteered for this task, so she abandoned the experimental piece of equipment. The group departed, wondering if they detected the distant sound of artillery, behind them to the left. A faint breeze carried the noise away. None was certain what it had been.

That same slight breeze kept much of the fog at bay and they enjoyed the best visibility of any day since they first landed.

It did not prove difficult to reach the river They took to the narrow track running alongside it. A few stunted trees grew along the way, but it was open country. In line with John's plan, they stopped to replenish their water bottles. Operation swiftly accomplished, they set on their way again.

The river flowed in the same direction the troopers were walking. A grassy bank led down to the water's edge. If John had his bearings correct, they were still heading away from the battlefield, deeper into the countryside.

Sergeant Ongogo took his turn leading and, soon afterwards, paused with his arm up indicating, "Alert!" The halt was so sudden that several soldiers bumped into each other, cursing.

"What is it?" John asked.

"Down there, but the waterside."

"Something moving?"

"No," the sergeant replied, leading his officer, plus a couple of others, down the bank. They needed to be careful not to lose their footing, but they all made it safely. The sight that greeted them was not a pretty one.

"Rebels," Ongogo said as he identified the bloated corpses in the water. A bend in the river meant the current depositing them there. Four or five bodies together, they had been dead a few days from the state of them. John's thoughts turned to their having filled up their canteens in the same water, but that had been further upstream and the water fresh.

"Enough," he said watching his footing as he climbed back to the track.

"They were victims of the bombardment," Ongogo speculated once reunited with the others.

"Yeah. We'll move on."

That they did, losing track of the river when the mist got heavier and the vegetation thicker near the bank. They cut out into open countryside and noticed the air was still once again.

On the platoon trudged, experiencing little change the rest of the day. Mid-afternoon, they passed through the site of a battle some weeks previously. Dead bodies still strew that plain; no one had thought to gather them up for burial. Now fast-growing plants grew up straight through the uniformed skeletons. A grizzly sight.

"God, I hate this planet!" exclaimed Della-Mura, adding a few expletive words for emphasis. Mumbles of assent met this. Meanwhile, their leader experienced unpleasant thoughts of his own.

'This is silly! I'm leading us blindly and getting nowhere. We have seen no enemy for a couple of days and we'll soon run out of food.'

As evening fell, they came across a small collection of trees, the tallest specimens encountered on Rakass-Hist to date.

"We'll make camp here," the lieutenant ordered.

He decided that if by midday the following day they had encountered nothing worthwhile, he would march his contingent back to the allied lines. Visions were forming in his mind of this entire enterprise ending in fiasco and him being held accountable. John tried putting such thoughts to the back of his mind and grabbed some vital sleep.

As the day-mist thinned, it was Liu Lau's turn to be on sentry duty. She stuck to her rugged individualism by serving her time up a tree. John saw no reason to object.

Having fallen into a deep sleep, it did not delight him upon being woken up. It was Liu Lau.

"What is it?"

"Lights, sir, and a building, a large one."

Without further hesitation, John got up. He climbed a tree to see for himself what she had spotted. In a swift movement, he got out his binoculars, he was wide-eyes at the sight. A huge, oblong building sat on a flat piece of ground a kilometre from their position. Lights beamed down from the eves while two sentries patrolled on the roof. He got Sergeant Ongogo to come and have a look before they discussed it.

"Some sort of warehouse, do you think, sergeant?"

"Most likely, sir, it could house an ammunition supply."

"Or even manufacture bullets and shells."

"Yes."

Turning to Liu Lau, he commanded, "Wake the others."

"Yes, sir."

Then, asking Della-Mura, he said, "You still got those explosives?"

"Of course, sir, lugged them all the way."

"Good. Now this is what we'll do..."

Three quarters of an hour later, the Allied platoon members were lying the other side of a natural earthen bank from the guarded rebel building. They could hear indeterminate noises coming from inside. Either a shipment was being prepared for the front, or they had stumbled upon a factory on nighttime working.

The observers detected four guards. Besides the pair on the roof, another patrolled the main entrance, well within their sight.

"Liu Lau, can you take out those guards from here?"

"Of course," came the confident reply.

"Okay, but not until I give the order."

He organised two assault groups. One, led by Sergeant Ongogo, would attack the main entrance, while the other, led by Corporal Bradman, approached from the rear. Lieutenant Thorn would remain with a reserve force. They may be small in number, but were resolved to storm the building. Once everyone was clear as to their role, the plan swung into action.

He set the attack for 0100 hours. As the seconds clicked down to that time, he saw Liu Lau stiffen as she prepared to fire.

"Now, sir?"

"Yes."

There was but a faint sound from the rifle, thanks to its silencer. Observing through his binoculars, John saw first one, then the other sentry on the roof drop like stones. The two at the entrance were unaware. Then it was their turn. The second man never flinched, let alone cry out, before he joined his colleague on the floor. The sniper's brutal efficiency was quite something to behold and more than a little sobering. He hoped the enemy did not possess such a beast.

Ongogo's squad leapt forward even as the last sentry fell. They entered the building at full pelt to the noise of automatic fire. A muffled explosion sounded from the other side of the enormous building, then further gunfire before silence fell.

For a few agonising moments, the platoon leader did not know the outcome of the fire fight, then Nicalino's diminutive figure appeared from the main entrance. In the light, and through his binoculars, John could see his smile as the short figure gave the all clear sign with his arms. As he rose, the officer ordered, "Advance!" and the reserves surged forward to see for themselves.

It had been a brief skirmish. The rebels never expected a raid this deep inside their territory and posted only a few guards, those taken out by Liu Lau. The troopers had been a little trigger-happy inside the building, killing most of the personnel they found, although they had taken a handful of prisoners unharmed. It delighted John that they secured the facility without a single casualty. In fact, they received not so much as a scratch.

Target secure, no enemy having escaped, prisoners taken, the lieutenant could not believe his luck. Now they must discern what the rebels were doing here. The victors soon worked it out. When they did, it shook them to the very core.

A fortnight later, it was New Year's Eve. John and all his crew celebrated back on asteroid 741998BQ, enjoying a wild celebration. The revellers were marking the end of the war, the year and, indeed, the century. Celebrating bringing the Third Intergalactic War to a conclusion was premature. Mopping up parties still engaged on

Rakass-Hist and, out in deep space, a few rebel raiders still operated. It seemed picky to point out these details on such a night. Folk simply wanted the year 2600 to be a fresh start.

As soon as they arrived back on the asteroid, they were told their group was being disbanded and its members de-mobbed. No time for sentiment there. Still, Senior Lieutenant Thorn enjoyed the undying gratitude of the troops who served under him. In all their time on Rakass-Hist, he did not lose a single one of them. It was an extraordinary achievement, considering what they accomplished.

It surprised John at the lack of publicity regarding his unit's shattering discovery when they got inside the building they stormed. It turned out to be a factory for battle robots. The rebels were breaking the ultimate taboo, or trying to. The first one was still being completed when they halted the production line.

"Wait until the Inspectorate sees this!" Ongogo had said.

"Would robots have even worked there, sarge?" asked Della-Mura.

John said, "They seemed to use a lot of low-tech, mechanical parts. They were aiming for the scare factor."

Such news should have been a tremendous propaganda coup for the Alliance cause. Yet, following an initial report, all news of it came off air. Why? Maybe, with the war won, it was no longer necessary. Maybe it was too horrific for public consumption. It was the one sour note on an otherwise magnificent achievement for the 968th Rifle Group. They held out there, throwing back several rebel counter-attacks, until the main Allied force arrived. They even made an excursion into the fog to rescue some hostages. It seemed like their amazing deeds were being overlooked.

Yet that was not entirely the case. There, at the party, a wealthy woman of influence was impressed by reports of Senior Lieutenant Thorn's exploits. So impressed she had a job offer to make him.

Meanwhile, Della-Mura had cornered John in the middle of the party, telling him a fresh tale for a change.

"Yeah, we played about in the building site. I know we shouldn't have, but we were only kids. A couple of older boys came along and we started a friendly fight, throwing mud bombs at each other. It was okay until one boy got hit on the head by a stone!"

He paused, for hovering by them (or was it over them?) stood a tall, imposing woman. Mid-50s, by the look of her, her make-up heavily applied, she wore her dyed blond hair piled high. She looked out of place amidst the military personnel, but John, in an excellent mood, did not resent her presence. With a broad smile, he asked, "Can I help you?"

"You're Senior Lieutenant Thorn," she stated in a nasally voice.

"I am."

"May I have a moment of your time?" she said, moving her body in a way to exclude poor Della-Mura from the proceedings.

John addressed the latter, "Excuse us a second; you can tell me what happened later." Then, as the trooper returned to the others, he said, "How can I help you?"

"Have you heard of Plerrania?"

Thinking for a moment before replying, he responded, "I can't say I have. I presume from the title it's a planet."

They moved to the edge of the throng and the loud celebrations.

"It is, in the Selucid Sector."

"That's closer to the hub, right?"

"It is."

"Can I get you a drink?" he said, after noticing she was without one.

Declining with the wave of her hand, she said, "I hear you are quite the hero. The universe needs heroes in these troubled times."

A fan then, not quite what he was expecting. When he struggled how to respond, she ended his confusion by getting to the nub of the matter.

"I have a job offer for you."

Her words coincided with a loud roar of laughter from the party, so he sought clarification. "A job offer?"

"Yes, I hear you are all being disbanded."

"News travels fast!"

"I don't know what plans you have, but we're recruiting members of the personal guard for the ruling house there. The House of Vaxon expects discretion and loyalty; rewarding those who serve them well.

"I'm unsure," John began, "the last time I accepted a job like that, I found myself in the middle of a revolution and was lucky to escape alive!"

"Whilst it's true there are... disruptive factions on Plerrania (which society is free of them?) I do not believe revolution to be at all likely. Emperor Leo is a magnanimous ruler and the vast majority of his subjects adore him."

She then detailed some duties of the job, such as ensuring security at state functions and ceremonies. He would have staff under him and access to the palace. When John mentioned his personal space ship, she assured him she would make provision for him to garage it there. They could avoid the subject of pay no longer, but she impressed him with the scale of remuneration on offer. He hoped it was not in proportion to the level of danger involved.

"And it's an open planet from what you've said," he commented.

"Actually, no, but it boasts the biggest domes in the known universe. They built them years ago," she said, then added, "but the engineers strengthened them last year and protect them with force fields. They are so big that an entire community has its dwellings constructed out of bricks and mortar. The hanging gardens are a wonder to behold too. Often you forget you are not on an open planet."

This last statement sounded pretty absurd, but John took it as mere hyperbole. As he stood on the edge of the party, considering the matter, he said, "I don't think you've given me your name."

"Eloise Caron, confidante of the Empress Madelyn."

"I see. I could try it..." he said.

"How does a four-week probationary period sound? You can see if you like us and vice versa?"

She, of course, meant, "If we think you prove yourself during that period," but it seemed a fair proposal for all concerned. It would be helpful to see if reality matched the lady's sales pitch before committing himself. Then another thought occurred to him.

"Would you mind waiting here a moment while I speak with someone?"

"I don't mind," came the nasally, but amiable reply.

"I'll be quick," he said as he disappeared into the crowd of party revellers.

Five minutes later, he re-appeared with Della-Mura in tow. Madam Caron was still standing there, detached from the celebrations. He presented his colleague to the lady and said, "I accept your kind offer, but with one proviso; that you employ Della-Mura here as one of my staff. I will vouch for his character,"

'Such loyalty to a member of his platoon!' she thought, 'most impressive,' and moments later she hired the retiring trooper as well.

They arranged to leave the following day. The military were hurrying to demob their personnel and the House of Vaxon wanted a swift answer. He learned that Madam Caron's transport was large enough to accommodate John's little runabout in the hold. That was for the morrow. After saying "Au revoir" to their recruiter, the men returned to the party and enjoyed a memorable night.

With the war over, Della-Mura had been wondering about his future. Having spent the last three years fighting for the Allied cause, it delighted him to start a new adventure. It took away uncertainty. Knowing that they would leave the following day, they said protracted goodbyes to the rest of the platoon.

It was interesting to hear what plans they held for the future. Nicalino decided to make peace with his parents and planned returning to Vonis to visit them. "But I sure won't be re-joining that cult!"

Corporal Bradman was also returning to his home planet to work on his farm. "I've earned a quiet life."

Peter Ongogo was uncertain what he was going to do. "I might try to join an army unit elsewhere, although I guess now that the war is over there'll be limited opportunities."

Patrick Chin was another one whose future looked uncertain. "I don't have to decide straightaway I've got enough money to take it easy for a while before making my decision."

Liu Lau was trying to get ahead of the game. Her parents had already set her up with a video interview at a food processing factory. "The manageress asked me what skills I possessed. I told her I could take someone out with a sniper's rifle at two kilometres. That seemed to halt the conversation in its tracks. Still, with my parents' influence I'm sure they'll offer me the job, anyway."

For John it was all a bitter-sweet experience. He built such a rapport with these people during the past weeks, it felt like he had known them years. It seemed a shame to break up such an efficient and well-balanced team. Yet, the fact they were being disbanded was good news. It meant an end to the war and all the suffering it entailed. That evening, everyone hoped the twenty-seventh century would be less bloody than the twenty-sixth, although he doubted it.

He received another piece of good news, learning that his brother, Frank, was on the planet Gan. It was further out from the hub than his current location, but close enough, with the asteroid's powerful transmitter, to get a message to him. As a new century dawned, it seemed like a worthwhile venture.

First, however, came the moment everyone had been waiting for. A clock on a large screen showed the countdown to the year 2600. They all joined in, "Five; four; three; two; one; hooray!" A tremendous cheer went up. There were handshakes, backslaps and even a kiss on the cheek from Liu Lau. They threw streamers amidst wild, but good-natured celebrations.

Della-Mura was getting drunk by this time. Still good natured, he was unfirm on his feet. His speech slurred, he could not get a coherent word out. With a last command to his platoon members, he got Nicalino and Patrick to escort him back to his room.

"And don't be late getting up in the morning!" John shouted before the trio disappeared from view down a corridor.

'Okay,' he thought, 'I'd better go to the transmitter room.'

He had booked an earlier slot and arrived hours after the intended time. The operator, a young woman with closely-cropped hair, was in a generous mood. She was having her own private celebrations with a little bottle of wine and a glass. Sober enough to function, she helped prepare the equipment so that John's brother would receive the video message later on this first day of the century.

What to say? He had such little contact with Frank since the latter left Marmaris when John was sixteen. In the end, he spoke off the top of his head.

"You're a hard man to track down, I just hope you get this. What in God's name are you doing in this quadrant, anyway? I thought you were supposed to be the other side of the galaxy!"

He then spoke a bit about his recent employment, without going into detail. His conclusion faltered a bit, ending, "Um... I guess I'd better say bye." It all seemed inadequate and, afterwards, he wished he had made out script. Then what could one say? He hoped the recipient got the message, that was what mattered.

It was late by now. He retired to his room and fell asleep almost as soon as his head hit the pillow.

John was sound asleep when there was a rat-a-tat on his door.

"I don't want you to be late, sir." It was Della-Mura.

When John went to bed, he envisaged having to wake the man up. In the event, the opposite happened. Amidst curses, he dressed and got his things together. Fortunately, most of his belongings were on board his spacecraft. As he left the room, he apologised to Della-Mura.

"That's okay, sir, I got here in good time. We can still grab a bite to eat before meeting up with the lady."

The former trooper was showing no adverse signs from the skinfull he consumed the night before. As bright as a button, he recounted two of his stories over breakfast. One tale John had not heard before.

Soon they stood at the hangar entrance and Madam Caron was waiting for them. John checked his TRAC (how nice now the thing worked!) and saw they were not late.

"It'll be the three of us," she announced.

John's case was stowed on board while he went to retrieve *Shooter* from a docking bay on the other side of the station.

"Hello, my beauty!" he said to the inanimate object as he climbed on board.

It had been a while since he flew her and he paid full attention to the pre-flight checks before lifting off from Asteroid 741998BQ. Docking with the large Vaxon ship proved easy enough. Soon nestled in the hold, a green light told him pressurisation was complete and he could come out.

"This way please, sir," said a servant, leading him along carpeted corridors to the ship's lounge.

Inside, Della-Mura was conversing with Madam Caron. He wondered how many stories he had subjected her to since they last met.

The luxurious lounge was quite a sight. The hostess sat on a cerise-coloured, velvet covered, chez lounge. As John entered, she said, "Your colleague has kept me entertained with some interesting tales."

'I bet he has!' thought the latecomer, but he merely smiled in response. He turned down a drink, asking the approximate journey time to Quella-Prime.

"Oh, the better part of a day."

"It's a fair way then."

"It is."

"May I ask how you came to be on an obscure asteroid near the war zone, so far from home? If it's not a secret. I'd like to think you'd gone all that way to recruit me, but I doubt it somehow."

215

She looked amused before answering, "My brother's the general. It was a second visit; we've always been close. You and... Della-Mura here are bonuses. We are - were - looking for fresh recruits for the personal guard."

Now himself seated, John plugged her for more background information on the personnel he would be guarding. "It would help to know a bit more before we arrive. It's a royal family, so a king and queen, I guess."

"Close, but not quite. Emperor Leo Augustine is, er... in charge, but you won't see a great deal of him. Empress Madelyn Augustine you will. She's a great lover of ritual and everything has to be correct."

"Of course."

"But you won't be organising things, just making sure the Royal Family are kept safe."

Madam Caron talked at some length about the Augustines. While she talked, John felt he was not getting the essence of the matter. If they were so popular, why the urgent demand for security and where did the threat come from? He discerned it was an internal menace and not a foreign power.

Another thing he learned was that the heir, ten year old Prince Frederick, possessed an older sister, Margaret. Their safety would fall within his remit.

Madam Caron was being sweetness itself, although John wondered what this privileged lady could be like if crossed. He would rather not find out first hand. John felt intimidated and did not ask any probing questions. It was also the reason he entered his new job more in the dark than he would have liked.

~ End of Chapter 11 ~

My Keeper's Brother - Chapter 12

People would often see John Thorn enjoying a drink in a dingy bar in the poor quarter of town. Four years had passed since he arrived on Plerrania. Four years since he saw sight of Madam Caron. The planet did not quite live up to the impression she gave, although it was hard to put one's finger on an actual lie. Except, perhaps, that he would be involved with guarding the Royal Family.

Plerrania was a rocky planet with a toxic, high pressure atmosphere. They chose it as a place to colonise because of its ideal gravity. Its twenty- eight hour day being long, they built a couple of daytime rest periods into the lives of most of its population.

Few inhabited the southern hemisphere. Scattered about were a few neo-colonist modules on the Great Sandy Plain. In the northern hemisphere, under their massive domes, the House of Vaxon ruled. Madam Caron had not exaggerated there. These were the biggest habitation domes John ever knew. They could easily be the largest ever constructed, as the locals claimed. This civilisation had built a vast city under the Great Dome, so extensive it was indeed easy to forget you were not living on an open planet. The expense and resources involved in their construction must have been colossal. These wonders were getting old now and needed constant checks, repairs and a powerful force field to keep the hostile atmosphere out. Theirs was an inward-looking world which possessed no juggernauts. Its few interstellar warships were obsolete, rarely leaving their launch pad.

The city was called Cilluda. Soon after landing, a guide told John that this was short for Ciudad De Mil Estrellas - City of a Thousand Stars - although no one ever called it by its full name. Tiny in population by old Earth standards, they divided it into two parts. The rich people lived in the Riqueza District. Private homes there possessed all kinds of security devices to keep the riffraff out: guards, surveillance, electronic disrupters and even localised force fields. They protected their way of life. The streets were wide and well-lit, its citizens wealthy and well connected.

John never saw the Emperor and his wife, except on the bar's vid screen. There he watched them open a new, shining hospital, or inspecting a police unit. Always present the cheering, adoring crowds. The man from Marmaris found their performance unconvincing. The propaganda portrayed the Royal couple as perfect role models for a married twosome, but the Empresses' fixed, sanctimonious expression was a little too much to stomach. It amused him upon learning that the ultimate Royal Lady had once been a maid on room cleaning duty when she caught the Emperor's eye twenty years before. 'I guess it proves social progression is not impossible in this society,' John thought.

Not impossible, perhaps, but rare. For this society had inertia for change. The ruling class was reactionary in the extreme. Representing the "haves," they wanted to keep it that way.

The run-down half of the city was known as the Erente District. The "have nots" lived there. They built much of it of a red brick made locally. Unlike the rich area, the streets were narrow and unable to support cars. The attitude of the people here, John found extraordinary. For a sizeable chunk of the population here revered the Royal Family and happily cheered them at the occasional public events they attended.

Another section of the poor people showed indifference. For generations, the social order remained unaltered and it was unlikely to change now. They wished to get on with their lives with a minimum of interference. Holding little time for Royal ceremonies, they neither sympathised with the revolutionaries.

This attitude was most frustrating for the small group who called themselves the Flistee. Dedicated to the overthrow of the regime, they were tiny, but determined in their aims. This group saw as legitimate weapons assassination and destructive acts. They projected themselves as freedom fighters; the ruling class classed them as terrorists. The vast majority of those in between reckoned them deluded "pains in the arse" as one typical citizen put it to John. "One of these days, they'll bring the Great Dome down on us all!" In short, the Flistee did not enjoy popular support. Most poor people were too busy scratching a living or aspiring to improve their plight.

Two forces jointly policed this area. The civil police, who wore dark blue uniforms and the Imperial police, who wore civilian clothes. In theory, both held jurisdiction over the whole of Cilluda, but the civil police rarely ventured out of Erente. Both found themselves under-funded and lacked equipment, especially the more sophisticated sort. Cars being a luxury beyond them. Few of the wealthy families provided personnel for these police forces. They were more likely to enter the Frem, the exclusive bodyguard for the Royal Family. In his ignorance, John thought he was being enlisted into their number when he first landed. Instead, he found himself a Comadant, junior officer, in the Imperial Police, investigating crimes in the seedy back streets of the poor district.

Lacking surveillance drones, CCTV cameras and half a hundred other modern policing methods, they operated with one hand tied behind their backs. Yet, they achieved results using their network of informers, plus threats, bribery, a little torture and a great deal of intimidation. On the plus side, the palace authorities did not interfere with their operations. As long as they kept crime away from the Riqueza District, they were left alone.

In any case, things were looking up. The authorities recently found funding for a new pathology laboratory. The money did not stretch to it being well equipped, but it still represented a huge step forward. A new pathologist had also been employed, John was yet to meet them.

As for sanctions, the death penalty was something the authorities readily used. Carried out behind closed doors, the culprit could avoid it if they enjoyed the right connections. The week before John arrived, a well-known case occurred where they sentenced to death a young man to death for murdering his girlfriend. In the event, he came from a wealthy family and they soon commuted it to exile for life. John was not alone in expecting him back soon, walking the streets of Riqueza.

It was next to impossible to keep up with all the statutes. Indeed, those who took the trouble to delve into them discovered many contradictions. It would have been a lawyers' paradise had they allowed the profession on Plerrania. A society minus lawyers might be called Utopia, but some families lobbied, so far without success, to allow advocates in from elsewhere when needed.

They possessed a court system of sorts, magistrates operating without juries. These volunteers came from high-born families. John attended many cases and, from the beginning, it surprised him at the humanity and common sense shown by many of the magistrates. It was not all "hang 'em and flog 'em" by any means. That meant there existed hope; not everything was corrupt.

Such, then, the state of the justice system on Plerrania in the year 2604. Flawed, but it worked after a fashion and not entirely without its merits.

With four years' experience in the force, John was well established. His superior rarely bothered him and he enjoyed freedom to conduct his investigations as he saw fit. That was how he liked it and he had enjoyed a string of successes operating his way. As deputy, the faithful Della-Mura still accompanied him. Now aged twenty-eight, he had grown up and was someone whom his leader relied on. There were also three detectives whom he could call upon:
- Miu Hung, twenty-five, taciturn to a T, but reliable
- Ching Cho, also twenty-five. Popular, she charmed everyone with her sweet smile. She was a marshal arts enthusiast.
- Lestrange, forty-five, very experienced. His worldly wisdom saved the day on more than a few occasions.

One evening, John walked from his flat (on the border between the two districts) to one of his haunts. It was that day's final time-section, but, feeling rested from a recent nap, he felt full of energy. The streets were dimly-lit and quiet with few folk abroad at that hour. His footfalls echoed off the rundown buildings he passed by.

A couple of days before, he had wound up a case. The terrorist Flistee had discovered an indiscretion by a female factory worker. They then blackmailed the woman into giving them information on goods shipments. Their plan had been to seize a valuable cargo to help fund their operations. Neither party realised that the courier trusted with their written notes was none other than Detective Ching Cho. The police copied the notes, altering the content using an expert forger in their employ where necessary. They set a trap and captured the group of would-be robbers. John hoped it meant an entire terrorist cell being eliminated. They believed the Flistee to be small anyway, he hoped this represented a major blow to the organisation. Whatever their cause, no matter how righteous, he believed that murdering people in cold blood (as they did) was never justifiable. Meanwhile, the Comadant put in a word for the blackmailed employee, for she acted under duress.

Still flush with the success of this operation, John submitted applications to join the Frem Imperial bodyguard for himself and Della-Mura. He knew he must not get his hopes up for a positive response, though.

One interesting effect of having such massive domes was that, if conditions were right, they could create weather phenomenon within. As he walked down a narrow road, he noticed a stiff breeze coming from behind. Flags on a large, dingy building to his left fluttered. They were more the remains of flags. One, battered over time, kept a mere stub which flapped wildly. It looked absurd.

No other soul was about and the sun went down as he walked alone, between closely-packed houses, deeper into the Erente District. Limestone walls, pale sand in colour, shimmered in the rays of the setting star. He felt the pulse pistol at his side, as was his habit.

Not long to go now. The buildings he passed were in a poor state of repair and they had seen little maintenance in recent years. He walked through a tight alley lined with tall old red-brick, one of the walls leaned in. In places, the bricks were crumbling away and long cracks appearing. Ivy lined the top and moss grew in places. Upon reaching the end of the alley, he stepped over some vomit before turning into the street where the bar stood. As he got closer, he heard amiable chatter and the clink of glasses.

Once inside, the barman greeted him with his favourite drink already prepared. John then moved over to join Della-Mura at their usual table near the end of the bar. They could monitor things from there. It looked a busy evening, but all the drinkers appeared to be regulars.

"It's a shame not having anything to do," Della-Mura said ironically regarding their having concluded their latest case.

"Don't talk a new job up!" his boss warned.

After a while, his deputy said, "Look at that girl's legs."

A young drinker at the bar displayed thin legs, accentuated by the short length of her skirt.

"They're like matchsticks," John said, a little above a whisper.

"Yes," agreed Della-Mura, who then began one of his little stories.
"Have I told you about the girl with the thick legs?"

"Go on," responded John in a resigned tone.

"It was a first date and she was pretty. The weather was hot, so I wondered why she was wearing knee-high boots. Me, being me, I commented on it. The words were barely out of my mouth when I realised she wasn't wearing tall boots at all. It was simply that her legs were as fat as tree trunks."

"I bet she liked that."

"The date went south after that."

"You don't say!"

They drank some more. It was a relaxed, peaceful evening... until they saw Miu Hung burst into the room and head straight or them. He looked serious.

"This doesn't look good," said Della-Mura.

Speaking to his Comadant, the new arrival reported, "A body in an alley, near to here."

The other two downed the remains of their drinks and rose to follow their colleague out.

Through the gloomy, ill-lit streets they went. Lestrange was standing at the end of a small alley. It was a cul-de-sac, wall one side, warehouse the other, with no one else about.

"I've sent Ching Cho to fetch the new doctor."

"The pathologist?"

When the detective grunted in confirmation, John added, "It'll be nice to meet them for the first time... bloody hell!"

The exclamation was due to the sight before them. The headless corpse of a naked adult male was laid out on the cobbles.

"Any trace of the head?"

"No, sir."

It was not long before the pathologist arrived and introduced himself.

"Dr Defage."

"Good health," John said, the usual Plerran greeting to someone not met before.

"Good health," the man replied. Then, turning, he said, "Which can't be said for this poor gentleman." Introductions all round followed.

One idiosyncrasy of their operations was that a qualified doctor must formally confirm death, even in these circumstances. It was therefore with an amused tone that John asked him, "Can you confirm that this headless man is, in fact, dead?"

Mirroring the tone, the team's new medical officer replied, "I can indeed confirm that this headless corpse is no longer in the land of the living." With that, he made notes and ordered photographs be taken. John studied the fresh team member as best he could in the gloomy surroundings. Young for a doctor, he had a hooked nose and a mop of dark hair.

The examination continued rather a long time. Impatient for him to say something, John chivvied him along a bit by asking, "Doctor?"

The man looked up and said, "Call me Defage, will you? I may be a qualified doctor and pathologist, but I hate worldly titles. It's Defage, okay?"

'An eccentric then,' thought the Comadant before replying, "You'd better call me John then. What can you tell us?"

"They did not kill him here, that's for sure. The perpetrators decapitated him without precision; hacked the head off."

"Ah, yes!" said Della-Mura, loud enough to make everyone turn to him. He needed to explain. "I've heard of a head transplant. No one's ever confirmed it, but they say it is possible. A wealthy old man has his head transplanted onto a fresh body... so he can live longer."

Clearly confused, Ching Cho responded, "Wouldn't that leave him with the old head in those circumstances, rather than the old body?"

"Not necessarily, they..."

"This victim was neither old, nor a wealthy man," Defage cut in, wanting to end this nonsense. "The hands are rough and his general condition is poor for someone his age at first examination. Not too impressive. I'll be able to say before when we get it back."

"Come on," John said, taking charge. "Let's take the poor bastard back to the lab. Seal this alley off and, tomorrow morning, get some civil police over to comb the entire area for clues. There are no houses here; we'd be lucky to find any witnesses. Anyway, let's get to work."

The following three days were busy for the team. Violent deaths were not rare in Erente, with pub brawls, or domestic murders being the most common. This was something different.

The detectives assembled to hear the pathologist's report. Only Della-Mura was absent. He had been called away, but they expected him back shortly.

"Someone has drained him of blood," Defage informed them. "There was very little left at all. Puncture wounds show someone with a modicum of medical knowledge has done it."

"Age?"

"Not old, mid-twenties, but in poor health. A short, but tough life."

"An operation gone wrong?" speculated Miu

"Why dump him in an alleyway?" Lestrange said. "They were up to no good."

John asked. "Has anyone identified him?"

Ching Cho advised they had not. Nor had any witnesses come forward.

"The body showed signs of physical abuse in the past, although no sign of alcohol or other misuse. It was someone who'd lived a hard life; manual labour."

To sum up the current state of affairs, John said, "A manual labourer from Erente, someone who would be unregistered."

Miu confirmed this by saying the fingerprints came up with nothing.

John said, "Unless a relative comes forward, we may never identify them. What about motive? I guess the head is missing to make it difficult to identify them. But why drain the blood?"

The conversation was still going nowhere when Della-Mura returned. As the others talked, he stood with a broad grin on his face. Frowning, John asked him what he was looking so pleased about.

"I might have a lead!"

"Well?"

"I had a word with a friend in the civil police. He reckoned they've taken a man into custody this morning who might help us."

"Go on."

After consulting the notes on his TRAC, Della-Mura said, "His name is Ivan Kovchenko and he's charged with robbery. He's said he saw something. It's worth a try."

"Without other leads right now, I concur. Let's have a word with our friends in the civil; see if we can speak to Ivan What's-'is-name. I'll give Comadant Wanolski a call."

Later on, John and his deputy sat in an interview room with Mr Kovchenko. The criminal was in an excited mood as soon as the interview began.

"I want to do a trade."

"What sort of trade?" asked John, giving the man freedom to speak.

"I help you and you let me off my charge."

"The robbery charge."

"Yeah."

"Okay. We're dealing with a murder. If you can give me information leading to the guilty party, I'll make sure you're set free with an official warning."

"I want it in writing!"

John was about to suggest he write a note on the prisoner's TRAC, then he remembered it would have been seized when he was taken into custody. "In writing?" he asked, seeking clarification.

"Yeah!"

It took a while for a piece of scrap paper and a writing utensil to be located before John wrote his note. It could be a good deal if this fellow had breakthrough information in his murder case.

He handed it over, but Kovchenko passed it back, saying, "Read it to me."

Realising the man could not read, he went through it word for word before handing it back, adding, "If you help me catch the murderer, then I'll be happy to make sure you get off. Now speak."

The criminal finally looked convinced. He folded the piece of paper away and said, "I know the alley where you found the body. I saw two men there before you discovered it."

"Can you describe them?"

"Too dark, but they were rich."

"Rich clothing?"

"Yeah. Two men."

"Description?"

"Couldn't see. They kept in the shadows."

"You'll have to do better if you want my help."

With a look of triumph, Kovchenko reached into his mouth and pulled something out of its hiding place. As he did so, John considered that the arresting officer had not done his job. He waited to see what this oral revelation would be.

"Hey!" the man cried gleefully, "this came off one of 'em."

It was a small brass object in the shape of the letter H. John was reluctant to touch it, but Della-Mura took out a handkerchief and gave it an intense wipe before picking it up.

"What is it?" asked John.

"The Holberd family," his deputy said in wonder. "A rich family from the heart of Riqueza. Someone was telling me about them a couple of weeks ago."

They quizzed the detained man at length after this, but he stuck to his story. Before they left, John got assurances that the relevant parties would put Kovchenko's case on hold until after the Comadant concluded his own.

"I'll get back to you," were his parting words.

It was getting late by the time they arrived back. They managed to update the team before the group retired. Further background investigations would have to take place prior to anything else happening.

John was at an unavoidable meeting the following morning on an unrelated matter. When he met with the team again that evening, he found they had made progress.

"What do we know about the family Holberd?" he enquired.

Ching spoke up, "Retired General Rafael Holberd and his wife, Silvia, are well connected."

"How well connected?"

"Friends in the highest places, including the judiciary."

This meant a great deal on Plerrania. It would not be easy to put pressure on them. Lestrange then spoke up.

"Miu Hung and I checked out their residence. It's nice! High walled enclosure with a single entrance, guarded, of course. The most sophisticated anti-surveillance electrics are available. No bugging devices could work there, or pictures taken, even."

"I see. Moving on, what about motive?"

Della-Mura speculated, "An employee got their displeasure, perhaps?"

"Must be more than that, surely."

"We looked into the employees and found them to be a tightly-knit outfit, difficult to infiltrate."

"Maybe," piped up Ching with a cheeky look, "Madam Holberd enjoys bathing in human blood."

Further speculation followed, but nothing made much sense. Miu Hung asked the Comadant if he was going to pay them a "friendly" visit.

"No. If they're guilty, it would only alert them to the fact that we're onto them. They don't suspect that right now. In fact, they have no reason to suppose we are."

"Unless Kovchenko sent us on a wild goose chase for the hell of it."

That did not convince John. "I'm sure he was genuine as far as the H is concerned. Anyway, it's all we've to go on right now."

He then set up an old fashioned surveillance operation, front and back of the Holberd property. Limited manpower was available, but with no other major cases currently, they could manage.

The first six days nothing of note occurred. The Holberds possessed a car with an anti-grav engine which sometimes did the rounds. Apart from that, nothing much happened. "We'll keep it up three more days," said John, but he was wondering what else to do.

On the seventh day, at dawn, a van entered the gateway. The officers on duty, Lestrange and Ching, saw nothing useful to the investigation. That evening, it left and headed for the Erente District at speed. They tried informing John straightaway, but the Holberds' jamming device meant the police could not get a call through. The van zoomed away into the distance.

The following morning, there was unwelcome news. A priest found a second body dumped on church steps in the poor quarter. As the Comadant and his deputy stood by the naked corpse, with Defage bending over it, John remarked, "At least they were kind enough to leave the head attached this time. We still haven't been able to identify the first one. Otherwise, it looks similar to the first."

The pathologist confirmed a connection between the two murders. "Same puncture wounds, same draining of blood," he said.

"No need to worry about identification," Della-Mura declared. "I know him."

"You do?" asked John

"Yeah. Name's Belgas, he's a lowlife from around these parts. He was new to the block."

"Known associates?"

"Not many; bit of a loner."

"Could be why they targeted him. Let's scan the area for clues and whether there are any witnesses. We might get lucky again. They didn't attempt concealing the remains this time, just dumped him outside a church."

"Must've been in a hurry."

"Hmm, either way, we've got work."

A couple of days diligent enquiries produced very little. No one had seen anything round the church. The deceased's few contacts could, or would not assist.

"Don't they care they might be next?" said John in exasperation.

The sole suspects to date were still the Holberds. The police saw their van leave for the poorer district the same evening the second body turned up. They had not seen it head in that direction before. They still had insufficient evidence to get permission in law to search the property. The magistrate for that district, Justice Akassa, who newly gained the position, was a friend of Madam Holberd. In that corrupt society, it made matters doubly difficult. John knew the realities within which they forced him to operate.

"I'm not giving up!" he vowed.

Ching said, "We've found out that one employee lives quite near my flat. I could try to befriend him."

Her Comadant was not at all pleased with the idea. Not that he held any better ones himself. "It's getting late," he stated, rubbing an eye. "We'll pick this up in the morning."

In the office early next day, John considered that he would have to update his superior on the investigation. The lack of movement amongst their usual informants was worrying, although fear was gripping the streets. Who would be next? In the event, the next fatality was unexpected.

The team assembled, but, not unusually, Della-Mura was late. John started without him.

"We have two dead bodies from Erente, both male, both with the blood drained from them. The first decapitated, but the other... oh, hello Della-Mura, nice of you to join us."

Smile undimmed by this sarcastic greeting, the deputy said, "You haven't heard the news then?"

"What's that?"

"The family has announced the untimely death of Madam Silvia Holberd."

"Cause?"

"Not divulged as yet."

"It can't be a coincidence," John considered, "this has got to be connected."

"Maybe she drowned in her blood bath," Della-Mura suggested, only to receive a look of disapproval.

"We need to get to an employee."

"Let me try my plan," Ching pleaded. "After all, I can look after myself."

Worried that the entire investigation might end up a dead end, John agreed to her idea. It would make a huge difference if she could entice a Holberd employee to confide in her. Yet it would take time; patience was called for. 'How many weeks?' wondered John.

Two days later, the employee sat in his office, wanting to confess all.

'Crikey, she's a fast worker!' he thought.

In fact, the servant Ching picked was seeking to extricate himself from the situation, anyway. It being a great relief to confess all, he told them with feeling, "Jesus wants me to come clean and tell you everything."

John said, "Good old Jesus! Pray continue, tell us everything."

He did. Madam Silvia proved an eccentric employer at the best of times. Recently, though, she became a lot more so. She became terrified at the prospect of getting old. Obsessed, she got it into her head that to have her blood changed for that of a younger person would make her younger, reverse the aging process. She kept reading about it on the intranet, some deluded person's ramblings. Her other employees were dedicated and had worked for her for years. The turncoat said that he went along with them, as he feared for his life otherwise. Their plan was to kidnap a suitable victim from Erente and take their blood. One employee had studied as a medical assistant, but they lacked expertise for this operation. That was why the first attempt ended in disaster: blood everywhere except into Madam Sylvia's veins.

Undeterred, indeed more determined than ever, she ordered them to seize a second victim.

"And were you involved in that?" questioned John.

"No, sir! I stayed at the residence. They'd knocked him out with some sorta drug. They did a better job this time..."

"Of the transfusion?"

"Yeah. They got the blood through okay that time... although she 'ad some kinda reaction to it."

"Why, what happened?"

"She gets this fever, chills. She'd trouble breathing and was sick. Chest pains she 'ad too. It stopped for a while, but in the end we found she were dead."

"Where is she now?"

"They 'ave a family tomb in the 'ouse basement. A morsa, morsa..."

"Mausoleum," stated John.

"That's it."

The Comadant considered the matter. He believed the man; it fitted all known acts. On Plerrania, this might not be enough. He muttered the word, "Evidence."

"This?" the man said, producing a booklet from nowhere.

"What is it?"

"Madam Holberd's diary. She didn't like to put personal things on her TRAC in case someone intercepted them. She therefore used old fashioned writing.

John grabbed it eagerly. He rifled through the pages. It was all there: her obsession with aging, her inmost thoughts, the first catastrophic failure with the unidentified victim, and more.

"You'll be our witness," he told the man, there would be no choice. "You'll then not face any charges yourself."

The servant just looked back at him, wide-eyed.

Justice Akassa pawed through her late friend's writings, unable to speak at the enormity of the revelations. She could not deny the evidence. She allowed the Comadant to say more.

"Defage, our medical officer, has informed us that the convulsions described by our witness show they transfused incompatible blood."

"The wrong blood group, you mean?"

"Yes."

"That's a pretty basic mistake."

"Indeed, but then the whole thing was an amateurish operation. Well, some parts perhaps, they still led us a merry dance."

"The identity of the first victim?"

"Still a mystery, I'm afraid."

"Why the inconsistency regarding the victims' heads?"

"We still don't know the answer to that one, either. These cases are rarely wrapped up with no unanswered questions."

"Hmm, eccentric woman," the magistrate then mumbled as she studied the dairy further. "The evidence is overwhelming, but matters on Plerrania are rarely as straightforward as they seem. This is what I propose..."

John sat back at his favourite bar in the Erente District with Della Mura alongside him. Three weeks had passed since his meeting with Justice Akassa, although it felt more like three years considering the big changes in his life.

If a magistrate put forward "proposals" on this planet, it meant, "This will happen." She meted out justice, of a sort, for the two unfortunate victims of Madam Holberd's insane quest for immortality. The three employees that John's informant pointed out were all arrested. They faced the death penalty and, for all he knew, the authorities had already carried this out. She allowed the informant employee off with exile from Plerrania with instructions never to mention the case. Madam H had, of course, paid for her folly with her life. A most painful death. Her widower, the retired general, turned out to be suffering from advanced dementia. They took no action against him. Maybe, John speculated, the sight of him in his condition prompted his wife's lunatic quest for the elixir of life. It was not clear from her writings.

The matter now closed, the Comadant and his team received commendations for solving the case. Justice Akassa made it known that John should come recommended because of his success and "great discretion in a sensitive case." The team got the message loud and clear not to talk about it. They filed away the matter under password security.

And the final bit-part player, he who implicated the Family Holberd in the first place? They let Ivan Kovchenko off with a warning, taking no further action over the robbery. The man was busy telling everyone what a reformed character he was now. "I'm glad to hear it," John said.

"If he sticks to his resolution, it'll be one less petty criminal off the streets," was Della-Mura's verdict. "I hear one of Miu's relatives has offered him a job. I hope that works out."

"Yes," said John, "Many positive outcomes to this case."

The most positive outcome as far as John and Della-Mura were concerned regarded their future careers. A pat on the back from the Comadant's superior, Kommissioner Chang, left him with a warm glow. But that paled compared with the job offer he received. He remembered the conversation from two days previously word for word.

"A major in the Frem?" John had said in disbelief. An officer position in the House of Vaxon's elite bodyguard was a proper step up. The Kommissioner gave a word of warning, though.

"Think before you accept, John. They're a cliquey lot even at the best of times. With your being an off-worlder as well, they may give you a rough ride."

"I can stand up for myself, sir."

"You'll need to be tough."

"I can be tough."

"I hope so. They like to see themselves as a cut above. Plus you're unlikely to be given any duties near the Royal Family themselves. They reserve those roles for the inner circle."

"It's true then, about their inter-breeding."

The Kommissioner laughed, "Don't repeat that one!"

"May I ask you something?"

"Of course."

"My replacement."

"You've decided, then."

"I have," John said. "I can't aspire for something for years and then reject it when it's offered me. I'm still very surprised."

"Magistrate Akassa put in a word for you."

"Did she indeed?"

"She did, but you had a question?"

"Curiosity, I guess, but I wondered if you'd decided on the new Comadant."

The Kommissioner responded, "Who would you like it to be?"

"Della-Mura."

"I knew you'd say that. He's proved himself. A little young, perhaps, but yes, I shall offer the promotion to him."

"I'm pleased. He'll do an effective job."

That conversation was the other day. Now John and Della-Mura sat at the bar in a celebratory mood. The latter, having only received his promotion news that day, insisted having a party at their favourite haunt the same evening.

"Hello!" they cried in unison as the rest of the team came in.

Much hugging and back-slapping followed before they settled down a bit.

"I'm sorry you're leaving us," Ching said, between smiles, "but we understand."

"Thank you. It's an opportunity I never thought I'd get. Um... where's Defage?"

"Couldn't make it."

"Oh."

After a slight pause, Ching said with a glint in her eye, "Say hello to the Emperor from me."

"I'm not sure I'll quite be moving in those exalted circles. It'll be more a matter of detective work weeding out terrorist cells."

"The Flistee, you mean?"

"That's right," John confirmed. "Could be quite interesting. And dangerous. As long as I'm able to keep the Royals safe from them, I hope to get on okay."

Della-Mura spoke for all of them. "We know you'll do fine, sir. You'll take them by storm!"

"I'm not sure about that, but I doubt if I'll be able to visit here often."

They all knew that the Frem did not frequent the Erente District of Cilluda, unless on a covert operation. Folk there knew John's face too well for him to be used undercover.

"You'll stay in touch somehow," the new Comadant said.

"Of course I will. I shall miss you all. We've been a good team."

They all drank to that.

John's first few weeks in the Frem, early in 2605, were not quite what he expected. The trainers kept him busy with a full programme even though he did not feel welcomed by those already in the organisation. He had to learn Plerran battle-language, a kind of shorthand speech used in a crisis to save precious split seconds. He needed to put in a lot of concentrated effort to master it. There were briefings on Flistee terrorists, their organisation, weaponry and tactics, plus a good deal of etiquette to learn.

Housed in a barracks on the edge of the extensive palace complex, he saw nothing of the Royal Family in those early days. He observed the top courtiers, or, as he thought to himself, "hangers on". The men wore tall hats, cylindrical with a broader band at the top. With their long, curly wigs and flowing capes, they looked quite a sight. Best to avoid such personages as much as possible, he was told.

One lady he wondered if he would see again was Madam Caron with whom he first travelled to the planet. She would never frequent the barracks and teaching room area. The area beyond was currently out of bounds.

They pointed him out another of the Empress' confidantes, albeit from a distance. "That's Madam Blanche Faubert," they told him, but the figure appeared tiny, the far side of an exercise yard, which meant he could not get a proper look at her. She glided through a walkway with a colonel in attendance.

"I'm not sure I've heard of her," John confessed.

"Not a lady to get on the wrong side of," his guide informed him. "I could give you her full name: Madam Blanche Bisset, Couture, Durand, Faubert."

"That's an awful lot of name for one person!"

"She's been married four times and keeps each man's surname... as trophies, perhaps."

"She's working her way through the alphabet."

The other man laughed before adding, "It's by no mean clear what happened to husbands number one and three. Best not to ask, but then she's best not gossiped about at all unless it's someone you know you can trust."

John considered this a big compliment from someone he did not know very well. In fact, spending his time in the training school with men a lot younger than himself, and from a different social class, making friends was difficult. At least the unpleasantness eased as he gained their respect. For news of his previous successes when in the Imperial Police got out. Not a huge amount stayed secret in that bubble for long.

One thing that fascinated him was the equipment available to the Frem. Special helmets with infra-red and an entire spectrum of other sensors, surveillance devices, the latest weaponry. Many new toys to play with.

One man he forged a friendship with during this period was the sole other mature student. Singh had a colourful background. Born to a middle-ranking family, he veered off the rails as a teenager and ended up killing a youth in an ugly brawl. Spared the death sentence because of a hefty bribe by his parents, they put him to work in a chain gang in the Royal gardens. He gained the confidence of his jailers who released him from his bonds occasionally to perform certain errands. On one of these he came encountered two Flistee would-be assassins preparing to attack the Empress. He thwarted their attack single-handedly, the reward for which was a Royal pardon and a position in the Frem. He and John saw each other as kindred spirits and became almost instant friends. This was good, because, upon finishing their training, they learned Singh would be John's deputy in a new unit being formed.

The rest of the squad were young, eager volunteers. John, confirmed with the rank of major, detected a note of arrogance amongst some of these highborn recruits. He gave them a stern lecture early on to knock any of that nonsense out of them. They got the message.

Orders then came to report to Colonel Hillier. At thirty-five, Philip Hillier was, in fact, five years John's junior, but much more powerful. He mixed in the highest House of Vaxon circles. It surprised John at the summons, because Hillier was not in John's natural line of command. It was therefore with a measure of trepidation that he knocked on the Colonel's office door.

"Come!" hailed a voice from within.

He entered and saw a casual-looking man sitting behind a desk.

"Ah, Major Thorn, do come in; sit down."

"Thank you, sir."

Hillier held an air of calculated calm. Somehow it seemed artificial, as if he were playing a part. John studied him. With his long, wavy hair and youthful appearance, he might have looked a dashing fellow. However, he possessed a deformed mouth, being over to one side. Cold blue eyes looked back at him, then he spoke.

"The Empress will attend the annual spring festival at the Colonnades in a week's time. Enormous crowds will be attending. Food poisoning has struck down the unit detached for her security at this event. We expect them to be non-operational for several days. I would like you to take on the responsibility, along with your unit, instead."

Seeing this as a great opportunity to show his worth, John said, "It shall be an honour, Colonel."

Unmoved, the senior officer said, "We've received a tip-off from a reliable source; the terrorists may plot an attack at the ceremony. You will have your work cut out."

"I see," John said, coming back down to earth.

Hillier gave him all the details, plus a list of dos and don'ts. A high-profile job without a doubt, with stakes even higher than he dare think about. If it all ran smoothly, it should help his career. Should the terrorists harm the Empress, the consequences would be too terrible to contemplate.

The Emperor was a figurehead, but in practice he exercised little power. His wife, Empress Madelyn, held and used the Royal authority. John realised the next week would be make or break for him.

He returned to his team and told them the news. Most were enthusiastic about the assignment, although some had trepidations. John's job was to motivate, equip and prepare them for the mission. This included a visit to the Colonnades ceremonial site and an intense training regime. Before the event took place, the authorities would issue them with special, performance-enhancing drugs to heighten their awareness and response times. The night before, John found it difficult sleeping, so great was the burden of responsibility weighing on him.

In the event, John and his team thwarted most successfully an assassination attempt. Seven terrorists killed. They sent John, promoted to Commander, on a mission into space to track down further renegades. Able to pick his crew, he ensured both Della-Mura and Defage came along. It took them to the remote planet Molten, where he met his brother, Frank, for the first time in years. Mission accomplished, John returned to Plerrania to a hero's welcome and a most interesting, responsible job.

[NOTE: For a detailed account of these events, please refer to *Secret of the Keepers*, chapters 1 and 9]

~ End of Chapter 12 ~

My Keeper's Brother - Chapter 13

Back on planet Plerrania following a fruitful operation, the court feted John and his crew as heroes. Their adventure had taken them to the galaxy's edge, but now they were back in familiar surroundings. A medal and the Empress's gratitude for a successful mission, it felt good.

How soon the euphoria faded. Della-Mura, Defage and the rest returned to their jobs, but John found his previous post filled. Colonel Hillier told him they would find a role for him soon. A vacancy had arisen in the Akaya branch of the Frem, the royal bodyguard. An officer's role. It meant a re-shuffle and a slot somewhere in the organisation for John. In the meantime, he would have to kick his heels.

He thought back to his stay on the planet Molten. A couple of weeks ago, but it seemed a lot longer. Spending time with his brother for the first time since their teenage years. Visiting a planet so remote that few stars shone at night. It brought back the same recurring dream he experienced half a lifetime ago. Such vivid dreams of a perfect society filled with beautiful people. The images and impressions were so real, as if he had actually experienced them. If only such a utopia could exist. These pleasant musings drifted through his mind as he sat on his bed. It was quiet outside and he studied the exquisite paperweight, acquired he knew not where or how, when he was much younger. The scene was mesmerising, the majestic mountain tops and the ripples on the lake in the middle-ground.

Back to reality and hopefuls were jostling and lobbying for position in the coming jobs shakeup. John left them to it. The snobbishness and power politics left him cold. Besides, he did not have half the senior contacts and patrons the other candidates enjoyed. If the colonel offered him a post he liked, he would accept. Should a position not arise, he would move on. Five years he had spent on Plerrania, the longest stay on a planet since he left home. It would not matter if he departed now.

After a week and a half, Della-Mura invited him for a drink. Back in the Erente District, he enjoyed walking the once familiar streets. Dressed in unobtrusive civilian clothes, he entered his once regular bar and was amused to see his friend sitting exactly where he used to. The faithful black and white chequered scarf still hung round his neck. They greeted each other and Della-Mura bought the new arrival a drink.

"Any cases on the go at present?"

"No, it's been quiet since I got back. It's given me the opportunity to catch-up on some paperwork; get everything in order."

John chuckled, "It's funny how we still use old expressions like "paperwork" long after it actually involves paper."

"Yeah, I'd struggle to write with a pen if someone asked me to."

"Me too. But there are lots of idioms we use with no relation to modern life."

"Such as?"

"'The whole nine yards,' meaning everything, taken from the sailing ships of old earth. Or 'beating about the bush' meaning avoiding the issue."

"Another one from old earth?"

"Yes, when they were hunting game and hired men flushed them out by beating the ground."

They ordered further drinks before Della-Mura resumed the conversation. "It was interesting having a spell on Molten. No modern technology; candles for light and old pens for writing. I can understand the appeal of the simple life."

"Can you?"

"Sure, the slower pace. My current breather won't last and I'll be hard at it again soon enough. Your brother's landed on his feet."

"You're right, he's done well for himself. If I hadn't become a soldier, can you guess what I'd have done?"

"No."

"Become an archaeologist."

Della-Mura's expression showed surprise at this. He said, "Not much opportunity for action, surely."

"Yeah, yet I reckon it would be interesting digging up the past and looking into it."

"Like detective work in a way."

"Yes! When I was little, about seven, I think, I mentioned it to my parents and they put me right off."

"Why?"

"They said there's no money in it. True, but there wasn't much money in farming either."

"It's sad what happened to your parents."

"Hmm. What about your mother and father? If you don't mind me asking."

"I don't mind," Della-Mura said. "My parents met working for the same engineering firm on Naramarr. They still live there, but both hoping to retire soon."

"Is that where you were born?"

" Naramarr? Yeah. I'm used to domed planets. I'm not sure how I'd cope living on an open one, all that infinite space. I'd be scared."

"Like Molten, you mean?"

"I suppose I'd get used to it, but domes give me a sense of security. I was born and raised under domes."

"Have you been to many worlds?" asked John.

"A fair few. I lived on a desert planet once called.... ah, the name escapes me now. Anyhow, they had a breathable atmosphere, but a hot, dry heat that most found pretty unbearable. We stayed inside the domes, but a few nomads lived out in the desert. Goodness knows how they survived, but they did. It was funny, though, 'cos when one of them was about to give birth, they'd come into the domes and get the best medical care... and for free! Many of the locals who'd paid their taxes to fund the service resented it."

"I guess that's understandable."

"Yeah."

"Were there the 'haves' and the 'have nots' on planet Naramarr? It seems to be the pattern wherever you go."

"Not quite. Big mining ventures settled Naramarr. so they're all company employees. The schools, the retail sector, all of it company owned. They're looked after and paid well. My parents used to talk about buying a place to retire off-world. I'm pretty sure they haven't got round to it yet. I didn't want for anything when I was a kid. my parents were financially secure. I didn't appreciate it."

"But you didn't follow in your father's footsteps."

"No, I wanted adventure, see the universe. And I can't complain, especially now I've got your old job."

John grinned in response and then listened further as the man continued.

"Now I need a good woman."

"Any on the horizon?"

"Yes, one I've got designs on. I hope my strategy works on her. Put it this way; I'm locked on target..."

"Not going in for the kill yet," John said, keeping to the military analogy.

They laughed. Just then, Ching Cho came in, minus her customary smile. She passed a cursory greeting with John, then homed in on her Comadant.

"We've found a body near the terminal. Head bashed in."

Della-Mura downed the last of his drink, stood and turned to John.

"Sorry," he said, "but you know how it is. Gotta go."

"Of course. I understand, you go."

"Nice to have a catch-up."

"Sure; see you again some time."

"Hope so."

He was gone, leaving John to finish his drink alone.

Over the following couple of days, John moved into a new flat in the Riqueza District. People might see it as a vote of confidence in his future there, but, he planned it prior to the space mission. With his commander's salary being paid, he could comfortably afford the rent. The flat came furnished and, not being fussy, it pleased him not to have to buy things for his new property.

He enquired about Della-Mura's love life, but possessed none of his own. John thought of Stella sometimes. His love for her had been genuine. Upon consideration, he realised how his selfish behaviour had soured the relationship. What was the use of regrets? Too late to make amends now.

One morning, he went for a walk. It was a bright day and when he looked up, shielding his eyes from sun's direct glare, he noticed the hexagonal shapes that marked the frame of the giant dome.

Wandering without purpose, he found himself near the palace complex. These were the widest streets of Cilluda, filled with cars. Driverless vehicles, the rich kids liked to show them off. As he progressed, he saw what appeared to be a family group taking up the pavement. As he got closer, he had little choice but to pay them attention.

A richly-dressed young woman was having a contretemps with a couple of her bodyguards from their uniform. Others stood in attendance. A boy, early teens, stood on the edge of the pavement, trying to distance himself from the affray. John was close to them right now and considering how best to negotiate his way past. A car drove by.

Then the boy, without looking, stepped out directly into a following vehicle's path. Quick as a striking snake, John lunged forward and pulled the boy to safety. It all happened in an instant, but several of the party saw it and praised the boy's saviour for his swift action. The car's emergency stop would have struggled to apply in this short distance. There was little doubt the stranger's action had saved the lad from serious injury or death. Moments later, with the argument halted, the young woman hugged the boy for all he was worth, although the lad himself seemed unmoved by it all. Meanwhile, a gaggle of people feted John as a hero.

"And what is your name?" enquired one large gentleman.

John gave it. As he spoke, he tried working out where he had previously seen the man. Then it came to him: Chancellor Vinner, one of the most senior figures on the entire planet.

"Ah, yes!" returned Vinner, beaming, "we've met before, haven't we?"

"Yes, sir. I was in charge of the hunt for the renegade Lynx. I am recently returned."

"That's right! Thank you for your swift action. We are most grateful."

Mumbling a reply, John saw the show was over. The group of people were already moving off, in the opposite direction to his. He therefore recommenced his walk and soon they were out of sight. It pleased him, though, at the thought of a good deed done. It would be nice to imagine Chancellor Vinner putting in a good word for him. After all, he saved the man's son. Then reality struck again as he told himself it was unlikely.

The following morning, he enjoyed a lie-in. With nothing scheduled before lunch, he possessed no incentive to get up. That was until he noticed a message on his TRAC.

"Commander John Thorn, report to Colonel Hillier."

He leapt out of bed, showered and changed into his black uniform. As he made his way to the palace office, inevitable speculation raced through his mind.

'Those in charge must have sorted out the jobs re-shuffle. They surely have a role for me, but I guess it could be to tell me there is no post available. After all, I'm not a member of one of their wealthy, influential houses with friends in high places. They'll be at the front of the queue.'

Cilluda's streets were quiet and did not take long to negotiate. Soon, he was being shown into the colonel's office to be greeted by the deformed mouth and cold eyes.

"Ah, Thorn; come in... sit down."

Even now, John found his mind trying to pick up hints. 'Would he be asking me to sit down if I'm to be told I'm surplus to requirements? Possibly another off-world assignment, or my old job in the Erente District...'

"I must add my thanks to everyone else's for the other day." When faced with a blank expression, Hillier added, "For saving the prince's life as you did."

The coin now dropped. So it was not anyone he pulled to safety, but Prince Frederick, the heir to the throne. It took a moment for his brain to process the information. He tried to recover the situation by saying, "That's okay," then thought how daft a response that must have sounded.

A rare smile flickered across the lips of the powerful man before him. He said, "You forced us into a jobs re-think, but we rose to the challenge. I have therefore brought you here to offer you a position in the Akaya branch of the Frem. That is the Royal Bodyguard."

John knew what it was, a place near the highest echelons of power. It would be interesting, if nothing else. He needed no time to decide.

"Thank you, Colonel, that is a great honour!"

"Indeed. You accept?"

"I do," John said, followed by more thanks.

Further details followed. While keeping his rank of commander, his responsibilities hinged on looking after the royal children. An intriguing challenge, but he was aware of his responsibility. His duties began the next day and he was told where to report for duty.

John walked back with a spring in his step, he received a call from Della-Mura telling him of a new post.

"I'm going to be in charge of an Imperial Police unit in Riqueza!"

"You're going up in the world."

"They say it's a sideways move."

"You and I both realise it's more than that "

This was true. A job in the city's upper class area held far more prestige.

The two men arranged a celebratory drink that evening, but John warned he must not be late home.

Back in their old familiar haunt in the Erente District, it surprised John to find the rest of the old crew absent. Della-Mura explained.

"They're in the middle of a hot investigation, hoping to make some arrests this evening. It disappointed them not to be here."

"But you got away."

"The new Comadant is with them. I'm starting my new job tomorrow too. No rest for the wicked."

"You must be looking forward to it."

"I am, although I'm not sure what to expect. Fewer stabbings down dark alleys, I suspect."

"Hmm, a more sophisticated type of murderer, no doubt."

"I'll have to wait and see; I'm meeting my new team tomorrow. Not sure quite what to expect, but I want us to keep in touch."

"Of course, we will."

John got up extra early the following morning, making sure he looked his smartest. An official car had been laid on to take him to the palace. He was outside waiting in good time and was therefore standing there ready when it arrived five minutes early. He got in and found an official sitting next to him, who spoke not a word as the vehicle whisked them to their destination. They then took John inside the palace.

Until this point, it never occurred to him he might meet the Emperor and Empress themselves that morning. In the event, he did not. Taken to an upper chamber, they left him alone a while before three personages walked in.

The person delegated with introducing him to his charges was Madam Blanche Faubert. He recognised her as the lady with four surnames and knew the importance of making a good impression on her. Therefore, manners to the fore, he sailed a course between extreme politeness on the one hand and obsequiousness on the other. It seemed to work.

"This is Prince Frederick," she pronounced, "whom I believe you have met."

She spoke with a twinkle in her eye, the reference being to his having pulled the young man from the path of a car. A formal handshake took place and it surprised John at how feeble Frederick's was. 'Someone should have taught him better.'

"Your Highness," the new bodyguard said with a slight bow. The fourteen year-old replied with a mumble and downcast eyes. There were confidence issues there.

"And this is the Princess Margot."

"Your Highness."

This was the young lady arguing on that pavement. At twenty-two, she was a fair bit older than her brother. Her bored look gave way as she greeted him with a smile that revealed a perfect, whiter than white set of teeth. She had a look of her mother with her brown, neck-length hair moulded round her face. Same distinctive eyes. 'Quite attractive,' thought John, 'without being beautiful.' She wore a magenta-coloured top and a single gold necklace.

Madam Faubert was supposed to instruct John on his duties, but she did not say a great deal. "Protect this pair with your life," lay at the heart of it. She provided him with a powerful, miniature communication and tracking device. To his surprise, though, he discovered he was a one-man band. Little threat hung over them while in the palace. An army of guards protected the area with a most sophisticated surveillance system in operation, plus the complex employed its own additional force field to prevent any threat from above. He wondered if his new role was a job in name only. The royal children (if Margot could still be called a child) rarely left the palace confines and then they had a whole posse of extra guards. No wonder the boy appeared pale and fed up and the young woman bored stiff.

"I'll let you get acquainted," said Madam Faubert, leaving him alone with his charges.

As the woman departed, the boy picked up a book, sat himself down and read. Princess Margot, with a look bordering on disdain, said, "I hope you won't be like the last one."

"What was he like then?"

"All rigid and boring," she said.

"I can't recall anyone ever describing me that way, Your Highness."

"Not now!" she snapped. Then, when it was clear, he did not understand what this meant, she said, "When we're alone, call me Margot."

"Okay, Margot."

"And you can call him Frederick."

Turning to the lad, who appeared absorbed in his slim volume by now, he said, "Hello Frederick," to see what reaction he got.

"Hello," came the reply with neither emotion, nor looking up.

"Good!" declared Margot, "that's a step forward."

"From what I gather, my role here is to make sure you're safe. I'm not your tutor or anything."

"God no! But I want to have fun."

John wondered what form this fun would take. He also considered that she was rather old to be treated like a child. Not wishing to say anything that might annoy her, he asked how she liked to spend her days.

With a shrug, she said, "I dunno, sitting around. Sit down, tell me about yourself."

That he did. The princess's bored aura disappeared, for the moment at least, as she listened to some of his adventures. It was a distraction and, in fact, quite riveting. A man of action from a distant quadrant should be far more entertaining, and pliable, than a home-grown Frem operative. John told his tales, leaving out some details, such as the remote planet Molten and his brother.

She said, "You must enjoy excitement and living on the edge. You are an adventurer!"

He said, "Adventure comes looking for me at least as often as I go looking for it."

"I think you will do."

"Thank you, my lady!"

She enjoyed his sense of humour and giggled before saying, "I go mad here in my gilded cage. One of your predecessors let me go out at night."

"What happened to him?" asked John, fearing the worst.

"Oh, they transferred him," she said before adding, "but not on account of anything he did here. It was a promotion or something."

"I see."

"I ache to taste that freedom again."

She was being theatrical.

"And do what?"

"Escape the palace grounds, walk around, feel the nightlife, mix with people."

"I'm guessing your parents don't allow it, so neither did my immediate predecessor, because he liked to stick by the rules. Am I right?"

"But you won't be stuffy like him."

"I'm not sure, I don't want to face the Emperor's wrath. I'd quite like to leave my head attached to my body."

"Don't be so melodramatic!" She cried. "I'm not asking you to face renegade spacemen or acid rain, merely to escort me while I have a bit of fun."

"Hmm, I'm not sure. Won't the surveillance machines pick us up?"

"Oh no, I've got a jammer to make us invisible to them."

"Have you? I bet the Flistee would enjoy getting their hands on that."

"I got it encoded by a technician here at the palace."

"But couldn't the terrorists copy the technology?"

"No, the surveillance devices operate on a random, oscillating frequency which synchronises with my jammer. They could never reproduce it. We will be quite safe from surveillance, plus there's another bag of tricks to make sure no one knows it's us."

"So you want you, me and the prince to wander the streets after dark?"

"Hell no! Not Frederick. He'll be happy to stay here and read. Won't you, Frederick?" Her tone sounded more like a command than an enquiry, but he shook his head. It seemed to be true.

Incredulous, he asked, "You'd like me to take you out for a walk tonight, then." "Incognito, of course."

"Just for a walk."

"I'd allow you to talk to me."

"Thank you!" he replied ironically.

Amused by this reaction, she changed the subject by offering to take him for a guided tour of the palace. It was an offer he could not refuse, but he was interested anyway. This planet was colonised early in interstellar history and he wanted to learn more about it. The enormous building appeared empty and, as she took him round, they were free to talk.

"Do you know much about Plerrania's history?"

She gave him a look which said it was a silly question, so he sought to justify himself.

"I'm interested in history, that's all."

"But that's in the past, surely?"

He laughed, "By definition; but it helps us to understand the present."

"I'm aware of my present. Hang about until my parents find a 'suitable' husband for me. I'm a commodity. It's as simple as that. I'd be more interested if history told me my future."

They walked on.

"Are we likely to bump into your parents at any minute?"

"Oh, God no! I hope not anyway."

"Might we get into trouble?"

"It's not that. Mother will be busy with her scheming and father... he's not too well these days."

"I'm sorry. I wasn't aware."

Margot passed this off as she took him, past a couple of guards, to the main vault.

"You might enjoy this."

"What is it?"

She did not answer, but led him through to the inner sanctum where a further guard stood. On a plinth central to the room sat a ceremonial crown. The lights in there shone onto the object. He stepped forward and inspected it close up. Jewel-encrusted gold glistened and the stones sparkled. The sight captivated him.

"How old is it?" he asked.

While he directed the question at Margot, the guard answered. A short, elderly fellow, he looked too feeble to stop a would-be thief. John listened as he spoke about the object.

"Eight hundred years old, sir," he said with a note of wonder. "It's our sole item everyone agrees comes from old Earth."

"Wow, magnificent," exclaimed the visitor, who then posed some searching questions. While the elderly man tried his best, he knew little other than the item's providence. John still enjoyed being shown. He also appreciated the fact that the princess took him there for his sake after he showed an interest in things historical. In fact, he was revising his opinion of her as a spoilt brat. Maybe if *he* stood in their shoes, he would get bored, cynical and wish to escape from it.

The rest of the day passed pleasantly. It was apparent the royal children saw little of their parents, who left them to their own devices. Frederick was self-contained and could sit reading for hours. Margot was a different proposition. Easily fed up and wanting distraction, she found few outlets and saw opportunity in a new, pliable bodyguard. That afternoon, she taught him a computer game and they played for quite a while. John surprised himself by enjoying the experience and liked it when she giggled when one of them made a silly move. Younger than him in years, she was a great deal younger than him in maturity.

As evening approached, she was getting exciting at the prospect of a perambulation outside the city walls. John still held severe doubts as to the wisdom of this. It could put his job on the line. After all, "She made me do it" sounded a feeble excuse. Yet her enthusiasm was infectious and he wanted to please her. Was it a matter of feminine wiles? John got the impression she could make his life hell if he did not comply with her wishes. That was the more likely fate of his predecessor. He wondered what the turnover of bodyguards was in this role.

He soon talked himself into going, it was either let her have her own way or face a sulky, overgrown girl. He knew nothing of the nightlife of this, the richest quarter of the city. It would be interesting to witness it first hand. What did wealthy types do for leisure? From everything Margot said, they should be safe. She seemed experienced in these matters and owned the required equipment. In short, he gave in to her.

"I've got a wardrobe full of clothes we can change into, plus we'll put on PFVs."

"Sorry?"

"The disguising devices I said."

He was pretty au fait with technology, but this was something new to him. She opened a cupboard and produced a couple of stiff bands of synthetic material. As she put one round her neck and activating it, her face suddenly changed to that of an old woman. Her voice sounded altered too, unidentifiable as Margot's.

John jumped in surprise, but watched, fascinated. It was not perfect, for the picture possessed an occasional flicker, plus a slight double-image at the sides, but if he had not known, he would never have guessed it was the Empress' daughter.

She explained, "It's obvious they are not real and there are devices to shut them down, but in the normal run of things, they protect one's anonymity. Everyone wears them at the casino."

Older and wiser, her bodyguard knew people are just as identified by their mannerisms and the way they move than by their facial features and speech patterns. She then told him more. The rich folk enjoyed a kind of "masked ball" nightlife, whereby they did not know, or at least pretended not to know, other participants. He thought it through. It was rare for the public to catch sight of Princess and her circle of acquaintances was small. Maybe she could mix without the others knowing they were next to the heir's sister.

"But we're going for a walk, nothing more?" he asked for clarification.

"That's right," she said with an innocent look.

The outfits she produced bordered on the comical. Hers was a long, flowing dress of inferior fabric. It would not get her noticed. His was a black leather jacket and brown corduroy trousers. They looked like a middle-ranking merchants with poor taste in attire. To Margot, it was all a big joke. When John donned the clothing and PFV, she roared with laughter. He took it in good humour, because he realised it was part of the game and she was not laughing at him. Nevertheless, he jumped back in shock when she held a mirror to him and he saw an ancient man staring back at him. Laughing himself, he wondered what people nearby in the palace would think. In fact, few frequented this wing of the building. She assured him they were quite safe.

The pair of them made final preparations for their evening adventure. She appeared an old, grey woman, he, a wizen man. That is until Margot synchronised the feedback coils. That meant while others would see their false images, the two of them would see and hear themselves as they were.

All set, they said goodbye to Prince Frederick. He dragged himself away from his book long enough to shake his head before returning to it. He showed no signs of wishing to accompany them.

"We'll leave by the postern." Margot informed her bodyguard and led him, via a secret corridor, through a concealed door in the palace wall. Soon they were progressing along the pavement through a part of the Riqueza District John had not visited before.

Everything amazed him. Crowds of people walked the streets in similar outlandish outfits and using the PFV disguises. A whole new universe opened up before him. Prior to that evening, he never guessed these goings on existed and continued nightly. They pedestrianised the wide road at this hour and there was no shortage of rich folk abroad experiencing it. They crammed the area and it was quite fascinating to observe the bizarrely dressed crowds. A lot more wealthy people lived in Cilluda than he realised.

The couple passed the casino and saw lots of people entering. John got the impression that his ward would have liked to join them, but, saying not a word, she picked up speed and sailed past. Soon they stood near the edge of the Great Dome, with no one else about. In an area of grass and bushes, the designers had placed a bench and she suggested they sit there. It was darker here and they could see the stars beyond.

"Best keep these on," she said, pointing to her visor, "you never know who's watching."

With the two of them seeing each other as normal, it was easy to forget they wore them. For conversation soon engrossed them.

"I've met no one who's visited as many planets as you," she gushed.

He relaxed more than he had all day when he said, "I guess I've been a bit of a nomad."

"Have you been to many open planets?"

"I have. In fact, I was born on one, Marmaris."

"I can't say I've heard of it."

"No particular reason you should. It's an unremarkable planet, a long way away."

"But it must be weird, knowing that there's nothing between you and the outside. What if an asteroid plummeted through the atmosphere and hit you?"

"That doesn't happen too often," he replied with humour in his voice.

"Even so."

"There are several huge planets with massive gravity in that solar system. They attract any passing projectiles. Not that one couldn't hit a minor planet like Marmaris, of course, but it's a rare event."

"What's space travel like?"

"I found it disappointing."

"Why?"

"I thought you'd get thrown about, but because of the inertia negators, it's nothing like that. There's no sensation of movement. When you look out of a porthole, for instance, it's like watching a vid screen. Not very exciting."

"Surely it's amazing, setting foot on another world. Don't you have a sense of wonder?"

"Yes, I do," John said, not wanting her to think him a cold fish. "There are some beautiful sights, it's true."

"I might travel to the stars one day," Margot said in a wistful tone. "It depends on who they get to marry me. No one is good enough, that's what they say... Mind you, we're so insular here on Plerrania."

"The House of Vaxon isn't looking to make alliances with nearby planets, then?"

"My parents rarely travel off-world themselves. They don't know anyone on other planets. They're sending ambassadors to find a suitor for me, so I've been told. It's been going on for... forever, it seems."

John said, "Isolation isn't entirely a bad thing. I've been on several planets where they were at war, or threatening war with their neighbours. It might be better to keep yourselves to yourselves."

"And marry a courtier here?" she said, pulling a face. The question went unanswered. The conversation resumed when Margot asked, "What would happen if the Great Dome cracked?"

"You have a force field over it. They're repair the crack as soon as possible, I'm sure. It would be safe."

"What if the force field also failed? At the same time?"

"It's improbable..."

"But just say"

"Um, worst-case scenario, you mean?"

"Yes."

"I understand the atmosphere on this planet is both toxic and under high pressure. So it would force itself into the dome,"

"The poisonous air?"

"Yes."

"And kill everyone?"

"I wouldn't dwell on it. You've been going hundreds of years, haven't you?"

"Yes," she confirmed with a sigh, "and nothing changes. What's it like on your home planet? How old were you when you left?"

"I was sixteen, keen to become a soldier. I fulfilled that ambition and have no desire to return to it."

"Have you ever been in love?"

Pausing before answering, John confessed he had. "Her name was Stella and we were together a few happy years."

"What happened?"

"I was too selfish. I shouldn't have put my own needs before hers."

"Do you regret that now?"

"Hmm, they say that one shouldn't have regrets in life. That's not being honest. Yeah, if I'm straight with you, I regret not making more of a go at it."

"Are you still in love with her?"

"It's a bit of an academic question, for I won't ever see her again."

"Maybe you'll find someone else."

"Maybe," he echoed. Then, following a long period of silence, he voiced a concern. "What if your parents find you missing?"

She was dismissive, "Oh, they don't care where I am!"

"Is that fair? I'm sure they must love you."

"Hmm. The staff who matter are already aware of my nocturnal habits. It wouldn't surprise me if my mother knows; she has other concerns. Besides," she continued, showing her wrist computer, "I have an alarm on here if the worst came to the worst."

"Good,"

"But I feel safe with you," she said.

"Pleased to hear it."

"I can relax when I'm with you."

"I'm pleased to hear that too."

"Even if others regard you as a funny old man in that PFV."

Their laughter cut into the still night air. In front of them was a small area of grass before the bushes began. Beyond those, the wall of the Great Dome stood. In the sky, stars were visible and an insignificant point of light traversing the heavens, a lone spaceship on its travels.

They chatted some more before the princess decided they should head back. The evening social life of Riqueza was still in full swing as they headed towards the palace. Their journey was without incident. Once inside, Margot read a message saying her brother had retired to bed. She and John divested themselves of their disguises and the princess said goodnight to her new employee, adding, "You're a lot better than the last one."

"Good. I've enjoyed the evening too."

He liked his room at the palace, near his wards' suite of rooms, but John knew he would have to decide what to do with his flat in the city. With its subsidised rent, there was no great hurry to give it up.

He woke up early and lay considering things. As his mind ran through the events of the previous evening, he recalled how struck he had been by Margot's appearance as she took her PFV off and shook her hair. What an enchanting smile, a pity she used it sparingly.

'I must be careful not to fall for her,' he told himself. 'She is out of my reach and only a little over half my age. But we got on well together...'

A quiet day followed. He tried to engage Prince Frederick in conversation, but it was an uphill struggle. John did not get the impression the lad bore anything against him, but he preferred his own company.

Evening could not arrive soon enough for Margot and John. As soon as they could, they donned their outfits and PFVs and prepared to go out.

"Tonight, we are going to the casino," she announced. Clearly she would brook no dissent.

Casinos were not John's favourite haunt, for he knew how they stack the odds against the punters. He recognised a mug's game. However, with mind set firm, Margot led the way.

As they entered the place, it amazed John to find that her words about everyone donning disguises there was not an exaggeration. All the players wore PFVs and the room was full of extraordinary-looking characters. "It's part of the fun," she said. Desperate not to appear disapproving, he tried to look keen.

Once inside, she got chips worth two thousand credits via her TRAC and headed for the gaming tables. 'Two thousand,' John considered, 'that would keep a whole family in Erente going for a year.'

It was another establishment set out in classical style. Why change something that worked? Folk liked the traditions. The princess plonked herself down on a stool at the roulette table, John at her shoulder.

"You'll be my lucky mascot," she informed him, then lost half her chips in next to no time.

John then dared to suggest they move to the blackjack table.

"I'm no good at that," she said.

"I can help you," he replied.

As he spoke these words, she lost another couple of counters. Not a single win so far. Turning round, Margot said, "I always get two thousand and when its gone, it's gone. I don't mind."

"It's going to be a short evening at this rate."

She declined placing another bet for the next spin of the wheel, she stood up and said, "You must be my *un*lucky mascot!"

"Blackjack?"

"Oh hell, why not? You'll have to help me."

"We'll still lose," he said with a wink that she alone could see, "but at least the evening's entertainment should last longer."

"Okay then," she said and moved.

They arrived at the table at the same time someone vacated it, she sat down in the middle. As the female croupier got ready, Margot counted her chips - eight hundred left.

"How many should I stake?"

"Let's start with a hundred."

"Okay," she said and, once they had all placed their bets, received two cards.

She began studying the other players, but John told her to concentrate on her own hand. She had seventeen, the dealer showed a queen up. Not a good start.

"Stick," he advised and she did.

One of the other players got an extra card, then promptly bust. With no more cards to give out, the dealer revealed hers, a ten.

"House pays twenty-one."

That was the first hundred gone. "Better luck next time," John whispered.

The croupier dealt; Margot got a king and a five. No choice: hit for another card. A four.

"Stick," said John, noting the dealer's seven.

When the dealer revealed her second card it was a six, making thirteen. They drew another one - three. Then another one, an eight. A win for the couple!

Third hand, the princess had fourteen, the dealer a jack. Not good. Hitting another card, it was a six. They stuck.

The croupier turned over a three, then a king. Another dealer bust, a second win. Margot squealed in delight; she was enjoying this.

The evening continued in a similar vein, they appeared to be holding their own rather than breaking the bank, but at least they were still in the game. It was hot in there, or was it the masks making them hot? Margot gave an enormous yawn, then John suggested they call it a day.

"We could do," she said.

"How much have we got left?"

She counted up. "Eight hundred."

"The same amount we started at this table with!" he declared as if it was a major achievement.

"We could stake it all on one last hand?" she offered. It was a suggestion, not a command.

"Let's cash it in."

She hesitated, then answered, "Yes, let's!" as if it was a novel idea to leave with some money, even if it was twelve hundred less than she started with.

They came away and Margot enjoyed the novel experience of having some money re-credited to her account. They went back to the palace in good spirits and she clung to his arm which he enjoyed. Once in the living room where he first met the royal children, they divested themselves of their headgear. She looked hot and sweaty, her wet hair clinging to her face. It was most sexy.

"Give me your TRAC code," she demanded.

He perceived why and he protested, but she was determined. "I want to share our winnings with you!"

"But they're not winnings."

"I know, but..." she said and gave a voice command to her TRAC, transferring four hundred credits to his account. It gave her satisfaction, so his protests turned into thanks.

As they said goodnight, she bent forward to kiss him. He turned his head and she had to settled for his cheek. Before she knew it, he was gone.

It was lie-ins all round next day. John woke late and hurried to get up when he realised the time. He need not have bothered, because neither of his wards were up.

The whole situation struck him as absurd. Margot and Frederick lived in a gilded cage with nothing to do. The pair expected no visit from their parents that day. In fact, the time dragged and, come evening, John could understand Margot's desire to escape the palace.

The young lady herself came alive at this hour and the pair were eager to get going. Frederick was reading a fresh book, a thick one which would keep him going.

"I thought tonight would never come," said Margot with a giggle as she donned her hi-tech mask. She was acting playfully and, from the smell, had been drinking alcohol. John hoped she would not act too silly when they went out.

Straight to the casino they hurried. This time, Margot needed no persuading to go to the blackjack table. They plied her with drink which was placed down on her right-hand side. Even before she placed her first bet, she knocked the tall glass over and send the liquid all over the table. They designed the advanced material to absorb the moisture and keep dry on top. It was still an embarrassing start and she apologised between giggles. The staff were especially nice about the spillage.

The other gamblers played that hand without Margot taking part. They produced a second drink, in a much shorter glass. Almost immediately, she almost knocked that over. John realised that this could not continue.

"Come on, we'll leave it for another night," he said and scooped her chips up.

"We've only just got here," she whined as he led her out of the building, holding her up as they departed. At least she ceased complaining after those initial words. They stepped out onto the pavement.

"I can't breathe," she complained, but dare not take off her PFV until they were round a corner and out of sight.

It was a gloomy service alley at the side of the casino. The fresh air hit her and her knees buckled. The bodyguard needed all his strength to stop her from keeling over. She took some gulps of air and the strength returned to her legs. Margot stood, propped up against a wall for some moments and began to recover. Then, realising this was no place to stay, she reapplied her mask and he led her along to the bench where they spent the end of the previous evening. They found no one else about when they arrived and sat down. They took the risk of removing their PFVs, but John kept a wary eye out in case someone came along.

He thought she would be sick at one point, but she was not. She felt faint and John made her stick her head down to get the blood back. It worked and they could lean back and relax.

The couple remained in silence and she felt better by degrees. She was sobering up.

"You don't think they saw me, do you?" she asked.

"No, I'm sure they didn't," came his reassuring voice.

"They probably know who I am anyway, but the mask gives us all the pretence of anonymity. The casino's continued existence relies on it. No one will say anything."

"No."

Then she said, "I embarrassed you!"

He sought to reassure her, telling her it was nothing. She gave a little laugh, then added, "Your predecessor would have given me a lecture."

"I'll give you a lecture if you want," he said in an amused tone.

"I'll give it a miss, thanks."

John liked this; she was talking to him as an equal. They sat looking at the stars allowing the time to pass. Then she grabbed his hand and took it across to her lap where she held it. The alcohol effects had passed.

"It might," she began, "be a good thing for us to go back; not be up so late."

"For a change."

"I was thinking about tomorrow."

"Tomorrow?"

"Don't you know?"

"What?"

"Tomorrow is the one day we have to attend court. It's boring stuff, but I have to sit there and look beautiful."

"I'm sure you'll find that easy," he said with a wink,

Margot liked the compliment and moved her head forward for a kiss. This time, he obliged her. The couple kissed long and passionately until their lips were tingling. John realised he was entering dangerous, forbidden territory, but at that moment he cared not one bit.

~ End of Chapter 13 ~

My Keeper's Brother - Chapter 14

Princess Margot was not far wide of the mark concerning the following day. Her attendance at court was compulsory for this one day a week. Empress Madelyn was holding court, because the Emperor was tired and unable to attend. She came over to her daughter to acknowledge her at the beginning.

"Everything okay?" she enquired, looking up at John. He was standing behind his ward, who was sitting on the mini-throne provided.

The session itself was stage-managed. Certain citizens, hand-picked for the occasion, came forth and presented their petitions one at a time. Their ruler could show her magnanimity by granting the requests. It was a heavily controlled show, of course, but that did not seem to concern anyone present.

One point of interest to John was when one courtier let slip that the House of Vaxon had no operative spaceships. Their fleet was small and in a poor state of repair anyway, but a recent accident rendered the last serviceable craft inoperative. No one appeared concerned, because interstellar travel was a low priority to this society. For all their pomp and ceremony, it impressed upon John that this was an empire in decay.

This section of the proceedings concluded with a top official giving an address in praise of their rulers. This was not too long.

The last part was a religious service. A cleric gave a talk half way through that went over John's head. The whole thing was novel to his senses, so he was less bored with it all than Margot. Anyway, she was on best behaviour and stifled any yawns that came her way.

That evening, she and her bodyguard were back outside the palace. On this occasion, gambling was not on the agenda. She wanted to go straightaway to "their" bench for a chat. They dispensed with their disguises once they got there. She wore a big hood, which she put down as soon as they sat.

Margot said, "I heard that the palace's security grid failed again yesterday."

"Again?"

"Didn't I tell you? It's failed several times last week. I thought I'd mentioned it."

"No."

"A courtier said this morning."

"I didn't realise it was on the blink."

"It is, like many things around here."

"I'd been told it was state-of-the-art."

"It was when first installed, but it's creaking with age."

"Do they know what's causing it?"

"That's just it, they don't. It's an intermittent fault they can't find. Like the dome, it's an ancient system in need of a good overhaul."

"Let's hope they fix it soon."

"Mmm. Tell me more about your home planet."

"Marmaris? You already know it's an open planet. Mining companies found no substantial mineral deposits. The soil is poor and not able to sustain a large population. I told you about the terrible plague that killed my parents. Most of the world was affected. They contained it by taking some pretty drastic action."

"I see."

"Afterwards, I gather they've undergone a big political upheaval. They've tried to introduce a worldwide government with a senate. I'm not sure how successful they've been. I'm not tempted to go back."

"You don't want to go back?"

"What for? There's nothing left for me there. It'll all have changed. I wouldn't be re-living fond memories of places I knew."

"Hmm, I wonder if I'll feel like that when I leave here."

"You think you will?"

"My parents told me when I was young that I'd travel to another planet and meet a man worthy of me." She laughed before continuing, "It must be all flattery. What makes me so 'worthy'? Born in a certain place to certain privileged parents. Does that make me worthy?"

"I think you'd be quite a catch," he said with sincerity. "Whether or not you're the ruler's daughter."

She let out another giggle before answering, "Thank you, I believe you mean it."

"I do."

"But it won't ever be possible for you and me."

"I realise that."

Margot was gazing up at the stars, but rested her head on his shoulder as she continued. "You've been in the Erente District; what are people like there? Are they all like those poor, obsequious souls we saw at court today?"

"I didn't meet any such there. The folk in Erente District, or anywhere else, aren't much different. They all have their hopes, concerns, ambitions and fears. It's the scale that's different. The two thousand credits you'd blow at the roulette wheel of an evening, and think nothing of it, would change a poor person's life."

"Do you think I should give my allowance to the poor, then?"

"I'm not telling you what to do; I'm saying that what is trivial to you is great wealth to them."

"Mmm."

"But I'm not convinced that giving your money away would help them. Yes, some would use it to improve their lot, but that's not the entire story. It would be such a shock to others that they wouldn't spend it wisely. They'd squander it on booze or something else harmful, or get robbed. There's no guarantee it would help their lives. I'm certain they'd enjoy the opportunity to give it a go, but not sure it would guarantee them a happier or better life."

"I remember someone saying that there will always be poor people, no matter what system you have to control society."

"That's true. It's true on every planet I've visited in the past and that's a fair few. Of course, throughout history, some political regimes that have tried to enforce the same amount of wealth on an entire population. The population ended up with the same amount of poverty and the entire system needed enforcing by brutal methods. That's not an improvement on here."

"No."

"On Plerrania, there may be a rigid class structure and a good deal of snobbishness, but people can improve themselves. I met prudent people in the poor district who were saving money and, bit by bit, getting better off, or better jobs. My friend Della-Mura is now in charge of a police unit here in Riqueza, so it can be done."

"But you believe there'll always be poor people?"

"Yeah, if you want an honest answer."

Margot thought for a moment before responding. "Okay then, what if explorers discovered a brand new planet? An open planet with lots of resources and good soil. You colonised it with... say, ten thousand people. They gave each one the same amount of money on day one. What do you think would happen?"

"What do you think?"

"I think some would become rich and others poor."

"And I think you're right. Within a year, there's be millionaires and beggars. It's the way of the universe. The rich get richer and the poor get poorer. Revolutions don't alter those facts, merely the personnel."

"So you will not run off and join the terrorists soon?"

"I am not."

With a chuckle, the pair snuggled up closer and Margot posed her next question.

"Do you believe God decrees some will be poor and some rich?"

"Ah, that's outside my area of expertise. I do not profess to know anything about God and his ways. You'd need to speak to my brother about that. He loves that sort of thing."

"But you believe in God?"

"I can't say I've ever thought about it. Doesn't affect my daily life at all. Why, do you?"

"I suppose I do. Someone's got to have made everything. It's absurd believing intricate things came about without an intelligent mind behind it."

"You've thought it through a lot more than I have," he confessed. "It's not something I've considered much."

"Mmm," she went again before reverting to an earlier topic. The poor here on Plerrania, they love mother."

"Do they?"

She pulled herself away with a frown. "How can you doubt it? All those crowds cheering her when she turns up for a ceremony. The people thanking her when she administers justice in court and grants their petitions. You don't think that's all staged, do you?"

"Oh no, of course not. You're right, she's a popular ruler."

John did not believe a word of what he had just uttered. The crowds were cheering her mother, because they were told to, or they bought into her as a figurehead for their nation. The petitioners showed gratitude, because their desires were met, even if the authorities had worked it out in advance. Yet he would not burst her bubble, for that might turn into an argument. He would not spoil the mood.

It was his turn to prompt the kissing and they sat for a long time passionately embracing. While aware this relationship had no long-term future, they wanted it for now.

They pulled themselves apart, only to return to the palace with one thing on their minds. The night was spent in bed together, making love. Only once they had sated their passion did they go off to sleep.

The following days followed the same pattern. They waited until evening before going out to their favourite quiet spot. Their conversation never faltered. They found plenty to discuss and were on the same wavelength.

Then, one morning, John woke up in Margot's bed. She was up and having a shower. He gathered his things together and crept to his own room, doing his ablutions. Getting dressed, he made sure he looked his best and, cheerful expression on his face, walked back to the living room. Seated alone, Prince Frederick looked up from his volume when the bodyguard came in. The latter enquired as to his sister's presence.

"Mother's summonsed her a few moments ago."

"Oh," went John, for that was unusual. He looked at his TRAC, noticing he had turned it off. That was also unusual. As soon as he reactivated it, the thing burst into life, telling him there were no less than seven missed calls from Della-Mura.

'I wonder what he wants,' he mused. He soon found out, for it rang again.

"John! Where have you been?"

"Oh, good morning to you too, Della-Mura."

His former deputy then produced a hurried sentence which would have been half the length had it not contained so many swear words. Excluding these, it ran, "I've been trying to get through to you for the last half hour!"

"Oh, why?"

"Your life's in danger, you must get out. They know about you and the princess. Get out now!"

As he went bright red, John mumbled something about, "How...?"

"Don't you think they have surveillance cameras?" an exasperated Della-Mura asked.

"But I thought..."

"And staff who would find out?"

"I..."

263

"Never mind. You need to get out now!"

John came to his senses, realising what he must do. There was nothing in his palace room worth salvaging, he therefore made for the secret passage and speeded along it. There was a taxi passing and he hailed it. It took him to his flat where he picked up some belongings, not more than he could carry, before hurrying to the space port. There, he made straight for the changing rooms.

It turned to his advantage that *Shooter* was kept outside a pressurised dome, for he could avoid contac. His mind was working overtime. How did they find out? Did an employee see them and report to the Empress? They had been increasingly indiscreet in recent days. Who tipped Della-Mura off? How did he get to the space port without getting arrested? Was the surveillance grid down again?

Few people were abroad and none appeared in a rush as he dashed past them. When he entered the changing rooms, he found no one else in there.

'What really happened to my predecessors? I never found out. She can't have seduced them all! I expect my offence is far worse than theirs. Della-Mura was right, I must get out fast. Most of my possessions are still on board ship, I never got round to unloading them; I'm glad of that now.' The account balance on his TRAC was not brilliant, but he believed his life was at stake which was more important.

It seemed to take longer than usual to put on his spacesuit. At least with his ship parked in an obscure corner on the surface; he did not have to rely on anyone else. He jumped into the airlock, but everything seemed to work in slow motion - the inner door closing, air pumping in to match the outside pressure... The light changed, meaning he could open the external door and enter the toxic atmosphere. Clutching his compact case, he stepped out onto the surface of the planet. He was unaware whether or not he was being pursued.

The act of walking to his ship, two hundred metres away, seemed especially difficult. The uneven ground did not help, but the real difficulty lay in pushing through this dense atmosphere. The moment he reached the machine, his internal radio leapt into life.

"Commander Thorn, you must return to the central dome."

That answered one question, they were onto him at last. He turned his radio off. A ladder took him up to the cockpit and he sat busily touching screens to bring *Shooter* back to life. Side-stepping many pre-flight checks, he did not even change the air in the cabin at first, but relied on his spacesuit.

The second he was ready, he lifted *Shooter* and she flew off, hugging the surface of the planet until the domes were out of sight. Then he sailed upwards and, utilising UDS drive, shot out into space and away from the planet Plerrania.

'I hope they did not intercept Della-Mura's call,' he considered. 'I have software on my TRAC to prevent that.' Then his thoughts turned to Margot. 'She might be in hot water, but, she'll probably tell them it as all my fault and I seduced her. I'd do that in her position. Oh well... Time to flush out the atmosphere and divest myself of this suit...'

He wondered whether the Empress would order a hunt for him... if they could get a spacecraft serviceable, that is. It took two and a half days to get to Vonus, his chosen destination. They would be unlikely to seek him there. He possessed plenty of water plus some iron rations to keep him going on the journey. Passing stars and uninhabitable planets, there was plenty of time to consider his future options. With this in mind, he checked the credit balance on his wrist computer. What he saw made his eyes bulge. There were twenty thousand credits more than expected. When he looked into it, he discovered Margot had transferred it into his account. She held the code. No hard feelings then. John shook his head and laughed. So there was one poor person she helped. He was grateful.

A week later, he was sitting in a hotel room on Vonis, still considering his future. His visit was proving to be a bust. He had hoped to catch up with his old wartime colleague, Nicalino Robles, but it did not happen. John learned the man, a native of the planet, had moved on. He wanted to tour the reservation, having been recommended it. Unfortunately, the site was currently off limits. This was because of renovation work, or an ongoing dispute amongst the residents there, depending upon whether you wanted the official or unofficial explanation. Either way, it did not impress the visitor. He moved on.

New Mars was not on his list. A domed, desert planet, it was subject to giant dust storms from time to time. None were in progress when he landed. All was calm. The planet held a thin, carbon-dioxide atmosphere and possessed a mean temperature of 220 degrees K - cold! It did not matter, because he had no intention of wandering beyond the dome. The days were a similar length to Plerrania's, too long.

One morning, he found himself mesmerised by the view from the observation window. A red, rocky landscape, there were a couple of huge, extinct volcanoes in the distance. The file on his computer informed him there had been no seismic activity there for several million years.

John was still unclear where his future lay. The rent on his room was pricy ("Artificial gravity doesn't come cheap!"), but his funds were good. He watched as a buggy crawled across the landscape, it looked tiny in the distance. Up above, one of the planet's two moons was visible.

"You like the view," a shrill female voice nearby made him jump. He turned to see a plain-looking, middle-aged woman standing beside him. Dressed unusually in his experience, she wore a white poncho with black edging over a long, dull-red dress. Her brown shoes were short and stubby.

"I do," he said, "quite mesmerising."

"Recently arrived?"

"I am."

"Marion," she said, holding out her hand to shake. He shook it as he gave his own name.

"Are you planning on staying long?" she enquired.

"Um, I don't think so. I've got nothing planned. I'm taking each day as it comes."

"You look tense."

"Do I?"

"Yes... I hope you don't mind me saying."

With a shrug of his shoulders, it occurred to John that he could not care less what the woman said. He then felt guilty for having such thoughts. His mind was thus in conflict when she spoke again.

"You should come along to our meditation session."

"Should I?"

"Yes, it's on tonight."

Torn between telling this complete stranger to get knotted, or quiet acquiescence, he asked simply, "Why?"

An ambiguous question, she turned it to her best advantage.

"It will lower the tension in your body and help you get your mind in proper order. Meditation is good for you."

John's mind flitted back to when he was a child. 'Eat up your food, Johnny.' 'Why?' 'Because it's good for you.'

She persisted, "At least try it."

In a battle of wills, his weakened mind stood no chance of winning. He said yes. She looked triumphant, telling him the group would be delighted to welcome a new member and gave directions to her suite of rooms where it would be held.

That was it then. The woman disappeared, to his great relief. It had been worth saying yes to get rid of her. Meditation? What in heaven's name was he letting himself in for? He preferred not to think about it as he moved on to an eatery.

There was a dearth of vegetarian options to choose from, but at least they offered a nut cutlet. It was tasteless until he showered it with a vinegary sauce. Then it tasted of... vinegary sauce. What was wrong? Why was he feeling dissatisfied with everything? He wished neither to stay, leave, or indeed do anything.

High on his "don't do" list was meditation, but, having said he would go, he felt committed. He could not have faced that forceful woman if he skipped it, then bumped into her the following morning.

'She must be quite wealthy if she has a suite of rooms,' he considered as he made his way there.

Walking along the corridor, fifty metres shy, he turned round and started heading back to his own room. 'I don't want to go!' he told himself.

'Yes, but you said you would,' his other side reminded him.

'What? Me? Meditation?'

'Let's get it over with.'

He turned back twice and turned round again twice. Finding himself outside the suite, he went to press the control panel. Up above, a surveillance camera whirred. 'Oh no!' thought John, 'I hope they weren't watching my performance in the corridor. Please, ground, swallow me up.'

If they had been watching his antics, they did not show it. A small group, a mere half dozen of them, they were welcoming. Marion introduced the recruit to them all, but the single name he took in other than Marion's was their leader. His name, Midge, struck him as most odd. 'I thought that was a small fly.' The small fly, with snow-white hair and beard, gave him a warm greeting and explained how the evening should unfold.

"I give a little reading, then we have half an hour's meditation. After that, there is a discussion period. We end with a blessing, okay?"

What was he supposed to say? - no? Anyway, he did not. Instead he surveyed the group. At forty-two, he was the youngest person in the room. At least they helped the novice by telling him what to do.

Midge said, "You can either sit or kneel, but keep your back straight. If you sit, keep your feet on the ground. Close your eyes to avoid distractions."

They gave him a mantra, a special word to chant in his head during the meditation period. If, or rather when, his thoughts wandered, he was to keep bringing them back to the word each time. It was not a time for thinking; thinking was verboten. One must concentrate on the mantra the whole time. There is only the mantra. Simple.

"And expect nothing to happen," warned the leader. "We're not here for mystical experiences. I've been doing it twice a day for over forty years and nothing has happened."

"What's the point, then?" John wanted to say. Instead he just smiled.

"We keep returning to the mantra."

"Okay."

Basics established, the session began. One participant read a passage which, to be fair, was succinct. John recognised the words from the common tongue, but it might have well been in Ancient Egyptian for all he understood it. Maybe that was the wrong approach. He considered that, maybe, he should let it wash over him and have it enter his astral body via the third chakra.

With the ringing of a tiny bell, the meditation began. He sat in his chair, back straight, feet flat on the floor. Marion, next to him, did the same. Most of the others knelt, but one elderly lady stood on her head in the corner. 'How long has she been there?' wondered John, 'I never saw her move.'

No time to think of it now. No time to think at all. Concentrate on the mantra, not allowing thoughts to interfere.

Mantra, mantra, mantra. John wished he had blown his nose before the session began. Too late now. 'Oh! Mantra, mantra, mantra. The silence is deafening in here, I daren't move a muscle. I wonder how long we've done; mustn't look at my watch. I know, I'll open my eyes momentarily to see what the others are doing. They've all got their eyes closed, all perfectly still. All Quiet on the Western Front. I remember reading that book when I was thirteen... Oh, mantra, mantra, mantra... Ah ha, someone's tummy rumbled, it sounded like a space rocket taking off from Marmaris. Even the tiniest sound in here is... oh! Mantra, mantra, mantra. This is all silly, isn't it? Mantra, mantra, mantra. Oh no, I need to swallow! My mouth is full of juices. I can't carry on like this, I've got to go for it... Oh my goodness, that was loud! Everyone else in the room heard it. I'm surprised the walls didn't vibrate. How much longer to go? Mantra, mantra, mantra... why in heaven's name - ha! someone's chair squeaked. That was far louder than my swallow. I'm not the loudest now. That's good.'

The session continued.

'Everyone else is quiet. How can they be this quiet? Oops, I should be saying the mantra. Mantra, mantra... oh no! I want to cough. If a tummy rumble makes the walls shake, what in heaven's name will a cough do? It'll blow the entire room apart. I'll give that lady on her head a heart attack. Hold it in, John, hold it in. I don't want to cough, mantra, I don't want to cough, mantra, I *do* want to cough! Oh no, if I can hold it in longer... Maybe I can hold it until the half hour is up. It must be up soon... it feels like hours and hours since we started. I can't hold it in any longer, here goes!'

He did cough. Even though he tried to stifle the sound as much as possible in his sleeve, to his ears it sounded like an atomic explosion. He took a quick peek; everyone else was perfectly still. 'I hope they'll make allowances for the novice. They won't invite me again.'

On the group meditation went.

'Mantra, mantra... oh, sod the mantra! When will this ordeal be over? It feels like we've been here for days. Maybe Mitch's watch has stopped. Will I be stuck here for eternity? Oh please, just finish!'

"Ding ding," the little bell sounded and the session was over. Had it lasted half an hour, or was it a couple of years? He felt a couple of years older.

It concerned him they might be upset with all the racket he had made. After all, the other half dozen only produced one tummy rumble and one chair squeak between them. He caused such a din that inhabitants on the planet's far side must have heard. Yet all were smiles. The lady in the corner came upright again to re-join the group, her face flushed.

"Right," Midge began, "does anyone wish to speak about the reading, the meditation, or anything else?"

"Yeah, let me out!" John wanted to scream. Yet he kept still and let the others speak.

They mentioned various books and passages, none of which meant anything to the first-timer. All sounded satisfied, while John was, by this stage, thinking that being thrown out of an airlock without a spacesuit a rather pleasant alternative to his current situation.

The discussion went on for some time. No one tried to bring John into the conversation. When the evening's events were over, they parted ways, following a blessing.

"Hope to see you next week," Marion said, her voice firm.

"Yes, I hope to be here," he lied.

He held his smile until he was out into the corridor, then, making sure no cameras were on him, he let it drop. John stalked back to his room and switched on the vid screen to clear his head. He needed to scream, but the noise would have carried through to the adjoining rooms, so he desisted. It was a rubbish programme on the vid screen, but he did not care. Anything to expunge that experience from his brain.

The following week on New Mars, he got into something of a routine. One patisserie in particular, he found, provided an excellent breakfast. He liked the olde worlde surroundings. He still wanted to move on. Where to go? That was the question. He dithered and could not decide what his next step should be.

"I look forward to seeing you tonight," came a woman's voice.

He spun round to find Marion standing behind him, to one side. With a forced smile, he replied, "Yes, that'll be great."

"Good."

He asked, "Have you been on New Mars long?"

"Yes, the years soon go by. It's over twenty years now."

"Is it true that this planet's population is only thirty thousand people? It seems low."

"I believe that's about right. It fluctuates according to the season, between thirty and thirty-five thousand, I believe."

"It's not many, is it?"

"I think it's plenty," she said, turning her nose up as she spoke. "They're talking about a new settlement south of here, domes for another twenty-five thousand people. We don't want that. It'll change the entire nature of our community. Still, as I'm on the committee, I'll do my best to ensure it doesn't happen... in my lifetime, at least. When I'm dead and gone, they can do what they like."

It struck him as a selfish attitude, but he was past caring. Maybe that explained why he found himself walking to meditation group for a second round that evening.

Greeted like a long-lost friend, he froze when hugged by the men. The format was the same. On this occasion, though, he did not even try to meditate as per their suggested method. Instead, he considered his recent life. It kept him occupied the entire half hour and he neither swallowed nor coughed once.

'I spent seven years on Plerrania, courtesy of the House of Vaxon. That's longer than anywhere since I left Marmaris. It was a mixed bag. I enjoyed a fulfilling time in Erente and we solved some tricky cases in between the run-of-the-mill. There was the mission to track and hunt down the renegade Lynx. It took us to the farthest reaches of the galaxy where my brother lives. He's done well, in charge of his own fiefdom. I wouldn't mind settling down in my castle one day. He's got everything: authority, a pleasant wife, a son and his faith in God. All things I don't possess. Where did I go wrong?'

One of the other chairs squeaked, but he did not even notice it.

'Then it was back on Plerrania. My status as a national hero didn't last long. Soon afterwards, I was leaving in fear of my life. But what if Della-Mura got it wrong? What if they had not discovered my indiscretion with Margot after all? I don't think that's true; I was called back when about to board *Shooter*. Plus, Margot would not have given me her generous donation if I'd walked out on her with no good reason. No, I was fortunate to escape, I hope she doesn't go back to the roulette wheel.'

Someone in the room coughed and John tried not to smirk. It was nice knowing he was not alone in this. His thoughts went back further.

'That war was a terrible business. I'm proud not to have lost anyone in my charge on Rakass-Hist. Beforehand, when I was aboard that space station, I heard of several people I knew who'd been killed. That's always horrible. The cause we fought for was just. The rebels needed showing up for what they were. I still don't understand why the robot factory didn't get more publicity. Maybe the authorities considered the truth too terrible to broadcast.'

Further back still, his mind focused on Kratos. 'Brother Keith, Ordinance Officer Erik, who went on to great things. I wonder where they are now. Erik was a good friend to me. Gosh, that's ten years ago now. They say it'll disappoint you if you try to re-live your past. Still I might as well go there. I've got the funds. It'll be an improvement on this madhouse. Anywhere would.'

The half hour went a lot quicker this time. John realised he was being a fraud, but decided it was kinder to humour than upset these people. When it finally finished and they said, "See you next week," he said, "Yes, of course," while thinking, 'Not on your life!'

He left the planet the next day.

Back to the Halma Sector he went. When he was there a decade before, Kratos and Typhon were in hot dispute over the important asteroid 542/SN. He had heard they patched things over when the greater was broke out. With that conflict concluded several years ago, John wondered what the current situation was. He was not in the mood for entering another war zone. 'I'm too old for that sort of thing,' he told himself.

As he approached the planet, traffic control scanned his spacecraft before directing him to a small landing bay. If he parked his vehicle outside the dome, the fees were a tenth those inside. While he was still well off thanks to Margot, it made sense to conserve his funds, so outside it was. This meant fitting into his suit again and walking to the airlock. He might stay for a while. It was therefore a small inconvenience worth enduring. He took with him a medium-sized case with anti-grav unit.

Once inside, he stored his suit in a locker provided and made for customs. Conditions had changed from the first time he arrived on

Kratos. They were then concerned with getting as many recruits as possible for their armed forces. Now he sensed a contrasting mood.

The customs officer looked as humourless as the worst of them. John knew not to joke with him. International treaty banned robots, but he wondered if a few had slipped through disguised as customs officials.

"Are you aware, sir, that your ship will be micro-scanned for forbidden items?"

"No, but it's fine with me."

"Are you carrying any weapons, mind-altering substances, or items forbidden under international treaty?"

"I have a pulse pistol on board, for personal protection. It's in the cabin."

"Hmph," was the response he got from this revelation. Both men knew international law allowed it. Then, "And the purpose of your visit?"

"I'm on holiday to see some old friends. I used to serve in your armed forces a few years ago."

"So I see," responded the official without emotion. He was viewing John's records, obtained via the face recognition software.

After a while, they allowed him to pass through. John's priority was find somewhere to stay. He was more inclined to the lower end of the market, luxury being low on his list of priorities. In the event, they spoilt him for choice. There were plenty of places available and at reasonable cost.

He had not enjoyed the extra-long days on Plerrania and New Mars. If, as he hoped, he was going to spend some time here on Kratos, he would enjoy their shorter days. After all the travel and customs inquisition, he felt tired and went to bed early, skipping the evening meal. He slept well.

Feeling both refreshed and hungry the next morning, he sat up in bed and checked the local database to see if he could locate Erik. It was a simple task, General Erik Lebouran being easy to find.

'That's good news, but he's probably at some high-powered meeting.'

Further enquiries found Erik should be available that afternoon. Good, no need to hurry then. John was staying in a small, family-run hotel which provided breakfast. It filled him up. Afterwards, he hit the town, planning on having a wander round to re-familiarise himself with the place.

Some streets were instantly recognisable, but they had boarded up a lot of properties and he found himself side-stepping beggars. Even as he ate his lunch outside a cafe, a young girl came up to him asking for money. She thrust a deformed limb in his face to make the point, but the cafe proprietress shoved her away.

"I'm sorry, sir, begging is illegal here. If you're caught giving them money, you could face a fine."

The proprietress noted his quizzical look, so she explained further. "There is state aid for the poor; there's no excuse for begging," she said before returning inside to do her chores. John reflected on a young girl with a severe disability having slipped through the net, but it was not his place to ask. He let the matter pass. He was about to finish his coffee and leave, when he received a call on his TRAC.

"Hello, is that you, John?"

The hologramic image showed an older, fuller face, but it was hardly surprising after the time interval. The voice was still the same. John replied, "Yes, I arrived yesterday. I'm sure you're busy being a general, but I wondered if we could meet up for a drink and a chat some time soon."

"That would be delightful. This evening suit you?"

"Yes!" John answered with enthusiasm.

"Good. You'd like to come to the servicemen's club?"

They arranged a time and a place to meet and John concluded the conversation feeling buoyant.

'Excellent! It'll be wonderful to see him again. I hope we can still converse on any subject like the old days. It'll be great to catch up and exchange news.'

So it proved. Over a tasty meal, they found plenty to talk about. Erik was keen to hear John's news. The latter spoke at some length about what he had done since he left Kratos. He did gloss over the Margot episode, however, saying that he left with a generous settlement.

"What about you then? How's life in the higher echelons of power?"

"Not all it's cracked up to be. I'm tired of chairing meetings. When the opportunity came up to command the grandly titled First Space fleet, I jumped at it. I spend as much time flying as I can. I'm usually

274

on board the *Santee*, a juggernaut, the newest in the fleet, which means it's five years old now."

"Is the *Astoria* still going?"

"She is, but mothballed."

"I see."

"Do you? The fleet's a fraction of its size at its peak. We could not sustain it on the old scale nowadays. Kratos has fallen on hard times since the war."

"Did your war go badly, then? You seemed pretty upbeat when I last met you towards the war's end."

"We played our part, but the huge build up of our armed forces needed to be paid in the end. Our planet was living beyond its means for a long time before economic realities set in. At least we settled the long-running Typhon dispute when both sides realised the futility of it. The war with Tangeot et al put everything into perspective."

"We're friends with Typhon now are we?"

"That's overstating it a bit, but we get along; we have to. The other three planets in our group helped to broker the peace. We now jointly own and mine asteroid 542/SN equally. The precious metals are about the sole thing keeping us afloat right now. Even then, the commodity price has fallen. Our economy has taken quite a hit. The goods and services that Kratos offers are being undercut by a new player from outside our system. How they can afford to quote those prices and still make a profit? Slave labour, I suspect. They have an advantage."

"Slave labour, or robots maybe."

"I thought you'd be the last one to joke about that."

"You're right," John said. "That was in poor taste, sorry."

"That's okay," the other was quick to forgive him. "I wish we'd been more directly involved in the war. After one major battle all we ever did was escort duty for merchant ships."

"I'm sure it all helped towards the ultimate victory. Not everyone lives at the sharp end the whole time. I spent two years sorting out wages before I got some action. Then someone has to do it."

"We're being silly, aren't we?"

"Why's that?"

"Wanting to be in the thick of it, risking our lives."

"I guess it is silly, but I don't regret doing it."

"You might have a different perspective if you'd come back maimed."

"I'm not sure that's true," John said. "It was a cause I believed in. The enemy threatened the status quo that has kept the civilised universe going for hundreds of years. I saw Tangeot nuked to oblivion, but I'm not sorry. They had it coming. I hope it's a lesson for the future. Civilisation is a fragile thing and needs to be protected, by force if necessary." He paused before adding, "I apologise if I'm preaching; I don't mean to."

Erik guffawed, then said, "We could do with you in the Halma Sector. There's a movement afoot on Pricus which is spreading over here. Groups of fanatics are rioting and destroying public buildings. Arson and looting, it's insane. It's also scary, because they'll brook no opinion other than their own. They are so intolerant. It's a mob mentality and woe betide anyone who dare speak against them. No individual is brave enough to and the government seems too afraid to act. The silent majority are just that: silent. When that happens then anything goes."

"I wasn't aware things are that bad."

"It's worse on Pricus, where it all began, but there are copycat groups over here. The government needs to get a grip. As for the perpetrators, it's incredible to witness how easily people are influenced, following sets of ideas which were unacceptable a short time ago."

"I see. When the radical becomes the norm, then heaven help society."

"True! They started off by talking about equality and fairness for all, cheap slogans. Before you know it, they 're telling others how to think, speak and act, like the very worst dictators."

"Or they chop peoples' heads off like the French Revolutionaries in the name of brotherhood!"

"How quickly worthy causes turn bad."

"It's true, you can see it throughout history. The more revolutionaries talk about fraternity, the more they repress their fellow man with torture and executions."

"You're right. We need to stop this nonsense on Kratos before things deteriorate further."

"As someone who's studied history, it's easy to discern a pattern. If a group, or a people, are persecuted over a lengthy period; once that

276

persecution has lifted, you'd expect them to learn something from it. You'd hope that a certain wisdom would sink in and they'd be the most tolerant. Yet history shows us again and again that it isn't the case. How quickly the persecuted become the persecutors."

"You think?"

"There are many examples. They persecuted the Early Church for their beliefs, first by the Jews and then by the Roman authorities. They underwent horrendous torture and martyrdom for holding fast to a set of beliefs. Then, in the fourth century, as soon as they held the power themselves, they issued edicts against other religions. A lot worse followed, with torture and execution in the name of the Church. Then there were the twentieth-century Jews. They underwent terrible things under the German administration. They shoved them into ghettos and systematically murdered them. After they became an independent nation, they built ghettos with high, impenetrable walls for the other races within the land they now controlled."

"I didn't know that."

"I'd say it's out of fear. After being persecuted themselves, they never want to return to that position. So, they take measures to avoid it which, all too often, mirror the actions of their former persecutors."

"It's a pattern then."

"If someone starts on at me about their ideas for equality for all, I think my question must be, 'On whose terms?'"

Erik said, "We don't learn from history."

"Too true."

"A spiritual man told me too many opinions exist in this universe. Opinions and ideas don't unite us, they divide us."

"It's hard to argue against that. But should we not have opinions, even sensible ones?"

"Who arbitrates what's sensible?"

"Opinions against the fanatics, I mean."

"The fanatics are going to call their opponents fanatics. One man's freedom fighter is another man's terrorist."

"What's the answer then?"

"I don't have one; I don't profess to be the fount of all wisdom," Erik confessed. "But the philosopher I met said something that I've not forgotten. He said that if you resist something, you end up strengthening it."

"Hmm, that's not as crazy as it sounds. You can feel resistance welling up inside you when you challenge these types. What is the answer then?"

"He said that one should not resist these things, but *observe* them. I don't quite understand it myself."

"It sounds like he was talking about the effects within oneself, not the rioters. A bit too deep for me, like the meditation group I attended. They were into this profound stuff which was beyond me."

"The philosophy book is on hold then," Eric said with a chuckle.

"I'm a fighter, not a writer!"

"So where's your next battle?"

John sighed, "I'm getting too old for fighting battles. I think I'll leave that for younger men. I'm not at all sure what my next step will be."

"Find a nice girl and settle down," Erik offered.

"Maybe. I did once and threw it away. I'm not sure fate is going to give me a second chance and I only have myself to blame."

~ End of Chapter 14 ~

My Keeper's Brother - Chapter 15

John Thorn woke late, but refreshed. In no hurry to get up, he lay there and considered the previous evening. Erik was excellent and a good friend, who had mentioned taking some back leave. John was unsure if he would see him again. A pity, because it was rare to find such a kindred spirit, someone you could discuss things without a pre-set position.

From a filtered observation window, John watched the sun rise. Which sun would the traveller watch in a week's time? He did not know. At the back of his mind, he still harboured fears that Margot's mother may have hired someone to either assassinate him, or kidnap him and bring him back to face her wrath. It was a fantasy, but it would not harm to stay alert. Each planet had computers keeping records of visitors. The information was confidential, but a skilled hacker, or someone with the resources to bribe, could obtain it.

John's hoped that if he could move about a bit more, either the trail would go cold or they would lose interest. Besides, it was just his imagination; most likely the incident was all forgotten. He hoped so. The regret of not having said goodbye to Margot was a bigger concern. He could do nothing now. She could not have held it against him if she transferred that immense sum of money. It was keeping him in good stead. At the present rate, her donation should keep him going several years yet.

Father had installed money sense into both his sons. Theirs was a poor family and they needed to watch every credit. Both parents warned Frank and John about the evils of gambling and the virtue of prudence. Some would say it precluded fun, but each had visited many worlds and seen sights their parents could only have dreamed of. That must count for something.

Right now, apart from going along to breakfast before the kitchen closed, his priority was to get his spaceship serviced. *Shooter* was long overdue and it would be wise to have her seen to sooner rather than later. After eating, therefore, he called the space port to enquire about private spacecraft maintenance. An automated system told him everything except what he wanted to know. None of the "frequently asked questions" was his and he almost wished for an "infrequently asked questions" facility! Frustrated, he travelled there in person to find a human being to talk to. He feared a long wait, but when he arrived, the place was quiet and someone saw him straightaway.

"Yes, sir, how can I help?"

The lady was plump, middle-aged and her face heavily made-up. More pertinently, she wanted to assist him.

"I've got a small spaceship. It's a private runabout and in need of a service." He gave further details, but the answer was negative.

"I'm sorry, sir, but all our facilities are currently full. The fleet's ships take priority, I'm afraid, and we have quite a backlog at present."

"Oh," he said, crestfallen.

"But I can recommend you a place nearby which takes private clients if you like."

"Yes please."

"Have you heard of Kostroma Shuya?"

"I have. I've been there."

"They have what you need. If you like, I can call them and arrange a booking."

How helpful! A grateful John accepted the offer, asking for an appointment in four days' time.

"I'm sure that won't be a problem, sir."

Back in the town, he walked to a museum he had seen advertised. Housed in a modest building, it was an eclectic selection of artefacts, some over four hundred years old. He found himself alone in a gloomy room, peering at a decoding device from the Second I.W. era. It appeared a mangled pile, difficult to make out. Why did museums do that? Was there a lack of serviceable items to display?

He heard several footsteps and turned to see a school party entering. A group of girls, aged about ten or eleven, all immaculate in their uniform, filed in. They were chatting and giggling, John could not help but smile at the sight. It took them a moment to spot him in the poor light. When they did, they broke into a spontaneous chorus of greeting.

"Helloo!" they cried.

John greeted them back and it was a happy, spontaneous scene until the teacher, following her flock, admonished them for making a din.

He moved to allow the group to congregate around the exhibit. In no hurry, he hung back as the teacher addressed her class.

After giving a few basic details, the woman continued, "The Typhons use similar devises against us today. We must remember not to trust the people from Typhon."

John had considered leaving. Yet, it tempted him to speak to the teacher in front of her charges. Her job was to inform these young, impressive minds, not to pass on her nation's prejudices to another generation.

In the event, he said nothing. After he finished with the museum, it played on his mind as he walked down the road. In fact, it annoyed him so much that, when his TRAC rang, he responded with a sharp, "What!"

"Oh," responded the voice.

Recognising the hologramic face as Erik's, he stopped and said. "Ah, sorry 'bout that. My mind was elsewhere. What can I do for you?"

"I wondered if you'd like to meet up again this afternoon. I mean, if you've got nothing..."

"Yes! If you're not too busy."

"I have a proposal."

"Oh."

"Have you plans for this afternoon?"

"Um, no."

"Have you heard of the Bourne Gallery?"

"No, where's that?"

Erik told him and they arranged to meet on the steps of the renowned national art galley of Kratos mid-afternoon. In the meantime, John got himself something to eat for lunch at a nice vegetarian restaurant. The waitress could direct the diner to the gallery.

'I could have checked my wrist computer,' he said to himself, 'but she was far better looking than my TRAC.'

Thus refreshed, he arrived at the Bourne Gallery in good time, only to see Erik already standing outside.

"Hi, I hope I didn't keep you waiting."

"Not at all. So you haven't been here before?"

"No, I can't say I've heard of it prior to this morning."

"I'm surprised," Erik remarked, heading inside.

"Sorry. During my previous stay, I had little opportunity for sightseeing, plus I left in a hurry to go to war. I'm trying to make up for it now."

The Bourne, being a national treasure, charged no admission fee. It was a classical art gallery with actual pictures as opposed to the reproductions on the large majority of planets. They believed some works to be seven hundred and fifty years old. The galleries were quiet, with few other visitors in evidence.

"I love this place!" Erik said with enthusiasm as they progressed down a corridor to the first gallery proper. "I've been here so many times that I know the exhibits inside out. I'm a bit of an aficionado, even if I say it myself." Then he paused and added, "You can download a guide into your TRAC if you like. That'll tell you about each exhibit."

"Will you tell me about these yourself? I'd enjoy that, besides, I don't want to have my nose in my TRAC the whole time."

"Okay," responded the other man with obvious delight.

"And you can set your explanation low so that I can understand!" John said, grinning as he spoke.

The pair had the most fulfilling hour and a half following that. A knowledgeable amateur and his eager apprentice spent a grand time looking round. The Vorn Strategic School was beyond John, though. He liked the landscapes from the New Akron twenty-third century masters. Then, with a note of triumph, Erik announced, "Let's finish with the collection's pièce de résistance, a painting that, we are told, came from old Earth."

"Really?"

"They tell us it has an impeccable provenance."

Through they went to a room where they exhibited a single painting.

"The Priestess of Delphi by John Collier," read the caption. John concentrated on this highlight of the gallery's collection.

'Horrible!' was his first reaction, but the longer he stayed and studied it, the more he appreciated it. This was what he saw:

A young woman sat on a tall, three-cornered, bronze stool with carved lion's feet. She wore a khaki dress which exposed her left shoulder and had draped over her head a long, red shawl, the excess of which lay over her lap. In the priestess' right hand sat a bowl, in her left, she held an olive branch. Smoke swirled round the bottom of the scene and she had her eyes closed in intense concentration.

"You like it?" Erik asked.

A pause ensued before John answered honestly, "Yes, I do!"

"It's nineteenth century Pre-Raphaelite. Few of their works survive. They had a distinctive style with powerful use of colour and a certain realism."

The two pulled themselves away and John enquired if his friend was free for dinner again. "I thought we might try that same restaurant if you like."

"Sure, that would be nice."

That evening, over the meal, Erik made a proposal.

"You've mentioned, John, that you want to move on from Kratos."

"I'm afraid so. There isn't a lot to keep me here. Not that I'm sure where my long-term future lies."

"Listen! I've got leave due me. One place I'd like to visit is Izangi, are you familiar with it?"

"Vaguely," John said. "In the Ithica region? I think that's right."

"It is indeed. A domed planet, but I'm told that it has the most wonderful scenery. I can look at holograms, but that's not actually being there. What do you say?"

"The two of us go together?"

"Yes!"

"Sure, why not?"

"Excellent."

"But I must return to Kostroma Shuya first. My ship needs an overhaul and I've been told they've got excellent facilities there."

"After that, we could travel to Izangi."

John took a moment to study the three-dimensional star charts on his TRAC. Then he said, "It's do-able; in fact, it would fit nicely. When can you travel?"

"I'll need a couple of days to get my affairs in order. The admiral has been encouraging me to take my leave. He'll be pleased."

"Great. Can we leave in three days' time? That'll tie in with my maintenance booking slot at Kostroma Shuya. It'll be good to have company."

Both realised this was a temporary arrangement, but it seemed a most agreeable one. Erik would finally see a sight he had hankered after for years. John would enjoy company for the next stage of his Odyssey to... goodness knew where. It was a match.

The maintenance facilities were on a large space station orbiting the planet. They would commandeer a taxi down to the surface. As they waited, the pair looked out of the viewing window.

"You said you've been here previously?" Erik enquired.

"Yeah, a little while ago. The government tax heavily the citizens. That's one reason they set up the servicing facilities up here at the station. It's a tax haven."

"Amen to that."

"Well, they've quoted me a good price, so I'm happy."

They peered down at the world below them, illuminated by the nearby star. John said, "I'd better warn you, it feels most odd when you first get out. The heavy gravity drags you down. It doesn't do to spend too long on the planet's surface."

"But I'd like to try," Erik responded. "It'll be a novel experience for me."

Off they went by taxi shuttle and landed on the surface. The ship's artificial gravity kept things normal until they disembarked, then they felt the difference.

"Most odd!" exclaimed Erik as he practiced a few steps forward.

A self-driving taxi took them to the main dome marked as the Forum. They were in for a further surprise upon arrival, for the gravity was earth standard. As John stood there in disbelief, a helpful local explained.

"In the last year, we've installed artificial gravity here in the Forum at substantial cost. We hope to extend it down the corridors and into the other domes."

John thanked him, then went sightseeing with his companion. They had been looking round for a little while when John received a message via his wrist computer that his ship's service was going to take longer than expected.

"Nothing serious, I hope?" he enquired upon calling them.

"It's the previous job, there's a delay."

"Oh, I see."

After a brief discussion with Erik, the two of them spent the night on Kostroma Shuya. They hired a cabin and found it was in an area unaffected by the modernisation works. It did not affect their sleep, but they felt most odd when they got up the next morning. They still felt hungry enough to search for somewhere to have breakfast. What John did not expect was a most extraordinary coincidence.

This planet, like most domed ones, supported a tiny population when compared with some open ones. There was neither the space, nor facilities to house more. Most of this world's inhabitants came on company contracts, anyway. They soon discovered there were few sightseeing opportunities. Unperturbed by this, the tourists spent a while chatting over their meal.

Erik said, "My younger sister's announced that she's gong to get married. That'll be a big celebration. She's like mother, doesn't do things by half."

"What's her name?"

"Drusilla. She's a lot younger than me."

"You said you possessed more than one sister."

"Yes, I have another, who was born between me and Drusilla. Her name is Poppea."

"Your parents liked classical names."

"I think that was mother's fault."

"Where did your name come from then?" John said with a laugh.

Erik said, "I don't know, I'm sure I should do. But what about you? You have a brother, don't you?"

"That's right. No sisters, one elder brother, Frank."

"So he's Frank Thorn."

"Yes. Do you and your sisters all live on Kratos?"

"We do. Neither of them has been off-world. They were going to go once to..."

He stopped, because a man they had not noticed before was hovering over them. So close, it was clear he wanted to speak to the visitors.

"Can I help you?" asked Erik.

The middle-aged man appeared awkward, but needed to get something off his mind. He moved his attention to John and said, "Did you mention the name 'Frank Thorn'?"

"Yes," came the reply with a frown.

"I'm sorry to bother you, but there was a young guy here enquiring after a Frank Thorn a little while ago. The name stuck in my head. An oriental guy, I don't know if you're interested."

John thanked him and he departed. Then, turning to his friend, they exchanged incredulous looks.

"What was that all about?" Erik asked.

"Don't ask me!" said John with a shrug. The words were barely out of his mouth when he saw a lone figure walk past who fitted the stranger's description. "Hang on a minute," he said and got out of his chair.

Going over to the young man, John addressed him, "Excuse me, I'm sorry to bother you, but were you enquiring about a Frank Thorn?"

"Yes I am!" said the man, astonished. "Do you know him?"

"I know *a* Frank Thorn. He's my brother, but I'm not sure if he's the one you want."

"My name's Ibuki Nakajima. My father was a close friend to a Frank Thorn on the planet Eden many years ago. Does that ring any bells?"

"It might do. What do you want with him?"

"Oh, my father always spoke highly of him. I've taken it upon myself to track him down. If I can visit him, I could report back to my father. I'm sure he'd love to hear."

They spoke further before John invited him back to the restaurant to talk some more. After a while, Nakajima convinced him of the genuineness of his quest and told him of his brother's whereabouts. He gave the young man the exact coordinates of the planet Molten, but he issued two warnings. "I'm sure Frank doesn't want the whereabouts of Molten broadcast near and far. He wants to keep their primitive society the way it is, which means you're not to tell anyone you're an off-worlder if you find it."

"Okay."

"And I must warn you there are rumours of Chang Tides in the area."

"Er, I'm not sure I understand about them, sir. Besides, I thought they were supposed to exist between galaxies, not close to one."

"They are, but it seems they frequent the region of space between the two arms of the spiral galaxy where Molten is placed. They distort space and play havoc with the space-time continuum. Like I said, they sometimes appear in that sector. So, if something weird starts happening, get away as quickly as possible."

Nakajima Junior departed, leaving the other two contemplating what had just happened.

286

"That was strange," was John's verdict.

"I'd call it fate, wouldn't you?"

"I don't know what the hell to call it, certainly a coincidence."

"He seemed a nice young man, genuine."

"I guess so. Not sure what my brother will say when he turns up on his doorstep."

A call came through saying that the engineers had completed the servicing on John's spaceship.

"We'd better get going then."

Next stop was the planet Izangi. It pleased John to have got his ship serviced, although it did not seem any different to fly. They landed outside the dome, but with a tremendous dust storm swirling outside, there was nothing to do but sit there. The pilot kept the force field on to ensure no particles damaged the engines or surfaces.

"How long?" he enquired of the local control tower.

"It's forecast to carry on for another eight hours," came the answer.

"Oh no."

"But they can stop abruptly."

"Thanks."

If they wanted to explore the planet, they would have to wait out the storm. Still, with pleasant company, provisions and air to sustain them, it was not all bad.

Erik said, "The guide tells me that Izangi is almost identical to New Mars; you've been there, haven't you?"

"I have."

"Tell me about it."

"What do you want to know?"

"With eight hours to kill, you can tell me everything."

"I'm not sure I know everything, but I'm aware that, aeons ago, there was a decent atmosphere on New Mars. It was dense enough for water to flow on the surface, evidenced by dry riverbeds. Extraordinary, if you think about it."

"When you say aeons, how long do you mean?"

"Oh, I'm not sure. A couple of billion years ago, thereabouts."

"That's what fascinates me, the scale of it all: billions of years in time, trillions of kilometres in distance... everything is amazing. Take the size of stars, for instance. Some are enormous, able to swallow Kratos's sun thousands of times over, and that isn't small. It's mind-boggling."

"Yeah, I've learned a lot since I left Marmaris. I guess with all those vast facts, it's not surprising that ancient man tried to bring everything down to scale. They imagined that the local planets and stars all revolved round the earth. It's easy for us to laugh now, but it was logical then."

"Do you know your Bible?"

"No, that's my brother's department."

"A similar process goes on there. They start with God like a human, walking in a garden. Later, he's a tribal god, then they came to recognise he made everything, but still has preference for one particular group. Later, still, they realise he is the God of everything in the universe. Which means it's a progressive revelation. In astronomy, the stars never revolved round the earth. As man's understanding grew, he realised it was all on a much bigger scale. In theology, God never really walked in a garden. As man's understanding grew, he realised God was all on a much bigger scale."

"So what changed was man's perception, not the facts themselves."

"Exactly!" Erik cried.

"And I expect we think nowadays that we have a full understanding, yet in a few hundred years, they'll look back at our limited ideas and laugh."

"You're right."

"You know that I'm interested in history. It's frustrating, 'cos twenty-first and twenty-second material is sparse. A lot of the records were on computer systems which don't survive. Funnily enough, books have a far better survival rate."

"I know that the nihilists deliberately deleted a lot of stuff in the Second Intergalactic War."

"But you mentioned New Mars. Of course, the original Mars was first colonised in the twenty-first century. It was a sea change in history. For millennia, technology confined our species to one planet. How vulnerable is that? At a stroke, we had twice the chances of survival."

"The number of colonisable worlds in any solar system must be limited."

"Of course," said John, "many solar systems don't have any inhabitable planets at all. The tenacity of those early explorers fascinates me. Did you know that the first interstellar fleet of ships set off before scientists developed UDS Drive?"

"Er, no, I don't think I knew that."

"They set off for the nearest star system, knowing that generations would pass before they arrived. The would-be colonists spent whole lives, many lives, travelling. It's astonishing to me, the single-mindedness, the sheer determination to succeed."

"I suppose if you were born on the journey, you had no choice how you'd live your life. The psychological strain must have been tremendous."

"The pioneers had no UDS, or inertia negators, plus the most primitive of force fields, it was such a gamble, but they were prepared to take it."

"And did they make it?"

"Ah, there the records contradict each other. Some say they did, others say they arrived, but discovered a group with UDS arrived first, whe..."

Erik interrupted with a laugh, saying, "That would be frustrating! You arrive, the great, great, whatever, grandson of the original explorer, then find some smart arse had made the trip in less than an hour!"

They both laughed at this, but John wanted to finish what he was saying. "Some records say they never actually made it. Or, if you enjoy crazy theories, there's at least one account of an advanced ship from the future that picked them up and taking them on to the planet."

"What do you think?"

"Early space travel was incredibly dangerous. They reckon a third to half of the fights never made it."

"That's terrible! You couldn't run a modern space liner operation on that success rate."

"Accidents do still happen."

"Of course, but it wouldn't be much of a selling point saying, 'Come on one of our cruises... you've got a fifty percent chance of coming through it alive."

"I'm serous."

"Sorry, I shouldn't be facetious."

"It's okay. But their tenacity inspires me. We've become soft now with artificial gravity, automatic pilots and advanced navigation aides."

"I've noticed you still like to fly your ship."

"Of course I do! But where have all the explorers gone? They're rare nowadays. A friend of mine, we called him 'XO' for Executive Officer, but I can't remember his real name now... Anyway, he was going on a flight into uncharted territory, I rather wonder if I should have tried to go along with him now. That was years ago. I've heard no report of an exploration ship returning with a marvellous discovery. I don't know what happened to him."

"It's still a dangerous venture then."

"Maybe, but where has our spirit of adventure gone, damn the danger? Mankind seems to have stagnated into pettiness, either involved in stupid disputes with nearby planets, or navel-gazing on one's own little piece of rock."

"You'd like us to mount more exploration missions?"

"Sure I would. Try to find old Earth, for instance. There's a massive chunk of the Milky Way that is still inhabited, but we've lost contact. Why doesn't anyone rediscover those worlds?"

"I don't know."

"I'll tell you why. We've become so small-minded that few folk see beyond the end of their noses."

"It would be an expensive business. There's an international slump in trade, as you're aware. No one's got any money to spare these days, certainly not Kratos. We spent all our money on juggernauts and other ships which are sitting around idle now. Besides, is it a good idea?"

"What?"

"Exploration. Take the matter of our making contact, re-contacting, the other arm of the galaxy's spiral a few years ago. It seems to be a bust now. Our respective civilisations moved apart over the centuries and now no longer speak the same language, both literally and figuratively."

John said, "It'd be great if we sent ships to another galaxy, say Andromeda. Even with UDS and favourable Chang Tides, it would take centuries to get there. As you said, the distances in space are..."

"Astronomical," Eric finished the sentence with a smile.

They fell quiet for a while. Then John said, "I'm feeling sleepy. I think I'm going to take forty winks. Wake me up if this storm even ends."

Erik might have, but he too fell asleep. A couple of hours later, Izangi control tower woke them, saying the storm was over and that it was safe for them to proceed to the dome.

"Oh, thank goodness!" said John.

They sent an automated buggy out to them and they needed to don their spacesuits in order to transfer to it. Once in the dome, they changed before looking around.

In the main dome was a large observation window. Some people were peering out, but dust particles swirling in the middle distance prevented a good view. John chuckled at the way observation windows in these domes held a magnetic power over people on a thousand different worlds.

John and Erik booked a room before finding an eatery. They learned they must order food on this planet and consume meals in one's cabin, which struck them as most odd, but at least their room had a dedicated little area with table and chairs. Such was the local law. They had dinner and then retired for the night on their bunk bed. As they ate, they allowed the information channel to play on the vid screen.

"Izangi is the single inhabited planet in the solar system. Outside the domes, the environment is hostile. Mean air pressure is eight millibars and the atmosphere is ninety-five percent carbon dioxide. The temperature varies between one hundred and fifty and two hundred and fifty degrees Kelvin."

"Chilly then," Erik commented.

"Giant dust devils kick up oxidised iron dust that covers the surface. These formed, over time, the famous 'needle' rock formations observable from the domes' windows..."

"Exactly what I came here to see."

"Let's hope it's clear tomorrow," John said, "and we can see them."

"Hmm, that's right. Now, though, let's get some sleep."

The next morning, the two men set out early for the observation window. The air was crystal clear and they could see to the planet's horizon.

"You'd never believe what it was like yesterday," John said.

"No," agreed Erik, "but look at those!"

Out on the plain in front of them stood the Needles. Tall, thin rock formations, these were the hard pieces that withstood the blast of the sand storms so prevalent on the planet. Some stood alone, like figures pointing up to the heavens. Time had joined others in strange shapes. All were the rusty, red-brown colour of the surrounding sand.

"Amazing!" was Erik's verdict.

"Worth coming for then?" John said.

"Definitely."

A tall woman standing nearby turned when she heard this conversation. She remarked, "You like our needles, then?"

"I do," the man from Kratos enthused.

"Your first time here?"

"Yes."

"I'm a contractor living here and have looked out at them many times. I never tire of the sight."

Later, back in their cabin, Erik said to John in an ironic tone, "You looked very interested in the Needles."

"Sorry?"

"You were drooling over that leggy woman who spoke to us."

He sounded amused, not critical. The accused gave a guilty verdict, though.

"Yeah, she was gorgeous. I mean beautiful! Didn't you think so?"

"I'm more into men myself."

"Oh," said John, he had not known this.

"I have a regular partner on Kratos, but we have to keep it quiet. The authorities don't allow same-sex relationships back home."

"Ah, the New Morality!"

"That's what they call it."

"There's nothing new about it, of course," said John. "It's the same throughout history."

"Is it, in what way?"

"People's ideas of what is morally acceptable in the field of sex. The sexual morals of the 1790s were completely rejected by the 1850s, for instance. The 2020s society completely set what was deemed right and wrong in the 1960s on their head. What had been acceptable was suddenly unacceptable and vice versa."

"I didn't know that."

"It's often to do with sex. I mean, no civilisation has ever held cowardice as a virtue. Many things remain static, but not sex."

"What about you?" said Erik. "You seemed taken aback by my revelation at first."

"Surprised? Yes, I hadn't been expecting that. I remember before my brother left home. He became all religious and started going on about sexual morality to me. I was a fourteen year-old virgin. I'd never even kissed a girl. It all went over my head."

"But what do you think now?"

"Now? I'm not into moralising. I leave that to other people. Different worlds have different ideas. I keep out of it."

"You say you've found different worlds have different morals?"

"Yeah, other subjects too. Attitudes to wealth. I guess I'm anti-gambling, but I don't see that as a moral stand, it's a practical thing. For every well-publicised winner there are a hundred under-reported losers."

Erik pressed, "But don't you think people are too quick to judge? They do it all the time."

"Are you judging the judges?"

"Maybe I am, but it seems something in human nature to be judging or confirming everything."

"Of course you're right. Some historians fall into the trap of judging the past by moral standards of the age they write in. It's absurd, because the people of long ago acted by the paradigm of the universe belonging to their era. Returning to the astronomical example, to criticise ancient people for thinking the stars revolved round their planet is absurd. They were acting on the level of the primitive understanding they possessed."

"What about witch burning? That was cruel, wasn't it?"

"Not in the eyes of seventeenth century people. They thought they were doing their society a favour by burning witches. For us now to say it was cruel, pass a twenty-seventh century judgement on it, is meaningless. If we take our modern ideas into our study of history, we end up understanding nothing."

"I see what you mean."

"I'm no prophet," John said, "but I'll make one prophecy that will come true."

"Go on."

"Society's morals will change again. Don't ask me how, but they will change."

"But will we *learn*?"

"Ah, now that's another question."

In no hurry to depart, they stayed another day. Early afternoon, they were back at the observation window. Unfortunately for John, the beautiful woman was not present on this occasion.

"My word! What are those?" Erik asked regarding the strange creatures accompanying a group of men in spacesuits in the foreground. They were walking between the Needles nearest to the dome.

"Those, my friend, are dakks."

"Ah, the frontiersman's friend, is that right?"

"I believe they were called that. Pack animals who are good at surviving space travel and breathing air other than oxygen-based."

"But the atmosphere's so thin here!"

"Yes, but they're artificial creatures, designed in the lab to cope with all kinds of environments. I encountered them in large numbers on my brother's current planet, Molten. Mind you, condition there were most favourable. It's got ideal gravity, atmosphere, everything..."

"And where is this utopia?"

"On the rim, a long way away."

"But you visited your brother there, didn't you say?"

"A mission took me there."

"Would you describe yourself as being close to your brother?"

"We'd not seen each other in adult life. It pleased me at how well we got on when I visited Molten. I might go back there one day."

"Do you think so?"

"Might do," John replied with a slight shrug. "It would be a nice planet to retire to for a quiet life."

"Would it?"

"On second thoughts, perhaps not. Frank told me he'd been involved in a battle involving ancient weapons, swords and spears."

Erik said, "So much conflict wherever you look. Whether it's juggernauts or swords, it's still the same."

"That's true. Maybe people should travel more."

"Travel?"

"Go to fresh worlds and meet different people. It's an old cliché that travel broadens the mind, but it's true."

"So, we're not being too judgemental are we?"

"Ha ha, yes!"

"Listen," Erik said, "I've heard of a planet in the next system which might be worth visiting."

"Have you?"

"Feronia has a lot of history attached to it. I know you enjoy that, what do you say?"

"Sure. I'll have to preview the route and docking facilities first, but I don't expect a problem."

And so it proved. Feronia a further domed planet, had not always been so, as they were to discover. They arrived at night and arranged a room, leaving everything else for the morning. A good night's sleep ensued.

"My name is Jorani and I will be your guide today."

John and Erik could have downloaded a talk for a fraction of the price, but they enjoyed the personal touch. This woman was accommodating, knowledgeable and patient, the perfect attributes for a guide. Along with eighteen other tourists, John and Erik sat in the modern "coach" as it glided over the sandy planet's surface. Safety procedures established, they were on their way.

This was another desert landscape, but displaying yellow sand and, while uninhabitable outside the domes, not quite such a hostile environment as Izangi. The atmosphere was mostly nitrogen, but ten percent oxygen and a balmy mean temperature of 280 K. They were passing a rocky outcrop when Jorani began her spiel.

"Feronia has a long and proud history. It was the first planet colonised in this quadrant, when the first colonists arrived from old Earth in the year 2142. They brought with them the very latest terra-forming machines, along with flora and fauna, and set about transforming this world. After twenty-five years, the pioneers established a breathable atmosphere and more people, both companies and unattached colonist families, flocked to what they hoped to be a model planet. A thriving population resulted and about this time they launched a huge number of artificial satellites into orbit around the planet. Some of these, now redundant, remain in orbit today."

"I know," whispered John, "I had to avoid the blooming things!"

"They made their Declaration of Independence in 2192. We celebrated our four-hundredth anniversary only fifteen years ago. It was a cause of glorious celebration.

"Around that time the terra-forming of the planet began breaking down. Keeping the atmosphere breathable and stable took a great deal of resources and the Mother Planet, not accepting our independence, refused to help. (Earth troops were still stationed here). As a result, conditions deteriorated and the habitation domes needed to be constructed.

"To your left, you'll see remains of the Great Forest that stood here."

They peered forth, but all they could see were some dead, bleached tree trunks sticking out of the sand. Nevertheless, they were a fascinating sight to the tourists, many of whom took pictures.

"The Great War of Independence began, erroneously known in other parts as the First Intergalactic War."

John was agog, for this was his favourite subject.

"The Earth Alliance sent a mighty fleet this way to bring the valiant colonists to heel. It took several years and Feronia was close to defeat at one point. Yet, at the Battle of Yorkavia, the Earth forces received such a beating that they had to concede our independence. It was a close-run thing, but thanks to Providence and the tenacity of the colonists, they beat the aggressive and undemocratic Earth forces."

Another member of the party requested details of the battle. It delighted the guide to be asked this.

"The Earth's fleet commander split up his forces and left the juggernauts unescorted while the rest of the fleet set off to bombard the asteroid Optan Riga. During that operation, the courageous colonist forces, heavily outnumbered, made a surprise attack on the juggernauts and, over the course of the day and a half, wiped them out. It was such a conclusive victory that Earth never recovered and it assured Feronia's future."

'Albeit stuck in domes overlooking a desert.' mused John.

That evening, Erik asked him what he thought of the guided tour.

"A most informative presentation, I learned a lot... although it was a rather one-sided account of events."

"Was it?"

"The dastardly earth people bullying the poor colonists."

"I must have missed that bit."

"She didn't quite say that, but that's what it sounded like. Also, she called them juggernauts, but they weren't called that then."

"Weren't they?"

"They were battle cruisers in those days."

"A little anachronistic then."

"Another thing, what sort of nation celebrates its independence from a date prior to them getting it?"

"How do you mean?"

"They celebrate their Independence Day from the Declaration of 2192, when it was a mere aspiration. The colonists could have lost the war, and nearly did in fact, and remain one of Earth's colonies."

"Aren't you being pedantic, John?"

"Hmm, possibly a bit, but they should get it right."

"Perhaps you should write to their President and tell him they've been celebrating the wrong independence date for the last four hundred years."

Erik said this with a twinkle in his eye and his friend took it in good humour. Then he became more serious, saying it was time for him to leave and return to Kratos.

"It's been great, though, I've enjoyed it."

"When do you want to leave?"

"Tomorrow?"

"Okay, we'll do that. I'll fly you home."

They set off the following morning, making one slight detour on the way back to take in an astronomical phenomenon.

"What are we looking at?" Eric asked.

"An unnamed planet, that's rare. It should be a gaseous giant, but it's orbiting far too close to its star. Being so close, it completes a revolution every seventeen hours which is ridiculously quick. The star has stripped away the planet's large, outer layers and all that remains is its core."

"How big is it? All I see is a black dot passing across the star. I can only look at it 'cos you've got the window filter on maximum."

"That's true," said John, who then looked at the read-out on his control panel. "Its diameter is about four times that of Kratos'. The star will soon swallow it up."

"I see."

"Thanks for indulging me, I wanted to see this and, as we were passing close by..."

"Don't mention it."

A couple of days later, they were back on Erik's planet saying their farewells.

"Thanks for taking me round. I was keen to visit Feronia, but the other places were worth seeing too."

"It's been great to have you for company. I wish you all the best for the future."

"And you. Do you know where you'll be heading for next?"

"Not really, further out from the hub, I reckon. I'll see where fate takes me."

"Goodbye, my friend."

"Goodbye, Erik."

They shook hands, then John released his grip and headed off for his ship. He was forty-four years old, without a home, job, or somebody to love. His future had never been less certain either.

~ End of Chapter 15 ~

My Keeper's Brother - Chapter 16

A year and a half passed by, time during which John visited innumerable planets. There seemed no purpose or plan to his wanderings. The year 2609 found him on an unremarkable rocky world named Janus Major. High doses of gamma radiation continually bombarded the surface from its volatile star. So, the people who settled there buried deep underground to fashion somewhere to live. Seismically, the planet, being stable, was quite safe.

John found the history of Janus Major of interest. It was originally a mining corporation venture. They believed there to be vast deposits of rare minerals within the crust, putting accommodation, infrastructure and other facilities into vast caverns hewn out of the rock. The deposits ran out far quicker than the original geological surveys predicted. Programmers made serious mistakes with the computer model they used.

The corporation made the decision to pull the plug on the entire operation and drew up plans to recover plant, machinery and everything else. Then the workers rebelled and stopped them. The corporation wrote everything off and an independent colony was born.

Now it sustained around thirty thousand people in a variety of industries. One of these was mining, which recommenced exploiting low-grade ore. They established trade with a score of other planets. An insurance industry worked out of the planet too, covering spaceships of all civilian types.

One lunchtime, John sat towards the end of a long table in a canteen. After finishing his meal, he looked up things on his TRAC. He realised, having been through his money, that his financial position was not as flush as it had been. He would need to count his credits going forward.

As he viewed the attractions on nearby planets, one caught his eye. He was further from the hub and unfamiliar with this quadrant's spread-out worlds. Tripek III, he read, was an open planet first landed on during the early colonial period. An archaeological dig in progress there. That should be interesting to visit.

"I don't know what I'm going to do," a worried male voice sounded nearby.

John saw someone with corpulent features a little further up the table on the opposite side. He was speaking to anyone within earshot and, as John was the only other person present at this late hour, he felt obliged to pay attention.

"My ship's gone missing," the man said.

"Oh, dear."

"It's a cargo ship, disappeared without a trace. How can such a thing happen nowadays?"

Instead of trying to answer this rhetorical question, John tried something more positive. He said, "I presume you insured it."

"No, I couldn't afford to insure it," came the reply.

'You could not afford *not* to, you mean,' thought John, but he held his tongue.

The distraught merchant pulled a face, stood up and hurried away without further ado.

'Poor chap,' John considered, 'but there's nothing I can do to help him.'

It was time to leave. He settled his bills and walked out to his own spaceship waiting on the flattened, rocky pad.

"You are cleared or take-off." Janus Major's control tower told him and the craft rose from the surface before shooting off into the void.

Just a quick hop to Tripek III and soon he was gliding low over purple mountains and green river valleys. How refreshing, travelling to an open planet again.

The space port was modern, clean and fresh-looking. Surrounded by mountains in the middle distance, the view was quite spectacular.

Post-flight checks completed, John exited the ship and gasped at the atmosphere. Hot and humid, it was unlike the air conditioned environments he had become accustomed to.

Passing through customs control, he realised there was a lot of the day unspent. 'I might as well visit the archaeological dig now,' he considered. His TRAC held the coordinates, but when he enquired about hiring a car, he learned that would not be possible. "The authorities do not allow private citizens control of motor vehicles here," a lady official informed him, "but we have plenty of state-owned taxis that can take you."

Deciding to leave his baggage at the space port for now, he travelled the few kilometres to the dig by driverless taxi. The automated system understood his instructions easily enough and he watched the bank balance on his wrist computer take a dive as the journey progressed.

The taxi sped through a nearby town. Like many "frontier planets," it appeared quaint and old-fashioned, the streets lined with individual stores. No automatic online deliveries here. John noticed friars like the Brothers of Compassion he had come across on Belovo and several other planets. Out in the country, the road passed along the bottom of a river valley. Tall, grey, craggy cliffs with deep gulleys filled his view. The sky, visible through the sunroof, was deep blue. It would have been nice to have company on the journey.

Unsure what exactly he would find at its conclusion, the locals had told him the archaeological dig was still in progress. An interesting visit was in prospect. It occurred to him he should have made notes about all the places he visited, or even kept a journal. Plenty of historical information that had come his way. He could be certain no one ever collated so much data from as many sources. It would make a good text file. With so much lost, it might do a service for posterity.

"Time to destination, two minutes," announced the taxi.

John braced himself. The taxi turned off the road and onto a narrow cinder track. It negotiated a rise, before descending a long slope. Grassland on either side, woods beyond that. In front, a large open area led down to a lake. The far side of the water was ringed with majestic, snow-capped mountains. It reminded him of the scene in his special paperweight. The thought flitted out of his mind. More pertinently, the encampment lay the near side of the lake. A collection of tents, all different shapes and sizes, formed a temporary "city" of sorts. He had found the dig.

He emerged from the air-conditioned vehicle and again the warm weather again hit him. The taxi came to rest next to the site's visitors' hut, so that was helpful. He stood for a moment and shielded his eyes from the fierce sun. The place seemed deserted, then the sound of conversation came from inside the hut. A man and a woman were talking. Plucking up courage, he ventured in.

301

A tall, thin man in his fifties was conversing with a much larger lady of a similar age. The latter had her ample back towards the visitor, so it was the man who spotted John.

"Ha! Hello there, tee hee hee."

"Hello, I've come to look around, if that's okay."

"Of course. We encourage members of the public to come and see what we're about, tee hee hee."

He struck John as a somewhat strange figure. Long, unkempt hair hung down to his shoulders from the side of his head. The top was quite bald. His funny little chuckle at the end of each sentence was disconcerting.

Meanwhile, the woman spun her great hulk around a hundred and eighty degrees and extended a fat hand towards him.

"I'm Scarlett," she said, "your first time here?"

"I'm John. Yes, I've not long arrived on Tripek. I'd heard about this site and decided to take a peek."

She gave him a warm greeting, exclaiming, "Good for you!" As she spoke, her large crystal earrings bobbed up and down. "This is Gilbert."

"Hello Gilbert," greeted John, hoping that repeating the name would help him remember it.

"Would you like a guided tour?" Scarlett asked.

"That would be great. Thank you."

"I'm sure we can find someone to..."

As she spoke, another man entered the hut. John's age, he sported a full beard and moustache... and a pained expression.

"... ah, Walban, this is John. Would you be free to give him the tour now?"

"Hmm. I vaz going up to trench 12. I can take him," Walban responded in a gruff voice with a heavy accent.

"Thank you."

Scarlett said, "Hope to see you later."

John left with Walban, walking beside the colourful tents where they billeted the archaeologists.

"Does everyone camp here?"

"Zertainly zey do. It's impractical to commute from ze town. The authorities ban camper vehicles on zis vorld, az are private cars."

"Why is that?"

"Huh! Zey come up viz many excuses, but ze truth iz ze government are control freaks and zey don't enjoy giving zer citizens freedom."

"Oh, you're not from Tripek III yourself?"

"Few of us are. I am from Lares Ballin. Vhere I come from is no zecret."

"It seemed an odd statement. The speaker followed up by enquiring how much John knew about the dig. His guide wanted to know where to pitch his talk.

"I know little about it, although I read the site here is pre-First I.W."

"It iz an early zettement, mid-twenty-zecond century. Zey suffered significant data loss in zat and ze subsequent conflict. Zo ve must rely on vot ve dig up, ze old-fashioned vey. Do you know much about archaeology?"

"Um, no, not much."

"On most sites zese days, a dig does not mean a dig. Ze ground-penetrating probes are zo sophisticated zat ve can learn everything ve need vithout disturbing the soil. Because of local conditions, zey do not vork at all vell here. Zo ve have to dig it up ze old vay, methodically."

"I see... oh, my TRAC isn't working."

"Do not vorry; it vill again ven you get back to town and vithin range of ze energy dampeners."

'How strange,' considered John, but did not dwell on it as his guide was telling him more about the site.

"Ze settlement here dates from around 2150 to 2300, or 2350. Not an enourmous expanse of time and rather a short vile after ze Second Intergalactic Var ze site vas abandoned and moved zeveral kilometres to ze north and vere the current town iz. Ve hope vun day to learn vhy zat happened. Zere are no shortages of theories, but nothing definite as yet. Zen zat is the vonder of archaeology, going through theories."

"I see."

They were beyond the tents by now. Left of the track sat small, irregular mounds amongst a landscape sunken from the level of the path upon which they walked. Nobody was in that area. All the personnel worked on the other side of the track, with a massive, oblong area where archaeologists had stripped away the surface, revealing the mid-brown soil underneath. A complex series of square holes and larger features studded the area. They had marked guide lines across the land with coloured string and twenty-five people were beavering away under the sun. A gazebo stood in the corner and Walban directed the visitor underneath so they could enjoy some shade. It was a relief to John, sweating in the heat. Nearby stood buckets, spades, wheelbarrows, pickaxes, mattocks and many other types of equipment. Once settled under cover, the guide showed him what was what.

"I believe zis to be ze site of ze first settlement. Indications are zat zey landed in vinter and zey vere in a hurry to build shelters. For zat reason, ze very first structures vere made of vood. If you look along zere, you vill zee vhere ze posts went. Of course, after four hundred and fifty years, ze vood has all rotted avay, but you can still zee vhere ze post holes vere from ze different coloured soil."

"Ah, yes, I see," John responded. It was a complete lie. He peered hard at the area being pointed out to him, but he was damned if he could see any post holes.

"Of course it takes a vhile to get your eye in. Experience, you know."

"Of course," the visitor echoed, trying not to go red.

"And beyond zat, over zere, vhere Elaine is vorking. Zat's believed to be Phase Two, ven ze first stone buildings vere erected. If you look to her left, you can zee zat grey area on the floor."

"Yes," said John. This time, he could see it.

"Zat's an area vhere ve believed a vall fell down, Zere are signs of burning zere, zo it may vell have been caused by a fire. But ve are alvays careful not to jump to conclusions. Ve have multiple theories; nothing is ever straightforvard."

"Right."

Walban offered a drink of water from his flask, which was accepted with gratitude. He then spoke further about the archaeological site in its twentieth season. Those digging seasons were long, the winters being short on Tripek III. Most volunteers could not commit for the entire period. This meant volunteers coming and going. Several qualified, professional archaeologists remained on site in season, but a high proportion of those present were students or willing volunteers. They travelled from near and far, even from different quadrants to attend, year in, year out.

Once his talk finished, Walban, wished to remain on the trench. He asked John if he would mind returning to the visitors' hut by himself.

"No matter," John assured him, "I'll find the way."

As he walked back by himself, there was plenty to consider. While interested in archaeology from childhood, this was the first time he visited a site and it enthralled him. He needed purpose in life following the previous couple of years, maybe this was it.

Scarlett and Gilbert welcomed him back and offered him a further drink of water.

"Oh, yes, please! That would be nice."

"You look hot," the woman observed.

"Is it always like this here?"

"Varies a lot. This summer seems to be a warm one."

They chatted some more and John was invited to stay. She said, "If you want to join us, you'll have to pass the introductory course held on your first week. A fresh one's starting in a couple of days' time and I'll be taking it,"

The two archaeologists explained to John about the fees involved and the catering facilities on site. He would have to purchase a tent and they gave him a list of personal equipment and clothes required. His resources were dwindling, but he could afford this and, once established, staying there should be inexpensive. Plenty to think about, but with his enthusiasm about the enterprise, he considered it was worth trying.

"Should I report the day after tomorrow?"

"If you get here early," Scarlett advised, "you'll get a good pitch. Several people leave at the end of this week."

It was a frustrating return journey, because the taxi broke down half a kilometre short of his destination. The thing crashed to the ground as the anti-grav engine failed. His seatbelt stopped him from hitting the windscreen. He was close enough to town for his TRAC to come back online, so he called the company and they said they would send a replacement vehicle along with a mechanic.

He opted to wait rather than walk in the late afternoon heat, but they seemed to take an eternity to arrive. It was frustrating. A couple of official-looking vehicles passed by during this time, but no one stopped to offer help.

Then the mechanic turned up and they swapped vehicles.

"I hope you get it to work."

No reply. John got into the replacement taxi, which returned him to the depot. In a bad mood by now, he kicked up a fuss in the office. They offered him a fifty percent reduction to the cost, which he accepted and went on his way.

Evening fell. Tired and fed up, he walked the short distance to the space port and slept inside *Shooter*. He was unsure if they allowed this, but security appeared lax and nobody saw him.

John woke in the middle of the night with rain pouring down, but he slipped back to sleep. When he surfaced, come the morning, the air was a lot fresher. He exited his ship and walked into town to find a hotel. A room was already available and he took a shower and changed his clothes. He felt a lot better.

"Now, to tackle that list!"

A tent was top priority. Scarlett's advice stuck in his mind: get one a reasonable size if you are going to stay any length of time. He held no idea whatever how long he would be there, but it seemed prudent to purchase a large one.

Hammer, trowel, travel bed, blankets, torch, sun hat, kneeling pad, insect repellent... there was a long list of things to get. He ate a quick breakfast, therefore, then set off with a purpose.

Gilbert's recommendation was a particular store in town which catered for the "arkies" as locals called them, so that was his first destination. He came away thinking he had bought half the shop, but at least he got most of the items on the list. Coming out of there heavily-laden, he needed to wait for a military transporter to go by before crossing the road to his hotel. He dumped the booty on his bed, then set off again to get the remaining bits and pieces.

It was a full, but fruitful day's shopping. The weather was still warm, but less muggy. He then committed himself to two weeks at the dig by transferring the relevant amount to their account while he could. The first week was the introductory course. After dinner, he sat on his bed to consider matters.

'I'll head off to the site early tomorrow. The taxi's booked. The last couple of days have been the most enjoyable I've experienced in ages. This dig looks most interesting. I hope it can bring me back some purpose in my life. Most people in their mid-forties have settled down, like my brother. Maybe archaeology could do it for me. I'll have to see."

The following morning went like clockwork. The taxi arrived promptly and took him to the site without a hitch. It pleased John that the vehicle did not choose this occasion to conk out. Once arrived, he found a good pitch to site his tent and set it up with the help of a young lady present. It took her to point out that he was trying to erect it inside out.

At the evening meal, he met a lot more people, including Elaine Derby, professor and head archaeologist of the entire project. Also a most attractive woman named Charlie, but who everyone called "Doc" because she was a qualified doctor. There were many more, but he struggled to remember their names.

"You've settled in then?" asked Scarlett. who waddled over to him. He smiled at seeing a familiar face... well, if not exactly familiar, it was someone he had met once before.

"Yes, thanks, a kind woman helped me get my tent set up."

"They're a good bunch here. I think you'll like them."

"I'm sure."

"And we'll start the course tomorrow."

"How many do you expect to attend the course?"

"This week? We have six people, something like that."

"I see, I just wondered. I like your earrings, by the way."

"You do?" she said, delighted to have attention drawn to them. "These are my favourite, clear quartz. A dear friend gave them to me a long time ago. This one," she said, extracting a rose quartz medallion from the depths of her ample bosom, "is my chakra stone. It helps me keep a balance in my life."

"I see," John responded, trying to sound as neutral as possible.

"You must think it's all batty," said Scarlett.

"Oh, not at all," he lied, "but I don't profess to understand a great deal about it." Neither did he want to, but he said nothing further. Best to keep on everyone's good side, his teacher in particular.

The next three days whizzed by. The course was gripping, having a good balance of both theory and practical work. He was gaining a lot from it, although after a few hours scraping back with a trowel, he found his back aching.

'I guess I'm not as young as I used to be,' he mused.

Whilst many older members came each season, a large proportion on the introductory course were young.

'They're half my age,' he considered as he found himself outside the set for banter and having fun.

Yet he did not feel excluded, because Scarlett was always friendly and others welcomed him. It was hard not to notice the large percentage of women there, John estimated at six out of ten people. Most men sported large beards. Not that there were no shaving facilities. One could describe the amenities as comprehensive for living in a field. It was simply easier to let it grow.

No one complained regarding the food on offer either, both quality and quantity. It was amazing how hungry one felt lunchtime following a morning's digging.

Each participant on the introductory course had one particular area to work on, under supervision, whilst on trench. It could have seemed laborious, repeatedly scraping back an area. It was necessary to reveal gradually the features. As the days progressed, John found he got his eye in. He even thought he could identify post holes and where a slot beam once stood.

A ditch circumnavigated the site of the first, twenty-second century settlement. The teacher showed the students different cuts in the ditch where rain water, long ago, silted it up and the sides had needed re-cutting. Walban, who was supervising them in the trench that day, told them, "Ze slope here means hill-wash coming down, in particular during a heavy storm."

"Do these still occur?" John asked.

"Zey do. Ve keep on vorking in the rain unless it gets too much."

Rain was not forecast that day. A fierce heat beat down and the archaeologists needed to take precautions against it. This included making sure they kept hydrated. One young woman on the course caught sunstroke and had to lay down in the shade.

Late afternoon, once the workers downed tools, the younger members charged down to the lake and splash about in the cool water. It was quite safe.

One evening after supper, John found himself alone with Scarlett. It felt good to talk, relaxing under a tree. She questioned him about his origins and he told her something of his life. Then it was her turn to speak.

"I was born and brought up on nearby Feronia, I don't know if you've heard of it."

"Yes, I have, I was there recently. A desert planet where the terra-forming went wrong."

She smiled. "When has it ever worked? If you try to get machines to do nature's work, that's asking for trouble. You need patience and work *with* Mother Nature, not try to force her against her will. Look at this place. When the first explorers arrived, neither trees nor grass existed. The most advanced indigenous life discovered were mosses."

"Seems hard to believe to see it now."

"It does. They seeded the planet, then left it for a generation before the first settlers landed. In the intervening period, grass and trees had grown like wildfire. The soil here is fertile. It's all nature's work, with a little encouragement from us, of course. One of the best artefacts from the early settlement is a paper diary kept by one of the early settlers."

"Was it found here, on the dig?"

"No. They handed it down through the generations of a family still inhabiting the town. The original is delicate now, but they have downloaded all its contents. The writer was an April Franco who was a keen botanist. She writes about them sowing grass seed after that first, terrible winter, and how it took like wildfire. When you survey the landscape today and see grasslands to the horizon, it's all from that initial planting."

"The soil must have been fertile!"

"Mother Nature is so wonderful, she can win against the odds."

"Not in Feronia's case, though," he pointed out.

"No," she conceded, "that was a step too far. Never enough open planets, not nearly enough. I love it here; the sky, the mountains, the fresh, non-recycled air. I'm trying to find energy lines here with my rods. I think we'll locate their worship place if I can find two intersecting."

John was lost by now and they fell silent. The light was fading fast as the sun had passed below the horizon. Effective artificial lighting was being provided by a rig set up on the branches above them. They both started speaking, then stopped. Scarlett insisted he say his piece first.

"I was going to remark that I saw several military 'planes going overhead for the second day running. Is there a base near here?"

With a scowl, she replied, "Blasted men with their guns! There's a row going on between Tripek III and Lares Ballin. Don't ask me what it's about; some silly dispute. Both sides are flexing their muscles. It's childish; high time they grew up!"

John considered, 'Possibly not be the perfect time to tell her about my former career in the space marines.' In fact, his beliefs had moved on a great deal since those days. With sincerity, he said, "Oh dear, there have been conflicts in so many places I've visited over the years. You'd have hoped mankind would have learned to live in peace by now."

"Fat chance!" she said. "The politicians talk about peace while preparing for war. It's all talk, but they're not serious. If they were serious, they'd know that peace has to start here," she fisted her chest, "and not with clever words or treaties."

They were both eager to change the subject and John enquired about tomorrow's itinerary.

"There will be a session on section drawing tomorrow and then, the following day, it's environmental archaeology. On the final afternoon, we'll have a little quiz to see what you've learned."

"Oh dear!"

"Don't say that. I've seen you making notes and taking it all in. You ask intelligent questions too. I like that."

"Thank you."

It reminded him of school and he wanted to please the teacher. Unlike school, they were all volunteers.

Next day, they worked on trench recording a feature and drawing sections. The teacher explained that the camera *does* lie, and even with the best hologramic photographic equipment available, they would only complement drawings. There were, he learned, certain subtleties which a drawing alone could pick up.

Walban was helping the trainees again and he came over to where John was sitting on a bench filling in his electronic context record sheet.

"And vot have you written for ze soil type?"

"Sandy-silt, firm. Dark greyish-brown."

"Good."

"Occasional, large sub-angular flint. Fill of cut three."

"Yes."

"And the pit is round in plan and on grid reference 32/16, fifty centimetres deep."

"Vot about the profile?"

"A U-shaped profile with a sharp break of slope at top and gradual at the bottom. Depth of fifty centimetres."

"Go on."

"There's a clear boundary between two and four. Not truncated. No natural disturbance (for example root damage) and the stratigraphic reliability is good."

"Excellent, John, you are getting ze hang of it."

That evening, he sat opposite Professor Derby, the head archaeologist. She reminded him of his late grandmother with her grey hair and worn, but kind, face.

"John, isn't it?"

"Yes, ma'am," he said, surprised that she could remember his name.

"Elaine, please."

"Elaine, right."

"How's the course going?"

"Very well, great, in fact. Scarlett's a wonderful teacher, but there's a lot to take in."

"There are always experts to consult and you're never alone."

"Thank you, that's nice to hear."

"Although," she said with a twinkle in her eye, "you ask five experienced archaeologists for their opinion on a feature and you'll get eight different answers."

While he chuckled at this, Elaine continued, "But we respect each other's opinions."

"Good. Have you been here since the dig started?"

"This is our twentieth year; I have been here since the beginning in '90. I say 'the beginning,' but they undertook a previous dig here during the '50s, of course."

"I didn't know that."

"A man named Diamond dug several test pits. He tried ground radar, magnetometry and some more modern non-evasive methods, but none worked to a satisfactory degree. It's rather fun doing it the old-fashioned way; getting down and dirty."

"How do you pass your time when you're not here?"

"Out of season? I go back to my long-suffering husband on Attis."

"What does he do?"

"He's retired."

"But he doesn't join you here on the dig?"

"He did one year, in the early days, but he decided it wasn't for him. Bless him."

As she spoke, a loud, low, throbbing noise filled the air as something big passed overhead. The intense sound was most unpleasant.

"A military transport," the professor explained before carrying on. "He has his own hobbies to pursue and doesn't seem to mind being apart from me for half the year."

It amazed John the level of commitment shown by many of the people here. Several had been there for two decades, returning year after year. He realised quite what a slow, patient enterprise it was. In stages, they built up a picture of the four hundred year old settlement. No end date existed for the project. He wondered what those first colonists, fresh from Mother Earth, would have thought about people raking over their lives and artefacts centuries later. The discarded tooth brushes and broken combs cleaned, preserved and put away in purpose-made containers. It seemed bizarre to him. In the year 3000, would a keen bunch of people be pawing over the site of his parents' farm on planet Marmaris? Possibly.

That night, he quickly dropped off to sleep. Absent were the flies that plagued them on the trench during the day. Why export those annoying insects to the planet? He supposed they were an essential part of the ecosystem, but it was a shame they could not have invented a different one, excluding them.

Next morning, following the daily early morning meeting, they gave the trainees over to the environmental section until lunchtime. The group crowded into the Enviro Hut, as they dubbed it. Shielded by some large trees, it was cooler there than out on the trench.

"It's a bit of a cushy number," joked Tom, head of the Environmental Unit. "We get to sit as we work... well, sometimes."

Early sixties, with a lively temperament and big, bushy beard, Tom was one of those ever-present since the early years. Always seeking a quick witticism, he pointed out a notice on the wall. It read, "Welcome to Enviro, a Politics-free Zone." To push the point home, he said, "So if you wish to discuss the Larens Ballin situation, you are more than welcome, but not while you're in Enviro."

The message was loud and clear. To date, John had only heard oblique references to a serious ongoing dispute between the planet they were on, Tripek III, and the other world. John had had his fill of current wars and rumours of wars and he was more than happy keeping off the subject.

"Environmental archaeology," Tom began, "is the science of reconstructing the relationship between past societies and the environments they lived in. Here in Enviro, we take sample buckets collected by the diggers and sort them to see what tiny bits they contain, but more of that later. We'll go outside and I'll show you the first part of the process."

Tom led the group out of the hut, explaining as they walked.

"We agree on a sampling schedule with the trench supervisors beforehand. This year, for example, we've set up a two-metre square grid over the feature at the south end of Trench Twelve. It's producing a lot of material to analyse. The diggers bring ten-litre buckets up from the trench and logged here. They electronically tag each one. We have to double-check that everything is properly recorded. If someone makes a mistake, then it can render the entire operation void. Before sampling, they make sure that their tools and bucket are clean and free from other deposits that may contaminate the sample."

The environmental supervisor then led them to the floatation tank. It appeared a crude piece of kit to John, but he supposed if it did the job, that was all that mattered. The group waited as he filled the tank with water.

"We empty the buckets of earth into the top of the tank and the resultant mud is worked by hand and allowed to fall through the close-meshed basket underneath. Other digs have tried automated systems, but nothing beats good old fingers and thumbs. What's left is the residue which we'll dry and sort later when it's dried. Come on," he cried, "you've all got to have a turn!"

The trainees took turns to place their hands in the water, washing the mud until it dissolved, falling to the tank's bottom.

"A pleasant job on a day like this," said Tom.

He was right. On that hot day, it felt most pleasant sticking one's hands into the cool water.

"But not so nice in cold weather!" he said.

Later, inside the hut, the trainees had a session at sorting samples of dried residue after being shown what to pick out by the supervisor. Snail shells, charcoal, small animal bone, fish bones, burnt seeds... there were plenty of things to watch out for. The course members struggled, as the tiny samples, often less than a millimetre long, appeared to mimic each other. It needed the supervisor's experienced eyes to say what was what.

"Is this an animal bone?" one of the young trainees.

"No, it's a stone," Tom advised.

"Is this a seed?" asked another.

"Stone."

"Bone?"

"Fossil; goes in the discard pile."

"Stone?"

"See the latticework on the other side? That's a sure sign of bone."

They had developed computerised systems for this work, but the authorities here rated them poorly. While instructive, John was unsure it was for him. He did not fancy sorting through tiny specs for hours. He slept well again that night, the fresh air and exercise helped with that. His back was no longer giving him gyp either.

On the last day of the course, they spent half the morning in finds. A pair of middle-aged women were pawing through labelled trays at an assortment of artefacts that the diggers unearthed. Remains of an old shoe, well preserved for its age, a dinner knife, a small, engraved case, part of a computer screen, jewellery mountings and half a hundred other things.

Scarlett, who stayed with her charges on this occasion, fiddled in a drawer for one particular find she thought they would enjoy.

"It's an early type of pulse pistol," she said.

The item, being crushed and degraded, John had trouble making it out at first. In fact, he remained unconvinced it was what she said it was, but he would not challenge her, particularly in pubic. Pulse pistol or not, the finds department held a particular fascination to him.

'I'm holding a comb that someone ran through their hair all those centuries ago,' he considered. Then a thought struck him.

"If this comb was from the first colonists, they could have manufactured it on old earth!" he stated with awe.

"It could have," Scarlett said. "We'll never know categorically. I'm aware that some of the finds team take things back to their home planets during the closed season and put them through the modern equipment there. It's one way we can find out more about them."

"Fascinating!" was John's verdict. He was hooked.

That evening, there was another conversation with the project head, Professor Elaine Derby. He sought her opinion on why the settlement had not stayed where it was, but moved up to where the current town stood.

"Ah! A cause of much debate," she replied with relish. "Earthquake, war, disease, the theories are legion. They appear to have abandoned it early in the twenty-third century, but experts dispute that date. I believe it was around the time of the Second Intergalactic War."

"You're going to tell me the records are limited."

"Indeed they are. However, there's a nearby planet, Milos, in the next solar system, which was settled round about the same time. There are far better surviving records there and it's fascinating stuff."

"And what happened to them?"

"They were colonists from Ithaca, a planet in the Domas System, one known for its binary stars."

"So the population here on Tripek III could've originated from Ithaca too."

"They might have, although diarist April Franco says that they were from Earth. The records show that, after the colonisation, but prior to the war, their own nuclear conflict ravaged Ithaca. It was an internal affair, but devastated the planet. They then ordered the colonists back to their mother planet to help re-populate and re-build it. But the worthy folk of Milos told them no."

"Not surprising in the circumstances."

"Indeed, but one theory is that the colonists here on Tripek III were also ordered there, but ignored the call."

"Do you believe that?"

"Would you give this up for a radioactive planet?"

"Hardly!"

"I'm keeping an open mind. Small-scale excavations up at the town show a quite different culture from the folk here. Then that's the fun of archaeology; building up plausible theories. It's genuine detective work. That's why I love it."

315

"I think I'm going to love it too," the onetime detective confessed.

"I'm glad. It has that effect on people. But tell me, what profession were you previously?"

"I was a soldier."

"Oh!" she responded, surprised, "in the war you mean?"

"I was indeed in the war, yes, but I was a soldier prior to that. I was a soldier for hire."

"A mercenary."

"I suppose that's right, I never used that word."

"You must be skilled in the art of warfare," she said.

It struck him a strange turn of phrase and he was unsure if she was being judgemental or not. It made him want to justify himself.

"I was young and full of ideals when I left my home planet. I loved history, I still do, and that's peppered with wars, of course."

"Indeed it is."

"And many large wars in history have had huge effects on mankind's future."

"You think so?"

"The outcome of the First Intergalactic War gave the colonists freedom from the Mother Planet's bondage and they could explore the galaxy in that knowledge. The Second Intergalactic War's aftermath produced international agreements to ban certain things in perpetuity. It also saw wide areas of the galaxy cut off. The recent, Third War kept the status quo."

"Succinctly put. You're therefore arguing wars are a good thing?"

"Hey, that's not what I'm saying at all. The point I'm making is that wars, no matter what our view of them, shape history. I've seen enough conflict for one lifetime and I wouldn't describe a lot as 'good.' The longer I live, the less keen on war I become. I wouldn't take up soldiery again."

"Not even for a cause you feel passionate about?"

"I'm getting disillusioned with causes that produce that sort of passion. We must find better ways to solve disputes."

"Amen to that."

"If things carry on as they are, I'll end up an ardent pacifist!"

While the professor was careful not to let on regarding her own views on the subject, she appeared interested in John's thoughts and the journey he had taken. She said, "But, from what you've told me, you're still interested in wars, but from an academic angle."

"The historical angle," he corrected.

"Yes, indeed."

"Surely in order to understand history, you need to know something about its conflicts. Yet, when I look at the finds here, the discarded shoe, or the comb with half its teeth missing, it helps me to appreciate the everyday, domestic side of history too."

"What are your plans for tomorrow?" Elaine asked.

"Our day off, isn't it?"

"Have you any plans, maybe visit the town? I know some people will be."

"I've not considered. Taken up with the course this week, I haven't thought beyond that."

"Have you heard of the Ignoss site?"

"Um, no."

"It's about forty kilometres from here, the site of a data storage and library facility that was destroyed during the Second War. It's quite a sight. If you are interested, I can take you there and show you around."

"Sounds amazing! Yes please. I'm surprised I haven't heard it mentioned this week."

"The old hands take Ignoss for granted. But it's worth a visit. There's not a huge amount remaining, but you get a feeling for the scale. Anyhow, I won't force you, but, if you're interested, we can catch one of the taxis getting here early tomorrow morning. That'll take us into town. Then take another one to the site."

"That's most kind. Yes, please, I'd appreciate that."

~ End of Chapter 16 ~

My Keeper's Brother - Chapter 17

In the year 2235, the Council of Yagishiri made an international decision to set up several data hubs around the known galaxy. With mankind spread out on thousands of worlds, they believed it desirable to concentrate all the centuries' accumulated knowledge on a few planets. They used them as centres of excellence, often, but not always, attached to universities. The Council organised the work with a sense of purpose and enthusiasm. It took less than twenty-five years for all the hubs to be installed. They set one of these up on Tripek III, which became active in the year 2251. No one anticipated the storm to come.

All too soon, the fateful year 2278 arrived. The Second Intergalactic War saw a huge attack on the facilities in a campaign to irradiate knowledge in a thousand fields and destroy records of the past. Their determination and efficiency matched their fanaticism. So much was lost.

John was enjoying his one-to-one attention from the elderly professor in charge of the archaeological project. He saw her as a mother figure who could hold conversation on many subjects. As they travelled to the site from the town, she told him how she met her future husband almost forty years before.

"We shared an interest in archery and met on the range. Holographic range, that is. I rather liked the look of him and we hit it off straightaway. Our having an interest in common helped, of course. We pursued a long-distance relationship because he worked off-planet. In the end, he transferred back and we got married. Ah! Here we are."

The taxi arrived at the site as the sun broke through the clouds and they disembarked. The air was warm and sticky. No one else was about.

"That's funny," Elaine remarked, "it's not normally as deserted as this."

They had the place to themselves. The complex consisted of a series of round white building. The jagged remains of a massive

318

dome dominated the central one. Caved in long ago, pieces of synthetic material mixed with the rubble that filled the interior. Also present were the twisted remains of data stores.

"It's massive!" cried John, awestruck.

"Yes, the library stretched back to that river. Nowadays, they employ people to keep the site from getting overgrown. There's usually a couple on duty, they could be elsewhere in the complex, I suppose."

The scale of the enterprise shook John. The nihilists had destroyed this vast housing of mankind's accumulated knowledge over millennia, along with its sister sites across the galaxy. What an act of cultural vandalism, a triumph for ignorance.

"I'm told," the professor began, "that the cadre who attacked this site was a group of students from Radon IV in the Omega Serpentis System, close to old Earth. The nihilist movement was strong there."

"I've heard of them. Crazy; why would students of all people set about destroying records, destroying their heritage? You'd have thought they'd be the last ones to act that way. Students should be learning, not destroying things they don't like, They seem to despise the past."

"Students of stupidity," she offered.

They explored by themselves in the absence of a guide. The information holo-suite stood closed "for essential maintenance." Elaine knew a basic outline of the facts, which John was aware of, anyway. Yet it was worth the trip.

"Mind-boggling," he said, "but it leaves you feeling the futility, the futility of conflict. Plus the idiocy of movements against individual thought."

The professor gave a slight toothless grin and nodded in agreement.

Back on site the next day, he revelled in his new status as a qualified beginner. The previous week's course was an excellent introduction and he sailed through the test, but he knew he had lots still to learn.

The first day as a qualified digger, he elected to dig on trench. "Digging," in this context, meant repeatedly scraping an area of soil, half a centimetre at a time. When completed, you started again for the next layer. It was slow, controlled work, but necessary, because by revealing the area in tiny stages, they saw everything and missed nothing. "Cos when it's gone, it's gone," as one supervisor succinctly put it.

By late morning, it felt hot. John licked his lips and tasted the salt on them. One digger fell faint and they took her away to the first aid tent. Soon afterwards, the supervisor called an early break.

He found himself with Scarlett over lunch.

"How was your morning?" she enquired.

"Too hot for me, to be honest."

"I'm back in finds this week. The dating results arrived back on the little girl's shoe found a fortnight ago. Spectroscopic analysis of the fibres shows a year of 2190, give or take ten years, so that's early. I hope to carry out further specific tests on it in-house. You'd be welcome to help us in finds for the a few days if you like."

"Cleaning items?"

"Yes. You'd be in the shade as you do it. There's a breeze, too."

"Consider me a volunteer!" he declared.

"Have a word with your trench supervisor over lunch. Tell them I've nobbled you for finds for the rest of the week."

"Thank you, I'll do that."

For the remaining days, therefore, John sat outside the finds hut cleaning a variety of artefacts brought up from the trench. The supervisor did not let him loose on anything too delicate or precious, but he took his time doing a thorough job taking the dirt off various items, including a damaged computer keyboard, a saw and some glasses frames. As well as Scarlett, he enjoyed Walban's company much of the time and they passed the hours with pleasant chat.

"What's that you've got there, Walban?"

"Zis is a child's silver necklace, delicate in the extreme."

"Beautiful!"

"Ve are not sure at zis stage vether it originated from Earth or here."

"So they could have manufactured it on the Mother Planet?"

"Or made here viz raw materials brought from Earth by colonists and zen made here on Tripek III."

"Ah, I hadn't thought of that third option."

"Ve are not avare of any silver deposits local to our present location. It vaz found in one of ze earliest levels. I think it vaz from Earth, but zere are still tests ve can do once it iz cleaned."

"Wow! It's unbelievable that you are holding something that might have originated on the long-lost Mother Planet," John said in awe.

"You vant to hold it?"

The rookie knew to handle it carefully. He held the delicate piece as if it might fall apart at any moment. It was strange the difference the act of holding it made from merely observing with his eyes. It enthralled him.

On another day, they spoke about families. Walban revealed in conversation that he had a wife and four children back on Lares Ballin. John trod with care, knowing there to be a dispute going on between the planets. He steered the conversation on to something different once t opportunity arose.

"I'm finding the food good here, considering they're catering out in a field."

"Yes, zey do a good job, viz limited resources."

"They always have a vegetarian option I can eat."

"Hmm, and are you a vegetarian on moral grounds?"

"Um, I don't know. Our parents brought us up that way, it's all I've ever known. I wouldn't want anyone to think I considered myself better than them for not eating meat."

Walban said, "In ze early evolution of man, ze eating of meat, carrion in ze first instance, ven our ancestors came down from ze trees, vaz an important step forwards. It meant zey did not have to send all day foraging for food and would use ze time to expand zere brains."

"You're not suggesting my brain has shrunk by not eating meat?" John asked, making it obvious from his expression that he was joking.

"No, no, not at all," Walban assured him.

"I know my brother is no longer a vegetarian. He said it was impractical in some places. If I lived somewhere where the options were to eat meat or die, I'd eat meat."

"You vant to live?"

"Yes! There are always fresh places to explore and learn... and interesting people to meet."

"Ja. Zere are a lot of intelligent people gathered in zis community. It makes for delightful conversation."

John was unsure if he qualified for the "intelligent" accolade, but Walban did not seem tired of his company.

That evening, over supper, he got a genuine sense of community that prevailed at the dig. An enormous pot was being used for a stew. It contained all kinds of food being boiled up together; the leftovers from the previous few days. A large group of them gathered in a ring of people, equidistant from the pot, amid much jovial chatter. Tom, the Enviro head, sat with his wife, Vicki. He stepped forward and popped a tiny piece of... something edible, into the large receptacle. As he retreated again, he announced, "That bit will make all the difference!" The others laughed.

When the cook served the meal, it turned out to be quite delicious. After about three spoonfuls of the stew, John paused. Unusually, there was no mention of a vegetarian option. He considered the conversation earlier in the day, but deciding it best not to make a fuss, he ate it up without saying a word. He would make sure he returned to his vegetarian diet the next day.

A group of younger volunteers, further round the circle, were exchanging anecdotes and laughing. John noticed how people gravitated to those around their own age. He never felt an "us and them" attitude creep in, though. It was quite refreshing.

He found himself with Scarlett again, someone whose company he enjoyed. She was telling him about matters back home.

"My son is hoping to buy a property in town here. The sale of his place, back on our home planet, is going ahead. I hope to help him find a property when he comes here."

"Is he an archaeologist?"

"He is not. A portrait painter - and a good one."

She took a long while to finish her meal, because she kept on talking while picking over tiny bits of food left on her plate.

"I shall have to sit in my tent this evening with my healing crystals. That will help me balance myself. Do some meditation..."

It occurred to John to mention his own meditation experience on New Mars, but overcame the temptation. This was no laughing matter and besides, Scarlett was talking more to herself than anyone else.

The following day, they were back by the finds hut. John did something different. Someone else had cleaned and dried small pieces of pot. Now he must mark each one with the site code for that year.

"We have a machine which does it in seconds," Scarlett explained, "but that's packed in. It had been used to destruction, but we cannot afford a new one right now. The project is on a tight budget. No matter, we'll have to mark them the old fashioned way with quill and ink."

It was a joke, their using the word "quill," but it showed her jovial mood that morning. Each tiny piece of cleaned pot needed to be marked with the data in ink, using great care. Some might have seen it as laborious work, but John enjoyed it. He tried hard to make his writing as neat as possible, taking a pride in his work. Scarlett inscribed a few alongside him at first, then left him to it.

Walban was still working on the necklace and the pair sat in the welcome shade, for the hot weather showed no signs of abating.

"I've noticed some of the grass fading from its rich green colour," John remarked.

"Not zurprising, considering zis heatvave."

"It's not this hot every year?"

"Most years ve have a spell of veather like zis. It rained a fair bit before you arrived. Zat is vhy it has looked lush until now."

"I must be the bringer of fine weather!" John said with a grin.

A young woman arrived from the trench. Breathless and excited, she was itching to tell her news.

"They've found a skeleton up on trench! It's in the church. You should have a look."

"Right, zank you," came the reply, but the woman disappeared to spread the news.

Scarlett's voice, from inside the hut, shouted, "Take your break early and have a look."

They needed no further encouragement. On the way, Walban gave a bit of background information.

"In ze early days of ze dig, ve concentrated on ze cemetery over zere. He pointed to the rough ground beyond the track. "Zey are being catalogued and analysed by the human remains team. They vere planned burials. Ve have not found a skeleton at ze site of ze settlement before."

They arrived as the diggers were packing up for their break. The young woman who discovered it stayed and talked to them regarding it, although there was little uncovered at this early stage. They had exposed a small section of skull, along with, five hundred centimetres away, some bones which even John could recognise as ribs. A huge amount of painstaking work still needed doing, but the unexpected discovery of a "body" was hot news at the dig.

"It's at the north end of the church, as you can see," the discoverer said. "Initial signs are that they'd laid it out flat."

'I'm not sure how they can discern that,' thought John, but he said nothing. Walban, meanwhile, wanted to take issue with a different aspect.

"Ze last I heard, ve have not identified zis area as a church building. Zat is von of several theories."

"Er, yes," the woman retreated from her previous statement, realising that here was someone more experienced than herself.

"Nevertheless, it iz a most interesting find. Keep up ze good vork."

The find caused a stir around the site and promised to get the "Find of the Season" award, unless they discovered the mother ship's remains in 2609, of course.

By evening, the arkies had at least half a dozen theories doing the rounds why the settlement had lain the body there several hundred years before. Yet, as the experienced Gilbert said to John, "Daft to speculate when we have so few facts, tee hee hee."

It remained light late and a bunch of younger people, both male and female, set off with purpose round the perimeter of the lake. John, along with some other members of the older generation, followed from a distance, chatting.

Once of these was Charlie "Doc" Dibson, a qualified medical doctor. They could usually find her sorting through human skeleton pieces. She possessed smooth, brown skin and wore her hair in a little topknot on the top of her head. As she looked up, she commented that one of Tripek III's small moons was visible in the still light sky.

"Hmm," Scarlett responded, "that might mean trouble coming our way."

John wondered what in the universe she meant by this and asked her.

"A moon coming up from that angle, particularly from behind mountains, predicts an argument, or disagreement. Strange, because we're such a happy little family here."

Was the woman insane? Her, a trained scientist with a string of qualifications from a prestigious university. How could she believe in such complete nonsense... or the crystals, for that matter? How could a brain contain such rationality and irrationality together? It beggared belief. With none of the others in their group saying anything, it did not incline John to challenge her. He found his mind leading to a question.

"You know, in ancient times, they read prognostications from the stars and made out constellations from the vantage point of Earth?"

"Yes."

"How can we square that system now we're in a different part of the galaxy? There's a fundamental difference in the stars' relative position, the old constellations don't hold up."

At that point, a tremendous cheer went up ahead. It took their minds away from the question and got Scarlett off the hook. John was not sure if she felt relieved, but decided it was a subject best dropped.

The leading group had found an upturned wooden rowing boat on the shoreline which caused the commotion they heard. A bed of reeds had earlier hidden it from view. With a collective effort, they flipped it over - hence the cheer.

"A storm last winter capsized it," a young man said with a note of triumph.

The boat was upright again, but in poor condition. Undeterred, the younger contingent gathered round and, pushing hard, launched the craft into the water... where it sank. The assembled crowd issued a mixture of groans and ironic cheers, followed by laughter all round. John looked about him at these people. He realised that, following his wanderings, he had finally fallen in with a group of people he could feel at home with. If they accepted him, it could be a long stay.

The next several weeks raced by. He spent most of his working hours with the finds team, cleaning, sorting, labelling and categorising items coming up from the trench. On occasion, a new discovery would surface, such as an enamelled broach of a previously unknown design. Most finds were mundane, but John was enthralled. Others appreciated his contribution, while his knowledge increased week by week. Periodically, the finds dried up and he would help Tom in the Environmental Department.

Most evenings, the arkies organised group events, some of which he joined in with. More often, he chatted with the members he knew best, or sat alone and read.

Once a week, he joined a group travelling by taxi into town to look round and buy some treats. John knew that his money ran low. This should have concerned him, but a conviction grew within him that "something would happen" to enable him to stay on at the dig. Life was relaxed and enjoyable.

The weather remained fair for the first four weeks he stayed, then broke in spectacular style with an electric storm and a deluge. It was a lot cooler afterwards, fresher too, then the temperature rose again, bit by bit.

"We're going to lift Lila next week," Elaine announced from the centre of the crowded taxi, taking a group to town on their day off.

"Exciting news!" Doc cried.

"It is, tee hee hee," Gilbert put in his contribution.

Lila was the pet name given to the skeleton discovered in the middle of the settlement. Weeks of slow work revealed that it was indeed female aged in the twenty to thirty year-old age bracket. The bones were ready for lifting now they had completed recording them in situ. The human remains experts would have plenty of work to keep them occupied.

Professor Derby said, "Petros and the rest of the team cannot contain themselves."

John asked, "Any more theories what she was doing there?"

"Theories? Yes, theories aplenty. For all that, we're rather shorter on hard facts. I think we accept we will never answer some questions."

Walban and Scarlett both began to speak. The man deferred, so the latter said, "I understand the skeleton shows no signs of trauma."

"None we can see now," Elaine confirmed, "but we'll know more once she's lifted."

With the taxi drawing up in the centre of town, further discussion ceased. They bailed out, reminding each other to rendezvous an hour and a half later. John set off by himself with a purpose, but stopped when his TRAC burst into life. It told him there was a message for him. Clocking in, he learned it came from the space port.

326

'Oh dear,' he thought, 'I hope they don't want more money for mooring fees. I tried to stick my ship out of the way where they would not see it.' He rang back.

"Information!" said the young woman at the port. The hologram coming from his wrist computer was fuzzy, but the audio sounded clear enough. She sounded officious, but at least it was not an automated system.

"There's a message for me."

"One minute."

He waited on the street corner, in a shaded area where he could see the hologram easier. A couple of military transports flew overhead.

"Yes, Mr Thorn, there's an international message for you."

"Oh! Put it through, please."

"No can do; you must come here to view it."

"Why? All I'm asking you to do is redirect the message to my TRAC."

The connection broke off. John was sure it was deliberate. Rather than try again, he set out on foot to the space port. The weather was clement and the distance short.

'It could be Frank, I suppose, or Erik,' he speculated. He must wait for it to be revealed.

"Hello, my name's John Thorn. 'I'm told you've an international message waiting for me."

With a faint look of acknowledgement, she directed him towards a booth to watch and listen to the message. When he played it, it astonished him at both the message and its author.

"John, this is Stella. I'm still on Belovo. I'm in danger. You should come and take me away from here. If you contact the Brothers of Compassion, they will take you to me."

That was it. He played it again. She was being demanding, no "please" or "thank you." No doubt it was her, though. She still wore her hair the same style, but looked older, of course. John could not remember how long ago it was since they parted, but it was fifteen years. Stella told him then that their relationship had run its course and he agreed. Leaving had seemed right. This cry for help, plus the prospect of seeing her again, made all his of his old feelings for her flood back. There was never any debate within him as to his next step.

"What does a reply cost?" he asked. Stella's message was three days old; he had no time to lose.

"A hundred and fifty credits."

" A hundred and fifty credits! That's an awful lot."

"That's for a hologram not longer than thirty seconds. You can send words only at ten credits a word."

"Hmm. Okay... so, if I sent a message, 'I'm coming, John,' that'll be thirty credits, right?"

"Forty - 'I'm' is two words."

Completely daft, but the woman was not one for talking round. After a brief consideration, he directed her, "Please send her a one-word answer: 'Coming'."

"That'll be ten credits, please."

They made the transaction. Unless Stella had sent messages to more than one person, which he very much doubted, she would know whom it was from. His former lover must be pretty desperate to call upon him in her hour of need.

'I'll leave straightaway, but I'll have to inform the others.'

He tried calling each of the people he travelled into town with, but experienced difficulty getting through to anyone. Finally, he made contact with the head archaeologist. John explained the situation to Elaine and her response was most reasonable.

"You go, John, I understand. Good luck and I wish you a successful mission."

Needing no further encouragement, he went straightaway to his little spacecraft. Food and drink were not a problem, because he always carried an emergency supply on board. The airfield was quiet that early afternoon. He planned to launch *Shooter* without obtaining permission from the control tower. Being parked on the edge, no one interfered.

Soon, UDS engaged and planet Tripek III was disappearing into the distance behind him. It would take twenty-four hours for him to get to Belovo. In the quiet of his cockpit, he pondered the situation. The thought of seeing his long lost love sent tingles through him. He noticed his heart beating faster.

'She didn't specify what kind of danger she was in. Why call me, of all people? I feel quite honoured that she has sought my help. I'm not sure what I can do to assist her.'

It was nighttime on the side of Belovo he needed to land on. His craft was on automatic, but the planet's space port was not picking up the "permission to land" broadcast. 'Oh hell!' he thought, 'I'm going to land, anyway.'

He remembered the space port as a small, amateurish outfit and found it little changed. Maybe a mysterious force caused time to stand still on Belovo. Stella only called him because she did not realise they split up a decade and a half before.

John dismissed such fantasies as he emerged from the cockpit, he strapped on his pulse pistol. It was dark.... and raining. After being confined in the cockpit, it was wonderful being outside with precipitation, a light, refreshing drizzle.

They had kept lighting on at the deserted facility and he soon found the track. A mere ten minutes later, he entered the town on this mild night. His hair was wet, but it did not matter. Passing the hotel he stayed in on his previous visit, he wondered if he could afford a room there again. It was not his intention to stay this time, though.

A couple of drunks lay on the pavement, a shop front propping up their backs. They paid him no attention and he assessed them as no threat as he walked past. Few folk ventured out at this hour.

She had mentioned 'The Brothers of Compassion' in her message, but where were they based? Then he remembered coming across one outside the establishment where Stella worked when he arrived the first time. He spurned one who asked him for a donation. John felt guilty about that now.

The streets looked alike in the gloom. Rather stupid, but he had left his night vision glasses on board *Shooter*. He was unsure which road to take.

"Can I help you, brother?" a deep voice issued from the shadows, which made the visitor start.

The figure, who stepped out into the partial light, looked innocuous. From his attire, John had stumbled upon someone from the very organisation he was looking for. It was not the coincidence it seemed, because the brothers walked the streets nightly, keeping an eye out for people needing help.

After clearing his throat, John said, "I've been told to find the Brothers of Compassion." When the other man did not offer any response, he continued, "My friend, Stella, er... I don't know what other name she goes by these days. She messaged me to ask me to come and help her."

"Your name?"

He gave it, then, as the drizzle eased off, began following the figure into the gloom. He fingered the pulse pistol at his side and was on special alert.

'If I'm set upon by thieves, they won't get much of a pay day.'

The taciturn Brother led him inside a building and up a flight of stairs. As John's eyes adjusted to the poor light, he surveyed the inside of a run-down property. Half way along a first-floor landing, the Brother stopped at a door and tapped it six times in a 2-3-1 code. After a brief pause, another of his kin opened the door. The friars exchanged a few hushed words which John could not catch, even from his proximity. After this, they ushered him in. There, on an assortment of cushions laid out on the wooden floor, sat Stella.

The utter relief showing on her face when she spotted him was easy to see, even in the dim light of a salt lamp. She shot up and gave him an enormous hug, which he reciprocated. He noticed how thin she looked.

"You came!" she exclaimed.

"I said I would."

"Yes, I got your message. Succinct as ever."

"I was trying to save money."

He looked round the room. Another, older woman, perched on the cushions, observing, but she did not stir. The walls were grimy and from the tops of the windows, hung hessian sacks, which served as curtains.

"My life is in danger if I stay here another day," Stella declared. "I need to get off-world."

"Where shall I take you?"

"As far away as possible," she said.

"I'm living on Tripek III on an archaeological dig. It's quite far from here... and from civilisation."

"Perfect! Can we leave now?"

"Now?"

"Yes."

"Um, I don't see why not. But it'll be a twenty-four hour journey in my tiny ship. Limited toilet facilities and I'm almost out of food."

"I have food!" she said, showing the bundle on the floor by the cushions. "And a little money."

"Um, that'll be handy."

"Can we go now, please?"

There was no reason for further delay, but, before they left, the brothers lent them both habits to don as disguises. John agreed without a fuss; there would be time for questions later.

"Keep your heads down," was one friar's instructions and the couple did so, flanked by two genuine Brothers.

Stepping into the street, they found the rain had abated.

"You landed at the port?" one escort double-checked.

"I did," he replied and they exchanged no further words until the group had navigated the quiet, night-time streets and were beyond the town.

"Oh, John, thank you for coming!"

She had not spoken like this before.

"Don't mention it," he said, "but I'll want a full explanation once we're on our way."

"You'll get it."

Their escorts walked all the way with them in silence. John and Stella took off their disguises by the ship and John swapped them for Stella's bag that one of the Brothers had been in charge of.

"Thank you so much, Brother Matthew!" Stella said with emotion as she gave the friar a large, but brief, hug. As she thanked the other one, John did his bit by shaking their hands and mumbling a few words of appreciation. 'What am I letting myself in for?' he wondered.

It was too late to consider that. He helped Stella on board the craft before getting in himself. Following a perfunctory pre-flight check, he took off.

The flight away from Belovo's solar system went smoothly. Then he put his beloved, trusty spacecraft onto automatic for the remainder of the flight. Turning to his passenger, he said, "Right, I think you have some explaining to do." But Stella, able to relax for the first time, was already fast asleep.

For Stella, many trials filled the years since John left. With him gone, she gave all her attention to bringing up her son. The teachers recognised Ben as a bright kid early on. It was no surprise, therefore, when he achieved a scholarship to enable him to go to the secondary school.

His mother kept the job at the bar and, with the money John left as a back-up, she could maintain her simple lifestyle. Occupied with her job and her son most of the time, she did not consider getting involved in another relationship. She experienced periods of loneliness and sorrow that her relationship with John had not worked out. Maybe, she reasoned, he had matured and over his need for "adventure." When she considered her other relationships, she realised that none of those men could hold a candle to John.

Some say that a mother's love is an irresistible force. Whether that is true, Stella's devotion to Ben was beyond dispute, if at times she took her possessiveness to extremes. For instance, she insisted on vetting any friends before he could play with them. The boy's father disowned him and took no interest in his progress.

Ben showed a natural ability in computer programming. When he came top of his year upon graduation, it surprising no one that an off-world software firm approached him. The job offer was too good to turn down and his mother encouraged him. She accompanied him to the little space port and kept a stiff upper-lip until he slipped out of sight. Then she wept buckets. She knew it was best, but that only softened the blow a degree.

More years passed. At work, plenty of male customers tried chatting her up. Now in her mid-forties, she was still an attractive woman. Normally, it was quite easy to dampen their ardour and brush it off using humour. However, one fellow was determined.

Ridiman was a draper by trade and a similar age to Stella. He was persistent and, finally, she capitulated and agreed to go out with him. Quite pleasant at first, if a little gushing in his praise for her, he then began insisting on her going to events with him, rather than asking. Alarm bells began ringing for Stella; she would not stand for someone trying to control her again.

Matters came to a head one evening when Ridiman entered the bar. He kept pestering Stella until she called the manager. Her boss was supportive and ordered the pest thrown out of the establishment. One local advised the barmaid, "You want to watch him, he beat up a woman once, left her disfigured for life." Others confirmed this story and warned her off him. Stella wished she had been told before and found herself shaking with fear.

Later that evening, the manager looked out of a front upstairs window and noticed Ridiman hanging about outside. He straightaway told his employee, offering her a bed for the night. Most grateful, she took him up on the offer.

When she emerged from the Majestic the next morning, there was no sign of Ridiman, but it spooked her. She found the fear welling up inside of her again. The man had showed genuine anger at his eviction and the fact that he hung about outside was worrying. Plus, the stories she now heard made her realise quite what an unsavoury, dangerous character this was. No telling what he was capable of. Afraid to return to her shack by herself, she turned to the Brothers of Compassion. She knew several by name and they were more than happy to assist her. For a first step, they put her into a safe house. Then two of them set off for her home to collect some essentials.

"I can't live with this," she told one of the other women there.

"Waddaya gonna do?"

After a long pause, Stella replied, "It's a long shot, but there is someone I can try to call. He might not help me after so long, but I'm desperate. I've got to try something; I can't carry on here."

She hoped John still flew the same spaceship as she got onto her computer and contacted the International Matrix Network. She found him easy to track down. With help from the Brothers, she sent a message to the planet Tripek III. All she could do then is wait. A pessimistic mood descended on her as she reasoned, 'He won't want to hear from me again after all this time. He will have moved on. He'll be married with kids...'

Three days she waited, it seemed like forever and towards the end of this period she thought she must pursue another option. Then she received his reply. It both amazed and amused her when it came. Audio alone and one word: "Coming." It was enough.

Shooter was behaving herself as she sped back to Tripek III. John considered what an excellent investment the craft had been. He had got his money's worth over the years.

After commenting on the lack of sensation on this, her first ever space flight, Stella slept the next couple of hours. She then woke up much refreshed and decided she needed the toilet. John directed her to his ship's modest facilities. Only later, when she was ready to talk, did her story came tumbling out.

333

She concluded, "So, on top of threatening me with violence, he wanted to own me. I couldn't bear the thought of someone controlling my life again. You never acted like that, John. I decided I must get away. Goodness knows what he would have done. I sought help from the Brothers of Compassion; Brother Aiden in particular I knew well."

"And he directed you to that safe house?"

"They took me there... I can't quite remember when, I've lost track of time in recent days. They hid me, fed me and calmed my frayed nerves."

"I see," said John, "but why me? We split up many years ago. I thought you were fed up with me. And how did you find me? I've been all over the place since we last saw each other."

"The second part is simple to answer. The International Matrix Network is an effective system. I'm sure you're aware every civilian ship has a ASL Transponder. It made it quite easy to find you."

He tried not to show emotion as a cold tingle went down his spine. How could he not know about this? It had simply never come up. Part of his reason for moving about a lot since leaving Plerrania was to escape the Empress' assassins. He realised now that, had this fantasy been a reality, they could have tracked him easily! Stella, unaware of this, was still talking.

"I'm sorry, but I was desperate and I needed you. You don't regret coming, do you?"

"Of course not, but how do you know I wasn't with someone else?"

"Are you?"

"No."

"You're my one big regret in life, John. I should've been more patient with you."

"I'm still trying to get my head round you tracking me down. It freaked me out a bit. I've abandoned planets in a hurry before now and..."

"Still the adventure seeker, then?"

"Not any more, those days have gone. I've found a place where I'm happy to stay and lead a simple life. My home is a tent. I have very little in my account and all my worldly possessions can fit inside the hold of this small craft several times over. I have got little to offer you."

"You think that's all I care about?" she asked, more puzzled than hurt.

"Um..." he began, but he could find nothing more to say.

"I'd like to give *us* another chance," she said, "and I don't care if you're a complete pauper. We possessed something special."

She had been considering this a lot. She therefore held an advantage over John. Following a deep sigh, he said, "A huge amount has changed since we were together, the war, a new century... and I know I'm not the same man I was. I'd like to think I've grown up a lot since then. When looking back, I realise how immature I was and didn't give you the attention you deserved and gadding off on every adventure..."

"But you held a sense of honour, that's why I was hopeful you would respond in a positive way to my message."

"Not because there was no one else?"

She ignored this and said, "So, what are you thinking? You came far to fetch me."

"And I don't regret it a bit. It overjoyed me when I got your message and the prospect of seeing you again. It feels even better now. If you want to give us another go, then I'm up or it."

"Good! Now your turn. I want to hear what you've been doing since we parted."

"Everything?"

"Yes, everything!"

It was one way to pass time on the journey to Tripek III. He told her about his wartime experience and his subsequent service for the House of Vaxon. He omitted to mention Margot at all. Stella was interested in John's visit to Molten, his brother's planet. He continued to describe his wandering period with Erik before his getting involved in the dig.

"Tell me about the dig," she enthused, "That sounds amazing!"

He did and the conversation flowed. For John, it was heart-warming, her reaching out to him after so long. The intervening years were not forgotten. He and Stella had been through a lot during that period. They were bound to be affected by those experiences. He had never forgotten her, but guilt still hung over him at how he had treated her, always going off on adventures and not accepting responsibilities at home.

The relationship with Margot was fun while it lasted, but Stella was his one true love in life. Upon seeing her now, he realised how much she still attracted him, both her personality and looks. The more he thought about it, the more pleased he became she contacted him.

Stella came to the present situation from a different angle. John held a unique place in her heart. For her, it was all about relationships. She concluded that all were pretty disastrous except the one with John. If only she had been more understanding. In the safe house, she told the Brothers about him. After listening, the friars encouraged her to do the hologram message. She did so, not knowing what kind of response she would get.

Ridiman, the Brothers told her, was employing a couple of investigators to track her down. Those helping Stella impressed on her the need to leave Belovo. She alone recognised the gamble that the John idea was. Stella had no viable alternative, but still hoped he would come good. She regretting them breaking up and hoped there was a possibility of them getting together again, although at the time she was aware it was a long-shot.

Never in her life was she more pleased to get a one word answer. It gave her hope. Now she travelled away from her homeworld where she had lived all her life. She prayed in the cockpit that she could make it work with John.

While the pair ate some of the food she had brought, the conversation moved to lighter topics such as favourite foods and meals. They relaxed. Later on, the subject of childhood memories came up. Stella spoke about an incident when she was a girl.

"I was with a group of girlfriends and we produced a play."

"Shakespeare?" John joked.

"Hardly! The play was one we'd written ourselves. I remember little what it was about, except that I played a boy. Anyway, we got all the parents in, we held it round a friend's house in town. There was quite a big gathering and the adults were on best behaviour so as not to belittle our amateur thespian attempts. It started off okay, but then... the second scene I think, quite early anyway... we all sat on a bench. It was part of the play, there were five of us, five or six anyway. Once girl, whose name escapes me, was on the large size and once we were all seated on the bench, it collapsed!"

"Oh dear."

"We all collapsed too - into screams of laughter. We rolled about the place. I've never laughed as much; my ribs ached. We'd stop, glance at each other and start all over again."

"And the play?"

"Abandoned, I'm afraid."

"That's a shame, but it sounds like you enjoyed yourselves. Frank and I rarely had friends round, because we were in a remote farm. Maybe "remote" is overstating it, but we didn't have any near neighbours. One thing I remember, though, and it's nothing to do with get-togethers, is that my parents always asked if I'd washed behind my ears. They didn't ask about other parts of the body, it was always, 'Have you washed behind your ears?' I mean, no one looks there, do they?"

"Their logic being if you washed in that hidden place, you must have done the rest."

"Hmm, I hadn't thought of it that way. Maybe you're right. That's a mystery solved!"

The couple gave each other an affectionate look before falling silent Outside, the stars passed by, matching the silence inside the cabin.

A sudden announcement by John finally broke this state.

"Another hour and we'll be landing on Tripek III."

"What time will it be down there?"

"Um, let me check... seven in the morning. Oh dear, that's bad."

"Why's that?"

"Hang on a moment," he said and touched a few controls. Although they felt no difference, the craft was, in fact, accelerating.

"What are you doing?"

"That's better. We'll arrived sooner now and I can park in the corner where she was before. It's concealed there and *Shooter* shouldn't incur any fees with a bit of luck."

Stella shook her head a little, but smiled. Then she sought confirmation. "Are we making a go of it?"

"After rescuing you from a dragon and hurrying you away on my trusty steed half way across the galaxy... yes, let's give it a go!"

"You're my knight in shining armour then."

"I am."

She changed tone, saying, "I'm sorry, this is all pretty crazy."

337

"Not at all; I couldn't be happier to see you again. There's been no one but you. I thought I'd lost you and that I'd never see you again. I'd like to make this work."

"So would I!" she said, squeezing his arm. Then, "Do you remember the first time we met?"

"In the bar in town? Of course I do. You still have the same hair style."

"Oh gee, thanks!"

"No, I like it."

"I liked you from the moment I laid eyes on you. I'm such a fool to've let you go."

"It wasn't only you, I was equally responsible. Now fate has given us a second chance."

"God has. Yes, he has."

~ End of Chapter 17 ~

My Keeper's Brother - Chapter 18

"This place is beautiful," Stella said, pointing to the majestic mountains in the distance.

John and she were making their way on foot to the town on Tripek III. She steered her one medium-sized case which employed an effective anti grav unit. They planned to travel to the dig by taxi. Stella did not seem disturbed at the prospect of staying in the archaeological dig's tent city. He concluded she was simply glad to get away from Belovo and would settle for almost anything if it meant escaping an abusive relationship. Her mind was elsewhere.

"I left a message with the Brothers to deliver to Ben. Some would say it's difficult to be apart from one's children, but the firm doesn't accept non-company employees where he is. Besides, I don't want to live under a dome all day. Neither do I want to cramp his style; he has his own life to live. He has an excellent job and I'd rather he enjoyed that and making a life for himself than living with me for the sake of it. I know he enjoys it, which makes me happy."

That early morning, few others were abroad. He responded by saying that when he retired, he would like to be on an open planet. "Frank, my brother, has got it made on Molten. Under populated and free from many of modern life's distractions. I liked it."

"It would be nice to hear..."

She broke off, because a military vehicle was coming up behind them quite fast. They moved to one side. It then drew up beside them and they halted. The front passenger sat nearest them, a young officer in an immaculate uniform. He addressed the walkers.

"You've just landed at the spaceport."

"Yes, sir," John said. He needed to keep on the officer's right side. He was fearing a demand for landing fees, but it was something different.

"Have you come from Lares Ballin?"

"Um, no," came the puzzled reply.

"You have a flight log?"

"Of course," John replied, fumbling with his TRAC.

The officer studied the data. He took it straight from the ship's log and it was almost impossible to manipulate. After reading for a few moments, it satisfied the military man and he told his driver to move on. They watched the vehicle disappear into the distance. Stella said, "Most curious, what's that about?"

"I'm not sure. There's a dispute going on between the two planets. They must be looking for spies, or foreign agents. I'm glad that's all."

It proved easy getting a taxi and before long, they arrived at the camp. The site's only difference being one or two fresh tents. John led them to the finds hut. A group sat outside, working hard, a few of whom the returnee did not recognise. Scarlett greeted them, saying the trench had produced lots of items that week and they had a blitz on.

"This is my friend, Stella."

"Welcome, Stella, are you visiting?"

"I was hoping for a longer stay, but it depends on John," she said, a little put out John had introduced her merely as "friend." Then she conceded she was a couple of steps ahead of him and should give him time. Scarlett then made a generous offer.

"I've got a spare tent you can use if you like."

"Oh, thanks!"

"I take it you haven't got one in there," the archaeologist said, pointing to Stella's case.

"Oh, goodness no!" the other woman said. "This contains the few clothes I was able to pack before coming away."

It intrigued Scarlett at the sudden appearance of John's "friend" and wanted to know more. She stifled her curiosity for the time being. With a bit of luck, they would reveal all in the coming days. Instead of asking probing questions therefore, she said, "I have a small tent you can borrow for the time being. I'm sure John can help you put it up. Conditions are a bit primitive, low tech, but most of us like it."

The new arrival was told that she could stay with John and the others cleaning finds before attending the introductory course the following week. She could not complain about that.

For the rest of the day, she was being introduced to people, erecting her tent and getting herself established. Her first impression was of a friendly community. Stella felt unsure archaeology was her thing, but she had committed herself to John and if he liked it here, she would give it her best shot. She found it relaxing being in a circle of people, young and old, chatting away as they cleaned four-hundred year old artefacts.

"How's the Lares Ballin situation going?" John enquired.

"Oh, don't ask me!" exclaimed Scarlett. "One benefit of living here is not getting news."

"I ask because the military stopped us after we'd landed and asked if we'd come from there."

"I see. They've a major base near here, but I don't know, I don't want to. I presume it's rumbling on still."

When the conversation turned to profounder topics, Scarlett got more animated. One middle-aged woman, whom John had not seen before that day, was telling forth some of her pet beliefs.

"I reckon that each one of us is given a specific task for their life, or lessons to learn, I should say. The angels give us each an assignment before we are born and it's our key purpose to work out what it is as early as possible, then run with it. I knew from an early age that I possessed a gift for spiritual healing. I've tried to focus my energies in that direction."

A lot of this was above John's head, but these women existed on a different wavelength.

Scarlett said, "I'm sure that I pre-arranged a knowledge of reincarnation before I was born this time. I'd learned this truth in past lives and wanted to make sure I didn't waste time in this life re-inventing the wheel. It's frustrating that I didn't apply the lessons that came with this knowledge. I realised the futility of worldly ambition and the necessity of always being kind. But I entrapped myself in the world's ways, being weak and easily influenced. When I got onto the corporate ladder, I was ambitious for worldly wealth and status. I realised how silly it was, but I kept telling myself that I remained in control and it was only a game. How wrong can you be? Ambition became my driving force and I got high up in a big company with power, position, prestige, influence, wealth - the lot. I hurt many people along the way, trampling over them as I climbed to the top. Even though I knew better, I'd become ruthless and ambitious."

"What happened?" asked John, now taking an interest.

"I retired early. People saw me as super successful, but I recognise that, in real terms, it's been a waste of a life. I've blown it. I should have got a lower-paid job serving others and not let a love of status seduce me. The annoying thing is, I'm pretty sure I learned the

341

lesson in previous lives, but haven't been able to move from that point. How stupid is that?"

"You're too hard on yourself," said the other woman. "You do a tremendous amount for the community and always act unselfishly."

Everyone nodded their agreement, not least Stella. The same lady continued talking, "You're not alone in making mistakes, my dear, but I'm convinced that it is through these that we learn. So the word 'mistake' is wrong. They are life's lessons reinforced. Besides, if you think you've been silly, it's not as bad as me! I was a girl when a wise woman told me I would learn the life lesson that worldly wealth would destroy me. I remember her telling me that. And it's not as if I dismissed her as mad or anything. I believed her, but I didn't let the knowledge influence how I went about my life. When I met a rich businessman, I wanted to get in with him. Not that I liked him particularly, but I fancied the glamour, the lifestyle, attending all the best parties and never having to wear the same expensive dress more than once. In the end, I cut off all my old childhood friends and even my family. It caught me up in this unreal dream. When he grew tired of me, I found myself outside the door before you could say knife. His fancy lawyers made certain I got very little and no one wanted me, either my wealthy "friends" who, it turned out, weren't friends at all, or the ones from earlier whom I'd discarded. I ended up moving away, living the simple life and re-connecting with my healing powers. I want my life to count with the time I've left, whether it's short or long."

A young, attractive woman who was also new to John, then said her bit. She spoke with a heavy accent he could not place.

"For those of you who haven't met me, my name is Kseniya. I got married a couple of years ago, because this young man asked me. But ever since then, he's shown no interest in me. He sits around the home and doesn't want to talk to me."

'Gosh!' thought John, 'she's gorgeous, although far too young for me. That young man needs a good shake!' Notwithstanding, with Stella sitting next to him, he realised it was best to say nothing. He looked skywards and saw a large military transporter flying overhead at low altitude.

The older woman gave her advice, born of experience, but John found his mind drifting until Scarlett put him on the spot with a direct question.

342

"What's your lesson in life, John?"

"Um, er... I've never thought about it."

"You should!" said she who had lost all her friends.

John wracked his brains. "Okay, I think I've learned that conflict isn't always the solution that some believe it is. But, I still agree we did the right thing, halting the Tangeot rebellion."

"But what about yourself in your life?"

"I've learned not to be influenced by others." Then, turning to Stella with a smile and extending a hand towards her, he said, "I've learned not to give up on love."

There were lots of smiling faces and heads nodding in response to this. They realised his words came from the heart, even though it was not as profound as some contributions.

Over the following days, Stella acclimatised to living in a field and camp life. Scarlett not only supplied her with a working tent, but also a bed and some useful equipment. She got into the routine during her first few days, then they put her on the introductory course.

John was still helping at the finds hut, but fewer helpers stayed that week. With someone else running the course, Scarlett sat with him. No one else was about when John began a conversation on a subject alien to him. Reincarnation was a topic John never normally considered. He knew it to be a widely-held belief, but he held no opinion. Neither did he want to delve into the subject. Yet, something Scarlett had said intrigued him. One quiet mid-morning, as he cleaned the dirt off an old ornament, he quizzed her.

"Did you say that you brought a knowledge of reincarnation with you when you were born?"

"I did."

"How do you mean?"

"It was something I was aware of from a young age. Not something I needed to learn. It's not the sort of thing my parents would ever have discussed. Indeed, I think 'reincarnation' was only a word to them. Only later did I begin meeting people of a like mind. Have you heard of the expression, 'Birds of a feather flock together'?"

"I have."

"Powers of attraction on the astral planes draw us to like-minded people."

John was not sure the astral planes needed to be involved. It was pretty obvious people are drawn to each other by having similar interests.

He looked up and saw a military vehicle progressing along the track towards the dig. A short time afterwards, a commotion began a couple of hundred metres from where they sat. Unclear what was happening, he heard voices being raised and saw further "arkies" swelling the crowd.

"I must see this!" declared Scarlett, getting up and waddled over to the fracas. John was more reluctant to get involved. He arose and took a few steps forward, but kept his distance.

"We forbid you to take him!" Elaine, in full, authoritative, Professor Derby mode, said to the two military personnel who were out of their vehicle.

The officer spoke loudly to be heard by the swelling, excited gathering.

"By the authority invested in me by the lawful government, we are ordered to take the illegal alien into custody for an indefinite period."

This drew a wide range of responses from the now frenzied people gathered.

"This is ridiculous!"

"Over my dead body."

"You can't take him."

"He's been here for years. We can vouch for him."

John realised that poor Walban was the centre of all the attention. He remembered that the man with the funny accent hailed from Lares Ballin, the planet in dispute with Tripek III. He never once heard Walban mention the issue, indeed he was most careful to keep off the subject of politics if it ever arose. For the arkies here, Walban was one of them.

The officer raised the stakes when he produced his gun. If this was supposed to force the unarmed archaeologists into submission, it had the opposite effect. Doc and Gilbert both put their bodies in front of the mass. Scarlett soon joined them with her considerable mass. So many protectors surrounded poor Walban that John could no longer see him.

He kept a short way off, observing, pleased Stella was not involved. Someone from the crowd's edge then turned and saw John standing off, some thirty-five metres away, and beckoned him to join them, but he did not budge. He quite liked Walban, but this was not his battle... and besides, there must have been at least forty frenzied archaeologists around Walban by now, many of whom appeared willing to sacrifice themselves for his liberty. One more would make no difference.

Meanwhile, the officer sheathed his weapon and cried out, "We'll return with many more men. You have only delayed the inevitable."

"We'll be ready for you."

"You shan't take him."

The soldiers returned to their vehicle, watched every step by forty or more beady eyes. The crowd waited until they were well underway before dispersing. Some slapped Walban on the back or spoke words of encouragement to him. John trudged back to his station at the finds hut.

One major topic of conversation dominated at the dig the following couple of days. Tensions remained high during this time. Walban himself thanked everyone, but told them that if the military came back in force, they should not offer resistance. He did not want anyone hurt because of him. Meanwhile, he strove to get on with his role at the dig.

John saw less of Stella while she was on the course. The lady herself wondered what she was letting herself in for. She was doing it for John's sake, determined to see it through to be part of the enterprise.

In the evenings, after supper, they would walk together through the countryside. With crystal clear air and impressive mountains as a backdrop, they ambled and chatted.

"You've visited countless worlds," she said, "but are any as beautiful as this?"

"One or two have been close, but I've always sought planets with smaller populations. I know that some are metropolises, attracting large numbers of people, but they don't appeal to me. With mankind spread out on thousands of planets, there are still wide-open, untarnished views like this."

"Mmm."

"Anyway, how did the course go today?"

"All a bit technical."

"Yes, they're a pretty clever lot here."

"The younger people seem to pick it up quicker."

"Are all the other course members younger?"

"No, I'd say about fifty-fifty."

"Oh, that's nice."

"They're all friendly, though."

"What are you doing tomorrow?"

"Enviro, I think. Is that very technical?"

"I didn't find it so. If we have another hot day, you'll be glad of time spent doing mud pies."

"Mud pies?" she repeated.

"You'll find out. I forget what they call the process, but you get the chance to stick your hands into cold water."

"I'll watch out for that."

Mid-morning the next day, John took his break in his tent. Thick cloud cover meant it was not too hot in there and he had a nap. He needed to catch up on his sleep after having a poor one the night before. By the end of break, he felt much refreshed.

He was leaving his tent when a young man approached with a message.

"Are you John?"

"Yes."

"There's a couple of visitors to see you."

He voiced his first thought, "Military?"

"Oh no, a posh couple along with a bodyguard so that we don't steal all the fine jewels they're wearing."

"And they want to see me?"

"Yup!" responded the young man, who promptly left. He did not want to be involved.

Speculation was useless, John ensured his tent was secure, then set off with a purpose. As he got closer, he saw Scarlett conversing with a couple of people. A tall, slim woman towered over her shorter male companion. Both wore the finest of clothes, not at all the normal archaeological attire.

The woman spotted him approaching. She removed herself from the three-way conversation and took a step towards him. Once he was the optimum distance from her, she greeted, "John!"

Good looking, that haircut, distinctive eyes... when he worked out who it was, he cried, "Margot!"

346

She allowed him to give her a peck on the cheek before introducing her husband.

"My darling, this is John who used to babysit for me in the palace.."

"Delighted," the short man said, extending his hand. "When Margot mentioned the archaeological dig, it intrigued me. I've never visited one before. Plus, with the opportunity of her meeting an old friend..."

"Darling," his wife got organising, "you have a good look round while I discuss old times and have a catch up."

The man agreed and Scarlett helped by volunteering to be his guide. Looking at his fine clothes, she said, "The weather's been dry, so you should be okay." The bodyguard accompanied them, leaving John and Margot alone.

With them gone, John took his former lover into a wood close by where they could talk unobserved.

"You look amazing!" he said.

"You've grown your hair."

"Um, not much chance to get it done here. Anyway, how did you find me? On second thoughts, don't bother, I know now about IMN and the ship's transponder. It's scary, knowing people can track you with ease."

"Unless you go to the far reaches of the galaxy, they can track you. I think the system operates as far as Gan, but not beyond that. Does it matter? I'm here!"

"Yes, but I visited multiple planets in a short space of time after leaving the House of Vaxon. It convinced me that your mother was going to send an assassin to kill me."

She laughed, "You silly thing! Mummy told me off after you'd gone, but I played it down and they forgot the whole matter soon afterwards."

"Was Della-Mura okay?"

"Who?"

"The Imperial policeman who tipped me off."

"I've not heard the name. We punished no one; the whole incident was forgotten, like I said."

John pondered. His worrying and moving about had been in vain. He felt silly, but he was happy with his current situation... and it was great to see Margot again.

"Oh yes!" he remembered, "thank you for the two hundred thousand credits, it made an enormous difference to my life. Thank you for that."

"You're welcome. I remembered what you said about money making a difference in some people's lives."

"It did. Thanks again."

"Don't mention it."

"And now you're married."

"A little over a year now. In fact, I have you to thank for that."

"You do?"

"We were the impetus behind my mother pulling her finger out and finding me a husband."

"Is he nice?"

"He's nice enough, although you could teach him a thing or two in the bedroom department."

Blushing, he replied, "I don't think I'll be giving him any advice today, if you don't mind."

She giggled, then said, "You always could make me laugh. No, he's a positive in my life... and I'm not saying that because of his money. Mummy would never marry me off to someone without a fortune."

"And he's got a fortune?"

"Put it this way: he'd give ancient King Croesus a run for his money. Amongst other things, he owns two planetoids. One of them is an entertainment moon where the rich come from afar to enjoy themselves. The income from that is astronomical. He's got plans for developing the second moon, but catering more for the "middle classes" if you understand what I mean. I'm probably going to become involved in that - after the baby's born."

She touched her tummy, but there was no discernable bump at this early stage. He congratulated her and Margot looked delighted.

"He doesn't keep you in a gilded cage, I hope."

"Not at all. Norbert allows me considerable freedom. I feel far more fulfilled in my life that I have ever done before. But, I want to hear about you. Have you been here long?"

"Um, I'm not sure, several weeks now."

"And does this fulfil you?"

"Very much so."

"You're hoping to stay for a while, then?"

"I'd like to, but the funds are running low now. Stella's brought some money with her, which should be..."

"Stella?" she interrupted and John had to tell her all about his rescue mission. She enjoyed the tale and said so.

He said, "You and your husband would be welcome to stay for supper. It's not the most exquisite cuisine, but they do a pretty good job." When she did not reply at first, he added, "And your bodyguard, of course."

"I don't think that's going to be possible, thanks. We have a busy schedule for the next couple of days. Norbert is visiting several worlds to see business contacts in person. He obliged me by visiting here. It was out of his way. What's with all the military vehicles in town?"

"I didn't know there were. There's a dispute with another local planet. I've been avoiding the news."

"You haven't thought of signing up for either?"

"Are you kidding?"

"I think I am. You wouldn't put your life on the line now that you've found your long-lost love."

"It wouldn't tempt me to sign up, anyway. My fighting days are over."

"I'm glad I came; wonderful to see you again and hear how things have gone for you since we parted without a goodbye."

"I'm sorr..."

"No, I don't need an apology, I understand."

They paused, then John said, "Seeing we never said goodbye, how about one final kiss to make up for it?"

Margot smiled, "Okay, but for however long the kiss lasts, I'm going to be the spoilt girl on Plerrania. That way, I'll square it with my conscience."

The pair moved deeper into the woods. No chance of them being seen there. A long, passionate kiss ensued. It was for old time's sake, the kiss they missed out on before.

"Mmm, that was nice," she said, her lips tingling as she looked into his eyes at the end. Pupils dilated, her cheeks flushed, she looked full of desire. He dragged himself away and the two of them began walking back to the site, keeping a respectful distance.

"I haven't got lipstick on me, have I?" he asked.

"No, I checked."

The others were chatting together, the tour completed. They stood in the welcome shade of the finds hut, for it was hotter now.

"I think we shall have to be on our way now," the husband spoke.

"Of course, my darling."

"Did you catch-up well?"

"We did; talked about old times."

It was smiles all round. John and Margot exchanged a quick peck before the visiting party got back into their taxi, which whisked them away.

"An interesting man," Scarlett observed. "How do you know his wife?"

"Margot? I served in the House of Vaxon for several years and ended up guarding her and her brother. That reminds me, I never asked about how her brother is. Mind you, she no longer lives on the same planet."

"Well, you must've made a big impression on Margot for her to travel several parsecs to look you up."

"Hmm, we did get on rather well together."

That evening, John and Stella took a walk after supper.

"The last day of your course tomorrow, isn't it?"

"Yes, I've enjoyed it. I wasn't certain I would when the course began. Mind you, I'm uncertain how much knowledge I'll keep. I was rather hoping to join you cleaning finds next week, it seems a nice cushy number."

"I wouldn't describe it in those terms to Scarlett if I were you, but it should be okay. You can have a word with her."

"Right."

"Shall we sit here?"

They perched themselves on a comfortable, mossy bank and looked out over the lake. It was still light and the still water reflected the magnificent, snow-capped mountains.

"What a view!"

"Yes, quite something. I want to settle on a nice, open planet to end my life," he said.

She was taken aback by his sentence being in the first person singular.

"So where will I be when you're settled on this nice, open planet?"

350

"Um, I was hoping you'd be by my side, but I don't want to presume."

"John!" she said, "I want 'us' to work."

"You're right," he replied, retreating, "but I'm still getting my head round it after all these years."

"I know, I'll be patient," Stella said as she grabbed his arm and rested her head on his shoulder.

How good to have her this near him. A tiny voice within him said that he should feel guilty about sharing that passionate kiss with Margot earlier the same day. But he did not. The kiss with Margot rounded off that phase in his life, finishing an interrupted episode. It brought closure and he could now place it firmly in the past. Stella represented his future, but he should at least make her aware.

She was thinking about her current situation. No longer living on Belovo, it felt strange, yet also good. Absent was the constant fear of the past couple of weeks. It was an immense weight off her mind. John seemed prepared to give their relationship a go once more, a real cause for rejoicing. Who knew? She might even become an archaeologist.

After a long period of silence, during which their minds moved in different directions, he came out with, "I'm sorry." Stella, not understanding what he meant, asked him.

He said, "I should have made myself clearer. I *do* see us having a future together. I hope so anyway. An open planet, but not here. I've had my fill of war. All theses military transporters flying overhead, the army making a show of force... I'm tired of it. Maybe, once we've finished here, we could retire to somewhere where life is uncomplicated and juggernauts aren't involved."

"You're not turning pacifist, are you?"

"No, don't label me! All I'm saying is I long for a quiet life."

"Have you somewhere in mind?"

"I don't know... where my brother is. That's off the beaten track."

"Remind me."

"Molten, out on the rim. A primitive society, they're not into pulse rifles, vimanas and what-have-you."

"A peaceful planet?"

"Yeah, I think it is... I don't know. That was the one time I've visited and we disrupted things. I'm sure it returned to normal soon after. The peasants are unaware of space travel."

"'Peasants?' that sounds patronising!"

"Sorry; the simple village folk on the pleasant planet Molten. How does that sound?"

"Just as bad!"

"Oh dear. My brother lives in a castle, did I tell you?"

"He's not a simple village folk, then?"

"No, he looks after them."

"A castle, you say?"

"Yeah, they have modelled it all on the old medieval ones back on Earth. Quite a feat of engineering, in fact."

"Is it luxurious inside?"

"No, pretty basic, in fact. I didn't see as much of it and the surrounding area as I'd have liked."

"You can take me there one day."

"It's a long way away. Makes you wonder why anyone would go to such a remote part of the galaxy."

"Like your brother?"

"No, someone marooned him there. I was referring to the early settlers."

"You said it was an open planet."

"It is."

"And it's unspoilt."

"Yes."

"That's your answer then."

"I guess you're right," John conceded. "Anyway, it's only a dream. I'd enjoy staying here longer if we can, if you'd like that."

"Of course I would! Why spend all that effort on the course and not apply the knowledge? Everyone seems friendly here, too."

"Okay, good. If we go into town the day after tomorrow, we'll transfer some money to extend our stay. After that, we'll have to consider our options."

Next day was routine. John enjoyed Walban's company on finds, but both men kept off the subject of the confrontation with the military.

Stella finished the introductory course, content to carry on at the dig for the foreseeable future. The arkies had the next day off. In the morning, John and Stella squeezed into an over-packed taxi heading for town. They planned to spend most of their time there, looking round and purchasing further provisions.

352

Once they bailed out of the vehicle. John and Stella walked off together. Whilst aware he must pay for their coming few weeks stay at the site, he was unsure if he held enough money in his account to cover it. They would have to rely on Stella's resources.

At an old-fashioned market, she stopped to look at some locally sourced fruit.

"I fancy something sweet," she said

He stood back out of the way and fiddled with his wrist computer. His eyes nearly popped out of his head at what he found. Someone had deposited a hundred thousand credits into his account! Only one person could have done that. 'She'd kept my TRAC code details,' he thought to himself with a mixture of gratitude and disbelief. This was an absolute game-changer. Yet again, Margot had assured his future. He was over the stars, but could say nothing to Stella in case it raised awkward questions.

"Everything okay?" she asked, coming over to him from a stall.

"Um, yes... yes!"

"You gave a funny expression."

"No, I'm fine. Did you find some nice fruit?"

"Can we afford it?"

"Yes, that'll be fine. I've just looked at my account and I have more in it than I realised." John said, trying to sound nonchalant. "You get the fruit. I'll pay our dues for the archaeological dig."

"I like it here."

"Good."

"It's quaint, as if it were a new settlement."

"Maybe. There's a big military base near here. I've never visited it. I expect they're more into modern technology."

Later that day, they were still working their way through the town. She was nibbling on a nebta fruit she bought as he watched the vehicles passing by. A sizeable military convoy was driving past. John wondered if he had talked them up from his earlier comments. Sparkling clean troop-carriers formed the bulk of the procession. Some vehicles' roofs were down, making the soldiers visible. Seated close together, they looked so young. All appeared to have the identical expression on their face, staring into thin air.

The couple progressed to a quieter part, where no one would overhear them. He chose this moment to mention the convoy.

"I wonder if a war with Lares Ballin has broken out at last."

"I don't know."

"Strikes me that the military run this planet, I've never thought of it before. I understand there are much larger conurbations over to the west. I've never visited one. They don't keep the folk of this outpost informed. We're in a backwater here. I'm only surmising because of the increased military activity."

"Forget it, John, not our concern."

"You're right."

The following few weeks passed by. The season was proving a busy one for the finds department with a steady trickle of artefacts coming up from the trench. The archaeologists discovered nothing spectacular during this period, though they made steady progress in unearthing the settlement. The diggers detected a fresh, large, oblong building and, inevitably, a multitude of theories arose regarding its original use. John and Stella visited the trench once a week to monitor progress. The diggers were always happy to give them a guided tour.

On the international front, the tension between Tripek III and Lares Ballin reduced. There was less military presence visible and no sequel to the Walban episode. The arkies, not privilege to diplomatic manoeuvrings, were ignorant of the reasons. Coming from a score of different worlds, few cared, as long as they could get on with the dig - and Tom's cabin remained a politics-free zone.

A mixture of volunteers joined the regular finds crew each week. Some, short-stay volunteers, were not seen again. One such was a man named Zarren. In his early thirties, he sported short, curly hair and had a curious habit of talking sometimes with his teeth clenched together. He would sit, staring into space, oblivious to the world about him.

One day, when Walban and Stella were elsewhere, John found himself alone with Zarren. The former expected a quiet morning ahead, but he was wrong. He was poking a small copper pipe, getting the earth out, when the newcomer began.

"You wife told me you were on Rakass-Hist."

"Um, yes, that's correct," John said, not correcting him regarding his marital status.

"Terrible business," Zarren said.

"All over a long time ago now."

His attempt at nipping this topic of conversation in the bud was unsuccessful, for the veteran was desperate to justify himself.

"I was on there for a year. It was right towards the end when we got relieved. What a hell hole, eh? The swamps, the heat, the rain. What unit were you in?"

When John told him, it meant nothing. It soon became apparent that the two men experienced different wars on the same planet. Zarren served in the equatorial, tropical belt, not the milder, temperate zone. He was also on Rakass-Hist a good deal longer; his tour of duty ending round about the time John landed to be involved in the final operations.

"It was hell in that jungle. Rain? I've never seen the like. It used to pour like a constant shower for days at a time. You were never dry, no matter how hard you tried. Damn bastard rebels weren't averse to attacking in the worst possible weather: at night, in the middle of a monsoon. And, of course, we couldn't use modern weapons. They'd come at us out of the dark and we'd set every gun we could on them. There were piles of bodies the next morning."

"Bad," John sympathised as best he could.

"An' those bastards used to hide up trees and snipe at us on patrol. Head wounds, they always inflicted head wounds. I'm pretty sure our equipment was faulty too. Either that, or they were using special ammo. The helmets they issued us with didn't appear too effective against a direct shot, anyway. I lost friends. When you see your best mate's head explode in front of your eyes, it's..."

He trailed off and John said, "Explosive bullets."

"Right. And we suffered more casualties through diseases than the enemy. It was murder... and the rations tasted horrible, but we ate them; we had no choice. An' the booby-traps left by rebs, wicked things."

Zarren's experience had affected him so he needed to talk about it.

"Towards the end of my tour at least two men in my platoon killed themselves. I saw one trooper blow his brains out, I saw it with my own eyes, I can't say the thought never occurred to me. It was one way out."

John said, "But I bet you're glad you didn't. I mean, life can get better, right?"

His fellow veteran had not expected this, it was not part of his script. It therefore caught him in indecision, not knowing what to

355

say. He was still undecided when Stella and Walban returned, much to John's relief. It was rare, in John's experience, for soldiers to want to re-live old battles, but there were exceptions. Zarren appeared mentally scarred and could not put his experiences behind him. John was not his therapist, though and would rather not re-live it. The women's presence shut the fellow up and John resolved not to be alone with him again if he could help it.

"Everything okay, darling?" Stella asked, noticing something unsettled about John.

"Yes, of course," he replied, wiping away his frown. "What have you been doing?"

"Down at the trench. They think they've made a new discovery. It's believed to be a plough, although they've still got a lot of excavating to do."

"I imagine they won't have to be as slow and meticulous as they were the skeleton. An important find, still."

"You're right. I'm pretty sure it's the first one they've uncovered here, but they must have grown crops in order to live."

"Of course," John agreed. "It would fascinate me travel back in a time machine and visit the settlement centuries ago."

Stella winked. "There'd be no point in holding the archaeological dig then, would there?"

"Ha, ha, no! Still, not much chance of it happening, so I guess we have to carry on with the project. I'll be interested to see this plough for myself. An important find; helping us build up the picture of what went on here."

Early evening, after supper, John and Stella took another walk down to the lake and sat on what was now their favourite vantage spot on grass overlooking the area. Following a long, dry spell, the water level stood lower than they had known before. Another hour of daylight was left.

Below them, on the water, a group of young arkies were in an inflatable boat, having great fun with it. Half a dozen of them clung on as the craft skimmed across the lake powered by a modern engine. The couple up on the bank enjoyed hearing whoops of laughter coming from them.

"They're having fun," Stella remarked.

"Yes, I wonder where they got it from."

After a while, she commented, "I thought you looked unsettled when I returned from the trench. I figured you'd be able to have a friendly chat with that Zarren chap if I wasn't about. Talk man-to-man."

"About Rakass-Hist."

"Yes."

"He said that you'd told him I'd been there."

"You mentioned it to me if you remember."

John, not wanting to argue, yet still wishing to make his point, continued, "The bloke's disturbed. It's one thing to reminisce about the good old days, but he wanted to relive the terrible conditions he experienced. He went on and on."

"Oh dear, sorry," She said, seeing things from a different perspective. She thought she was doing him a favour.

"You weren't to know. Besides, I think he's only here for the one week from what I can gather."

"And you," said Stella, with a positive spin, "did him a favour by letting him get it off his chest. It was an act of kindness. To be there and listen, you were someone he felt he could talk to."

"Hmm," was all John's response. He did not sound convinced. Best to put it all behind him.

Further laughter from the lake as the inflatable streaked by. Some congregated on the shoreline below where John and Stella sat. They cheered and shouted encouragement.

The boat went further out now. It was speeding across the centre of the lake when it somersaulted, shooting the occupants into the air. John was watching the moment it happened. It was as if they hit something below the waterline which catapulted the craft over and landed its contents into the water.

He and Stella stood up, there were gasps from the shoreline. A rescue boat was soon speeding its way to the middle of the lake.

"I hope they're okay," Stella said.

~ End of Chapter 18 ~

357

My Keeper's Brother - Chapter 19

John and Stella sat on seats on the snowy bank overlooking the frozen lake. The ice appeared quite thick, but they would not risk walking over to the object in the centre. The water level dropped still further before the freeze came. It exposed the tip of a fin believed by some to be a large boat, others a spaceship. The dig's season ended too soon for it to be investigated, but it would be a priority for the following year. John dreamed of it being a 1.I.W. fighter. It was possible, but, like everyone else, he must wait to find out.

Whatever it was, it was the object that the speeding inflatable hit. To everyone's relief, no one drowned or suffered more than minor injuries. In the end, the young people involved passed it off as a laugh, although the craft had to be written off.

"Everything's so still," he said.

"At least there are no flies this time of year," Stella commented as she moved closer.

"Yes, every season has its compensations."

"Are you cold?"

"Why, do you want to go back?"

"I'm okay for a while. I'm enjoying the view."

It was quite breathtaking, the blue ice stretching out to the far bank, then an unbroken white landscape to the distant mountain tops. These latter had dark veins of rock which the snow could not cling to. Earlier, it amused them at the sight of the permanent cabins, such as the Enviro Unit's, left over winter. They were so many white mounds following a big snowfall.

The couple elected to stay on Tripek III over winter, although most arkies had gone to their home planets. They got a room in the mid-range hotel charging less for their off-season rate. Stella told John about her visit to a virtual art gallery in town earlier that year.

"I moved on to the medieval religious section after looking at old masters."

"You moved on, did you say?"

"I'm speaking figuratively, of course. I sat in my private booth; they have some bigger ones for groups. The pictures are presented to you and you choose which one to view. There were some lovely ones there. I like *Madonna of the Book* by Botticelli. The rich, the deep blue of her gown dominates the picture. Her delicate face is mesmerising too. If my TRAC worked here, I'd show it to you."

"You'll have to show me when we get back," John said, showing an interest.

"A group of schoolchildren entered the building as I left. They were going to be shown round by their teacher. It was nice to think they'd see the old masters and he would teach them, broaden their minds."

John told him of his previous experience of the teacher at the art gallery passing on his prejudices. This tale outraged Stella. "That's dreadful!" she exclaimed. "It's a teacher's job to educate, not close the kids' minds."

"Would you have said anything?"

"I don't believe so, it's difficult. Besides, they'd write me off as a batty old woman if I did."

"Oh, I don't think you're a batty old woman!"

"You're too kind."

"Just old."

"Hey!" went Stella and pretended to punch him. They laughed, but then became serious when John said, "You remember that Rakass-Hist veteran last year who couldn't stop talking about his experience?"

"Yes."

"I wish now I'd said, 'Don't dwell on it;' that would have been good advice. Instead, my single desire was for him to go away. He was a brother-in-arms to me. I should've been more understanding, more humane."

She put a mittened hand on him, saying, "Don't let it bother you. You were unprepared and, besides, we all have off days."

Soon after this conversation, they headed back before they got too cold. They trudged through the snow to the driverless taxi waiting for them.

On the return journey, John said, "Did I ever tell you about the planet with funny-numbered moons?"

"No," she said, amused.

"I've come across several planets where they have numbered the moons rather than given them names. There were seven moons round one planet I visited. Guess what they were numbered."

"It wasn't one to seven?"

"One, two, three, Four A, Four B, five and Six!"

"Huh?"

"They thought Four to be one mass, but then they discovered it was two rocky bodies orbiting the planet close together. When they found out, instead of re-numbering any of the others, they decided on the solution I told you. It just tickled me."

"Were any of the moons inhabitable?"

"No, they were all tiny and uninteresting."

"I see. Did you hear on the news about a planet explorers have recently discovered, or re-discovered?"

"Go on."

"The natural bacteria, the report said, had a strange effect on people. They flew into rages for no apparent reason."

"That's weird! Where was it?"

"I can't remember. It was on the news. They should have a follow-up report."

"Or," he said, "they'll never make another mention of it. That seems to happen; you want to know how the story goes after reading a report about it. Then you never hear another thing. It can be frustrating."

The new, 2611 season began with a buzz. The committee's decision was to make excavating the object in the lake the priority job that year. Preliminary investigations showed it was the remains of an old spaceship. It would be a major enterprise, taking a lot of resources and costing a lot of money. The overwhelming majority of the archaeologists agreed. They mothballed the trench for the winter, as usual, and would only re-open part of it for this season as the team would concentrate their efforts on the ship.

"Quite a sight, isn't it?"

John aimed his question at Elaine, Professor Derby, back again for another season.

"It is, we're making progress," she replied.

They were standing on the shoreline as a specialist barge hovered over the centre of the lake, dropping another pile into the soft silt of the lake bed. The barge's anti-grav engine was causing ripples to form and move away from where the ancient spaceship lay.

"Good, this is the second day, right?"

"Yes. We've hired the barge for a week and should've completed this phase by then. This part of the operation, anyway. It has to be, 'cos this thing is costing us a fortune to hire."

"Once the piles are positioned and a seal established, we'll pump out the water, correct?"

"That's right, then we'll work out what sort of ship we have. If indeed it is a spaceship as we suspect. I hear you are an expert on 1.I.W. ships of the line."

"Um, it *is* a subject I have taken an interest in."

"'Cos there's not much information I can glean online. The Intranets, both here and on my home planet, are pretty poor and neither allow data capture from off-world."

"No, not a great deal exists online. I possess some old books, which may come in handy."

"Excellent."

"But, frankly, I'm a bit surprised we're going to all this trouble. Divers could have gone in, leaving it in the water."

"The committee considered that, but we'd have to train our own people. Plus, we got a good deal on the barge, believe it or not. I mean, it's expensive, but less than the full cost. The difference in price between doing it both ways turned out to be negligible. The ship has attracted much interest this year. That means we attract more volunteers for this season and more money to fund this project. We should be okay, barring mishaps."

"Changing the subject, I haven't seen Walban about. Is he coming on later this season?"

"I don't think he'll be able to," Elaine said. "The Tripek III / Lares Ballin situation has flared up again. I suspect he thought it best to stay at home and hope things settle down once more."

"Oh dear, more sabre-rattling then?"

"I'm afraid so. Boys with their toys."

As if to emphasise her point, at this moment a formation of military ships streaked overhead.

He asked, "Aren't bookings up? You'd have thought they'd be put off."

"I think they committed before it kicked off again. I'll have to see, but I'm hoping they can resolve the situation amicably. If volunteers cancel, the project will be in a serious financial crisis. We contracted all this," she pointed to what was going on above the lake, "before the renewed dispute with Larens Ballin appeared likely. It's rather sprung back out of thin air."

"Do you know why?"

"Do they need a reason?" she countered.

"I don't know, but it seems to have flared up again quickly."

Elaine concluded by saying, "I'm hoping that if I ignore it, the situation will go away. I've no control over that, so I'm going to concentrate on this."

The next fortnight saw one or two minor setbacks in the operation, but, by the end of that period, the piles formed a three hundred and sixty degree circle round the area. They had established a seal and pumped the water out. A select number of arkies then took a launch, skimming across the water towards the crashed spaceship. John, in his vaunted capacity as spaceship expert, was amongst them.

Travelling by old-fashioned motor boat (for it was cheaper than an anti-grav sled) they slipped across the still waters to the now drying area. They drew up to the edge of the barrier formed by the piles. The quiet waters lapped at the barrier. Having secured the craft, they stood and gazed inside.

Elaine apologetically explained, "We're soon going to have a proper landing place constructed here, plus a ladder down inside, but we can take a preliminary decko now."

Stuck into the mud, front-first, at an angle fifteen degrees from vertical, the spaceship's hull stood, pock-marked, grimy and with water still dripping from it.

"What do you think, John?" asked Elaine. She sounded like she wanted instant answers, which was not like her normal self.

Once close to, he got an idea of the scale of the space craft. Small by interstellar standards, but big enough. It dwarfed the archaeologists peering over the barrier. It must have been a tail end fin that caught the inflatable the previous year. That the craft possessed such fins indicated it was built for atmospheric flight and space travel. It was the standard size for a 1.I.W. destroyer, only it was not. Feeling it unwise to say anything until he had taken a good peruse, he studied it some more. Then he felt confident enough to speak.

"It's not a 1.I.W. ship."

"No?"

"It's not a military ship either. See the lines and the fuselage shape. It's a civil transporter from... um, the twenty-fourth century, or the twenty-fifth.

The professor swore, which was not the language John associated with her. She said, "This won't attract students like it was supposed to."

Gilbert, who was also present, said, "We can always advertise it as a 1.I.W. planet destroyer. They will not know the difference, Tee hee hee."

Letting the flippant comment go, Elaine shook her head. Then John said, "There's no reason why, in the coming weeks, we can't force our way in and discover what cargo she was carrying. There might be something valuable, either historically or intrinsically. It might even force the re-telling of the story of Tripek III."

"Or a load of corroded nuts and bolts," said the expedition leader. It convinced her it was a bad day.

It disappointed John that she did not look upon his idea favourably, but he seemed to be the one optimistic person at that moment. Leaving the matter there, they returned to the shore. There, as they disembarked, Stella was there to greet him.

"Why all the long faces?"

"It looks like it's a lot more modern and far less interesting than people were hoping. I think we all got carried away on the tide of speculation."

That season, John and Stella were staying in one tent together, with another one next door for storing their equipment. They had given Scarlett back the one she lent them.

After supper, the pair liked to sit outside their tent and chat. It passed the time pleasantly, catching up on the day's events.

"There are fewer people here this year," Stella remarked. "Someone mentioned a rash of cancellations since the preliminary findings on the ship."

"Um, it's early days yet; more people should arrive later. That's what the committee is hoping. I've heard there are only four people on the introductory course this week. That's not viable, but they're carrying on, anyway. We're pretty sure it's the unstable political situation here putting people off."

"I keep hearing that too, but I know nothing about it."

"Neither do I, other than another planet, Lares Ballin, where Walban comes from, is involved. Let's hope sense prevails and things settle down. You're right, though, it feels funny with the place half empty."

"Not as many flies around either."

"A bit early for them. They'll be out in droves when the weather gets hotter."

"I watched a group of men cutting back an entire sea of stinging nettles down by the spoil heap. It's a bumper year for them if nothing else."

"I wonder," said John, lowering his voice, "if the professor regrets putting all the resources into the ship project. She had convinced herself that it was to be a major find, bringing in more volunteers plus sponsorship to fund the project. A twenty-fifth century cargo ship isn't sexy enough to do that. It's a big disappointment. I think we got into a collective mindset where we were certain, without evidence, that it was a First Intergalactic War fighter. A rare find which would generate a huge amount of interest."

"Can't you re-paint it and pretend?"

He laughed at this before saying, "Nice idea, hadn't thought of that."

"Having gone to the effort, I presume we won't abandon it," she said.

"The committee are discussing that now, but I think you're right. They can't invest so much time, money and effort, then just leave it. They've got to make the best of a bad situation. I'm expecting to be involved with the ship as they open it up and look inside. The entire enterprise hangs in the balance currently, I've heard it said. We'll have to wait and see the outcome."

"I see. I've still got plenty of finds to clean at present, we left them at the conclusion of last year's dig when there was a big flurry towards the end. Not many finds this season so far."

"I feel that we're at a pivotal moment for the project."

One evening, two weeks later, the two of them waited until dark before returning to their favourite spot by the lake. Once seated, Stella indicated she wanted to kiss and they spent some time in a warm embrace. They pulled apart and looked at the scene. Light reflected from one moon lit up the scene to a small degree; it was not pitch black.

"Shall we turn in?" suggested John, but the words were barely out of his mouth when the most extraordinary firework display began in the heavens. Rumbles, which sounded like thunder, followed brilliant flashes of light, high in the atmosphere.

"Is it a meteorite shower?" asked Stella.

"They don't look like that."

"Or an electrical storm?"

"I don't think so," John said. "I think it's a battle going on, far above our heads."

"In space?"

"Not quite; more like the exosphere. Look!" he added as he pointed up at a ship coming down in flames. "No meteorite would fall like that."

As he spoke, a burning hulk spiralled down from the sky. They watched, hypnotised by the sight, until it disappeared behind a mountain. Other arkies came out to join them and watch the display.

"What does it mean?" asked one young woman.

John said, "It should become clear in the morning."

"I'm scared, John."

"We'll be okay, an archaeological dig is not a strategic site."

The following morning, the sound of many vehicles woke John early. Some sounded quite large, too. He crept out of the tent's sleeping compartment and stuck his head out. The sight that met his eyes concerned him. A convoy of military vehicles was stopping and soldiers disembarking. Their uniforms looked quite different from those they had seen before on this planet.

Darting back in, he woke Stella and in an excited whisper, told her, "We've got company!"

"What?"

"Many soldiers are here."

"What do they want?"

"Dunno, but looks like they mean business."

John dressed in double-quick time and returned to his tent door vantage point. He spotted a dozen soldiers, but was aware of more. Professor Derby was striding out to meet them and a couple of arkies were with her. He decided to join them, so, after telling Stella, he exited his tent and hurried to where the parlay was taking place.

On his way, he studied the uniforms. They were cream, overlaid with a camouflage pattern, quite different from the khaki of the soldiers who visited the site the previous season.

Elaine finished her conversation with an officer at the same time John joined the growing group of archaeologists.

"We are being ordered to leave," she announced in a tired, monotonous voice.

"Who are these people?" a voice asked

She replied, "The People's Army of Lares Ballin. They will occupy this place and want all aliens, that's us, to leave. I've convinced the colonel that we don't have any native Tripek citizens here, but he needs us to leave... and leave now."

There were no dissenting voices; this was a distinctly different atmosphere from when the local soldiers tried to arrest Walban.

Just then, a loud alarm sounded from one of the military vehicles which brought the remaining somnolent arkies stumbling out of their tents. Professor Derby announced they had only twenty minutes to gather what possessions they could carry before being escorted to the space port. She concluded, "You will have to leave your tents behind."

No one argued; they would not mess with these soldiers. A flurry of activity followed, not least by John and Stella. They did not have many possessions in their tents, not compared with some folk. Still, they were laden down, making their way out towards the military convoy. There, along with others from the dig who were ready, the soldiers placed them on board a military transporter.

The evacuees said little. Many still seemed half asleep and no one wanted to antagonise these victorious soldiers. Herded like sheep, they moved up to the front of the vehicle and sat down amidst piles of their possessions. Those awake enough realised the implications of what was happening, looked concerned. John's imagination was running riot; were they being carted off to a quarry where the soldiers would shoot them and dump their bodies? The soldiers were not heavy handed, but efficient with emotionless faces.

The motor started and the transporter lifted off the ground and took the track toward town. Worried faced glanced at each other. Stella gripped John's arm, but no one spoke a word.

366

There was some relief felt as they entered the space port; that must be a good thing. The convoy stopped and the soldiers ordered them to disembark. They bundled out with difficulty, because some arkies had brought a tremendous amount of with them. Once they were all out and herded into a group, an officer addressed them. He instructed them to walk to a military space transporter, which would remove them from the planet. The speaker never stated an actual destination, but many got the impression that the main point was to evacuate them from Tripek III. As the people moved off, Stella and John caught each other's eye. He said, "I'll have to speak to him."

"No," Stella contradicted him, "let me do the talking."

He deferred and watched as Stella set off for the officer in charge, moving against the flow of people heading in the opposite direction. John followed from a distance.

"Excuse me, general," she began, putting on her sweetest smile.

"Colonel," he said, a frown disappearing from his face at the sight of this attractive woman.

"Colonel, we have our own private craft. If you want us off planet, please would you let us take that? We will be away from Tripek III straightaway, I promise."

The commander was putty in her hands. Turning to a subordinate, he ordered, "Escort these people to their ship."

"Yes, sir!"

Breathing a sigh of relief, the couple headed off for *Shooter*. They picked up their pace and it did not take them long to arrive at their destination. Not wanting the military to change their minds, they wasted no time storing their things, but heaved them into the cabin.

"Are we able to leave straightaway?" John asked.

The soldier gave a shrug, which he took as permission to take off. Therefore, without further ado, they shut the cockpit and John engaged the engine. Moments later, they were hovering in the air before UDS kicked in and they shot off.

'I hope the Lares Ballin battleships don't blast us out of the sky,' thought John, but he was careful not to say anything. He did not want to alarm Stella. It made no difference, because she was having the same thoughts.

"What course have you set?"

"I haven't. I just want to put distance between us and the battle zone."

If confronted, he would do his best to explain the situation. As it was, they made their escape unmolested and, as they passed out of the solar system, they issued an enormous sigh of relief.

"You've still got what it takes!" John said. "The colonel took to you."

"Hmm, it was time to be submissive," she said.

"We're safe now. Where shall we head for?"

"Hello, brother, it's me! I know I've been the worst person ever at keeping in touch, but I thought you might like to hear how I'm getting on..."

John was working a communications array on the space station that was their home. It orbited the recently re-named planet Encontrar (previously Axon Three), where a most unusual archaeological dig was taking place. Following centuries of trying, this was the first unequivocal evidence of an alien civilisation ever discovered.

"... You know we missed them by quite a margin. They had thought it was about five million years ago, but more research revealed that the cataclysm that killed them all happened nearer fifty-five million years ago..."

It was a verbal message only, but he hoped his brother would receive it on the equipment that John left with him on his visit to Molten.

Encontrar was proving an alien world in more ways than one. For a start, there was no atmosphere. The scientists believed it used to have breathable air, breathable by the aliens, that is. The current theory was that a single catastrophic event had it stripped it away, and that was responsible for their demise. A rogue star, or a large planet passing close by could have done it.

Geological surveys showed the sphere cooled for a crust to form a mere hundred million years ago. They believed the current crust to be thin with a huge, hot molten core beneath. Earthquakes, volcanoes and other seismic activity were prevalent on Encontrar 's far side. This was not the case near the dig site where, they suspected, the crust may be thicker. The site was near an ancient lava flow.

Strange, massive structures covered an area of a hundred square kilometres. As ever, theories abounded, one popular being that the aliens originated elsewhere, because the timescale between the crust forming and the evolution of an advanced civilisation was too short. They had not yet discovered this birthplace.

The project was a high profile, high status enterprise which John and Stella were lucky to get in on. Now well established, they lived with the team on a space station in synchronous orbit over the site. Occasionally, select personnel transferred to the surface, but with the transportation involved and the need for space suits, the project director did not encourage it. The space archaeologists carried out most of the work remotely from the orbiting headquarters. A thick layer of fine dust covered the surface and anti-grav motors had the effect of kicking it up. They therefore rigged a framework over the area under consideration. Tools and equipment ran up and down rails within this. While something was being excavated, they applied a suction pipe which vacuumed up the dust and lose particles from the immediate area. John had taken over operating the controls for this from orbit. Excellent cameras aided him, set on the ground and on the space station. The latter were powerful and, with an absence of atmosphere, showed an excellent aerial view. Another help was his colleague Samantha Van Leer. Sam, a real brain-box, was a sensitive soul and, fortunately for John, extremely patient. He enjoyed working with her.

The director put Stella in charge of logistic supplies and she threw herself into the role with a determined efficiency. She kept each department on their toes, because she needed them to assist her so that she could help them. Proactive in her work, Stella was proving a popular addition to the team.

The overall person in charge was Professor Mary DuBois. An able facilitator, as well as scientific brain, she possessed a firm grip on what the project needed for the way ahead. She was also good with people. This latter skill was proving necessary with some characters in the limited room available on board the platform. Joni McCann (engineer) was bad tempered and liable to explode without warning. Irene Metaxas (finds) was at the opposite end of the spectrum, a loner who always avoided confrontations.

John and Stella enjoyed spending their free time in each other's company. Their relationship was thriving, although she would still have preferred being in a formal marriage. He had docked *Shooter*, his trusty spacecraft at the station, which meant he did not have to worry about that. The dig paid them a modest salary, generated by the funds raised across the quadrant because of the great excitement generated by the discovery.

A genuine alien site was something mankind had dreamed about for centuries. Reality dashed all those early hopes of encountering multiple other species in the galaxy after man discovered the ability to reach the stars. The explorers soon learned quite how a hostile universe stacked the odds against life of any kind, let alone intelligent life. False claims and hoaxes abounded, but Encontrar was the first genuine site discovered.

It was still early days. They were yet to decide what appearance the aliens took, although signs were they dwarfed the average man. They interpreted markings uncovered as writing, but the station's resident linguist expert, Allison Piper, was finding her work cut out, trying to make something meaningful out of it.

John and Sam were taking a break one morning after a busy session. An earnest-looking Mary popped her head into their compartment. Her face was long, but longer still was her wavy hair cascading down both sides beyond her shoulders. She was a lady on a mission. John thought he would try to engage with her.

"Hi, do you want a hot drink? Come and join us?"

She hesitated for a moment and then, suddenly, her face changed as she relaxed, replying, "Sure."

"It'll do you good to take a break," Sam informed her, "as you always tell us to!"

"I get the point," the professor conceded, looking amused. She got her drink from the dispenser and joined the other two.

"John said, "Sam was telling me about her university dissertation. Will you tell us what you did?"

He sat back with a cheeky expression, awaiting the response, but Mary was up for it.

"If you're interested... My degree was in astrophysics, not archaeology."

"Quite useful here, though."

"I think so. But to answer your question, my dissertation was to do with the ocean of Shui Gui." When the others laughed at the name, she smiled and confessed that it sounded funny. "But it's a large moon orbiting the giant planet Hao Xi'an. The latter's a fascinating astronomical body. It has an iron core fifty percent of its radius, which drives a magnetic field so vast that it stretches to the orbit of the next planet out, some seven hundred million kilometres. It revolves round a binary star system."

"They're quite common, aren't they?"

"Binary stars? Yes, of course. But I was concentrating on Shui Gui, like I said."

"Why did they call it that?"

"It's Chinese for water demon. The moon has its own magnetic field and water below an immense layer of ice. Scientists believed the vast subterranean ocean to have the energy and primordial ingredients for life. I began my studies when a drilling exercise was close to breaking through. They were happy to have me on board and took me under their wing. It was a perilous operation and needed to be automated."

"So what happened?"

"They got through and, contrary to all hopes and expectations, the water was sterile. It was devoid of life and, from its chemical composition, could not support any type known."

"Oh dear."

"Putting a positive spin on it, a negative result is still a result. It'd be far more exciting to write a dissertation explaining the viability of alien life in this ocean, but it wasn't to be."

"All the same, you got the qualification."

"I also had a fascinating experience and established lifelong friendships. I don't regret any of it."

After this, John and Sam told the project leader how their morning was going. Then Mary dropped something of a bombshell.

"I'm going to call the crew together for a meeting this afternoon."

"Oh?"

"I may as well tell you now, but keep it to yourself until after I've announced it."

"Of course," the other two chorused.

"There's a meteor heading our way - towards the planet, I mean. We've known about it several weeks, it's been no secret. It's been difficult to predict its path. Some models suggested it was going to pass us by, but as it gets closer, they reckon the predictions are getting more accurate. I'm not convinced, they keep making excuses for the changes. Anyway, with a week to go, they think it's going to hit Encontrar."

"Near the site?" asked Sam.

"Again, they keep emphasising how difficult it is to predict. Their latest idea is that it will hit in a week's time and at a shallow angle, a hundred kilometres from their dig. When I do the presentation this afternoon, I'll show all the data. In a nutshell, it's likely to kick up a great deal of surface material. I estimate it could disrupt our operation by at least a week. Then," she added with a wink, "an enforced break from excavating won't be too hard to bear."

John agreed, "There's lots of data to keep us busy if there's a big dust storm down there, don't worry."

That evening, after the presentation, John and Stella were together in their quarters.

"It won't affect me much," she speculated. "I've got lots of finds to sort through and catalogue."

"How's that going?"

"It's difficult, so difficult. Knowing little about their civilisation, I'm guessing what things *are* half the time. That's following consultation with the experts here. An artefact may be a foot covering, a washbowl, or a piece of equipment. We do our best and write up the reasoning behind our decisions. I'm sure in future years, when we know a lot more about them, we'll redefine a lot of the finds. I mean, we haven't even settled on a *name* for the aliens yet."

"No, I know that Mary is reluctant to be hurried into doing that. She's under pressure in that regard, but would rather Allison made a breakthrough with their language first. We need to establish what they called themselves."

Stella said, "That presupposes they possessed voice boxes like ours. They might have made noises we couldn't even imitate, or were beyond our range of hearing. We still know so very little."

"You're into this now, aren't you?" John said with a laugh. How refreshing to see her so happy and committed.

As for Stella, she had found a worthwhile purpose in this enterprise and it delighted her to play a part. It was no longer about pleasing the man she loved, although that was a bonus.

The following three days passed by. John and Sam had developed a close understanding of operating the excavator together. Plenty of concentration was involved. Sometimes they would work for a full half hour without a word being spoken between them. Thinking alike, they worked as a smooth, efficient team. The pair seemed to

372

others to be toiling especially hard that week. At the backs of their minds was the spectre of a meteorite disrupting their work for several days. They wanted to achieve a lot before being forced to down tools because of large, swirling dust clouds.

One break period, they were in the station's rest room with Stella. The trio were enjoying a rather superior cup of coffee from a supply that Mary procured on her last visit to her home planet. The unselfish professor shared it amongst the crew.

Stella asked, "Sam, is it true that you've been with the project from the beginning?"

Finishing a long sip, she replied, "It is. I'm the sole survivor of the original team. I presume you know a bit about what happened."

When the questioner shook her head, she continued, "It was a bit of a disaster. There were horrible personality clashes and little cliques formed. I hated it. The whole thing degenerated. The personality profiling should have forestalled such a breakdown, but it didn't. A major problem was having too many of us crammed in here. The current staff numbers are smaller, plus they added another module, the recreation room."

Grinning, John said, "Would that be the recreation room stuffed so full of extra supplies you can't move?"

"Hmm, Mary assured me a week ago that she'd get it sorted. I might have to have another word. I don't like to criticise, though, because she's a brilliant director. She holds the entire project together and tries to shield us from external pressures."

"Such as?"

"The Scientific Grants Council and the Space Exploration Society for two."

"Maybe," began Stella, "we'll all be able to lend a hand next week if there's an enforced..."

She broke off when Allison Piper burst into the room with an excited expression. The linguist expert asked, "have you heard the news?"

"You've cracked the alien language!" joked John.

Stella was close enough to give him a kick. She did not like it when he was flippant.

"No, it's Joni. They rushed her off, planet-side, in an ambulance. Something to do with her heart."

"A heart attack, you mean?" John enquired, trying to be sensible.

"Not a heart attack," Allison replied, "but serious enough for her to be taken off immediately."

The messenger disappeared as quickly as she arrived and the three of them discussed it, saying they hoped their engineer would make a swift recovery.

"She'll miss all the fireworks on Friday," John declared.

"Let's hope it doesn't come to fireworks," Sam said. "I'm hoping they've got their calculations wrong and that it passes us by, like they first said. I won't welcome a disruption to our work."

The following day, Stella and Sam sat together in the rest room when the former began a conversation.

"John's always extolling your virtues. I know he enjoys working alongside you. You're making progress. It was a major lift yesterday, wasn't it?"

"It was. A piece of machinery, although it's hard to tell when everything's fossilised following millions of years. But we got it up in one piece and onto the transporter. It'll keep the analysts going for a long time, I'm sure."

Then, wishing to change the subject, Sam enquired, "What was that holo-cast you were watching when I came in? If you don't mind me asking. You seemed gripped by it."

Stella glanced down at her TRAC before replying, "Have you heard of Joan Stenx?"

"Mmm," the other looked thoughtful. "She's a religious leader, isn't she?"

"I'd say more of a philosopher. She doesn't endorse any religion or sect."

"Oh."

"She said that in any given situation we shouldn't focus on ourselves, but the needs of others. Each time we have company, we should remember we're here for their sake and not our own."

"What about a relationship where someone is wants to take advantage of you? Or an abusive relationship, she's not saying we should be doormats to be walked over?"

"Sorry, I'm not expressing myself well. It wasn't so much about letting other folk have their own way, but doing what's best for their soul's development. If someone tries using you, or manipulate you, it'd be better to get out of that relationship. You're not doing them any good by indulging them."

"Isn't that a big ask, though, your having to discern what's best for everyone else's soul?"

Stella hesitated. She realised Sam was being genuine and not trying to pick this philosophy apart. After a while, she said, "Maybe you're right. I'm sure I'm not putting it across as well as Joan Stenx does. Maybe I should watch more of the holo-cast."

The rest of that busy week flew and, before they knew it, the meteor approach was a standard hour away. Joni was still off site receiving medical treatment, but the doctors considered her condition not too serious. She hoped to return in a couple of weeks.

Nearly everyone present on the space station took up positions on a crowded observation deck. Meanwhile, engineers manned monitors in another room. They evacuated the personnel from the surface as a precaution. Most joined the regular station personnel to watch the event. It was one thing to look at it on a screen in your room, but nothing beat sharing the experience with others and having both the observation window and screens showing close-up views. Hence all the people gathered. They brought extra seats in and Professor DuBois was given the place of honour in the front row. All the others sat except John and Kahill, the youngest member on the station.

Something of a party atmosphere prevailed and people were munching snacks and drinking.

"I don't know what people expect to see," John said, turning to Kahill. "This thing will whiz past at a trillion kilometres a second and we'll see nothing."

"They say it's likely to give it a glancing blow and kick lots of dust and debris up."

"As long as it doesn't hit this space station!"

Some stared at the observation window, others glanced at the screens as well. Two smaller screens to the side were showing numbered read-outs and one a real-time diagram showing the course of the projectile in relation to the planet. Its trajectory was erratic, buffeted as it was by various gravitational fields. This made it difficult even for their sophisticated computers to predict what would happen. The data readouts were jumping about as the meteor got closer.

When it got near, the chatter level in the room dropped. A voice said, "Three minutes out." Stella turned round and exchanged an affectionate look with John.

Closer it came. "I think it's going to hit," opined Kahill, although he knew no more than anyone else in the room.

As the final ten seconds arrived, the people began a countdown.

"... Six, five, four, three, two one..."

There was a tiny puff of dust as the object hit Encontrar straight on, a mere fifty kilometres from the site... and disappeared.

Silence rained for a moment. Then Kahill asked with a puzzled expression, "Did it hit, or pass by?"

Even as he spoke, the screen showed a slow-motion replay. The meteorite, travelling at ultra-high velocity relative to the planet, had gone in like a bullet. No angle was involved, it went straight in. No great dust cloud; nothing.

"Huh, that was a damp squib!" declared Allison, sounding most disappointed.

Almost immediately, John shouted, "Look!" and the audience re-focused on the point of impact. The ground where the projectile hit was rising. Soon a conical shape appeared and, before anyone else could speak, a jet of magma shot up into the sky.

Mary jumped from off her seat and, heading for the exit, ordered a selection of people to follow her. These included Ruhakana who piloted the space station for orbit corrections.

The new volcano kept growing, spewing out increasing amounts of molten rock. Meanwhile, further fissures nearby wept. Stella looked round again, this time her face was one of alarm. Amidst others rising from their seats, some to get closer to the screen, she hurried to John's side.

"Did you see that?" she asked. Then, realising the stupidity of the question, continued, "Of course you did! It's, it's..."

"I know," he whispered. "We always knew Encontrar had a thin crust with a large, active interior. The meteorite must've punched through like a missile and it's releasing all that pent-up energy."

"How long will it go on for?"

Even as she spoke, more cracks opened up near the archaeological site and fresh magma poured out. A sea of molten rock flowed out and drowned the entire area.

"I think I might be out of a job," Kahill said, demonstrating his ability for understatement.

"We all are," said John.

They watched as the planet moved further away, Mary having ordered a higher orbit to be on the safe side. Meanwhile, there was no end to the lava pouring out, quite the opposite. Soon it was hard to pick out pieces of dry land. They all knew it meant the end of their venture. Until a fresh crust formed (months, years away?) the entire surface would be a boiling, seething mass.

Shock gripped the people; most of them staying inside the observation dome. They could not tear their eyes from the screen. "I don't believe it," one man kept saying again and again. The party was over.

"So that's that," said John.

"Succinctly put," Stella said.

"I guess we'll have to look for somewhere else. I can't see them keeping us on, my darling."

"No... and just as we were contributing. It goes to show you never know what's round the corner."

Everybody knew that the project was over regarding fresh evidence. Further research would continue for years on the artefacts salvaged and the hologramic pictures taken. They would do this inside a dome on the scientific research moon Cantor 967, requiring less than half the current staff.

For the next forty-eight hours, most of the space station's inhabitants went round in a daze. They understood the disaster's implications, although the facts still took time to sink in. The strike had eradicated this priceless, unique site in less than an hour. It was irredeemable. Research would still continue for years, but they would excavate nothing fresh.

On the third day following the disaster, Professor DuBois met with her staff. They congregated in the one room large enough to accommodate them, the observation deck, but the window was shuttered and the screen switched off. Mary had been the sole person full of energy since the catastrophe, co-ordinating with the project's sponsors and committee and deciding what would happen. She had not had a blink of sleep as she fought for the best deal for her staff. It was therefore a somewhat dishevelled Mary who addressed the subdued archaeologists.

"We all know what happened on Friday," she began, "so I won't waste time going over that. You probably know that we lost all our surface equipment, but, having recalled the maintenance crew, there were no casualties.

"A ship is coming from Shistua to tow the station back there. They will carry out further research under the domes of Owen Base, planet-side. I've done my best for you, but we're only able to retain a third of staff."

She then read out the names of the members being kept on the project. As she did so, neither John nor Stella held out any realistic hope of staying on. They were correct, they would leave at the first opportunity. There was no point dragging it out.

Sad, protracted, sometimes emotional goodbyes took place as those who were leaving got ready to go.

"I can't believe they're not keeping you," Stella told Sam with feeling.

With a resigned shrug, the other said, "Wrong skill set."

"You'll be able to get a job somewhere else I should imagine."

"I hope so; Mary's agreed to give us all glowing references. After all, we were an effective team."

Stella and John made sure they thanked Mary before departing. She had fought for, and won, a generous redundancy package for them.

"You're welcome," the professor replied. "I hear there's a new dig being set up on La-Negros in case you're interested. I'll be working on the reference over the next few days."

"Thank you," said a grateful John, glancing at Stella. "La-Negros, you say."

"A domed planet not a million miles from here.... actually, it's many millions of miles, but you know what I mean."

They smiled at the sleep-deprived professor's attempt at humour. Once the couple had everything packed, every goodbye said and no excuse to stay a moment longer, they boarded John's old, but trusty spacecraft.

"So," he said with a sigh, "one door closes. Let's hope another one opens."

~ End of Chapter 19 ~

My Keeper's Brother - Chapter 20

The following three and a half years in the couple's archaeological careers were less fulfilling. Accepted on the La-Negros excavation when positions were scarce, they stuck with it, because there seemed nowhere else to go.

Not an open planet, they spent all their time within one particular dome excavating a site which was a hundred years old. Archaeologists were sifting through the rubbish left by the early colonists. It was all too recent for John's liking. They put Stella, the former nurse, in charge of first aid at the site. To date, she had dealt with minor bumps and scrapes. She spent the rest of her time cleaning finds. She went along with it to please him, but as he seemed unhappy, so she began seeking outlets elsewhere for the two of them, but without success.

An autocratic style of leadership and underfunding did not help the project. Neither did the fast turnover of disaffected staff. Matters culminated one day John pushed a squeaky wheelbarrow full of artefacts (or "junk" as he would have put it) to where Stella sat cleaning an old toothbrush with... an old toothbrush. He looked worn out and every bit his fifty-six earth years.

"All the anti-grav ones have broken down," he complained, glancing at the wheelbarrow. "I'm having to use this old thing."

"John, sit down," she directed, patting the mat next to her. He sat on a spare stool and looked at her. Stella decided she must tell him how she felt.

"I've been thinking," she said. "It's silly to stay here when we're both unhappy. It's crazy. I want us to settle down. I'm tired of all this. I've had my fill of archaeology too, if I'm going to be honest."

"Me too," he said. In the silence that followed, he looked round at the other workers pulling out a battered handbag, a crumpled push-chair and a bent bedstead from the junk heap. He pursed his lips and let out a long exhale. "Where to go?" he asked.

"I've got an idea!" she chirped, sounding far more full of energy than he was.

"What's that?"

"You spoke about your brother Frank on the planet Molten. Why couldn't we settle there?"

She half expected a negative response, but when the reply came, John was more thoughtful. "You realise it's a backwards planet?"

"Yes, you told me."

"There are no real luxuries there."

"Like we've been enjoying these last few years?" she asked ironically.

He laughed at this. Then a supervisor came over.

"Come on, you two, we don't start break for another twenty minutes!"

"We're taking an early break," Stella informed the young man.

"Who gave you permission?"

This annoyed John, who snapped, "Leave my wife alone! Go away."

The man did so, muttering to himself. John glanced up and saw that Stella was smiling.

"'My wife'? It's about time!"

"Um, I... maybe when we go to Molten."

"We're going then?"

"They don't even have hot running water," he continued the list of disadvantages.

"Okay."

"Or electricity."

"I know all this. It's a medieval society, you've told me before."

"And we wouldn't be able to discuss interplanetary travel."

"Oh dear," she said with a glint in her eye, "my favourite topic."

"Hmm, I won't to put you off, will I?"

"Would you rather stay here?"

He pulled a face before perking up as he said, "I'll send a message to Frank. I left a receiver with him; he should get it."

"Ask him if we can come?"

"I'll *tell* him I'm coming."

Stella looked startled at the firmness of this declaration, so John changed his tone.

"It's okay, I'll tell him nicely; I'm sure he'll say yes."

"When shall we go? I wouldn't mind if we never spent another minute in this hole."

"Me neither," said John, appreciating her depth of feeling for the first time. Then neither had he realised his own. He had drifted along for too long, it was time for a change. Their being on short-term contracts meant they could leave at the end of the week. The call to Frank was successful and he got a positive response. John spoke to his brother about informing "the others," but there was only one companion who would travel with him. The pair spent the rest of their time well, getting their things together and collecting provisions for the trip.

"It should take about fifteen days," he said, "but I've packed emergency supplies for a lot longer. Rumours abound of Chang Tides operating intermittently in that area of space between the ends of the spiral galaxy."

"Brilliant," she said, "so we'll either land there in 33AD or the year 3000!"

(Chang Tides were still very much an unknown quantity and no one understood their effect. Some refused to believe they existed at all).

John replied, "You're not having second thoughts, I hope."

"Nope! I will not be put off. Let's get going."

Two weeks later, following an uneventful journey, they were approaching their destination. Stella felt it was high time she learned more about he whom they were going to meet.

"You've mentioned he's religious, but that's about all."

"Um, yes. I've only met him once since he left Marmaris when I was a teenager. He's still religious, but has plenty of other things to fill his time. I've told you it's a backwards planet. Frank's in charge of a little fiefdom there. He's fallen on his feet, I'd say. But it's not all relaxing, he has to administer his domain. Seems to do pretty good job. He learned administration skills during his time on Eden. But this is a whole different matter. I've said he lives in a castle."

"Yes."

"It's an impressive structure, better than the hovels his subjects live in. I guess it needs to be that way if he's in charge of them."

"But what's he like?" Stella pressed.

"Um... like I said, I've had few dealings with him for most of my life. He's earnest, but still capable of joking. He's well organised and... I don't know. We should be able to stay awhile, get to know him better. We'll get along, I think."

"Did you tell me he's married?"

"Yeah, although I can't remember her name for the life of me. I hope you get on well together."

"So do I," she responded before changing the subject.

"I can't believe how few stars there are."

"Yeah, it takes a bit of getting used to. The planet is between two spiral arms of the galaxy and towards the end of them, on the edge of the Milky Way. Next stop after Molten is Andromeda, two million light years away."

"I see, so if we find ourselves in Andromeda, we'll know we missed your brother," she quipped.

Later, in a more serious mood, she said, "I'm glad we contacted Ben before we left."

"Sure, it's good to know how he's well settled."

"Yes, a mother never stops worrying, but he's where he wants to be. And he seemed pleased for us."

"Plus, he's got the details so that he can contact us if he has to. He will be fine, I'm sure of it... ah, here we are, see?"

The white dot in the middle of the screen was expanding before their eyes. Once it filled the whole monitor, John stated, "Coming out of UDS... going to enter orbit round the northern hemisphere." Then, after a pause, he added. "We'll approach where Frank is from the east, It'll be night time."

He checked the read-outs and declared everything to be in order. "We can enter the atmosphere now. Once we're in the Troposphere, I'll switch over to manual control. I'll fly in slow and low; don't want to wake the neighbours."

The automatic systems brought the ship down through the increasingly dense layers of air. Ever since the initial space flights, this had been a critical point, although mishaps were few in the twenty-seventh century. On this occasion, everything ran smoothly. John took over the controls, making sure *Shooter* cruised at sub-sonic speed in a cloudless, dark sky.

"What's that?" asked John, more to himself than to his companion.

Something had set a customised sensor off, which got him very excited. "It can't be!" he exclaimed.

"What?" Stella said out of curiosity, for he did not sound worried.

"I don't believe it... there's a ship down there. I'm going to circle round."

"Is it one of ours?"

It was a curious enquiry, for it begged the question as to whom "ours" referred to. John ignored it anyway. As they came round a second time, he ensured a flypast above the object so that the sensors could pick up the maximum amount of data.

"It's old, it's ancient, in fact."

"Oh no," she knew his fondness for classic spaceships. "You're not stopping now!"

"You're right," he said, "but I'll want to analyse all this once we're landed."

"Hmm."

"Not for now. We'll carry on to our destination."

After logging the location of the find in the ship's computer, he steered the craft westwards, sweeping low over the undulating terrain.

"Almost there," he announced as the spaceship swooped down over Thyatira's Castle and landed in the nearby woods. The ship settled into the soft ground and the engine turned off.

"Best bring as much as you can," John told her. "I don't want to keep coming back here."

"But you'll engage the cloaking device?"

"Of course."

In the event, they could only take a fraction of the ship's contents. Stella held a large case, but with the anti-grav unit engaged, it weighed nothing. John was so encumbered that he ended up putting some back before finally disembarking.

"Lots of lights on," his companion observed.

The Castle was indeed lit up. Flickering light came from every window. John commentated the occupants must be staying up late before handing Stella a pair of night vision glasses.

"Remember, we must take these off as soon as we meet anyone."

"What about that great big TRAC on your arm?"

"Ah, yes," he replied before taking his wrist computer off and stuffing it into his pocket.

A slight chill filled the clear night ait, but the travellers were warm enough walking across the grass. Stella glanced back, the woods were fast receding.

"We'll skirt round this way to get to the entrance."

"Okay."

The courtyard entrance was closed, so they walked further round to the main entrance. As they got closer, the pair noticed a steady stream of people leaving, each holding a lantern against the pitch black. John and Stella stopped to see the stream turn into a trickle, followed by the occasional straggler.

"They must have held some kind of important meeting," John observed.

"Never mind, let's carry on."

Two hundred metres further was the entrance, manned by a couple of guards. Torches on the walls illuminated the area. Their flames danced in the slight breeze and moved the shadows about.

The visitors took their glasses off and hid them before approaching the sentries. The soldiers had seen a lot of comings and goings that evening because of the harvest supper being held in the Castle's hall. They would have let the strangers pass unchallenged. As it was, John halted and addressed the nearest one.

"My name's John Thorn, I'm the, um, Despot's brother. Please, will you take me to him?"

Startled by this revelation, the sentry jumped to it and offered to escort them to the keep.

"Yes, thank you."

"Be right back," the guardsman addressed his colleague. He then offered to carry Stella's case, but she declined. It appeared light from the ease at which she carried it.

They crossed the dimly lit bailey towards the keep's ground floor reception room. On the way, their guide mentioned they were late for the party. The comment went unanswered.

"Oh!" exclaimed the soldier upon finding the reception room deserted. "That's most odd. Never mind, I'll take you up there myself." As they ascended, the sound of chatter in the main hall got louder. Top of the stairs, the sentry opened the door and ushered them in. Keen to return to his post, he left them to it and disappeared back down the stairs.

Stella and John took in the sight before them. It was a large, brightly-decorated hall with tables laid out, filling most of the space. The celebrations looked to be over, with empty chairs abandoned at odd angles. The tables had used plates, cutlery and leftovers scattered across them. A small army of servants was busy clearing up.

Meanwhile, a gaggle of people were standing, talking, some twenty metres away. They did not notice the couple at first and continued conversing.

Stella stared in amazement at the room. It was like the ancient castles she had seen pictures of when she was a girl. The whitewashed walls had a pattern painted on them. Various rooms and stairways led off the hall. The servants all possessed identical, snow-white hair. There was a lot to take in.

As he scrutinised the group engaged in conversation, John noticed two men talking, one a cleric, plus another couple, a man and a woman. It took a few moments, but he soon recognised one speaker as his brother, Frank. As if drawn by John's stare, the interlocutor looked up. He gave a broad smile of recognition and asked to be excused. He strode over to the pair a short way inside the entrance. Stella released the anti-grav unit on her large case and it sank slowly to the floor.

"John!" Frank exclaimed, taking his hand, "how great to see you again!"

The visitor was delighted with the warm welcome. It intrigued him that his appearance at that moment had not surprised Frank.

His brother seemed to read his thoughts, for he explained, "I heard your ship coming in to land, even through these thick walls."

"Ah, of course... and this is Stella."

As the Despot greeted her, his wife came forward and John introduced her to those present. There was warmth in Hannah's greeting and it put them at ease. Further people came across and they found themselves introduced to the former steward, Natias, and Bishop Gunter.

"I met you last time," the former reminded John, who nodded, although he could not remember.

The two regulars then made their excuses and departed. In the background, the servants were helping Alan and Karl get up. John noticed, commenting that some revellers must have enjoyed a merry time that evening.

Hannah, who looked quite tired, said, "I've never seen those two so worse for wear. However much did they drink?"

Ignoring this, Frank said, "We'll get a room set up for you. I know it's late, but join us for a nightcap before we retire."

It was an offer they could not refuse. First, though, the Despot called two passing servants to him and said, "Our guests will stay in the northwest tower room tonight. Take their cases and prepare the room for them."

"Yes, My Lord."

Turning to John and Stella, he said, "Small, but not uncomfortable. We put our VIP guests in there."

"I'm glad we qualify," John retorted with a grin.

As they stepped forward to sit at the end of a cleared table, Stella noticed a servant try to lift her case. He was most surprised at its weight and struggled with it up the stairs. She felt guilty, realising that she could at least have put the anti-grav unit to minimum. It was too late now.

"How lovely to see you," Frank enthused.

"And you too, big brother."

"Don't call me that," his elder brother said with a pained expression. "'Frank' will do fine."

John mumbled an apology and made a mental note. He remembered how little he knew his sibling and hoped they would get on.

"So, you're from Oonimari," the Despotess stated, looking straight at Stella.

"That's right," the other woman replied casually, John having primed her about her cover story. "We're hoping to spend a while here."

After glancing at her husband, the hostess said, "You can spend as long as you want. I'm looking forward to getting to know you."

"That's right," Frank supported this statement. His brother's previous visit had been brief and the time taken up with a crisis. Now, the quiet domestic and international scenes presented an opportunity to properly get to know him.

Hot drinks were served, but none of them wanted to stay up very late. They therefore retired to bed soon afterwards, with promises of spending quality time together the next day.

The following morning, Stella and John woke in good time. They found crude, but clean washing facilities in their small tower room and took advantage of them before getting dressed.

"Everything's quiet," Stella commented.

"It's the thickness of the walls."

"I looked outside and it's quiet there too."

"Mmm. Frank mentioned breakfast being in the same hall in which they met yesterday. I'd rather not be late."

"Okay, let's go down."

They exited their tower room and found their way to the spiral staircase, working their way down to the hall. It was deserted, apart from a couple of guardsmen and some servants. John hesitated at the foot of the staircase, but Stella gave him a surreptitious shove, hissing, "Go on, then!"

The tables, rearranged after the night before, looked bearer. They stood at the one nearest them, the couple were a long distance from anyone else. They were hovering aimlessly when a servant appeared and took their breakfast order.

A short while later, Stella was trying out a hamble cake and John was tucking into some porridge. They sat together in silence until they heard a voice behind them giving a hearty greeting.

"Good morning! Did you sleep well?"

"Frank!" John said with some relief. "Yes, we slept well, we've found travelling to be pretty tiring."

"Not as tiring as late night revelries, it seems," the Despot observed, looking round at the empty places. "Hannah's having a lie-in; it shattered her last night." He then added, "I'll join you," as he took a place opposite them.

Breakfast went well. Hannah's lie-in did not last too long and she was soon joining them, along with their son, Joseph. The five of them sat together. Elsewhere, more Castle workers had come down to eat.

"How's Oonimari?" enquired the Despotess.

John hesitated before replying, "Um, we haven't been there in quite a while, we've been doing a lot of travelling."

"Visited some interesting places?"

"Yes indeed, we..."

"I thought we could go for a walk this morning," Frank interrupted, wanting to curtail this line of enquiry. "I could show you the senate building and some of Castleton. We've come a long way since your last visit."

"I hope I'm included," his wife put in, concerned that she might be marginalised.

"Of course you are."

As she saw the low numbers attending breakfast, Hannah noted Alan was missing.

"I'm not surprised. The state he was in last night. Goodness knows how much he and Karl drank between them."

"Not like either of them."

"Well, they had a skin-full, I saw them."

After breakfast, Hannah, Frank, Stella and John set out together, Joseph having gone off with his tutor. The host led them the short distance across the road to the fringes of Castleton. The weather was warm, but a thick covering of cloud hid the sun that morning.

"I don't remember any of this," John confessed.

"When was it you visited before?" asked his brother. "The years roll by and it's hard to keep track of them."

"Um, 2606."

"Well, everything's changed in the last fifteen years. Thyatira has expanded tremendously in that time, both in terms of population and size. Castleton, as it's now known as, was called the Castle complex before. It has grown organically. It started off a few dwellings. Now it's a town in its own right."

"Impressive houses too!" John remarked.

"Yes, especially up this end. It's still expanding to the west."

"That's the other end?"

"Yes. And this," he pointed to the extensive building behind the whitewashed wall, "is the senate building."

"Also new?"

"It's been going for some years now. They run the day-to-day business of Thyatira. It was getting a bit much for me after the first major expansion. Now I have a dedicated personal assistant as well. Tristan has the day off today."

Meanwhile, Hannah and Stella were engaged in their own conversation. The former asked, "How long have you been married?"

Looking sheepish, the visitor admitted they were not married, adding, "Not that I wouldn't like us to, but every time I broach the subject, he shuts me down. He avoids the issue."

They took a tour of the senate building which quite impressed John. Back outside, Stella was more taken with the mansions.

"It did not lead me to expect buildings like this," she said.

Frank replied, "No, things have come on a long way since John visited. Some wealthy blacks began settling here when we had suspended the building regulations for a time. It's grown and grown since then."

As they passed a magnificent dwelling, he said, "This is where Deejan Charvo lives. He's a merchant and a friend. Nice man. And this is where the bishop lives."

John quipped, "Typical of the Church to own an enormous mansion."

His brother's head spun round and gave him such a glare that John apologised straightaway. He thought, 'Dammit! Me and my big mouth... if we're going to ask to stay here, I don't want to upset him. Note to self: be more sensitive and think before I open my mouth.'

Stella then rescued the situation by asking, "Is there a hospital here?"

"No," Hannah confessed, "not in Castleton. In fact, the despotate's only place is the monastery infirmary. The facilities are pretty crude, to be honest. We built and ran far better ones in Ladosa."

"Ladosa, that's where you're from?"

"Yes."

"Is that part of.. Hoame?"

"No, it's the country north of Hoame. It's where I grew up."

Frank, who had been listening to all this, blurted, "I've an idea! You know relations between us and the Ladosans are probably the best they've ever been?"

"Yes."

"We could see if they'll take one or two of our serious medical cases from us. You said they have better facilities."

"Proper hospitals, yes."

"What do you think?"

"I think it's worth considering. We could put out some feelers."

They moved on and, as they came past the next mansion, Frank said, "This one's unoccupied. It was owned by a wealthy black who passed away recently. He died with no heirs, so it's reverted to me as despot. I must decide what I'll do with it." Then, stopping, he said, "Well, I reckon we've shown you the best part. Let's turn round and head back, shall we?"

As the Despot turned on his heels and began walking briskly in the opposite direction, the party realised it was more of a command than a suggestion.

Hannah proposed. "Shall we skirt round the Castle rather than go straight back?"

They agreed, although Frank warned that the grass might still be heavy with dew.

Stella, meanwhile, enquired, "You mention 'blacks' quite a lot. John told me a bit about this, a rigid social structure split between blacks and whites who are a race apart. Is that correct?"

The Despot took it upon himself to answer that one. "Well, it's a complex situation. When I arrived, the whites were a complete underclass, but the situation has changed a lot since then. We have some white senators here in Thyatira, plus there is even one white in the Inner Council based in the Capital. I've been striving for a gradual change to improve the lot of the whites. Things have been improving elsewhere too. I know that conditions for the whites in Aggeparii - that's one of our neighbouring regions - have got a lot better in recent times. The Inner Council has been encouraging change in other despotates, too. I believe in a gentle approach for gradual change. It needs managing."

"Is there pressure from the whites to speed reform?" asked Stella.

"Not on the whole, although we get the occasional revolutionary trying to disrupt things. The correct way is gradual change."

"And this Inner Council, they run the show?"

"That's one way of putting it. They are in overall control, but we have a federal system with the regions, despotates, autonomous in mundane affairs."

"You're a despot, in charge of this region, Thyatira, right?"

"And a member of the Inner Council," he was quick to point out.

"Right."

"Folk call the Inner Council members the 'Keepers,' because they keep control of the country."

"I see," said Stella. These answers must satisfy her, for now at least. She would not rock the boat by pressing him further.

Soon they were due north of the Castle and John recognised the wood beyond the grassland where he had hidden his spaceship. Coming alongside his brother, he said in lowered tones, "We parked our ship in those woods."

"Cloaked?"

"Yes."

"Well, it should be safe enough there. I don't think you've got anything to worry about."

Meanwhile, Stella and Hannah were talking together once more. The latter commented, "There are still a lot of superstitions existing around here. Last week, one woman told me she slept with a few coins under her pillow, hoping that it would bring her good fortune in the future."

"I'll have to try that!" Stella joked before adding, "I don't think we can confine superstition to here, though. I've come across plenty if superstitious people on my travels. Some people believe in the craziest ideas."

Once back at the Castle, the two couples split up. Stella and John ascended to their room in the tower where the former unpacked and hung up her clothes. John liked the view and peered out the window for some time.

"There's a minor road leading up that way. Lots of trees wherever you look. I thought Tripek had lots, but I don't think I've seen a planet with this many trees."

"I thought you said we shouldn't talk like that."

"Huh?"

"Mentioning planets."

John almost said that it was okay between the two of them. Then he saw the wisdom in trying to quit the habit while they were on Molten.

"Yeah, you're right."

"Hannah's nice," Stella commented

"Lovely; I'm glad you've made a good start here."

"I confess I held quite a few concerns coming here, but the reality is looking a lot better."

The pair ventured back down to the hall late morning. Stella took with her a handbag. Hannah and Frank had arrived shortly before them and were sitting at a tables. The newcomers moved over to join them.

"I got things sorted out in our room," Stella mentioned.

Following a smile, Hannah said, "I hope you've got enough room."

"It's fine," Stella replied. It was quite small, but they had left most of their possessions onboard the ship.

392

"It won't be long before lunch. We sometimes eat up in our room, but usually we join the others in the hall."

"I like the design on the walls. It looks fresh, is it a recent thing?"

"They painted it a while ago, but the colours are holding. I'm glad you like the design."

"I do."

Alan joined them. He looked rough and, as he took his seat next to John, moaned, "Remind me never to have an alcoholic drink again."

Frank introduced his guests, but the drone was in a poor state following the previous night's revelries and took little in.

Meanwhile, Stella was searching in her bag and, after a while, produced a pill box. She took one out and said to Alan, "Swallow this with a glass of water. It will make you feel better."

He would not question this and, after grabbing a passing servant for a drink, he soon downed the pill.

Then Hannah addressed John. "Last time, you arrived in a flying machine. Have you come that way again?"

"We did. It's hidden from prying eyes."

The Despotess was on a different tack, but she decided not to pursue it.

"Can you ride a dakk?" Frank asked.

"I don't know," said Stella, "I've never tried."

"Oh; they're the best transport if we go to Vionium."

Hannah looked puzzled. "Why do they want to go there?"

"I thought they'd enjoy having a look round there this afternoon."

"Give them a break, my dear. I expect they'll want a rest this afternoon. We can show them another day."

With his wife so firm, and the guests not contradicting her, Frank yielded before her wisdom and deferred. A messenger then entered the hall. As he walked over to the group, he produced a communication in an official-looking tube. Frank put up his hand to receive it, but the messenger told him it was for Master Alan.

The drone took it and, with his head clearing, extracted the contents and began reading the letter. All conversation at the table stopped as four pairs of eyes watched him. He spoke.

"It's from Charlotta..."

Frank explained, "She's in the government of bordering Ladosa."

John and Stella nodded.

Alan continued, "Hmm, interesting. She says the news of our helping the Neo-Purples during the civil war has leaked out..."

"Well, it was bound to come out."

"It sounds like it was a good time for it to happen. Opposition parties are divided and, with the economy doing well, and a favourable international situation, the government is popular. I think the revelation did little damage."

"Good news, then," Hannah said. "It would never remain a secret forever."

Frank chuckled before remarking, "I don't suppose our new ambassador to Ladosa, Count Wonstein, will give me any updates if he can help it. He'll be sending them straight to the Inner Council."

"Someone you don't like?" said John, picking up on his brother's tone.

"Not particularly, he was a thorn in my side at the Inner Council."

"Ah. They're based in your capital city down south. That's right, isn't it?"

"Asattan, that's right."

"That must be a trek, having to attend their meetings?"

"True, but I don't go to many meetings these days. With the despots in charge in their individual regions, the country runs itself. It's in times of national emergency that the Inner Council comes into its own. I've got a lot of allies in the Council and they keep me informed of any developments. As for Count Wonstein, now he's away from there, I hope he does well in the ambassador role. It's not in our interests for him to fail."

"Politics, eh?"

"Hmm, yes," Frank said, then spotted Squad Leader Darda hovering nearby and called him over to introduce him to their guests.

"This is Darda, well known around here for his bravery and acts of heroism."

His Despot's words embarrassed the young man, but he said hello to the visitors before making his escape.

"You made him blush," Stella said with a chuckle

"Oh, did I?"

"Yes," Hannah said.

That afternoon, the Despotess led Stella outside to show her the gardens outside the Castle wall.

"I had them made from designs I worked on, with a bit of help from others," she said as they approached. "I meant them to be organised into a traditional Ladosan layout, but it never came about. It's a bit of a mish-mash now of plants, flowers and vegetables I'm not sure what you'll make of it."

"I saw it from a distance, of course, when we skirted round the Castle wall. It's nice to see it close to. Ah, a herb section."

"It is."

"I think it's enchanting; you should be proud of it."

"Thank you; I'm pleased with some of it. These apple trees are coming on. As you can see, I'm having them trained to provide a screen next to the path."

A couple of white gardeners were toiling, not looking at the black women. They moved on to an area where the grass was fifteen centimetres high except where pathways were mown. One of these led to a wooden seat which they took advantage of. There they soaked in the atmosphere. The sun was out, but a screen shielded them from the heat.

Swatting a couple of flies away, Stella said, "Do you come here to meditate? It's so beautiful and peaceful too."

"Alas not. I don't frequent here as often as I'd like to. It's nice to have someone to share it with."

"Frank's not too interested then?"

"No, he sees this as *my* project. He'd be happier looking at the accounts, drafting new laws, or even listening to a sermon he considers good."

"I see."

"Talking of which, tomorrow is the Sabbath and we'll have a service within the Castle walls, in the bailey. You and John would be welcome to attend if you like."

"I'm afraid it's not for John, but I'd love to attend."

"That's good," Hannah said with enthusiasm. It's held mid-morning and I'll make sure they take an extra chair out for you. Bishop Gunter normally presides. I understand Keturah will give the address. She's such a young thing, but quite precocious. If it's only half as good as her last one, it will be worth hearing."

The following day, John did indeed opt out of the church service. There was an enthusiastic crowd in the bailey ready for the proceedings to begin. It was a sunny day and it relieved Stella to be amongst the group of VIPs, because it meant she was in the area shaded by the keep. She sat next to Hannah which pleased her, because the two women had hit it off. To Hannah's left was her son, Joseph, then her husband who followed the proceedings avidly.

Bishop Gunter was in an ebullient mood and the service ran with a swing. Hannah knew Frank was looking forward to Keturah's talk with great anticipation. It concerned her it might not live up to his expectations. She need not have worried.

Some whites, standing with the sun in their eyes, wore hats with wide brims to cut down the glare. It delighted them seeing Keturah, one of their own, take to the stage for her first address at this service.

"This morning, we heard Jesus' tale of Lazarus and the rich man. Sometimes it's known as Lazarus and the rich *black* man, but there is nothing to support the insertion of the word, "black" into the text.

"During their earthly lives, the rich man has all the benefits of comfort and wealth, while Lazarus is a poor beggar. In the afterlife, the roles are reversed, with the poor character in heaven and rich Lazarus in hell. And a great divide stood between the two states.

"It concerned the rich man that his brothers may end up in the same eternal predicament as he and wants them warned. In the climax to the story, Jesus says the brothers already have the Law and the prophets to teach them. If that has no effect on them, then even someone returning from the dead won't move them.

"What is the story's meaning? Some scholars have build whole theologies of the afterlife on the contents of this tale. But let us remind ourselves what a parable is. Jesus used parables to get across a point, a *single* point. The individual details are unimportant, they are not to be treated as allegories.

"The parables of Jesus were a *verbal* form of communication. Unlike us, the people could not read them and pick them apart afterwards. At the end is the important part, the nub of the story. The rest is a device so that they will remember the message.

"In his ministry, Jesus could have used bland words such as, 'Be kind to everyone regardless of race.' Instead, he gave us the story of the Good Samaritan. Jesus could have stated that God is a forgiving God. Instead, he told the story of the Prodigal Son. Those stories stick in our minds far better than mere statements.

"What are we to understand from the account of Lazarus and the Rich Man? Unfortunately, we have lost the context and we do not know which group he aimed it at. We know the one group he singled out most for their obstinacy, the religious leaders of the day, the Pharisees and Sadducees.

"'Look!' Jesus tells them, 'we have the most wonderful religion, but you have degraded it into a bunch of academic rules and squeezed the life out of it.' If the Jewish leaders did this when they had the Law and the prophets, it wouldn't move them even when God raised someone from the dead. He was, of course, referring to his own resurrection and prophesying, correctly, that they would not accept him even then. It is a message condemning obstinacy of heart and disbelief. Please God, grant us open minds and hearts to receive your messages and not block your blessings out."

Upon her concluding her sermon, Frank turned to his right with a look of satisfaction. It had met with his approval. Stella whispered to Hannah, "I wish John had been here to hear this!"

Once the proceedings concluded, the crowd dispersed. Some whites had travelled from Vionium and faced a long walk home.

Frank jumped to his feet and was about to stride over to Keturah, but Hannah put her hand on his arm making him hesitate.

She said, "Don't be too generous in your praise of her, it wouldn't be wise."

Frank hesitated for a moment before he saw sense in his wife's words. Encouraging is one thing, but gushing praise quite another. He still moved across to Keturah and spoke briefly before inviting her and the bishop to join him for lunch in the hall. The latter declined, but Keturah, after her consulting her father, Deejan Charvo, accepted the offer.

The hall that Sabbath was fuller than Stella had seen it. She smiled when John came down to join them. The Despot and his family sat at the end of the table, then Stella and Alan. John was stationed opposite Keturah who, being shy in this situation, listened rather than join in the conversation. To deliver a sermon through the power of the Spirit was easier than sitting amongst these powerful black citizens.

Alan pronounced, "I'm thinking of visiting the Capital, calling upon friends I haven't seen for a while. Things are quiet here."

"I see," said Frank, "when will you leave?"

"I'm not in a hurry and won't leave for a few days."

They discussed the outdoor service and lots of positive comments were voiced. "An uplifting event" being the consensus. This annoyed John, who felt Stella was being pulled into the religious fold by Frank and his wife. With the others engaged in their conversation, he issued a challenge to coy Keturah.

"Isn't it a rather crude idea, that God would sacrifice his Son so that those who believe can get off scot free? What sort of father lets his son go through that?"

The girl went wide-eyed, not expecting such a question. In order to gain time to gather her thoughts, she asked, "How do you mean?"

"This idea that one man gives his life in the most horrible way to purge everyone else's sins."

"I see," Keturah responded. Her speech was barely audible. Yet, once she got going, she sped up and her voice became firmer. "Whilst I would agree that Jesus Christ was fully man, he was fully God too. True understanding of the doctrine of Atonement means we have to ask, 'What does it mean to give a life?' Does one side's gain, the sinner, necessarily mean loss on the other, in this case, God? Looked at it this way, giving one's life means giving it up. An eye for an eye.

"But we should see Jesus' words differently. God is love and when we give away love, we enrich the universe. It's the one thing you can give with no diminishing effect on either side. God is infinite and can give of himself without loss. A mother gives life when she has a baby, but it doesn't diminished her as a result, quite the opposite.

"Bible, sacrifices aren't always a life being given to atone for sins. Peace offerings and thank offerings, for instance, were to do with reaffirming the Covenant between God and his people.

"At the Last Supper, Jesus inaugurates a New Covenant where he gives his life for everyone. He is still alive today and gives life to us, to believers... feeding us with his body and blood at the communion service and inspiration throughout our lives.

"Through Jesus, we become one with God in an ongoing process. He said that he wishes to give life in all its abundance which is what Christians experience today."

At this point, John shut up.

That night, as Stella finished preparing for bed, he was surveying the view again.

"It's so dark out here."

"Yes, darling, come to bed."

"In a minute. Will you blow the candle out?"

"Are you sure? It'll be jet black."

"I want to look at the sky."

With no light pollution, the few stars became visible as his eyes adjusted to the darkness. He never found time for such contemplation when he visited Molten before. On this occasion, it fascinated him how few stars were visible to the naked eye. It was as if he remembered somewhere else where he saw an empty night's sky like this. Yet he knew he had only contemplated such a barren sky here on Molten.

That night, he experienced vivid dreams of beautiful beings, not just on the outside, but deep inside too. He almost seemed to recognise them, but doubted such perfect beings could exist in this imperfect universe. He slept long and woke feeling happy and content with life.

~ End of Chapter 20 ~

My Keeper's Brother - Chapter 21

Another morning and John and Stella woke early and chatted in bed.

"How are you finding it, then?" he asked.

"What? Life on Molten?"

"Yes. You seemed to be enjoying yourself."

"I'm loving it."

"Enough to want to stay?"

Stella paused before answering, "Yes, I'd like to settle here. How about you?"

"You don't miss your TRAC, electricity, anti-grav engines?"

"Not one bit. Maybe they've only shown us the best, but the people here seem contented enough. Your brother doesn't have an autocratic style. He's in charge, but he eats with the commoners and is not aloof from them."

"I guess not."

"Plus, he seems to have everything under control. And I adore Hannah; she's easy to get on with. I could be friends with her. But tell me your thoughts, I wouldn't be happy here unless you wanted to stay."

"I'm tired of planet-hopping. It would be great to settle down somewhere as peaceful and uncomplicated as this. I'm unsure what Frank will say. It's one thing being a guest, quite something else settling down. Then there's the money situation. The credits on our TRACs count for nothing, would we be asking to live on handouts?"

"Talk to him. He seems sympathetic."

"Or should you speak to Hannah first?"

"No, he's your blood, I think you should put tell him straight. We would love to stay if possible, but... I don't know. Do you ask for a role that would bring us income to live on?"

"Okay, I'll speak with him, but I think I'll have to play it by ear... catch him in a good mood."

"He seems quite affable."

John recalled the fierce glare his brother gave him when he made the sarcastic comment about the bishop's house. He also hoped that

Frank had not heard his remarks to Keturah. Not that she did not deal with his challenge admirably, but he realised that, if he was going to stay, he would have to watch what he said about Christianity.

Then, well motivated, he arose and exited the tower room before Stella was ready. As luck would have it, Frank was in the hall and unoccupied

"Can I speak to you?"

"Of course," the other said, rising because of the serious tone in his visitor's voice. "Let's go into the Throne Room; no one will disturb us there."

The pair sat down and the Despot looked on, waiting for John to speak.

"Frank, we've been here a short while now and we're hugely enjoying it. I've discussed it with Stella and we were wondering how you'd feel about staying longer."

"Longer?"

"Um, indefinitely, if possible."

His sibling looked delighted. "That's wonderful!"

"Like I said, Stella and I have discussed the idea of settling here.. It seems such a tranquil place after some we've been to."

Frank guffawed at this, saying, "Oh dear, you mustn't get the wrong impression. I've lost count of the number of wars I've been involved in since I first arrived. Still, I suppose things are improving. When I arrived, the Ma'hol were our enemies; now they're our friends. Later, we had a war with the Ladosans. Relations with them have never been better. Conflicts can arise out of nothing, as we discovered in the Chogolt War. I'll grant you that things are looking up. I just don't want you saying I promised you peace on Molten."

"Noted. So, what do you think?"

"It would be lovely to have you here long-term, John. I want to know you better. And Hannah and Stella seem to have hit it off right from the beginning. But I'm afraid I would have to lay down one condition, I..."

"I know!" John interrupted, rolling his eyes, "I mustn't say anything bad about the Church!"

"Well, I suppose there is that. But what I was referring to was your getting married to Stella. I can't expect to impose moral values on my subjects if my brother is living in sin."

It was an unfamiliar expression to John, but the meaning was clear. It was a small price to pay. Besides, he knew it was something Stella wanted.

"Okay, but can we keep this conversation between us? I'd like her to think the idea came from me."

Frank appeared satisfied as he nodded his agreement. Yet John still had one thorny issue that needed tackling.

"Is there a job for me? We need money to get by and the credits on my TRAC are useless."

"Oh, don't worry about that," Frank said in a matter-of-fact tone. "You can have a modest pension; I can't have you starving. Being serious, I can make sure you're given regular money so that you'll be able to make ends meet. I don't want you worrying about that."

"Thank you, but it would be only right to contribute."

"If you want a job in our army, I'm sure we can procure an officer's role for you."

John pulled a face before answering, "I finished with my soldiering a long time ago. Besides, my heart is no longer in it."

The two men discussed this at length as the former marine recounted his experiences. He explained his disillusion with military life.

"Well, never mind," his brother said, still upbeat, "I won't force you to do anything. If the two of you wish to live in retirement, then... oh, I remember! That big house in Castleton; you can have that. I think you'll find it rather nice."

"You're pulling out all the stops for me. I am most grateful. I know Stella is keen to stay... as am I."

"Well, we'll organise a visit for you to see the place. I think you'll like it."

They exited the Throne Room to find the hall considerably busier. Servants had reserved spaces at their favourite table and they took their seats amongst their loved ones.

"I wondered where you'd got to," Stella told John, "until someone informed me you were in there."

"Um, yes," replied John, who then lowered his voice to add, "I've got something to tell you, but I'll wait 'till later."

Stella raised her eyebrows in response, but did not speak. He then contradicted himself by whispering, "Frank's agreed for us to stay if we want to."

"I do," she said, her face aglow with happiness.

The approach of two young men, heading straight to the Despot, distracted the others.

"My Lord," began one, may we speak to you about an idea after you've eaten?"

"You can talk to me here and now if it's not confidential."

Joseph and Hannah, having finished their meal, volunteered to vacate their two places so that the petitioners could take their seats opposite her husband. They accepted this proposal and Tristan and Ayllom sat down. The Despot's assistant and his friend wished to put an idea to their ruler. Stella and John listened on.

"Thank you, My Lord. You remember Ayllom?"

"From Ladosa, yes. I noticed you at the party."

"Yes, My Lord," the foreigner said.

"So, how can I help?"

Tristan began, "Ayllom and I have been discussing the facilities available in Castleton. We possess no proper hospital. In fact, there's no modern hospital in the whole of Thyatira. We have the hospice for the dying run by Azikial and the infirmary at Muggawagga's monastery, but no real medical facilities such as they have in Ladosa. If we could erect a proper hospital and staff it, then it would ease suffering and be a tremendous boost for the despotate."

"I see," Frank said, wondering how to respond. "That would incur an enormous cost, would it not? And I expect you'd be looking to me to finance it."

"For the initial cost, we think that Ayllom and I could foot the bill. The cost of the building and the internal fittings such as beds, etc."

The Despot looked incredulous. "How big are you thinking?"

"A hundred beds, My Lord, split between male and female, black and white."

"That would be a massive undertaking!"

"The need is there. Plus, we've spent some time costing it out. We've come into a lot of money. We have got some plans to show you."

As the young man produced some drawings, he admitted, "We will ask you to assist with the wages of the staff as an ongoing cost."

"Hmm, this'll have to go before the senate," Frank mumbled as they laid the papers before him. He took time to study the plans. The operation might have been better on the wider Throne Room table, but with everyone present peering at them, no one suggested it.

Everything hinged on the Despot's decision. Even if the senate approved, he possessed the final say. Nothing would go ahead without his agreement. He inspected the neat drawings in front of him and they impressed him. They had gone into it in great detail.

"And where would this be situated?"

"The far, western end of town."

A long discussion ensured with everyone joining in and taking an interest. They needed a proper hospital. Thyatira possessed a head physician with a team under him, but their stretched resources were inadequate for the modern, expanded despotate. In the outlaying villages, they resorted to remedies little better than witchcraft. If they could build such a facility and run it properly, Thyatira would be dragged into the, if not the twenty-seventh century, the seventeenth.

Natias approached and stood behind, listening and, after a while, Hannah rejoined them. Alan was keen on the idea. He told the two young visionaries that he was heading for the Capital shortly. With his connections, he could secure the best surveyors and architects. They should be able to give expert opinions on the suitability of the site and calculate more accurate cost figures. There was an overwhelming enthusiasm for the project amongst the assembled group. They debated many practical considerations and Ayllom, who until now said little, spoke about his experiences.

"During the civil war, Tristan and I were ambulancemen. Since then, I've been working at the hospital in Laybbon, training to be a doctor. There's a circle of Laybbon city medics there whom I could encourage to work here once it is ready. The government of Ladosa wants to increase ties between our two countries and I am confident of getting backing. Even if only short-time, I might convince them to pay the salaries of any who moves here."

"I am a qualified nurse," announced Stella to the surprise of most present. "I'd love to get involved with the care side of things."

John, who, of course, was aware of Stella's past, asked her, "Would you really want to involve yourself in this?"

"Yes," she said. This delighted him, because a long-term project would give her meaning and purpose here on Molten.

"It'll be ages before they would be up and running," Alan pointed out.

Looking at Tristan and Ayllom, Stella responded by suggesting they set up some tents in the interim. "It would serve as a temporary home until they completed the building. We could train volunteers, begin treating patients in a small way at first."

Frank pointed out that, while the weather was fine now, the winters were harsh. Tents would be inadequate. "Maybe come the spring..."

Hannah, not wanting to put her new friend off, said, "We've got plenty of abandoned wooden huts unused to the northeast of here. The old refugee camp. They would be adequate for the temporary measure you are suggesting. In the meantime, we can undertake detailed planning and make it known throughout Thyatira in order to raise interest in the project." She said, "We'll need to fence off the land and erect notices to ensure no one else builds there."

The Despot called the impromptu meeting to order. "All right. Well, there's still much to discuss. I would want the two of you to present your plans to the senate. I *am* in favour in principle, but it needs a huge amount of thought. All the fine details need working out."

Tristan said, "I'm sure Ayllom and I can prepare a presentation to give before the senate." As his friend nodded, he said, "We commit ourselves to this and would like to see it through."

With a sigh, Frank said, "I suppose I'll have to release you from your current role as my assistant."

"Yes please, My Lord, but I am happy to stay on until you find a suitable replacement."

"Good, that will be helpful. I'll give it time to consider. I can't have just anyone in the role... and you'll be a hard act to follow."

Tristan took this for the compliment Frank meant it to be. On the way back to his house with Ayllom, they were ebullient.

"That's the best response I could have hoped for," he said.

The Ladosan agreed. "If it comes off, it could have far-reaching consequences."

"Improve the welfare of the sick, you mean."

"I'm also thinking of Hoame / Ladosan relations. We've signed a treaty, but this could be the project that cements that initial step."

"I see what you mean?"

"There's much endeavour ahead, like the Despot said."

"Of course it's early days. We'll have to spend time on our presentation to the senate."

"Will that be soon?"

"Despot Thorn isn't for hanging about once the ball has got rolling."

"Good. After that, I'll return to Ladosa a while. I've got friends who can help me, help us, both in the medical profession and the government."

"Friends in high places," Tristan joked as they neared his home.

"I'm sorry, I wasn't boasting."

"I realise."

"But they're going to be vital if we're going to get help. I also need to collect the bulk of my money and bring it here."

"I should come with you."

"No, you'd be better use to our cause staying. I need you making more converts here and keep this issue in the spotlight. I think Stella will be a useful ally. Don't worry, I shall stay for the senate presentation before I leave. I'll return with company, all being well, so I'll be safe."

"God willing," Tristan added with a smile, which his friend reciprocated.

"Yes," the Ladosan humoured his friend. "We'll need his help if we are going to pull this off. We'll need all the help possible."

It was time for John to bite the bullet. Marriage was not his thing, but if it satisfied both Stella and his brother, and ensured they could stay on, it was worth doing. After all, he loved her. The idea of spending the rest of his life with her was most agreeable.

Not the most romantic person on Molten, or any other planet, he was determined to seize this opportunity. He arranged to have their evening meal brought up to their room. With Stella out most of the afternoon with Hannah, he prepared the table himself, lighting candles even though the mid-summer days were long.

"Oh my goodness!" a hot Stella exclaimed when she came in and saw the effort John had gone to. This was not his normal style.

"You like it?" he asked.

"Y-yes, it's nice. What's the occasion?"

"No occasion, I thought it would be nice for a change."

She was speechless, but a knock on the door broke the silence before it became embarrassing. It was a couple of servants with the meal. The couple stood in silence while they laid the food out. Once alone again, they sat down. Even with the window open, the air was heavy and humid.

Baked mascas was a rather filling starter. Stella welcomed the ham salad main course.

"Sounds like thunder," she observed at the distant sound.

"Yes, a good storm will make it more bearable," he said. "I keep getting electric shocks."

The conversation stayed light until near the end of the meal. They were eating a selection of fruit when John asked, "You're happy here on Molten?"

"Yes, I am."

"And would you like to stay?"

"If you want to; I told you."

"I *would* like that; settle down after all that travelling about. Settle down for good. Frank's offered us a pleasant house to live in. I thought perhaps we could go along and view the property tomorrow if you'd like to."

"Of course, is it far from here?"

"It's that large house he pointed out when we walked into town together."

"The one next to the bishop's?"

"I believe so."

"I'd love to look at it."

Heart racing, this was the time to seize the moment. After swallowing hard, he asked, "How would you feel about us getting married here?"

"How would I feel?"

Annoyed at how his words had come out, John said straightaway, "Will you marry me?"

After a brief pause, Stella said, "Yes."

"Good."

She looked now at the table lay out in a different light. She said, "So that's why..."

"Um, I wanted to set the mood."

"You thought it would improve your chances."

Stella was teasing him now. How long had she waited for this moment? She would make the most of it. With no comment forthcoming from John, she said, "Yes, I'll marry you, John Thorn, but I don't want to wait another thirty years before the ceremony."

"Gosh, is that how long we've been together?"

"Almost that, on and off."

"No, we won't wait. I've spoken to Frank and he confirmed the bishop will do the ceremony. It'll be a grand occasion."

"My darling, I don't care about the grand occasion, but I want to tell the world about my commitment to you."

"And this world will do?"

Laughing, she avoided the question, but corrected herself, saying, "Showing my commitment before God and the world. I love you, John."

For John, there was much to consider. Stella's reply delighted him as did the thought that, with the hospital, she had a long-term project to sink her teeth into. Her enthusiasm for Tristan and Ayllom's idea remained high. She was jotting down notes to present to the pair the next time she saw them.

Meanwhile, he was uncertain how he would occupy his time here on Molten. Yet there was one task he needed to accomplish soon. In the morning, he caught his brother alone in the Throne Room. In front of the Despot sat a large pile of papers, but he was prepared to put his immediate duties to one side to listen to John.

"I've spoken with Stella and we've agreed to get married at the first available opportunity."

"Excellent!" Frank cried.

"We're grateful for all you're doing for us and would like to settle down here on Molten... here in Thyatira, I mean."

"Good."

"And we'd like to accept your offer of the house."

"Of course. Have you seen it from the inside?"

"No, we haven't."

"Well, I'm sure we can arrange that."

"But before any of that, I must do something."

"Go on."

"You could describe it as one last adventure."

"Does this adventure entail another trip to the stars?"

"On no, nothing like that."

"What, then?"

"This country is called Hoame, right?"

"Yes."

"And you have experience of your neighbouring countries?"

"I've visited Rabeth-Mephar and Ladosa."

"What about to the east?"

"The east?"

"Tell me about the country east of Hoame."

"I know little, I'm afraid. It's the other side of Hoame. The eastern Hoame seem to know little beyond the border. As far as I understand, the central desert encroaches there, forming a natural barrier. Beyond that, I do not know. There's supposed to be a mythical land of Oonimari, but it's only a name."

"That name rings a bell," said John, "isn't that our cover story?"

"That's right, I'm a prince of Oonimari." They laughed before Frank continued, "I've lived here so long now that I'm sure no one thinks about that now. Anyway, where's all this leading?"

"It has fascinated me, the history of the First Intergalactic War all my life, especially the hardware. Precious few ships of that era have survived. I visited a museum once and the 'battle cruiser' was a pile of junk metal. It could have been anything. On our last sweep to get here, my ship's sensors detected an old ship on the ground. It registered as a space destroyer of the First I. W. era. Before I settle down, I've just got to see it! I'd never be at rest if I didn't try."

"When you say, 'see it,' do you mean fly past to see what data you can pick up, or..."

"No, I want to land and explore the ship on foot. I've been giving it a lot of thought; I'd like to go at night and cloak my landed ship."

"And Stella would go with you?"

"Oh no, it's not her thing at all. I've spoken to her and she's given her blessing on the understanding that it's my last hurrah."

"How far away is it?"

"About three hundred and fifty kilometres."

"You realise that if you end up in an Oonimari gaol, no one will come to your rescue. Not even me, it's impossible."

"I understand that," John said.

Frank observed, "I can tell your heart's set on this."

"It is."

"I mustn't lose you after only recently reconnecting."

"Don't worry, I'll be careful."

"I'm concerned about you going alone. You can have my blessing, but I must insist on someone going with you."

"Oh."

"I have someone in mind."

"I'm glad to hear it, because I don't know anyone here."

"Darda, a squad leader here at the Castle. He's resourceful, brave and has a taste for adventure. I'm sure he'd love it and I could rely on him to watch your back."

"Has he ever flown before?"

"Of course not! We'll have to swear him to secrecy."

" You must trust him."

"I do. Besides, you'll find most whites here compliant; he won't give anything away if we tell him not to."

"I see."

"I'll call him in and explain. Let me do the talking."

With a shrug, John agreed. Darda was then called for.

"What I am about to tell you is top secret and you cannot divulge it to anyone. Do you understand?"

"Yes, My Lord."

"I know we've introduced you to John here. He wants to go on an assignment to the east, east of Hoame, I mean. We would like you to accompany him, hold his hand." When the young man frowned, he said, "I mean, be his bodyguard. But it's not a command, it's a request."

Darda's first thoughts turned to his new girlfriend at the Castle. Their relationship was taking off and he did not want to jeopardise it. Bearing in mind the "east" was a great distance away, he questioned the operation's expected duration.

"A day should do it," answered John.

"A day?" asked Darda, incredulously.

John looked to Frank, who responded, "John's got a flying machine, you'll be travelling in that."

The squad leader's face changed from confusion to amusement. Of course, the two brothers were having a joke at his expense, "I see," he said with recognition, "you're mocking me, this is all a jape; you're making fun of me."

"Oh no!" John assured him, "this is quite serious."

The frown returned to Darda's face as he listened to the stranger's plan. They would set off by night in the flying machine, travel east, locate the object and land nearby. Then travel by foot to inspect the "ship" (whatever that was) before returning home.

410

"I don't understand half of it."

"You won't have to," Frank said. "Your assignment is to protect him while you're on the ground. We don't know what conditions we'll face. As a nighttime operation, the cover of darkness will help you."

'How in heaven's name will I see?' Darda thought, 'especially in an unfamiliar land.' However, instead of voicing this, he asked whether he should don armour and take his sword.

"Oh no," assured John, "I don't think that will be necessary. I'll have my pulse pistol."

"No, you won't!" his brother insisted. "It could get lost, or stolen. We can't risk that."

John conceded this point without an argument. He needed to keep on his right side. The pulse pistol would remain in the cloaked ship.

"I'll take my dagger then," said Darda, who had not understood this exchange.

They agreed this and John explained further details before swearing Darda to secrecy once more.

"When do we leave, then?"

Glancing over to his elder brother, John said, "Tomorrow night?"

Frank nodded.

"You're doing what?!"

Stella wanted to scream when she heard John's plans. Far from having cleared it with her, as John told his brother, this was the first she heard of it since they first arrived. Yes, she knew he had caught an old spaceship on the sensors during the flight in, but he had mentioned nothing since they landed. She hoped he had dismissed it. Now she realised she should have known better.

In the argument that ensued, he stayed firm in his resolve, but at least she got a firm promise of no more such adventures after this one. How cruel would it be if fate snatched him away shortly before they got married and settled down? Yet he was adamant. Stella gave in, because shouting at him was neither helping nor changing the situation. Best to stop now before she said something they would both regret. She knew this was his dream. If he did not scratch this itch now, it would only worsen. She was still cross, though.

411

"And you need to take a local along with you? I thought you told me we're supposed to keep spaceships a secret from the population here."

"Um, it's not a complete secret, They saw my other ship last time I came. I don't think they're aware of the 'travelling to the stars' bit. And I'll be taking someone whose job will be to protect me. Frank insisted on it."

"And can we trust him?"

"Frank thinks so."

"Hmph! I suppose if neither of you is worried about it, then neither should I," she said.

As for worry, she was far more concerned for his safety than Hoame's social consequences. Why undertake a fool's errand and put yourself at risk?

"I'm going to hold you to your promise that you'll do nothing like this again!"

"I swear."

"Huh."

In time, she calmed down. She had made her point, her feelings clear. If there was nothing further she could do, she would grin and bear it. At least it should be over quickly. Earnest private prayer would be her answer.

Next morning, at the breakfast table, her mind was a thousand light years away as Frank and Natias discussed domestic issues.

"I have heard sevewal people, My Lawd, telling me that there has been a sharp incwease in the number of Ladosan twaders."

"Really?"

"Yes, My Lawd. Some operate at the market here at the Castle while others choose village twade."

"The villages?" Frank said, surprised.

"I should say, the towns," the former steward corrected himself.

"I see. Well, it's good news, we want to increase our ties with the Ladosans. Every little thing that improves our relations with them is to be welcomed."

"Yes, My Lawd."

"What about the other way?"

"I'm sowwy?"

"Are our traders crossing the border and plying their trade over there?"

412

"Not as far as I know."

"A pity. We're too insular in our outlook, Natias, we need to encourage our people to do more, seize the opportun..."

He did not finish his sentence, because he noticed that Stella, deep in thought, was picking at her food and eating very little. He asked her if she was okay.

"As well as I can be."

Knowing what she must be worrying about, he offered soothing words. "I'm sure he'll be back safe and sound, it's only a brief visit."

Stella shook her head, but remained silent.

"Have you got everything?" John asked in hushed tones.

Darda nodded, replying, "I've got everything. Ready to go now."

From the confines of the hall, they departed without further word. Half an hour after sunset, it was getting dark, very dark. They left the keep and crossed the bailey. The flaming torches above the sentries' heads were already casting shadows.

The pair hit the track leading towards the Ladosan border. Once they were away from any prying eyes, John produced two pairs of night vision glasses and handed one to his companion.

"Here, put these on."

"Wow!" Darda exclaimed, seeing night turn to day. "How?... these are fantastic!"

"Keep your voice down."

"Oh yes, sorry, My Lord."

"Um, 'John' will do."

"Okay."

"Come on, we'll cut across the grass."

He led them on a beeline straight to his ship. Once it was de-cloaked, Darda stood looking at it in disbelief. This, then, was the flying machine. Almost having to pinch himself in disbelief, he realised the reality of the situation.

After giving his companion a moment to comprehend, John showed him how to mount the machine and where to sit. Darda complied, struck dumb by it all. They took their glasses off.

Soon, the pilot was alongside him and the canopy closed. John played with the dials and, although the observation screen in front of them was black, a smaller screen on the pilot's side showed numbers and symbols in green. He made a few incoherent grunts as he fiddled about, touching the symbols on the monitor. This seemed to take a while. The passenger wanted to know when the flying machine would start flying. In the end, he had to ask.

"Oh," said John, surprised at the question, "We're half way there now."

Darda, having felt no movement, sensed again this was an elaborate hoax at his expense. He got out of his chair, but John held out a hand to restrain him and he stopped.

"What are you doing?"

"We haven't moved a centimetre."

"Sit down, listen. They fit all ships with inertia negators which means you have no sensation of movement. It has to be that way. Even the mild acceleration we've just had would pin you to the chair's back, making it impossible to breathe. Out in space, with the speeds involved, your body would be squashed into... I don't know what. Anyway, look at this little screen here. The journey won't take long; we should be there shortly."

Darda remained silent. He must accept the pilot's word, at least for the time being. Part of him would remain in denial until they landed and emerged from the cockpit. His scepticism was soon put to the test.

"We're here!" John announced with a note of triumph. "Right, put your glasses back on and we'll climb out... and remember, we must keep quiet. Only speak to me if it's absolutely necessary and then in whispers."

The other's nod was wasted in the darkness. They re-applied night glasses, with all the clarity that brought. As they emerged from *Shooter*, it disappointed Darda to discover they were still in the same woods. So it *had* been a practical joke all alo... but wait. The temperature was lower here and the wood held an unfamiliar smell.

His fellow adventurer was peering at something now strapped to his wrist which glowed before its green light went out.

"This way, about three hundred metres."

The ground here was sandy, with odd tufts of spiny grass, unlike anything Thyatira offered. Darda finally believed it was true. He had flown to a foreign land, a weeks' long journey in a matter of minutes. The reality was hard to comprehend and it lost him in wonder before remembering that he must focus on the task in hand.

John considered taking communication devices for the two of them, but dismissed the idea as a step too far for his accomplice, brought up in primitive conditions. They got to the top of a rise and scanned the view ahead. Similar, unbroken ground fell away in front of them. There, at the bottom, was a huge, oblong hangar. His TRAC informed him that the object he most wanted to see was inside. With heart beating faster as a result, he surveyed the area further, but there was no sign of life. A few, much smaller buildings sat a short distance beyond, some with lights flickering in their windows. They were far enough away not to concern them.

"That's the building we need to get into," he explained and began leading the way down the slope towards it.

'This is unlike anything I've seen in Frank's domain,' he told himself as they got close. The walls of the mammoth construction appeared to be made of metal.

"We've got to find a way in," he said, somewhat stating the obvious.

With that, he began walking along the bare wall, feeling it with his fingers. Meanwhile, Darda, forgetting his bodyguard duties, seized the initiative. An external, metal ladder, attached to the wall, rose out of sight. He climbed it. Up the top, he found a small window ajar. Peering in, he saw a gantry running along the inside of the building, with a spiral staircase leading down. He had found a way inside.

Darda hurried back down and caught up with John, who was having no success. The Thyatiran told him his discovery and John eagerly followed him back to the ladder.

Up they climbed and, at the top, Darda showed him the open, horizontal window. John could not believe their luck, but it occurred to him that the people here might not consider this facility required security. There was neither sight nor sound of any security guards.

Darda climbed through the window first and did it with ease, landing on the metal gantry. This went along the building's entire length at a height of ten metres.

Meanwhile, John found it much more difficult to negotiate the window and his colleague needed to hold it open for him. Soon they were both established on the walkway.

Being cautious, the older man peered over the railing and inspected the gigantic room first. No sign of anyone in the enormous building. Just an immense empty area. At one end was the item he had waited a lifetime to see. It appeared to be housed in a tent open at the front. With a canvas roof obscuring his view, it was hard to see much from his current position.

The adventurers made their way along the gantry towards the spiral staircase. Their footfall echoed around the cavernous building, even when they tried to tread softly. The same happened descending the staircase. John paused, wondering if he should take his boots off, but decided not to. It would be painful stepping on those cast iron treads. They continued on down, still no one else about.

Reaching the bottom, John waited until Darda was on the floor before they walked over to the exhibit. The special glasses ensured it was as light as day. Heart beating with joy, John advanced to the rope strung across some three metres from the ship. He studied it there first, intending a closer look in a moment. As his young companion came up beside him, he spoke softly.

"From my ship's read-out, I thought this was going to be a space destroyer, but it's a larger, battle cruiser. It's 1.I.W. all right, a government ship from old Earth. See the markings?"

Darda strained to see the faded lettering.

John said, "It's from the 2nd Air Fleet, 294th Squadron."

"Oh."

"And it crash-landed by the state of the bow, but a low speed impact, or rather its force field did its job until the last moment. I've never seen a specimen in such good condition. She's far from home, if only she could tell her tale."

His companion thought these words most strange, but he asked, "It's old then?"

"Ancient, about five hundred years old."

Darda was not stupid. Despite of the novelty of this entire experience, he added two and two together, asking, "And it came from the stars?"

"It did, a huge distance. I don't know exactly how far."

Head spinning, the Hoaman struggled to take it in. The implications of it were mind-blowing, but the evidence appeared undeniable. A craft that came from outer space. How did this man know? How much more did he know? Where was he really from? These and many more questions arose, but he dare not ask them. A sound to their right cut his musings short. A massive door crept open and some figures walked in.

Two giants accompanied an elderly gentleman with long, blond hair and flowing white garments. The former held flaming torches in one hand and heavy wooden clubs in the other.

John had taken the TRAC off his wrist to get the best hologramic pictures of the spaceship. He stopped this and watched in silence as the men approached. At five metres away, the old man halted and his guards followed suit, one either side of him, but a step behind.

"I am the Guardian," he announced, "what do you mean by violating our shrine in the middle of the night?"

The flaming torches would have interfered with the visitors' sight, were their special glasses not fitted with automatic filters. Darda felt for the dagger at his side and weighed the odds.

'Two of them with clubs in a wide open space like this... we don't stand a chance. I wish I'd brought my sword...'

The Guardian, his expression one of intense displeasure, not to say disgust, called out, "You are under arrest. We will interrogate you, come with me. Be under no illusion, you are in deep trouble!"

Back at the Castle in Thyatira, Hannah and Stella were up late, talking. In the comparative luxury of the Despot's suite, they sat in the living room. Neither of them was in a hurry to retire.

Stella enquired, "You said you were from another country. That's right, isn't it?"

"It is, Ladosa, north of here. They brought me up in a politically active family. There, most citizens are obsessed with politics. My father was a leading light in the Purple Party. Mother and I fled when our enemies assassinated him."

"Oh my dear, how dreadful!"

"Yes, it was. We headed for the nearest border, even though it was Hoame, Ladosa's long-time protagonist. We sought political asylum. It was not a certainty they'd grant it. For there was a price on our heads and the Hoamen might consider it expedient to extradite us. We were at their mercy."

"You came here?"

"Yes. Frank had recently been appointed Despot of Thyatira. He took us in and assured us of Hoame's protection."

"The first time you met your husband-to-be?"

"It was."

"And was it love at first sight?"

"To be honest, no. The first time I saw him, mother and I were tired after our journey across the mountains. I was in no fit state to fall in love with anyone!" They both gave a little laugh before she said, "But he was kind to us. He accommodated us, thank goodness. Life was simpler in those days. Thyatira and its population were a fraction of the size they are now. They didn't require a senate, or half the laws on the books we possess now. Then came the war."

"I'm sorry," said Stella, "but which war was that?"

"Between our two countries. It went on for... I don't know, but too long."

"What caused it?"

"A lot has happened since then. I can't remember all the causes now, but my coming here didn't help. Although I said nothing then, I wonder if my coming here provoked it."

Stella, resisting the temptation to mention Helen of Troy, said, "That must have been difficult for you, being in Hoame, with them fighting your countrymen."

"I wanted Hoame to win, because Ladosa were the aggressors. Goodness knows what would have happened if they'd lost. On a personal level, I needed Hoame to be victorious for my and my mother's sakes."

"So, I presume they did."

"Kind of, it all ended in stalemate in fact. The effort wore both countries out. In the aftermath, two changes occurred affecting me."

"Oh?"

"A revolution occurred in the Inner Council and Frank found himself in a position of enormous power in the country; a position he keeps to this day."

"And the other?"

"The other was more personal; he asked me to marry him."

"Did you say yes straightaway?"

"More or less, I didn't keep him hanging on. Fifteen years later, I'm still pleased I said yes."

Stella smiled, then changed the subject, saying, "I can't get my head round this black and white thing."

With a sigh, Hannah said, "It's unique to Hoame. For countless generations, the whites were an underclass whose purpose was to serve the blacks. The vast majority of whites are conforming by nature, they've accepted it. Frank was unhappy with the status quo.

418

Ever since he established a power base in the Capital, he has used his influence to improve the lot of the whites. I admire him for it. Yet he's felt it necessary to take a soft approach. He fears that too much change too soon will lead to revolution. Frank prefers evolution. Still a long way to go. There's resistance to reform, even from some whites. Less so in Thyatira which has attracted more progressively-minded people.

"There's still a far to go, but we've made remarkable steps forward. Christianity, once the sole domain of the whites, is being embraced by more blacks. In fact, it's becoming something of a fashion statement in certain black quarters."

"Is it?"

"It is, but I'm unsure that's desirable, for fashions come and go. Anyway, the whites' lot has improved immeasurably, particularly here in Thyatira, which Frank wants us to be a model for the whole of the country. There's even a white Keeper in Asattan."

"I was told that. The white hair is quite striking; I'd seen nothing quite like it, like wool. You're a black from the colour of your hair. What about me? Does my blond hair make me a white?"

The Despotess burst out laughing at this. "No," she replied, "you need not worry. As a foreigner amongst us you don't fit into Hoame's social groups."

"Ah," went Stella, who, after a moment, continued, "I've enjoyed our talk. I wouldn't have been able to sleep."

"Worried about John, it's understandable."

"I want him back in one piece as soon as possible. I don't want him to get caught up in a silly, unnecessary, dangerous situation."

~ End of Chapter 21 ~

419

My Keeper's Brother - Chapter 22

John assessed the situation in a flash. Arrest and interrogation were not on his agenda. Besides, he would never have forgiven himself for putting his young companion into this situation. As he held his TRAC in his hand, he fingered a sequence which he had never expected to use.

"You must come with us now!" the Guardian demanded.

"Have a look at this," John suggested, lobbing his wrist computer at the trio.

As it reached them, there was a colossal explosion and it blew the torches out. Temporarily blinded, the three men staggered in the dark. In the confusion, John scooted for the open door. Darda needed no telling, but ran close behind him. As he passed the guards, one groped across his path. Darda gave him a strong shove and hurried past.

Once outside, John said, "Our ship's this way. Come on!"

They sprinted toward his small craft, only pausing for breath at the top of the ridge. Glancing back, no one was following them. Darda laughed, but the older man, a lot more out of breath, commanded, "Save it... until we're safe."

The pair walked the rest of the way, finding their transport, they climbed aboard. Cancelling the usual pre-flight checks, the pilot got *Shooter* airborne. His passenger needed to check.

"Have me left yet?"

"Yes! See my screen? We're at seven thousand metres and heading west again. We'll be back before dawn."

The prediction proved accurate and the pair walked from the ship to the Castle aided by the special glasses. They took them off as they neared the sentries at the entrance and Darda handed his back. He acted like an excited child, wide awake because of the adrenalin rush still coursing through his body. The last time he experienced this much fun was when he progressed, semi-naked, through an enemy camp with nothing but his sword for protection.

John needed to calm the young man down. In the confines of an otherwise deserted hall, he reminded him, "Remember your oath. This must remain a secret to your dying day."

Sobering up somewhat, Darda said, "Of course. You can count on me."

"Good. We should retire and get some sleep."

"Sure."

John crept into his temporary tower room, but a voice came from the darkness, saying, "It's okay, I'm awake."

"Ah."

"How did you get on? Did you get to see it? Are you still in one piece?"

Too many questions at bedtime, but he told Stella he was okay.

"And the boy?"

"I think he enjoyed himself. He's okay too."

"Good."

"But I'll tell you the rest in the morning."

"Will I want to hear?" she asked, unsure she wanted to learn about any close shaves he might have encountered.

"I hope so. We're both back safe and sound... and I got to see the ship."

"Good. Tell me in the morning then. Come to bed; I want to go back to sleep."

Morning came and, while some Castle residents lay-in, Tristan went there early. After making enquiries with the staff, he learned the Despot had already gone to the senate building. He made his way across the grass, his shoes getting wet from the heavy dew. Upon arriving, he knocked on the office door.

"Come in!"

Tristan did, finding a cheery face before him. He needed him to be in a favourable mood.

"Ah Tristan! Good morning. No Ayllom today?"

"Not right now."

"You two have been inseparable since he arrived."

"He's a good friend to me."

"Indeed... and now you're working on the hospital project together."

"Yes, My Lord."

"You'd like to discuss that? I've got the time."

"Thank you, My Lord, but I' here on a different matter."

"Oh, well sit down. What is it?"

"I'd like to talk to you about my mother."

Frank gave an involuntary sigh. He knew all about Wanda Shreeber, guilty of plotting the murder of her husband, Tristan's father. Instead of imposing the death penalty, he heeded pleas for clemency and ordered her bricked up in the monastery for life. Recently, Hannah had been pleading for her friend's release. He agreed to consider it, but to date had not come to any conclusions.

"Okay, I'm listening."

"I wondered if you might possibly commute her sentence? Not that she was not guilty, or that she deserves less, but I'm asking for clemency."

"I see. Commuted to what?"

"Exile, My Lord. That you send her away, never to return to Thyatira."

Frank remained silent as he considered the matter. It got wearing having his wife, and now Tristan, putting pressure on him. He knew they meant well, but he was concerned about the precedent it might set. The Despot could do without this problem. He liked Tristan, and he loved his wife, and it would please them.

"Where would she go?"

"I thought Asattan, My Lord," the young man replied, pleased that the Despot might at last consider the matter.

"Why there?"

"She has friends in the Capital, as do I. She would far away."

"Hmm... and how would she manage for money?"

"I can provide for her."

"Oh yes," Frank said, remembering that Tristan had come into money. He warned, "She could never return. Never."

"No, My Lord, I would make that quite clear to her."

"And the release must be done clandestinely. I don't want a fanfare of trumpets."

"Of course."

"Although the news will no doubt leak out; it always does. But a period between the release and it becoming well known will help."

"Yes, My Lord! Thank you."

A knock on the door and John poked his head round. "You got a few minutes?"

"Give us a moment."

His brother disappeared and he sat alone with the petitioner once again. He said, "All right then, I agree. But you must do it before the population is abroad.... and the monks and nuns sworn to secrecy. I'll have to speak to Abbot Muggawagga."

"That won't be necessary, My Lord. I'm sure the Despotess and I can go through it with him."

It was apparent the two of them had been conspiring together. 'What does it matter anyway?' he asked himself. 'It will take a thorn from my side and make people I care for happy.' He said, "Will you go along there with the Despotess?"

"Yes, My Lord, if it is not against your wishes. We will make sure that we comply with the conditions you have stipulated."

Tristan was close to euphoric. This was something he wanted. He could not hide his joy and thanked Frank several times.

"Well, off you go then. You'd better see my wife."

"I will, My Lord. Will you be requiring my services this morning?"

"Er... no, I can give you the day off."

"Good." Before leaving, the assistant said, "I don't suppose you've found a replacement for me yet?"

"Not as yet, no."

They said nothing further and Tristan left, to be replaced by John.

"You survived your little escapade then," Frank observed.

"Yes," his brother confirmed as he sat down, unbidden. "Quite an adventure, though," he added. When asked, he confirmed Darda was unharmed. He followed this by the tale of the night's exploits in every detail, a much fuller account than he gave his fiancé.

Frank said, "The elderly man and his guards never learned your origin?"

"No, they didn't."

"They might have guessed by Darda's hair."

"But I thought you said you had no contact with Oonimari."

"That's true."

"They showed no sign of recognition."

"And the explosion destroyed your TRAC."

"You can say that again! I'd owned that thing for years and I never thought I'd use the self-destruct. I didn't want to, but it got us out of a tight spot. It was after I'd taken a couple of hologramic pictures of the ship before those men entered; now they're lost."

"You're not thinking of going back there?" asked Frank with a worried expression.

"Don't worry, I wouldn't put Stella, or you, through that again. I want to grow old here. Besides, with the move to the mansion coming up soon and the wedding planning, I'll be too busy."

"How *is* the wedding planning going?"

"We have an appointment with the bishop."

"Gunter."

"Yes, later this week."

"You're settling in then?"

"We are; and enjoying it. Stella's.... um, I've never known her more content. She looked very pleased when, this morning, I reiterated my promise not to go on any further adventures. And the hospital will give her a long-term interest."

"And you?"

I'm not sure yet, Frank. I'll give it further consideration after the move and wedding."

"Yes, there's plenty happening currently."

"But exploring old spaceships won't be one of them. I've scratched that particular itch."

The morning came when Hannah and Tristan set off for the monastery. Ayllom was another passenger in the wagon; he came to offer moral support. They said little on the journey. It pleased Hannah that her husband relented, but resolved not to crow about it when she got back.

An early mist was burning off, heralding a nice, late summer's day. Their wagon was followed by a second one. Some men Tristan was paying to get his mother to the Capital manned this. They had informed the abbot the previous day and he set about having a wall of the prisoner's cell demolished in order for her to come out.

They pulled into the monastery forecourt to be greeted by Abbot Muggawagga. As they disembarked, it occurred to Tristan that the abbot, Despotess and Ayllom were all raised in Ladosa. He alone was a born Hoaman. He dismissed the thought, it was irrelevant.

"My Lady! Tristan, me ol' bucka and... who's this?"

"This is my friend, Ayllom."

"From the old country, from your attire."

"Yes, sir," Ayllom confirmed with a bow of his head.

424

"All are welcome, but I know that you're here for a single purpose, so we won't delay you."

The small group left the hired men and entered the women's section of the monastery. An elderly nun met them inside. She was short and, when she opened her mouth, revealed the most uneven set of teeth ever. They were jagged and some stuck forward, it was most disconcerting. She passed words with the abbot before he led them into a small room where Wanda Shreeber sat. Springing from her chair, she first embraced her son, then Hannah. It shocked Tristan at her skin's pallor, but then she had not seen the light of day in quite a while.

"How can I thank you both for... for everything?" she asked the couple while Ayllom and Muggawagga held back. "I could not believe the news when I first heard it yesterday."

She and Hannah held a brief conversation during which the latter informed her it was her son's plea which tipped the scales in the Despot's mind. Wanda thanked Tristan, the Despot, God, indeed just about everybody until her friend said that they should leave.

"Now, you understand that you will be in a covered wagon. The men Tristan has hired will escort you to the Capital; men he knows and trusts. You may not leave Ephamon, ever. You understand?"

Wanda did. To enjoy an entire region to roam in rather than a tiny, bricked up cell, that was freedom indeed. She possessed friends in Asattan and, thanks to her son's generosity, wealth enough to live a comfortable life. She had every reason to be grateful for this act of clemency.

"You will write?" she asked both Hannah and Tristan, "and visit occasionally?"

They told her they would. Muggawagga cleared his throat and they took the hint to get going. Wanda was bundled into the second wagon. She waved at them before disappearing into the interior, the canvas flaps at the back closing. The conveyance pulled away and the small group watched in silence.

The abbot broke the spell by asking if they would stay for a drink. Hannah said she appreciated the offer, but declined, which meant they could go. Turning to their wagon, they almost bumped into an elderly woman carrying a huge bundle of sticks on her back.

"Oh, I'm sorry!" Ayllom said, for he was the one closest to her.

"That's all right, sonny, I'm stocking up for the winter."

425

They let her move on. Muggawagga informed them that the monastery was doing the same. "We got loads o' wood stored everywhere, enough to withstand a siege in winter."

The return journey was soon underway, but, unlike Wanda's wagon, theirs travelled with the sides down so that they could enjoy both the sunshine and the view. They pursued an indirect route to see some of the countryside.

Progressing through some woods, an unusual birdsong drew Tristan's eyes up into the branches.

"Look!" he said, pointing upwards, "that's a crested bankel."

"I think I see it," Ayllom said, "that little yellow one."

"Yes, they're quite rare nowadays."

"I didn't know you were an ornithologist," commented Hannah, who could not see the bird however hard she tried.

"I wouldn't say that, but my father taught us to identify some species. Victor and I used to look out for certain birds... until we grew out of it."

A short while later, they were progressing beside a field of oilseed rape. They could hear cows lowing in the distance, but the beasts themselves remained out of sight.

They drew into the Castle bailey and, upon the vehicle stopping, Tristan helped the Despotess down. After saying their goodbyes, he and Ayllom made their way back to their house. The Ladosan was wary about saying the wrong thing regarding his friend's mother, so he kept quiet. Instead, it was Tristan who spoke first.

"I appreciate you coming along and giving me support."

"I did nothing."

"You didn't need to. Your being there was support enough. Now we can concentrate on planning the hospital."

Another visitor came to see Frank. He was still sitting in his senate office when Captain of the Guard Rodd entered. This was someone he had known since his first days on the planet Molten. He watched him join the guard, rise to his present position, get married and start a family. Rodd was someone sober, brave and reliable, an asset to the despotate.

"May I have a word, My Lord?"

"Yes, of course. Come in and sit down. What can I do for you?"

Coming straight to the point, Rodd said, "I'd like to volunteer for the job of Despot's assistant now that Tristan is moving on to pastures new."

This was a big surprise to Frank, whose immediate response was to ask if he had grown tired of army life.

"No, My Lord, but I've been in the army since the Ma'hol invasion. I thought that being your assistant would be something fresh and a welcome challenge. I am well organised and I hope you know you can rely on me."

They discussed the matter. The Despot liked the idea of having an enthusiastic volunteer. This was unlike Tristan, who was sceptical at first, but grew into the role. Frank said, "Yes, I'd be happy to have you."

"Thank you, My Lord."

"I'll make sure that your pay is at least commensurate with your current role. You'll need to speak with Tristan to find out what's entailed. I'm pretty sure he made notes and a chat with him will prove most useful to you."

"I shall get in touch with him without delay. When do you want me to start?"

"Well, it'll be another Sabbath in six days' time. How about then?"

It was a tight schedule for Rodd to prepare and speak to Tristan. He wanted to start now it was decided.

"That will be fine, My Lord."

They settled the matter to both their satisfaction. It left an important role needing to be filled: the Captain of the Guard. What better person to fill that role than the Despot's brother? Someone with military training and experience. While interstellar warfare differed greatly from neo-Medieval, the principles were the same. Yet, he was not expecting the response he got.

"Are you telling me I must take up this post?"

"No, I'm not *telling* you," said Frank, surprised at the question. "Why, don't you want it?"

With a pained expression, "Not really." Had his brother not taken in their previous conversation when John made it clear his army days were over?

"But you like soldiering. Okay, so it'd be bows and arrows instead of pulse rifles, but similar principles apply. I'm sure that your skill-set would fit well. I'd get Rodd to go through everything with you.

We've got experts who can teach you sword skills. Not that you're likely to wield one often. It's more to do with management, training, tactics and suchlike. You'd be answerable to General Japhses, he's a..."

"Frank!"

"Yes?"

"If you insist, then of course I'll take the job. But the truth is I'm tired of soldiering. I told you. Besides, I haven't done it for years. I've been an archaeologist since '99. I have no desire to return to the army, any sort of army."

"Oh, okay, it's best that you tell me straight," the Despot said. He had indeed forgotten their previous conversation. Whilst surprised at the response, he soon got his head round it.

"Can you think of an alternative role you'd like to do... after your move and wedding?"

"I'd rather like to help with the hospital project. Stella's got her heart set on it and I'd enjoy giving her whatever support I can. Those two lads mean business."

"Tristan and Ayllom."

"Yes."

"I see. Well, I won't force you into the army role. I'm a little shocked, that's all."

"Sometimes people need a change in their lives, Frank. After all, isn't that what Rodd's doing?"

"It is indeed!" Frank said, looking happier. "No, it's okay. I'm sure I can find someone else for the captain's role."

"Me?!" exclaimed Darda, finding the Despot's words hard to take in.

They were in the Throne Room and it was getting late. Frank wanted to get the matter resolved without further problems.

"Yes, you've always impressed me as a squad leader. I'm confident you possess all the qualities to be Captain of the Castle Guard."

"I accept!" the young man said. He wanted to do so before his ruler changed his mind.

"I will speak to Rodd, get him to explain what your duties will be. Take notes."

"Yes, My Lord."

Relations had not always been perfect between Rodd and Darda. The former took a lot of convincing that the youthful fellow was leadership material. Yet, Darda proved himself well in the squad leader role after a shaky start. He won the more experienced man around, but how would he react to this news?

The Despot was still talking. "I'll get Rodd to explain everything with you as a matter of urgency, because the timescale is short. No point in hanging about. I need everything in place next Sabbath."

"Yes, My Lord."

Darda trying not to look wide-eyed at the suddenness of it all. He considered the matter: better to start as soon as possible as to hang about worrying about it. He would be the youngest ever Thyatiran captain, but he was certain about accepting the job. The Despot was presenting an opportunity for Darda to prove himself. He would rise to the challenge.

The young man departed the Throne Room on Cloud Nine. Wait 'till he told his parents, his friends, his girlfriend. Captain of the Castle Guard. He needed to pinch himself to make sure he was not dreaming.

Stella was getting stuck into Thyatira's life. In particular, she was meeting Tristan and Ayllom regularly to discuss the hospital project. She was becoming their official advisor. In fact, her previous experience, which she remembered well even though it was years before, was proving invaluable. After having helped them prepare for their presentation before the senate, it delighted her to learn it went well. The senators were enthusiastic about the idea, the white members in particular, when they learned the plan was to assign some wards to their kind. All members were delighted to discover the setting-up costs would be privately funded. Alan said, "Au revoir" and set off for the Capital to drum up some experts to help with construction, scheduled to begin when the winter snows abated.

Meanwhile, John was both amazed and impressed at how hard Frank worked. His image of his brother as sitting with his feet up, enjoying lording it over his minions, could not have been further from the truth. Not only did he work hard, but cared about his subjects. He lived modestly and mixed with both black and white. The man led by example.

429

One morning, the Despot received an early visitor in the hall after breakfast. Bishop Gunter was reporting on his latest visit to Norland. This was an area, formerly in the Aggeparii despotate, now ceded to Thyatiran jurisdiction. The takeover had not occurred without its problems, both ecclesiastical and secular. It sounded like the bishop was getting a handle on the former.

"I'm instituted re-training for the Norland clerics. It is going to be compulsory."

"Theological lessons, you mean?" Frank asked for clarification.

"That's right, because they need it."

"Well, we must leave them in no doubt as to your authority over them. I'm sure they'll come to appreciate your guidance and devotion to your pastoral duties. Give them time; it's a big change for them."

"You're right," Gunter conceded. It then lost him in thought before he started a different topic. "The Chequers is being demolished, along with a few buildings around it."

"Ah, the hotel in Carnis that burnt down..."

"The same."

"... the one that Emil and Darda escaped from."

"But not everybody," the bishop reminded him.

"No, indeed; a terrible tragedy."

"No, not that corner, *that* corner!"

Stella was directing workmen as they put their few possessions into their new abode in Castleton. The previous owner had died with no living relatives and the Despot granted the house to her and John. This included the furniture. It was not her style, but she could change things in time. Meanwhile, she would not look a gift horse in the mouth. A large building with sizeable rooms and a well-planned garden, it had great potential.

The night before, she and John had made a further trip to his cloaked ship and retrieved the rest of their possessions. A modest collection, but it felt good to have everything together in their own home.

"We've landed on our feet!" she said, surveying the spacious living room. "The servants begin tomorrow; we're so fortunate."

"We are."

"Then being the Despot's brother must be a help," she pointed out.

None too pleased at this comment, John said, "I want to pay my way here on Molten, I just haven't found my niche yet."

"Yes, dear," she said. "I'm going to speak to Tristan and Ayllom about a salaried administrative role for you at the hospital once it's up and running. You expressed an interest in doing that and I get the impression they're less interested in the admin side of the operation. I'm sure they see the need for it."

She was absent, though, when the pair visited the site again. A temporary fence was now in situ and notices erected. These advised the purpose for which the land was earmarked. They needed this to deter unauthorised building which still occurred despite the authorities' best efforts. If anyone tried it here, they would find their structures being torn down.

Tristan was in a buoyant mood. He had, the day before, received a letter from his mother saying that she was safely arrived in Asattan and was settling into her new digs. A messenger had delivered the welcome news in record time.

The pair had returned to Castleton following a visit to the site of the former refugee camp. They stood now, surveying the large plot of land in which they invested all their dreams.

"I'm glad," Ayllom said, "that we visited the site of the temporary hospital prior to ours being built."

"The huts require attention, but should match our short-term needs."

"It's a good use of the asset."

"I agree. They were due to be demolished, but they're holding off now until after we've used them."

"I see," said the Ladosan. "Stella's still as keen as ever."

"It's good, she'll be a useful ally up in the Castle as well as helping with her medical expertise."

"I'm visualising the completed hospital in my head. I keep coming up with fresh ideas and jotting them down before I forget."

"Good idea. This facility will make a massive difference in Thyatira."

Ayllom chuckled before asking, "Remember when we served in the ambulance corps during the war? That was life on the edge!"

His friend could never forget. Ferrying the wounded back from the front to the mansion-turned-hospital. It had been the fire in which they forged their close friendship.

The following day, Ayllom was due to head back to his homeland, both to collect his money and recruit medical staff for the spring. He was a man of his word, Tristan knew, and would return, helping the dream turn into reality.

They were still overlooking the site when a couple, man and wife, approached them. Tristan only noticed them when they were quite close. He recognised the pair as Tsodd and Katrina, owners of the Selerm, the largest eating and drinking establishment in Vionium. After an exchange of greetings, they explained the reason for their visit. Katrina was their spokesman.

"We've heard about your plans for a hospital here," she began in her distinctive gruff voice. "Have you given much thought to catering yet?"

The two young men exchanged glances, but said nothing. That answered Katrina's question.

"You'll need a ready supply of meals," she said, "and the Selerm has got the facilities and expertise to provide it."

It was Ayllom who loosed his tongue. He said, "It's a good point, but we're not getting into such fine detail as yet. We won't be operational for a while yet...."

"We're at the planning stage," Tristan added.

"... which means we can't say for definite yet. But it sounds like a good idea. Maybe, nearer the time, we could discuss your ideas."

His colleague nodded, saying, "We've got time right now to discuss it now, if you like."

Ayllom, although considering it premature, agreed there was no actual harm in going through a few ideas. A conversation ensued regarding catering for an institution still on the drawing board. It proved to be a useful discussion, although they settled nothing other than that Katrina and Tsodd's establishment would be the first one considered for catering.

"That's funny," remarked Tristan once they were alone again, "it was an aspect I hadn't considered before now."

"Me neither. I expect we'll find several other things we haven't considered as time goes on."

"Never mind, we'll rise to the challenge. We will make this hospital a reality."

"And a success," Ayllom said with a determined look.

A couple of evenings before the wedding, Frank and John were alone in the former's Castle living room. The weather was a good deal cooler than of late and they sipped warm brankies to keep the cold at bay.

"What's that you've got there?" Frank asked of the object he noticed John fingering earlier and now lay in his lap.

"This? I brought it along to show you. It's a souvenir I got... I don't remember where and when, but it's very special to me."

He continued to speak after passing the paperweight across. "This might sound daft, but I love to look at it and it cheers me up if ever I'm depressed."

"That doesn't sound daft at all," his brother assured him. "I think it's beautiful. The mountain scene, the waves rippling, the colours, the three-dimensional effect. Quite exquisite. It's unlike anything I've seen. It seems to draw you in and is more realistic than any hologram I ever saw."

John beamed; it delighted him that Frank liked it as much as he did. Before passing it back, Frank noticed the inscription on the bottom and said, "I see it's personalised. A pity you can't remember where it came from. I want one!"

John took it back. Although saying nothing further about it, he seemed to feel an energy being given off by the paperweight. It held a special quality for him. Frank then produced a piece of paper and said, "I received a letter from Despot Schmidt."

"One of your neighbours?"

"Oh no, he's from Capparathia in the deep south. A good man, though, a trusted ally. I took a quick scan of the letter earlier. I'll have a careful read of it, tomorrow."

"It's not containing bad news, I hope."

"Nothing like that. On our last visit, we discussed their idea of starting up a university down there. There are none in all Hoame and it's a revolutionary concept around here. Despots are reactionary by nature, but Schmidt is of a new breed. I hope this university will be a model for the entire country and attract students nationwide. That's the idea, anyway."

"You'll be supporting it?"

"One hundred percent."

"And sending candidates from Thyatira?"

"When the time comes."

"I see. There are no further education places on Molten then?"

"I can't say regarding the entire planet, but in Hoame, no. The letter is a progress report."

"I'll try to get this right," said John with deliberation. "Ladosa to the north, Rabeth something to the west?"

"Rabeth-Mephar, you were close."

"And do they possess universities?"

"I haven't a clue."

"But didn't you tell me you've visited them both?"

"Yes, but seeking halls of higher learning wasn't a top priority on those occasions. In fact, in Ladosa, my highest priority was trying to stay alive. But you're right, I don't know everything about their social conditions."

"Staying alive? What was that all about?"

"Well, the first time, I was on a pre-war spying mission. The second was *during* the war when we laid siege to one of their towns. It was a bloody business, but I guess I don't have to tell you what war is like!"

"Hmm, I get the distinct impression that I had it easy on Rakass Hist. The final stages of the operation were when I served. I spent most of the conflict on a space station, away from the slaughter. During the final stages, I was planet-side. Afterwards, I met a man who'd been there earlier and evacuated due to battle fatigue. He'd been there during the rainy season, when they were up to their knees in mud half the time. He said they couldn't keep dry and many illnesses and suchlike were the result. They suffered more casualties because of the conditions than they did from enemy action!"

"Must've been horrible. In one place I stayed, a group of veterans came in and one of them told me about his experiences. I think his name was Ivan. Anyway, he needed to tell me, get it off his chest, I suppose."

"A few men react that way."

"The whole episode sounds grim."

"It must have been. Several people I knew died down there in the early stages. The rebels were expert at concealment, they'd creep up at you from behind. It shredded the nerves."

"That was the place where they couldn't use modern weapons, wasn't it?"

"Yeah. Good old firearms and gunpowder."

"Gunpowder?" said Frank.

"Not exactly, the modern equivalent."

"Oh."

John said, "You know, it's funny. If a bullet flies close by your car, you hear a distinctive 'pop' sound. You got to recognise it, used to it."

"It must make you duck down!"

"Of course."

"And be more than scary."

"Better to hear it. The time to worry is when you don't, it's because they've hit you!"

"War, eh? I've done my best to establish peace on this planet."

"So I've been told. Friendly with the neighbours that you once fought against."

"That's the idea."

"Don't you believe," began John, looking at the ceiling dreamily, "that there could be a perfect society where wars have ceased?" As he spoke, he as he once again felt the paperweight in his palm.

"Not before the Millennium!" Frank said.

"No," his brother complained, "I'm serious. I feel it in the depths of my being that a perfect community is possible. One where fear is unknown and they work together for the common good."

"Hey, I thought I was supposed to be the religious idealist, not you!"

"But I'm serious, Frank. Sometimes I have dreams where I am amongst these beautiful people. They're perfect and will never harm other people. Don't laugh!"

"I'm not laughing," his brother said. "If I smiled, it's because you've never talked like this to me before. I guess it's showing me how little I know you. I still think of you as the young lad committed to becoming a soldier. You told me yourself that those images are way out of date. But where's your 'beautiful people' stuff coming from?"

"I'm not sure," the other admitted. "Sometimes I feel like I've met these wonderful beings for whom kindness is all they know and to act in a selfish way would never even occur to them. I suppose this all sounds daft to you!"

"I wouldn't say that. I don't profess to know everything. An advanced species could exist somewhere in this vast universe, we don't know. But I've heard that, while we sleep, our astral body leaves our physical body and can communicate with other beings. It sounds good, but if that's the case, why don't we remember it upon waking? My dreams are crazy! You dream of perfect people, I experience nonsense dreams."

"You admit the possibility of a perfect world then?"

"We have to be careful. I've read Plato's *Republic* where the discussion is on a perfect society. It goes into a lot of detail."

"You've read Plato?" John asked.

"Sure."

"Heavy, isn't it?"

"Not really; not once you get into it. It's a group of characters discussing with each other. I don't remember the details now, it was many years ago. I seem to remember he held a low opinion of actors and wanted them banned from the city."

"Not a bad idea."

"But I remember little else. I do recall it was quite frustrating to read, because the conversation used to develop in a direction I didn't want it to."

"If you'd been there, you'd have steered it in a different direction?"

"Yes!" Frank confirmed before carrying on, "but we must be careful of fanatics trying to impose their ideals of a 'perfect society' on others. They end in the most horrendous, repressive regimes. You must remember what's happened in the past: communism, or that commune on Karnak Five."

"Okay, but I'm thinking of something other than political ideas. This is above politics. I know you've always been the religious one, but I have this feeling within my being (dare I call it my soul?) whereby such a perfect society *is* achievable, but it's because of an inward revolution within people's hearts, not because of a political dogma."

"So, changing the way folk think and feel?"

"That's it! A fundamental change in attitude, an end to self-centred living."

"I see. Have you ever read The Sermon on the Mount?"

"No."

"In it, Jesus tells in similar terms to what you are saying. I think so, anyway. It's been an ideal for generations of Christians, but it's often seen as impossible to live up to. It remains something beautiful to aspire to. I'll show you where it is in the Bible, I think you'll enjoy it."

"Okay, I'll try it."

"Good."

"Huh! You must think I'm pretty bonkers with all these ideas I've been coming up with," John said with a quick shrug of his shoulders.

"Not at all, it's most refreshing. It's good to contemplate higher things."

The big day arrived and Stella was getting herself ready in her dressing room. The hairdresser was finishing, standing back admiring her handiwork. Stella was to wear a small tiara for the ceremony, but, when they handed it to her, she found her hands shaking and she got one of her handmaidens to put it on her.

She told herself, 'I've been with John for a good proportion of my life. Why is it so different getting married?' Yet she knew why. It was the commitment before God that she longed for. It might not hold the same power over her fiancé, but it meant everything to her.

She was ready and, surrounded by a veritable army of servants, she tottered to the waiting wagon. It was a standard vehicle, ready for the brief journey to the Castle, but they had decorated it all over it with flowers and bunting. What surprised her, though, was the crowd waiting outside. Blacks and whites, young and old, they cheered as she emerged from her new home. What was this all about? She never realised what a public event it would be, having requested a small, intimate ceremony to be held in the Castle chapel.

"They're well-wishers, My Lady," a handmaiden whispered in her ear when she hesitated.

"Oh, yes," Stella responded, forcing a smile.

With help, she stepped up into the wagon. Someone had placed a special, padded seat. Sitting there, she was high enough to be visible to the assemblage. She waved back at the strangers.

A short time afterwards, even at the dakks' slow pace, she was passing through the main entrance into the Castle bailey. She breathed a sigh of relief at leaving the multitude behind. This was premature, because further people, Castle workers this time, stood and cheered her final progress to the keep entrance.

Guards stood to attention and servants came forward to help her down. As she passed one soldier, she overheard him say, "She's late!"

'They'll have to wait!' Stella thought defiantly as she ascended the internal staircase to the hall. Then her musings softened. She would rather contemplate the fact that she was about to marry the one man in her life she had ever truly loved.

After traversing the hall, she was soon standing at the entrance to the chapel. The ten guests seemed to fill the small chamber.

An usher urged her to come forward and, as part of the ceremony, Frank took her by the arm and escorted her up to his brother.

"You made it then," John whispered, followed by a wink.

Stella gave a quick smile before turning back to face Bishop Gunter in his finest vestments. Then, following a period of silence allowing the assembled gathering to clear their minds, the ceremony began.

"The grace of our Lord Jesus Christ, the love of God and the fellowship of the Holy Spirit be with you."

"And also with you," the congregation chorused.

"God is love and those who live in love, live in God and God lives in them." The people sat down before the bishop continued, "In the presence of God, we have come together to witness the marriage of John Michael Thorn and Stella Elizabeth Green; to pray for God's blessing on them, to share their joy, to celebrate their love. Marriage is God's gift in creation through which husband and wife may know the grace of God.

"It is given that as man and woman grow together in love and trust, they shall be united in heart, body and mind, as Christ is united with His bride, the Church. Marriage brings joyful commitment to the end of your lives...."

The ceremony proceeded at a stately pace and the bride's mind wandering as she awaited the all-important vows. When the time came, Gunter gave her the precise words to say.

"I, Stella, take you, John, to be my husband. To have and to hold, for better for worse, for richer for poorer, in sickness and in health, to love and to cherish, from this day onwards, till death us do part."

Afterwards, everyone told her it had been a beautiful ceremony it had been, but it was a blur to Stella. She remembered the last pronouncement, "You are man and wife," and the modest congregation cheering. It was an all-consuming moment, but she was as pleased everything was concluded, they were finally married.

They held the reception meal in the hall. It, too, was on as modest a scale, as per the couple's request. That was the way she wanted it and John's sole wish was to grant her desire.

Two men present were on their first day in their new posts. As the Despot's fresh assistant, Rodd had little to do on this occasion. His wife was away visiting friends, so he was by himself. He found himself opposite Natias and Eko. The former steward and his wife he had known all his life.

"A beautiful ceremony to be sure," Natias declared. "We are happy they're our new neighbours."

The other one starting a new role was Captain of the Castle Guard, Darda. His meteoric rise was raising eyebrows, but Rodd was being supportive, helping as much as he could. The more experienced man's blessing meant a great deal to Darda, who turned to his girlfriend sitting next to him.

"Look at this spread! I don't know where to start."

"I'm sure you won't take too long to decide," she said with a cheeky expression.

Meanwhile, in the centre of the proceedings, were the families Thorn. John looked to his brother and said, "I've done the deed, big brother, are you pleased now?" His tone was a bit mocking and Frank gave a somewhat wry smile as he said, "I am; it's not before time."

Then John turned to his new wife, her face radiant as she surveyed the scene.

"Happy?" he asked.

"Yes," Stella replied, "the happiest day of my life."

~ The End ~

The Keepers Series

1a. The Keepers of Hoame - Part One
1b. The Keepers of Hoame - Part Two
1. The Keepers of Hoame (in one)
2. Secret of the Keepers
3. The Journey Hoame (a prequel)
4. The Molten Fire
5. The Vortajer Plot
6. Death in the Senate
7. Return From Azekah
8. Prospects of Peace
9. My Keeper's Brother

Printed in Great Britain
by Amazon

87827836R00251